# THE TWICE-SOLD SOUL

## THE McKENNA ELLERBECK SERIES: BOOK 1

# KATIE HALLAHAN

orbitbooks.net
orbitworks.net

This book is a work of fiction. Names, characters, places, and incidents are the product of the author's imagination or are used fictitiously. Any resemblance to actual events, locales, or persons, living or dead, is coincidental.

Copyright © 2024 by Katie Hallahan

Cover design by Alexia E. Pereira
Cover illustration by Miranda Meeks
Cover copyright © 2024 by Hachette Book Group, Inc.
Author photograph by Katie Hallahan

Hachette Book Group supports the right to free expression and the value of copyright. The purpose of copyright is to encourage writers and artists to produce the creative works that enrich our culture.

The scanning, uploading, and distribution of this book without permission is a theft of the author's intellectual property. If you would like permission to use material from the book (other than for review purposes), please contact permissions@hbgusa.com. Thank you for your support of the author's rights.

Orbit
Hachette Book Group
1290 Avenue of the Americas
New York, NY 10104
orbitbooks.net
orbitworks.net

First Edition: November 2024

Orbit is an imprint of Hachette Book Group.
The Orbit name and logo are registered trademarks of Little, Brown Book Group Limited.

The publisher is not responsible for websites (or their content) that are not owned by the publisher.

The Hachette Speakers Bureau provides a wide range of authors for speaking events. To find out more, go to hachettespeakersbureau.com or email HachetteSpeakers@hbgusa.com.

Library of Congress Cataloging-in-Publication Data
Names: Hallahan, Katie, author.
Title: The twice-sold soul / Katie Hallahan.
Description: New York, NY : Orbit, 2024. | Series: The Mckenna Ellerbeck series ; book 1
Identifiers: LCCN 2024021899 | ISBN 9780316580199 (trade paperback) | ISBN 9780316580182 (ebook)
Subjects: LCGFT: Fantasy fiction. | Romance fiction. | Queer fiction. | Novels.
Classification: LCC PS3608.A548247 T85 2024 | DDC 813/.6—dc23/eng/20240513
LC record available at https://lccn.loc.gov/2024021899

ISBNs: 9780316580182 (ebook), 9780316580199 (print on demand)

*For Cass, because without her,
there would be no story*

# Chapter 1
# A Demon Comes to Call

It was well after sundown in Paris and taking everything I had to keep myself upright and stumbling down the cobblestone street. Empty—good. I was shaky and desperate, and the last thing I needed right now was a Good Samaritan. Harder to get rid of than a mugger. Three vials of my drug of choice, an anti-magic elixir, clattered in my pocket, no good without my injection kit. I could drink one—they were burning a hole in my resolve not to—but it was a waste of elixir, not as effective, and I had to make this batch last a week.

Grabbing the building as I turned the corner, I halted, gasping for breath. My heart was racing, fever-sweat making the late-October chill even worse. My nails raked over the inside of my wrist, digging at the itch that lived under my skin and coursed through my veins.

*Come on, it's a few more blocks. The McKenna Ellerbeck story* does not end with *"American Woman, Missing 10 Years, Found Dead in Paris."*

I could make this all go away anytime I liked. The matching tattooed runes on my wrists taunted me as I scratched, somehow more tempting with those red lines running across them. Cross my wrists, whisper the spell, it'd all be over in a second. No pain, no itch, no sepsis in my blood, all gone. Blissful relief was right there, was *one word away*...

Laughter at the far end of the alley, from the cross street. I shrank back against the wall, sliding to the ground, and strained my neck to peek at the scene. Luckily, it was just a group of normal twenty-somethings, drinking and fucking around. Seven hells, to be like them...but if I let my magic out this built-up, it would take out a building in the process. Those kids would die, the police would be everywhere, and the cherry on top, I'd have to book it back to my apartment, pack up everything I could, and flee before the demons showed up. I'd gotten pretty fast at that by now, though, and on the bright side, I wouldn't have to pay my bastard landlord next month's rent.

*No. Not again. I've made it a year without unleashing. I can make it another hundred yards.* Gritting my teeth, I pushed upright, but the street tilted and sent me back into the wall. One glass vial of glowing blue liquid slipped out of my pocket and tumbled in the air toward the cobblestones. I lunged for it, my knees jolting painfully on the ground, catching it just before it could shatter on the stones.

"Seven hells," I panted. But before relief could replace panic, a new terror hit: the corruption in the air seeping along my skin, the vile smell of rot and sulfur, the growl of an approaching hellhound.

It emerged from the shadows at the end of the block. Hairless, mottled, bruised skin, damp with unknown fluids. Shadows writhed around it as it stared at me with fiery pits for eyes. From its back sprouted the ragged bones of useless wings, hung with shreds of skin. It smelled overwhelmingly *wrong*, of the Pit and cobbled-together flesh, stolen to give itself a body in the mortal world. Another growl behind me reminded me that they always hunted in pairs.

Every time in the last ten years that I'd unleashed my magic, these vicious and unrelenting minions of the Archdemon of Madness had shown up to hunt me down.

But this time, I *hadn't* used my magic. I was half dead from *not* using it, so how the hell did they find me?

No time to think. If I was going to live and stay sane and free, I had to act.

Step one: Play dead.

I collapsed onto the pavement, slumping forward, seemingly passed out. My heart pounded as their paws thumped wetly on the pavement toward me. The one in front reached me first, thrusting its head down as the writhing shadows coalesced into teeth. As it made to bite me, I smashed my hand against its head, shattering the vial. The glass shards sliced into both its flesh and mine, the anti-magic elixir seeping into the cuts. While I instantly began to feel better, the hellhound did not. Its flesh withered, suddenly denied the demonic magic that held it together, falling apart into ash and wet clumps on the cobblestones. I dragged my hand against its jaw, pushing up onto my feet and smearing as much of the drug on it as I could. One down, one to go.

I knew the other hound was almost on me, but I had emergency measures for this. And thanks to that last vial, enough of a clear head to use them. I thrust my uninjured hand in my pocket for the stored banishing spell I always kept there—only to learn I'd left it at the apartment.

"Shit!" I backpedaled, reaching for another precious vial, but the hound was already springing into the air—

—and met its end on a blade of shadows that snapped into existence along with its bearer right in front me. The gorgeous dark-haired woman flashed me a familiar smirk over her shoulder.

"Hello, darling. Be with you in a moment."

She pulled the shadowblade free and the hellhound slumped to the ground, gravely injured but not dead yet. It tried to come at her again, but she expertly lopped off its head with another slash. A thin shadow rose from it, the wispy form that was all most demons could manage in the mortal world without a fleshy form to host them. It was joined by another as the first hellhound's body finally collapsed entirely.

"Run along, little doggies. This one's spoken for," she snarled. She snapped her fingers, and the remaining body burst into flames. The two shadows blinked out of existence in this reality, back to the Pit and their master.

The woman turned to me, her shadowblade vanishing with a thought. "How *do* you keep finding yourself in these situations, McKenna?" The wicked smirk on her red lips hadn't changed; nor had much of the rest of her, though she could shapeshift into any form she wished. But that smirk was Remiel Blake's trademark. The Archdemon of Desire. My ex-girlfriend.

Before I could answer, a wave of weakness and vertigo overtook me. I stumbled, but Remi caught me before I fell into the wall. "Get...get me back to my place," I panted. "A few blocks...that way..."

"If it's all the same to you, I know a shortcut." She secured her arm around me, fire flaring in her eyes. One moment we were there; the next, darkness. Then we were in my apartment. She helped me onto the couch, flipping the lights on with a gesture. I was unused to demonic teleportation these days, but I wasn't about to complain.

"Bathroom. Black bag," I gasped. She set off to get it while I took the last two vials from my pocket. Setting them on the coffee table with a shaking hand, I pushed my shirtsleeve up past my elbow.

Remi returned, kneeling and unzipping the bag. "What do you—" She halted when she saw its contents. "McKenna. This is a drug kit."

"Prep the needle. Explain later." She reached for a vial, but I grabbed her hand, staring her in the eyes. "*Don't* spill it. Not a drop."

Between us, we got my arm prepped for the injection. I tried to take the needle for the act itself, but I couldn't hold it straight. Remi rolled her eyes and did it for me, though not gently. Even so, the needle prick was familiar, a sign of oncoming relief rather than of pain, and the glowing blue liquid brought a rush of blessed cool as it entered my blood. I pulled the tourniquet from my upper arm and slumped back onto the couch, finally letting myself slip into darkness.

---•---

When I woke up, the smell of sautéed garlic, onions, and pasta filled the air. I blinked and slowly sat up. My fever and chills were gone, my head had cleared, and I was shaky only from hunger instead of an overabundance of magic in my blood. My left hand, the one cut by the vial shards in the alley, still stung but had been cleaned and bandaged. A glass of water was on the coffee table. I picked it up with my good hand and gulped the whole thing down. It was still dark outside, a little after midnight according to my clock. Over in the small kitchen, my Archdemon ex was cooking dinner for me.

I couldn't remember the last time anyone had cooked for me.

She looked over when she heard me approach and smiled. "Welcome back, darling. Feeling better? I must say, hellhounds and intravenous drugs are not exactly the reunion I pictured."

"What are you doing here, Remi?" I asked.

"Gee, it's nice to see you, too. Is that any way to greet an old friend who saved your ass *and* made you dinner?" Remi retorted. "You're welcome, by the way."

"We had a deal."

She shook her head as if this was a silly misunderstanding and began dishing out the food. "We did, and surely you realize that as someone with an outstanding debt to me, I'm always able to find you, darling. Not to mention having a certain sense of your well-being, especially when it takes a sudden nosedive. Want to tell me what that's all about?"

"So you've always known where I was." I shook my head. It figured. "Right down to my address and apartment number?"

"I plead the Fifth." She set the plates down on the table, which was set for a lovely little romantic dinner for two, complete with candles and two glasses of wine. The only thing off was that the centerpiece consisted of my needle kit and the remaining two vials of glowing blue elixir, one of them now half empty. "What is this stuff, anyway? Doesn't look like any drug I've ever seen, and that's saying something," she asked, picking one up.

"Anti-magic elixir. Why? You want to try a little in your Bordeaux?"

She dropped it so fast it thunked on the table and began to roll. I grabbed it before it got too far. "Hard pass. Do you have any idea what touching that stuff could do to me? Even a drop of that—"

"Would cancel out the magic keeping your host body alive and habitable and crumble it into dust. Why do you think I told you not to spill any?" I set the two vials into padded slots in the kit bag and zipped it. "This is hardly the first time I've been in danger. So, again, why are you here?"

"It's the first time you've been in *that* much danger," Remi said. She took a seat, gesturing to the other for me to sit in. "And you'd be a whole lot worse without me, so, again, you're welcome. Can we get back to why you, a witch, are injecting anti-magic elixir into your arm?"

I could've tried to dodge the question, but I knew she wouldn't let up. "Because it turns out too much magic in your system, like anything else, is a bad thing. If I don't inject that, the magic in my blood starts to poison me. That's why I was in bad shape tonight." I eyed the chair like it was a trap.

"The chair won't bite, McKenna," Remi said.

"And what am I gonna owe you for all this?" I asked.

"Seriously? It's not a favor, it's food. Entirely from your depressingly sparse cabinets, at that. All I did was add heat. Like I do." She smirked.

I rolled my eyes. "I know how it works, Remi. Nothing's free."

"Consider it me protecting my assets, then. You owe me a debt, and you're no good to me dead or half starved. Sit. Eat. There's no price tag on this one, I promise."

Instead, I looked at the door. "I don't have time to eat. Those hounds won't be the last. I need to get out of here."

"What are you talking about?"

"I'm talking about being *hunted*, Remi, like I have been for the last ten years!" I snapped at her. "I don't know how they found me this time. I didn't even use my magic. But I've got a few hours tops before they tear down this building trying to find me, and I don't plan to be here when they do!"

"McKenna!" Remi was on her feet, hands up in a calming gesture. "I'm sorry—please, take a breath, okay? I know it's been a long time, but if anyone or anything tries to hurt you, I'd still end them merely for thinking it. I can protect you. You're safe with me."

She'd said that to me before, when I'd made my deal with her. My answer was the same. "No one's safe with me."

"Not what I said. And if it comes to it, I'll manage," Remi

said. Her dark eyes held mine for a long moment. "Now, I intend to eat something before we get into whatever our next argument is going to be. Join me if you like. Or stay hangry, whatever." She sat back down, made a show of placing her napkin on her lap, and started eating.

I considered saying she was missing my point, but it wouldn't make a difference. And, honestly, she had a point, too. She was far from defenseless, and the minions of another Archdemon ranked well below her in terms of power. That, and the delicious smells were setting my stomach rumbling, so I finally sat down and dug in. For the first time in years, I became aware that my table manners had gotten a bit lax and found myself sitting up straighter in an attempt to maintain whatever dignity I still had here. Out of the corner of my eye, I caught her smiling, but for once she held her tongue.

In the silence while we ate, I couldn't stop myself from looking over my ex, taking her in. Remi could appear however she liked: male or female, any ethnicity, blond or brunette or redhead. In days long past, as a teenager discovering and exploring my sexuality, I'd enjoyed that flexibility more than a little. Right now, Remi was wearing the same face and figure she'd worn day-to-day when we were in high school. When we were together. A lean young woman of average height with nearly black hair, her curves were enough to be enticing, not enough to be ostentatious. She had dark-brown eyes that became pools of shadow and promise when the light was low, as well as clear, naturally tan skin. She liked to joke that she had the "face of the Mediterranean." She was hot, of course, and she knew it, of course.

She did look older, however. Remi was the only demon who

had a human host body to call her own. At some point, while the original owner was still alive, the body had been designated for Remi's future use—through circumstances that were, I'm sure, less than pleasant. Then they perished, their soul moving on to whatever came next, and Remi moved in. I wasn't familiar with whatever dark magic ritual and runes had made it possible—no witch alive was—but long story short, magic had preserved the body as a vessel for her use and hers alone. Now she could pass as human while having access to all of her demonic powers. She could change her form and heal virtually any wound, though I knew she was not totally invulnerable. She never suffered from human ailments. She could not, however, alter the body's natural age. When she was in the demon dimension known as the Pit, she didn't age at all, but when she was in the human world, she did. Sustained by magic but limited by mortality: The passage of time and the inevitability of death were beyond even an Archdemon's ability to change.

Judging by her appearance, she was still of an age with me. Surprising, given I knew that her body had lasted her more than a century before we met.

Still, even next to a demon in illicitly gotten flesh, I felt underwhelming by comparison in my unspectacular outfit of jeans, a black blouse, and comfortably worn boots. My brown hair was pulled into a messy bun, and my makeup was currently nonexistent. I'd probably gained some color back since the alley, but I wasn't exactly runway-ready. Working as a library assistant might require being clean and put-together, but it did not require dressing to stand out. Very few things I'd done in the last decade had, and that was the way I liked it.

"So. Why exactly is there too much magic in your blood, then?" Remi finally asked, losing the quiet game.

"Aren't you supposed to be good at small talk?"

"I also remember how much you hate it, but if you insist. Hey! Our ten-year reunion is soon. Did you RSVP in the affirmative?" she asked with an overabundance of cheer.

"Shockingly, I didn't get an invitation."

"That'll happen when you go off the grid and assume a new identity. You must admit, I did a very good job of covering your tracks," Remi said. "I mean, when even Reunion Committee chairwoman Brooke Luppino can't find you..."

I rolled the stem of my glass between my fingers. "So...she did take Lucca's last name."

Remi nodded. "A debate she was no longer interested in having by the time she and the furball got married. Six years ago, by the way, right out of college."

"Did you go to the wedding?" I asked.

"I did. Not that they knew, of course. I lurked in the back of the church and wore a different face," Remi replied.

I cracked a smile. "And you didn't burst into flames just walking in?"

"I know, right? I lost some serious street cred for that." Remi chuckled. Her eyes glinted as she looked at me—gazed, really. I looked away again, clearing my throat and trading my wineglass for another forkful of pasta.

"What other news is there?...Leo?" I asked.

"She's been busy. Living in the Commons again now, though."

"She was somewhere else? Where?" I asked, questions tumbling out of me. "Do you ever talk to her?"

"Patience, darling, one at a time. She lived in Boston for a few years after college, moved back a few years ago. We stayed in touch for a while after you first left, less so lately."

"What about..." I had to physically bite my lip to keep from asking about my brother Cameron and my mom. "What about everyone else?"

"All busy with their own lives. You know—college, jobs, engagements, weddings, affairs, babies, et cetera."

I raised an eyebrow. "Affairs?"

"Not nearly enough of those," Remi pouted. "Your friends are exceedingly human and boring sometimes."

"Don't you mean *our* friends?"

This time Remi raised a knowing eyebrow at me. "Let's not pretend they didn't tolerate me purely for your sake, McKenna."

"Leo liked you!... Eventually," I was forced to add. "Whatever. At this point, you've seen them more recently than I have anyway. I can't call myself a friend to people I haven't seen or spoken to in ten years."

"They would beg to differ. If they knew you were alive, that is." Remi sipped from her glass as I stayed silent. "It's been a lonely decade. I'm rather looking forward to the reunion," she continued.

"I'm sorry. It's easy to forget that you..."

"Used to be a normal high school student?" Remi forced a smile that didn't reach her eyes.

I wore one that matched. "We both know you were never that."

"Indeed." She swirled another bite of pasta onto her fork. "And what are you doing for work these days, darling?"

"Don't call me that," I replied. "I've had all sorts of jobs since leaving, but lately, I've been working as a library assistant. Guess that's over now."

"You ever get your degree?" I shook my head. "Even after ten years? That's got to be killing you."

"I don't love it, but it's been kinda hard when I've had to keep moving."

"Keep moving?"

"Don't act surprised," I said. "You didn't drop me off here, and you already admitted to having McKenna GPS installed."

"True, but it's not like I was checking it every day," Remi said. "And I know you wanted to come here. Junior year abroad, wasn't that the plan?"

"Took me a while to save up for the cost of living here. But hellhounds mean it's time to go," I said with a sigh, looking out the window. It's not as though I had an Eiffel Tower view or something, but she wasn't wrong. I'd been here nearly a year, the longest I'd been anywhere, and I wasn't thrilled to be ousted yet again.

"Right, or else they come along and ruin the neighborhood, something like that?" Remi said, seizing upon the opening with a wide grin. "Please, do tell me more."

I sighed again, put down my fork, and held up my wrists to show her what looked like simple charm-bracelet tattoos around each. "After you got me out of Arcadia Commons, it didn't take too long to figure out that using my magic was like pointing a neon sign at my location. The Archdemon of Madness sends hellhounds every time I unleash it. So I got these wards tattooed on me. They protect my mind, prevent anyone from scrying on me, make passing unnoticed easier overall." I indicated a few of the charms as I mentioned their purpose. I'd hidden the runes within designs that looked perfectly mundane—a modern dancer with her body dramatically posed, a cat raising a playful paw, an angled chessboard, a maple leaf. I turned my hands to display the ones inside my wrists, the largest and most obviously witchy "charms": a matching pair of seven-pointed stars. "And these ones keep my magic locked up. I can unlock it if I have to, but then the hellhounds come running, so I don't. However, since my power lives in my blood, after a while it's too much, and I get sick. Blood poisoning, basically. That's what was going on when you showed up tonight."

Remi frowned. "And the elixir takes care of it? That would explain the fast recovery."

"The elixir helps. For a while. But it's...it's not working like it used to." My gaze drifted to the lit candles, wax pooling beneath the flickering flames and running down the sides. "I've been building up a tolerance to it. It's not dangerous at normal doses, but...with how much I need to take and how often..."

"...now *that's* what's poisoning you, isn't it?" she finished for me.

"Not yet, but it will be soon."

Remi was silent, taking this in. "What are your options?"

I smiled without humor. "I don't have any. No good ones, anyway. Unlocking the wards and letting off a blast of magic will help for a while, but that also means it's time to run again. Doesn't solve the real problem."

"Clearly. Sounds like you're in need of a more permanent solution."

"Like what? I can't get rid of the tattoos," I said.

"Then get rid of your magic." Remi peered at her glass, spinning it between her fingers.

I blinked in surprise. "What?"

She looked at me sidelong. "It's not like you're using it."

"It...it's not that easy."

"Why not?"

"For starters, it takes seven witches to sever one from their magic," I pointed out.

Remi shrugged. "Seven witches or one Archdemon." I glared at her so sharply, she put down the glass and held up her hands. "I'm just saying! It wouldn't be a sell-your-soul-level Bargain, and you know I'd never try to trick you into one, either."

"Not gonna happen. Not with you, not with any Archdemon. Not again." Remiel's predecessor, Forneus, had made that kind of Bargain with me once. When I was a young and stupid sixteen-year-old who thought she knew everything.

Still...yet again, Remi wasn't wrong. It would solve my problems. No magic, no outbursts, no septic shock, and no more demons dogging my every step. I could have a life, friends, a permanent address. Everything I'd left behind.

Maybe I could even go home.

No. That was the one thing I could not do, with or without magic.

Besides, it also meant *no more magic*. Permanently. I hadn't used my magic in almost ten years, not really, but I knew it was there. I could still feel it in my blood, wards or no. I couldn't imagine *not* feeling it, the same way I couldn't imagine losing one of my other senses. Living without magic was survivable, sure. Most of the world got along fine not even knowing it existed. But for me, for any witch, it was the sixth sense, as much a part of me as my eyes or ears. And I admit, I liked knowing that if I ever truly needed it, if things got desperate, I had it. Magic was my security blanket. It just happened to be one that might choke me to death.

"Or," Remi went on, "you could unlock those pretty little chains of yours and let your freak flag fly."

That brought me out of my reverie. "You know I can't do that."

"Do I?"

I scowled. "Better than anyone else alive."

"Mm." Remi finished her glass and picked up the bottle to refill it, standing as she did and looking around the small apartment. "Well, that's a shame. It's a decent place. And you've got a lot to pack in a short time," she said a little too casually. "I'll be happy to help you finish off the wine so you don't have to pack that, too."

"How considerate." I put my glass down and stood up as well. "Remiel. You didn't come here to catch up and drink wine. And I get the feeling none of this is actually a surprise to you. You could've swooped in to play savior against the hounds dozens of times since I left. Tell me why you're *really* here."

Remi grimaced in a way that still somehow looked like a smirk. She set her glass down on the table. "I guess the foreplay's over then. I'm here for two reasons. The first is that I truly did sense you were in danger, and I couldn't *not* help." She stepped closer, pretense falling away from her face, and took one of my hands in hers. Her hand was smooth and comfortingly warm, and I found my fingers interlacing with hers on instinct. "I could feel you dying, McKenna. I felt how close you were to it, and—and I had to come." She smelled like burning candles and dark wine. Her eyes held mine with a magnetism that had nothing to do with demonic powers, and I was keenly aware of the color of her lipstick and the suddenly vivid memory of how her lips felt on mine.

No, now wasn't the time to get swept up just because my ex showed up when I was on death's door. But it had been so long since anyone looked at me like that...if this wasn't the time to get swept up, when was?

I delayed the notion with a question. "What's the second reason?"

Remi sighed softly, a sound of resignation. "To take you back to Arcadia Commons."

# Chapter 2
# A Matter of Trust

I jerked back from Remi. "Very funny. Try again."

"I'm not joking, McKenna. That's why I'm here."

"Why would you even—I can't—I'm not going anywhere near that town again and you know it!"

"No need for dramatics. It's been ten years. I know you miss your friends and your family—whom I noticed you *didn't* ask about, by the way. One little visit, a week, seven short days. Why not?"

"You *know* why not!" I snapped. "Sorry you wasted your time, Remiel, but the answer is no."

She sighed again. "I knew you'd say that."

"Yeah, well, it's not my fault you decided to waste your time." A beat passed and realization hit, my eyes snapping back to her. "No. No, you wouldn't."

"As you've no doubt realized, my asking is purely a formality, McKenna. You still owe me for your escape plan ten years ago. And that debt has come due."

"I am *not* going." My hands clenched. "And you can't make me. You *won't*."

"Won't I?"

"You promised, Remi," I rasped. I knew I sounded desperate, and I hated it. "When you got this power—when I helped you get it, intentionally or not—you promised you would never use it against me."

Remi didn't blink as she met my glare, her face no longer open but occluded. "You knew one day I would come to collect. And you had to know that odds were you wouldn't like it when I did."

My jaw tightened as my heart began to race and my stomach to twist. I started to speak, but she held up a finger.

"You're about to threaten to banish me, but as we've discussed, you can't. You're trying to run the logistics, weigh the consequences. But it's been a long time since you played the role of the demon's witch." She leaned in close, her voice an edged whisper that I could hear perfectly, as if she were speaking aloud my own thoughts. "I doubt you'd get off the spell against someone like me before I whisked us both out of here. It doesn't come to you quite like *that* anymore, does it?" She snapped her fingers. "You can't act that fast, not with those chains you've put around yourself. Even if you could, you couldn't control it like you used to. You might remember all the words, all the runes, but your reactions are dulled from disuse. *Tsk-tsk*." I could swear I saw flames flickering in her eyes as they broke away from mine to wander over my face, my body, a gaze that was intimate and alien at once. They landed on my wrists, and she clasped her fingers around one and lifted it. Her warm fingers slid along the inside of my wrist and the delicate lines of the tattoos.

"An impressive artistic endeavor, but I can't say I approve of their purpose, darling," Remi said as she admired them, her fingertip lazily circling one of the charms.

I yanked my hand out of her grasp.

"Don't. Call. Me. That."

Spinning on my heel, wanting Remiel's eyes off me, I stalked to the table, picked up my glass, and drained it as anger filled me. Anger at Remiel, at her request, her assessment. But most of it, older and more familiar, was for myself.

"Why would you make me go back there?" I asked, my back to her. "It completely negates the deal I made. It puts everyone in danger. It puts *me* in danger."

"Not precisely. You bargained for a new identity, untraceable, somewhere far away from Arcadia. I gave you all of those things. Your cover is still secure, none are the wiser, and none of them need to be. What sort of profile you keep once you're there is up to you. Hole up in Motel Six for a week if you like, enjoy the basic cable and the snack machine. All I require of you is that you return to your hometown for one week, starting in one hour."

"One hour!" I sputtered, spinning to face her again. "Even if I left right this second, I wouldn't be there by then!" Much like Fae, demons were damn picky about the details of their deals, and breaking one was never a pleasant experience.

She waved away my worries with a delicate hand. "Please. As if I would make you suffer through customs and a transatlantic flight. Pack a bag and we'll travel my way."

She was serious. This wasn't hypothetical, this wasn't a joke, and she wasn't trying to convince me. She was going to make me. Fear gripped me, fresher than it had been in years, as I tried to wrap my head around the idea of setting foot in Arcadia Commons.

"Remi...don't do this. Please," I pleaded, trying another tactic.

She looked at me with sympathy this time. Well, almost. "McKenna. I don't *want* to force you. But we both know I can, and if I must, I'm afraid I will insist. I would never ask of you something you could not handle."

"Clearly a lie. I can't go back there, not...not after what happened..."

"McKenna," she said in a soft voice, bending her head to catch my eyes. "I know what you're thinking. But that was ten years ago and Arcadia's been nothing but quiet ever since. Don't let fear of the past stop you."

"If it's been quiet, then that means I made the right decision," I replied firmly, straightening up and turning away. I heard her sigh.

"McKenna." She said my name for a third time as she stepped around to stand in front of me again. "I trust you. I always have. I trust your abilities and your limits. Your moral compass," she added with a smirk. "We all know it's better than mine. Hell, it's been guiding me since we met, and I mean that. You asked me to help you run, even when I didn't want to, and I trusted your decision then. Now it's my turn. Please—will you trust me?" she asked, lifting a hand in supplication. Her voice was softer now, her gaze plain, the smirk gone, no fire in her eyes and no suggestions, either. "You used to. Even when things were at their worst." A melancholy smile. "Fact."

*Fact.* I hadn't heard that one in a very long time. Not since we'd been together.

"I'm not going to lose you. I won't *lose* you." I cupped her face in my hands, meeting her eyes. "Life, death, or demons, nothing is taking you away from me, Remi. You and me, we're a team. We're a fact."

*"Far be it from me to argue with McKenna Ellerbeck,"* she said, smiling in defeat. *"Fact . . . I like that."*

Remiel Blake would never have come here and proposed this if she weren't going to enforce it. If I didn't pack, she would still take me back to my tiny Massachusetts hometown, ready or not. She'd already laid bare the fact that my magic wasn't up to the task of stopping her, even if I did break my own wards. Assuming the resulting blast didn't bring down the building and kill her altogether, and maybe me and my neighbors, too. None of which I wanted.

The thing was . . . Remi might be an Archdemon, but she wasn't wrong about trust. Mine or hers. Sure, her moral judgment was skewed by millennia of being a demon, but she'd been changing since the day we'd met, and that was what I'd believed in when it came to her. I'd heard plenty of people talk like they were on the side of the angels just to cover their own asses. I'd heard my dad talk about how much his family meant to him, only to repeatedly cheat on my mom and then walk out on us entirely. Heard the Witches Council claim to represent practitioners of all power levels, only to continue to cater to the wants and needs of the elite. Words didn't matter if the actions weren't there, and Remi had proven herself through actions more than once.

So why did I break up with her? Suffice to say that I hadn't been ready to fully believe that absolute power couldn't corrupt absolutely. Plus a heavy dose of trauma.

And then the fact that I went and fell in love with someone else.

Still, if there was one thing that I had always been able to count on with Remi, even after our actions got her unwillingly promoted and after I had a new boyfriend, it was that she had my safety and well-being at heart. If nothing else, I could trust that Remi would not do me harm. Although the same did not necessarily apply to anyone else. Remi knew everything that had happened, knew exactly why I ran away. She wouldn't bring me back if there was a chance that would happen again.

I let out a heavy sigh. Like it or not—and I definitely did *not*—I was going back to Arcadia Commons.

"Fine. I'll go."

Remi beamed at me. "Excellent! Okay, you go clean yourself up and pack a bag. I'll wait here while you get ready. I'll entertain myself." She jauntily picked up her wineglass and brought it into the sitting room to look around, leaving me staring after her before shaking my head and retreating to my room.

One week. It wouldn't be so bad, right? Like Remi had said, all I had to do was hole up and make sure no one saw me. Then my debt would be paid and I would be free to return to my life, free from any further obligation to Remiel or anyone else. No more strings. No more favors. Life would be on my terms again.

As much as a life on the run and under a false name and the constant threat of death ever could be.

The real question was, of course, what was Remiel really up to? I had decided to trust her, but I wasn't going to be blinded by that trust. Why did she want me to go home, and why now? If I'd stayed more informed on the goings-on back home, maybe I could answer that. But that had been one of the first lessons I'd learned: Reading news from home was too painful. Especially any news about my mom and brother. Seeing a news clip from a local station about my disappearance with the once vivacious Wendy Younger Ellerbeck looking tear-streaked and broken, holding on to my despondent-looking little brother, nearly broke me, too. I'd slammed my laptop shut and sworn off looking up anything about Arcadia Commons ever again. If the news was good, I couldn't share in it, and if it was bad, I couldn't do anything about it. I had always been a doer, a planner, and yes, fine, kind of a control freak. Removing myself from the equation had been harder than I anticipated.

So I stopped torturing myself. I stopped reading, stopped watching, stopped myself from wanting to jump back into a life I could never return to. Eventually, it got easier. There was never a day when I didn't wonder about home and my family and friends, but not knowing became familiar. Whatever awaited me there, I would have to find out when I arrived, and try to figure out what Remiel's real plan was.

After a quick shower, I threw on jeans and a clean blouse

and pulled my damp hair into a braid before I started packing my clothes, keeping comfort in mind. My laptop went in, a few books, and some bathroom products. I threw in some sneakers to have a second pair of shoes.

"All right, I'm packed," I said, heading back into the living room. To my surprise, Remiel handed me a mug of coffee as I set my bag down.

"I didn't see any sugar or cream," Remi said.

"I take it black now," I replied. "Why do I need coffee if I'm planning on crashing once we get there?"

"You never know. You might decide you want to stay up and take a spin around the old neighborhood," she said with an enigmatic smile.

I narrowed my eyes. "What are you getting at?"

"Just drink the coffee." Warily, I sipped. "That's a nice French press, by the way. Or do they just call it a press here?"

"Ha ha."

Remi eyed the packed gym bag at my feet. "That seems a little...light. Sure you're not forgetting anything?"

"It's everything I need to sit in a motel room for a week and keep from being bored out of my mind."

Remiel shrugged with a faux-innocent look on her face. "No garment bag? Dress shoes in case you go somewhere nice? Jewelry, makeup? Maybe that grimoire under your bed?"

"You snooped around my room? Dammit, Remi," I cursed. "That is *not* okay. I don't care if you're an Archdemon and I owe you."

"You took your time getting ready, darling. I got bored." Remi shrugged again as I scowled at her.

"*Stop* calling me that."

"Sorry, sorry. Old habits." She didn't sound sorry. "Seriously, though, you should pack it, and some nicer clothes."

"What exactly is going on in Arcadia Commons that you aren't telling me?" I asked. "Why would I bring that grimoire, of all things, back to that town?... Are my mom and my brother okay?"

"I'm just suggesting you be prepared in case you decide not to sit around shunning the light of day for the next week. Come on, you used to pack more than this for a quick weekend trip to the city." Her smile became flirtatious again, and her eyes gleamed with a familiar heat. "Granted, most of what you packed for that trip didn't take up much space..."

I made a quick exit back to my room before she could see me flush. Remi clearly wasn't about to share further information, and I no longer knew how to deal with her looking at me like that.

I eyed my closet's contents. My wardrobe wasn't as extensive as it had been back in high school. I grew up in the middle class, and clothing was one of the luxuries I used to indulge in. Now I lived much more practically, and options were limited. I grabbed a decent little black dress and some heels to go with it and called it good.

Next, I bent to retrieve the grimoire from beneath my bed. Had Remi actually poked around down here? Nothing looked out of place, not that I could've said precisely where the assorted shoes and other items had been before. Maybe she'd sensed the latent power in it. Many of the spells in it were designed with harming or containing someone like her in mind, after all.

Before I could clearly see the book, I could feel it. The thing pulsed with a quiet promise of power that any witch would notice, but since this book was mine, I felt it even more keenly, wards or no. When my fingers brushed the old leather, a wave went through me: power slipping over my skin, teasing me with what lay within. I grabbed the book by the spine and pulled it out, holding it with both hands in my lap, letting the magic wash over my whole body. I couldn't connect to that magic, but I could feel it. It was nostalgic and new, comforting and exciting all at the same time. It felt good. It felt *right*.

The thick tome had unevenly cut pages edged in gold, with a large handprint pressed into the leather cover. Only my hand, or my mom's or Cameron's, could open it. Grimoires contained the intimate details of a witch family: their magic, their history, their stories. Their secrets. They were practically living things, made from and brimming with magic that built up over time the longer a family line continued. They changed as the family did, too, growing in strength along with the bloodline.

The weird thing was that my family's magic—which I got from my mother's side—had always been too weak to have a grimoire. Until I made my proverbial deal with the devil.

Arcadia Commons Academy, the school I'd attended after sixth grade, was a magnet school for children of supernatural families. Though it masqueraded as a standard, exclusive private school, on its grounds, safe and hidden from the rest of the world, students could learn about the supernatural and how to use their powers as they came into them. Or didn't, in my and my best friend Leo's cases. It was her and her brother Lucca's birthright to be werewolves, but even though they were twins, she never changed. And while I'd always known my family's magic was at the meager level of hedgewitch, I had hoped for something more when I came of age. Instead, I saw my former friends and peers growing in power and turning their noses up first at me and then at Cameron. I tried to ignore it, but how they treated us infuriated me to the point that I sought out another answer.

What can I say? As teenagers are wont to do, I made a spectacularly bad decision.

The idea got into my head that a demon could give me the power I was after, and everything I learned about Forneus made him sound like the decent sort. I took advantage of my after-school job at our local library and my access to the Uncommon Collection, the secret section for supernaturals. I found the restricted books, I learned the ritual, I practiced drawing the circle until I knew it all backward and forward. I was convinced I had everything under control. I ventured outside Arcadia's anti-demon barrier to perform it, and it went perfectly. Forneus showed up, I asked him to give my family more power, and he happily agreed, saying only that for as long as I had that power, I would owe him loyalty. It seemed so innocent—why wouldn't I want to help the creature that had helped me? We had a Bargain. I didn't realize until too late it also meant he owned my soul and, when and if he wanted it, my body.

Of course, once I figured it out, I took steps to fix that problem, too. Fixed it with a magic demon-slaying sword in

Forneus's back, a plan that almost got me and all my friends killed, and inadvertently made Remi his successor in a moment that still cropped up in my nightmares.

*The sword glowed a brilliant white as Forneus, black blood pouring from his wound, screamed. The inhuman sound shook the air and shattered the floor beneath him.*

*Within that light, a cloud of impenetrable darkness hung, the Archdemon stripped to his barest form, before the explosion of power threw us all to the ground. I heard his voice one last time, all around me, yet so close it was an unwelcome whisper in my ear:*

"Remiel, I crown thee."

Thanks to my friends and no small amount of luck, we survived. To everyone's surprise, my family's magic remained, along with the partially filled grimoire that had appeared the night I made my Bargain.

Remi told me once that demons couldn't create something from nothing. Which meant that somehow, that magic *did* in fact belong to us. I still didn't know why it had dwindled for generations, though I suspected the missing grimoire had something to do with it, but post-Bargain, we were powerful banishers and summoners, especially when it came to demons. My mom and brother would've become less powerful without the grimoire close by, and that was a big part of why I took it with me when I left. They were safer that way. Safer without this power, safer without me.

As I sat holding the book, I realized Remi's flirtation had been a distraction that I'd played right into. In my eagerness to escape the conversation, I'd sought out the book. Now that I had it in my hands, with its whisper of spells and magic, I didn't want to put it back. Not now that I was remembering the feel of magic on my skin and in my blood...

Before the thought could tempt me further, I shoved the grimoire in the bag. It was a good thing I didn't need to take a flight. People surely would've stared at me for fondling an old book filled with Latin and arcane symbols. I headed back out to the living room.

"Okay. Grimoire, black dress, heels, are you satisfied?" I asked.

Remi was flipping through a French magazine now. "European *Cosmo* really is the superior publication," she said without looking up.

"Don't be crass."

She grinned crookedly at me. "As if you don't get something out of it, too."

I rolled my eyes. "Do you want to look at my internet history before we go, too?"

Remi's grin broadened, and she tossed the magazine down. "Now, *there's* a tempting offer." I gave the demon a dark look, and Remi held up her hands. "All right, all right. You're in a rush, so be it. Last call on the coffee before we go."

I considered that, then took a large gulp of the warm, dark liquid. Carrying the mug to the sink, I reclaimed the anti-magic elixir kit from the kitchen table on my way back. "Sufficiently caffeinated. Let's get this over with."

Remi nodded, picked up the duffel bag and slung it on her shoulder, then grabbed me around the waist and pulled me close against her body. Once again, we were nearly eye-to-eye. The scent of fire along with a nice perfume surrounded

Remiel. For a moment, the demoness was still, a solid presence, her arm and her warmth sensations I had known so well in another lifetime. For a moment, Remi looked at me like she still loved me, and I wasn't sure if she might try to kiss me. I wasn't sure what I would do if she did.

But only for a moment. "Hold on tight, darling." Darkness enveloped us, and the world was ripped away.

# Chapter 3
# A Grand Entrance

My lungs were burning when we popped back out of the darkness. I grabbed the nearest wall and sucked in lungfuls of air.

Remi cocked an eyebrow at me. "You didn't remember to hold your breath?"

"It's been a while," I gasped after a few moments. Looking up, I did not see anything resembling a forgettable, carbon-copy, find-it-anywhere cheap motel. No, instead I saw a simple but nicely appointed room with the words WELCOME TO THE ARCADIA COMMONS GRAND HOTEL painted in fancy script on the wall across from me in several different languages.

I glared at her. "Tell me this is a hilarious joke I'm just not laughing at, and that you did not bring me to the portal room of the Lemaires' *fucking luxury hotel*." Being a hotel in a supernatural-heavy town and run by a family of portal witches, it and all Lemaire properties boasted rooms specially designed for portaling in and out via magic.

"Please, like I'd put you up anywhere but the best," Remi said, straightening her jacket. "Before you fret and give yourself premature wrinkles, relax, it's under your pseudonym, Miss Kendra Moureau." It was the name I'd used ever since leaving Arcadia, the identity she'd helped me establish when we made our deal.

She went to take my arm, but I yanked it away. "I can't be here! Someone is going to recognize me."

"Would that really be so bad?" Remi replied.

"If someone finds out who I am due to your negligence, that's a broken deal on *your* end, Remi. You know, I've always wondered what happens if the demon's the one who breaks the deal."

Remi pouted at me. "You're no fun. I suppose I could disguise you. But it can't come for free, McKenna."

"Seriously?"

She shrugged. "You *could* do it yourself. You just refuse to."

I heard muffled voices from outside the room. Was someone coming in here?

"I hate when you do this. How much?"

"Not much. A small favor."

"Fine. Just do it, *now*."

"My pleasure." Remi reached into her pocket and pulled out a necklace with a charm made from a black knight chess piece. One I hadn't worn in years and would've sworn was sitting on my dresser back in Paris. She'd given it to me for my seventeenth birthday. When we were still together, before we'd killed Forneus, freeing me and making her his successor.

*"A black knight?"*

"*Because you're no one's pawn, darling, and we all know you don't need a white one.*"

I shook off the memory. "You went through my stuff?"

"Like I said, I got bored. Now, since you're in such a hurry?"

Remi reached up, her arms snaking about my neck as she slipped it on me, brushing my hair aside so it could settle. Her warm fingers skimmed over my collarbone, a light, teasing touch. When she lifted the charm to her lips and kissed it, her dark eyes not leaving mine, a rush of warmth like a full-body blush spread over and through me as her power settled on my skin.

A bellhop poked his head into the room. "Good evening, ladies! Welcome to the Grand. Can I help bring your things to the check-in desk?"

While I hesitated, Remi gave him a wide smile. "That would be wonderful, Seth, thank you," she said, getting his name off the tag on his vest. She handed him my single bag. "Shall we, darling?"

With a dark look, I eschewed her arm and followed Seth to the lobby.

With marble on every surface, a chandelier of operatic proportions, and more employees like Seth in crisp uniforms that were tastefully old-fashioned, everything was luxury, down to the sparkling water offered to each guest upon check-in. The ceiling displayed an immense mosaic featuring sea gods, imposing war galleys, mermaids, and crashing waves. The art decorating the large atrium all matched the ocean theme. The Grand sat on a rise overlooking Ipswich Bay, after all, and like everything else in the tourist-loving town, it cashed in on the oceanic kitsch. Here, however, it was done with tasteful elegance and opulence.

On the far end of the lobby, an immense staircase hugged the curve of the wall and wound its way to the second-floor balcony, where cocktail tables and a bay of windows let patrons of the hotel bar, Titan, take in the view while they enjoyed their handcrafted cocktails and small plates. The main ballroom was up there as well. To the left, doors led to the four-star restaurant called Siren, with the fanciest and priciest seafood selection between here and Boston. A bank of elevators sat in an offshoot hallway between the restaurant entrance and the concierge desk.

Trailing behind Seth, I felt very exposed, as though every eye were on me and judging me, despite logically knowing that none of them were. My darting eyes landed on a boisterous group taking pictures on the stairs and suddenly I saw the place not as it was now, but as it looked ten years ago, filled with teenagers in tuxedos and fancy dresses. Senior prom. Remi hadn't been the one on my arm that night, however. By that time, I was dating Bastien Lemaire.

Much to the dismay of Bastien's family, their golden-boy heir apparent had fallen for the upstart young witch known for consorting and cavorting with demons. The Lemaires weren't just your standard uber-rich white folks, either, but also one of the most prominent witch families in the eastern United States. While Bastien's parents had always been nice enough, his grandfather, who held the most senior of the seven seats on the Witches Council, was never a big fan of mine. Not surprising, since he once tried to have the Council brand me a supernatural criminal and strip me of my magic.

As for how Bastien went from grudging ally who negotiated his aid in taking down Forneus for my confession to the Council in the first place to the next great love of my teen years, well... that was yet another long story.

Remi talked charmingly to the woman at the desk as she checked "Kendra" in. I was relieved to overhear that she had shown some restraint and wasn't checking me into a penthouse suite. Remi had always been prone to extravagance, and she enjoyed being a scooch, as Lucca would put it. Still, housing me here was a bigger risk than either of us needed to be taking.

"All set, Miss Moureau," Remi said, handing me a key card. "I know that look. Thinking about taking off?"

"Considering it. Why are you really putting me up here? This isn't what I'd call keeping a low profile."

"There's no reason to stay in squalor. Now, are you taking that sparkling water or am I free to claim it?"

Half out of spite, I grabbed the bottle and cracked it open as we headed to the elevators. "A cheap motel is hardly squalor. I've lived in worse. You're up to something, Remi."

Remi smirked broadly. "Has it been so long that you forgot? I'm *always* up to something."

We stood at the back of a chatty crowd by the elevators. The middle elevator dinged and opened; everyone shifted, parting to let the occupants off first. I stepped to the side to let them pass, and my eyes caught on a chin-length crop of copper hair that, for a split second, I thought belonged to a dead girl. My breath caught. But the figure shifted and it was revealed to be that girl's younger brother: Tom Harwell, another local witch who'd been in my brother's grade.

What was he doing here? Didn't matter. Disguised or not, I didn't want to see him.

"We're taking the stairs," I hissed, turning away.

"But you'll miss getting to say hi," Remiel said, still with that damn grin on her face. "You have a lot to catch up on, you know."

"It's in your interest as much as mine that no one sees or suspects me, *especially* not a Harwell."

"I hardly think he's going to suspect anything, *Kendra*. Unless you think he's going to read your thoughts?"

"I've got telepathy wards handled, that's not—"

"Good, because it's too late," she whispered, then broke into another overly friendly grin. "Tom Harwell, as I live and breathe! Aren't you a sight to see."

"Remi Blake." Tom's tenor tone greeted her with mild surprise. My gut twisted as I slowly turned to face him. He gave me a brief glance with no recognition whatsoever. Remi's disguise was as good as her word.

"So good to see you again," Remi said smoothly. "How have you been?"

"The usual," Tom said. He was unexpectedly casual with her. He hadn't looked at me at all, but my heart still hammered in my chest all the same. "Are you here for the reunion?"

"Of course," Remi replied. *That's tonight? Here? Remi, you bitch!* I struggled to keep my outward composure. "Yourself? Crashing so you can hang with the big kids?" Remi teased.

Tom and my brother Cameron had been two years behind us in school.

"Something like that." Tom's eyes flicked to me. "I don't think we've met, I'm Tom Harwell." He held out his hand.

Remi tsk'd. "Where are my manners? Kendra Moureau," she introduced. "My friend and plus-one for the evening."

I swallowed and put on a smile, taking Tom's hand. His grip was loose and mine trembling; it wasn't a great handshake. "Nice to meet you," I replied, doing my best to sound perfectly normal and uninteresting.

"You, too. Don't worry, whatever she's said, I'm no one to get nervous over," Tom replied with a kind smile, apparently noticing I was on edge. "I'm distinctly not a big deal around here."

That he truly had no idea who I was or what I'd done should've been a relief. Instead, I felt sick.

Thankfully, Tom looked at Remi again, leaving me to cower inwardly in peace. "I don't think anyone's expecting you to show up."

"I wouldn't dare miss it. But do me a favor and don't ruin the surprise," Remi replied, eyes twinkling.

"Don't you usually charge for that kind of thing?" Tom asked, following us back onto the elevator. I was surprised both that he was coming with us and that he was turning the request back on her.

"Clever boy. And what would buy your silence for an hour or so?"

Tom hesitated for only a second before suggesting, "How about an hour or so of your tab at Titan?"

Remi nodded. "Done. An equivalent block of time it will be. Try not to run it up so high this time." She held out her hand.

The elevators dinged for the mezzanine level, where the bar was located. Tom shook Remi's hand, looking satisfied, but his smile still didn't reach his eyes. "Pleasure doing business with you, Remi." He tucked his hands in his pockets and headed for the bar. He looked even more like the male version of his older sister Jackie now than he had years ago, but he lacked a certain vitality that she'd always had.

I guess losing a sister will do that to you.

———————•———————

After that, I was brimming with questions, but I waited until we stepped into Room 1402.

The suite was very nice: a kitchenette, a plush couch and armchair in front of a wide-screen TV, with a queen-size bed in a room that could be made private by closing the French doors. The view overlooked the bay, which was largely empty, what with it being late October. The walls were covered in a tasteful, inoffensive pattern of matte white and shiny off-white. The rest of the decor and upholstery featured bolder color choices than your standard chain hotel, and the quality was of a higher caliber, most of it in ranges of blue and green. The bed was covered in a brilliantly white comforter and more pillows than anyone had ever needed.

I dropped my backpack at the foot of the bed and pulled off my shoes before padding to the floor-to-ceiling windows along the outside wall, gazing out at the bay I'd grown up with. Just looking at it, I could smell the salt air that carried a thousand memories on it. The hotel beach curved below us, and the lights of docks and yacht clubs led both north and south along the coast. Farther inland, the average household income took a dive, but waterfront property was the prize of the elite here as in any town. My family's home, while nothing to scoff at, was well out of view from here, on a cul-de-sac called Fox Hill Road, where it had sat for generations.

"A sight for sore eyes, I hope?" Remi stepped up next to me.

"A lot of memories out there," I said, looking out at the water as it peacefully lapped the shore. After the night I'd had, it was pleasantly calming.

"Mmm, like that time we went skinny-dipping off the boardwalk?" Remi prompted, smiling slyly.

I gave a wry chuckle. "You never change."

"Whatever do you mean?"

"Still the incorrigible flirt." I turned away from the window and began to pull a few necessities from my bag. "I didn't agree to go to the reunion."

Remi sat on the bed, leaning back on her hands. "Oh, come on. It's *right* downstairs, filled with friends you haven't seen in a decade. How could you say no?"

"Because I don't want to see any of them."

Remi gave me a look. "Lies do not become you, McKenna."

"What? It's true." I tossed my black dress on the bed—now I knew why she'd insisted I bring it—and pulled out my pajamas and toothbrush.

"No, it's not true. What you don't want is for *them* to see *you*," the demoness emphasized. I pressed my lips together, trying to ignore her. It was, as always, not easy. "See? I knew it. But here's the brilliant thing, darl—McKenna. None of them will see you, they'll only see Kendra." She gestured to the mirror on the closet door; I paused to see exactly what my disguise looked like.

My hair was dirty blond, my eyes bright blue, my nose rounder, my figure more filled out, though my height was unchanged. The necklace that was holding the illusion appeared to be a small, simple diamond pendant, though my other clothes remained the same, as did the bandage on my right hand. I pulled up my sleeve and noticed that my tattoos were still visible. And while the old scar in the middle of my left palm was not, I could still feel it when I rubbed my thumb across it. Remi's work was purely visual, but it was good to know that my wards were good enough to be unaffected. "While Kendra may be lovely—she is my handiwork after all—she's got nothing on the real deal," Remi went on, her eyes lingering on me.

I reached back and undid the necklace; the illusion fell away and I saw myself again. Tired, pale, still too thin and strung-out looking. I sure didn't feel lovely.

"The enchantment will remain on the necklace for the rest of the week, in case you were thinking that taking it off now would be the end of it."

I scowled. "And what do I owe you for it?"

Remi waved it off. "We'll figure it out later. Now, are you going to put on that little black dress or what?"

"I'm not going, Remi. I'm here, I'll stay here for the week, but I'm hermiting up, exactly like I told you I would," I reminded her. "I'm going to put on my pajamas and go to bed. I've got a long week of pay-per-view to rest up for."

Remi rolled her eyes. "I forgot how stubborn you can be."

I shrugged. "If you wanted more, you should've asked for it before we left."

I crossed to the bathroom to deposit my toothbrush, shampoo, and so forth, while Remi poked around in my makeup bag. "So you're not at all curious to see Lucca and Brooke, ask how married life is treating them? To find out how Preston Chang's burgeoning wedding planning business is going? Ask Chris what's new in his life? Ooh and ahh over Mariposa Perez's big shiny engagement ring?"

I gave her an odd look as I came back in. "Who's Preston Chang? And why would I ooh and ahh for the ultimate mean girl convincing some poor fool to marry her?"

Remi shrugged. "Harsh. Isn't that what one does when someone gets engaged? Friend or no. As for Preston, he was still known as Nancy Chang when you knew him."

"Oh—*ohh*." Well, that was unexpected. Although, now that I thought about it, maybe not.

"Why is there a rune carved on this?" Remi asked, peering at a closed mirror compact. I snatched it out of her hands before she could open it.

"Insurance policy. Look, I'm happy for Preston and everyone except maybe whoever Mari got to propose to her, but I'm not going, so it doesn't matter who's who or who's engaged or whatever," I replied. "In fact—why are you still here?"

"You haven't asked me to leave."

"Easy to fix. Remiel, please show yourself out. I'll talk to you in a week when it's time for me to go."

Remiel stood up from the bed, straightening her jacket and walking toward the door, in no hurry at all. "Very well. If you change your mind, you know where to find me and the rest of your classmates," she said. "And Tom Harwell, of course. I imagine he'll be well into his cups by the time things get going."

That finally made me hesitate. "...How many times have you made that deal with him? The whole exchange sounded a little too familiar."

Remi shrugged again. "Here and there. He's a teacher now, you know, at the high school. History. And Arcadia Commons Academy might have a nice endowment, but teaching only pays so much."

I looked down at my backpack. My grimoire was still in it, and I could swear it was whispering to me even from here. I reached down, zipping it closed and shutting it up. "I wanna say he always seemed straight and narrow, but I didn't really know him."

"Things change, people change," Remi said over her shoulder from the door. "Especially when they lose someone so close to them. Well! Enjoy the room and your pay-per-view. I'll let the staff know that my tab is open to Miss Moureau as well; room service is on me. Ta-ta!" With that, she finally let herself out.

I sank onto the bed. The quiet that followed, which had often been my companion in the last decade, was suddenly alien and unwanted and far from empty. Without Remi's playful presence, the space filled with memories I'd held at arm's length for so long that I'd forgotten they might still be there at all. Laughter, tears, magic, love. Pain, fear, guilt.

Secrets.

Blood on my hands.

"Dammit, Remi," I cursed under my breath. I got up and grabbed the little black dress. I had a high school reunion to go to.

———————•———————

Half an hour later, I was exiting the elevator in that black dress and heels, made up for the occasion and with my hair brushed back into a chignon. The reunion hadn't started yet, but there were more people filling the bar area now. Some were familiar. Thankfully none were my close friends.

But I wasn't here to mingle. I was just here to check on Tom, make sure he wasn't drinking himself into oblivion thanks to me. This was purely to ease my conscience. And if he did have a problem... well, I wasn't sure what I would do, but I'd deal with that if and when I had to. For now, I was merely looking in on him and escaping before the reunion started.

The fact that I was dressed up was... purely to blend in. That's all.

The mellow piano music in the lounge stopped as I approached the bar, scanning for Tom. A moment later, a pop hit from my graduating year began playing at a louder volume, and a familiar, perky voice exclaimed, "Perfect!"

At the end of the bar, nearly looking like she'd stepped out of a time capsule, was Brooke Luppino née Bellerieve. Her beachy-blond hair hung only to her shoulder blades instead of her waist now, swaying as she moved to the music. Her skin still glowed with a perfect natural tan, and her wide green eyes were recognizable even at this distance. She was about my height in her white heels, with long legs and a lithe but curvy build, and clad in a short, swishy blue-green dress. Her look was all summer all year round, and somehow she made it work. On her left hand, she wore a set of gold rings, one glittering with a small princess-cut diamond. She offered me a friendly smile as she passed, and I returned it out of reflex.

"Are you here for the reunion?" she asked.

I blinked, surprised at being addressed. "Me?"

Brooke smiled and nodded. "I know you weren't in our class, since I don't recognize you and I'm excellent with faces. But you look like maybe you're here for it. Are you someone's date?"

I hesitated—was the bar closed for the event? If so, I'd have no chance to find Tom. I forced a smile and cleared my throat. "Yes. I'm here with Remi Blake."

Brooke's blond eyebrows went up. "Oh! Really? I didn't know she was bringing anyone. Actually, I didn't even know she was coming! Well, I'm Brooke Luppino, it's nice to meet you," she replied, offering her hand.

I shook it; it was very odd introducing myself as though for the first time to someone I'd known so well. "... Kendra Moureau. Nice to meet you, too."

"Come on, let's get you a name tag," she said, hooking my

arm with hers and leading me back to the sign-in table. My feet stuck to the floor for a second before I stumbled to keep up. My skin felt alien and ill fitting, like it wasn't mine at all, like I wasn't in it but witnessing this moment from outside my body. Seeing Remi was one thing, running across Tom was another, but this was jarringly foreign and familiar all at once. The first day I'd met her, in eighth grade, we'd walked together just like this.

---

*Sixteen years ago*

"That's the new girl, right? Brooke Bellerieve?" Lucca asked me at our lunch table.

At the end of the lunch line, a blond-haired, green-eyed girl looked around nervously.

"Yeah, that's her. Moved here from New Orleans, she's like a... third or fourth cousin to Dorian Bellerieve," I replied.

"New Orleans? Why'd she move up here?" he asked.

"The Bellerieves split off a long time ago, half the family moved down south and half stayed here," I explained. Witch 101: Know your family trees. "I guess everyone but her died when Hurricane Dalia hit this summer. So now she's living with Dorian and his mom."

"That's awful! No wonder she looks terrified. C'mon, let's invite her to sit with us," Leo suggested.

"Sure, sounds—oh, no." I made a face. "Looks like Mari's claiming her."

Mariposa Perez, flanked by some of her other adept-level witch friends, approached the girl. "Brooke, right? I'm Mari Perez, nice to meet you."

"Thanks! Yeah, that's me," Brooke said, smiling at her.

"I wanted to ask you to sit with us—" Brooke's face brightened with hope. "—but then I heard this *awful* rumor that you're just a hedger water witch whose family drowned. So I just had to ask, because, I mean, that can't be *true*, right?"

Brooke froze, speechless, tears gathering in her eyes at Mari's mocking. Leo and I looked at each other and, without a word, stood up and swooped over.

"Hey Brooke. I'm Leo, this is McKenna," Leo said, linking arms with the new girl.

I linked up on her other side and smiled at her, ignoring Mari. "And now that you've met the worst Arcadia has to offer, how'd you like to meet the best?"

"Y-yeah. I'd like that. Thanks." Brooke sniffed but smiled gratefully. Without another word or ever looking at Mari and company, the three of us walked back to our table together.

———•———

Leo and I had always been each other's ride-or-die, but once Brooke arrived, we were basically a trio. Now here Brooke was, taking in a supposed stray the same way, looking precisely as happy and bubbly as ever. Meanwhile the dissonance of my night—of my life—was making my head throb.

"So are you a friend or a girlfriend? Or a... *co-worker*?" The word practically winked at me.

"A-a friend," I stammered.

"Oh." Brooke sounded disappointed. "How did you meet, then?" she asked as we reached the table. She handed me a HI MY NAME IS sticker and gestured to the array of colorful Sharpies. I took a purple one and wrote KENDRA on it.

"Through mutual friends."

"Oh, you should write I'M WITH REMI on there. That's what I'm having the plus-ones do," she helpfully suggested.

*Won't Remi love that.* I scribbled the line below my name. "So, what have you been up to since graduation?" *Nope, too familiar.* "I mean—what do you do?"

"I'm an aesthetician and massage therapist at Pasithea—you might've seen our card in your room?" she asked. "It's the hotel spa. Just down the hall from the pool on the first floor. You should check us out while you're here!"

"Sure, maybe," I replied. That was surprising—she'd always wanted to go into medicine back in high school. Then again, it wasn't exactly like I'd gone into my intended field, either. "You must be pretty busy with people in town for the reunion."

"We are. We still have some availability, though. Next weekend is when we're really busy, since my manager is getting married. I'm the maid of honor!" She beamed.

"Congratulations. I'll keep that in mind if I make an appointment." I pressed on my name tag, very much wanting to get away from this conversation, and forced another smile. "And now that I am properly labeled, I think I'll get myself a drink."

"Sure—find me later, we'll talk!"

I was grateful to slip away before Brooke could launch into a series of twenty more questions or start going on about wedding minutiae. We had lovingly teased her with the nickname Babbling Brooke for a reason. I took a deep breath, shoving that whole interaction into a box labeled THE PAST: DO NOT OPEN in my brain, and scanned the bar for Tom. He was at the far end, with several empty seats next to him. I strode over and took one, leaving a chair between us.

"Water with lemon, please," I ordered—tempting as it was to get something stronger, I already had a weird mix of wine, coffee, and teleportation lag going on. "Tom, right?" I continued, turning to him. "Kendra. We met by the elevators, I'm Remi's friend."

Tom looked up from his glass of scotch. It reminded me of my father's nightcaps. "Kendra! Right, yeah. How's it going? Have a seat," he invited magnanimously, with a wide sweep of his arm at the empty barstool next to him. *Yep. He's drunk.* "Oh, ha, you already...never mind. So a friend of Remi's, huh? What kind of friend?"

"The old kind. We go back a way," I replied.

Tom nodded with a knowing smile. "Ahh, yeah, I bet you do. How'd she get you to come here?...Hey, wait, you're not gonna cause trouble, are you?"

The bartender set down my water. "No. Causing trouble is the last thing on my mind," I said.

"Well, here's to that, then—no more trouble," Tom toasted, wagging a finger and holding up his scotch. I obliged him, clinking his glass and drinking.

Unlike Brooke, Tom looked nothing like I would've once

expected. Not that I'd known him well, since he'd been younger than me, and Jackie and I hadn't really been friends. He hadn't been close to Cameron, either, though they were the same age. But the young man before me didn't feel like he fit with what I could recall. He was drunk, sure, and maybe that's why he looked a little rumpled, but even his drunk smile wasn't real. It didn't fully reach his eyes, much less deep down inside of him. I knew what it was like to wear a smile like that.

"So this isn't your reunion?" I asked him. "Remi told me you graduated a few years after this group."

Tom nodded, looking at his glass. "Yep. My older sister was in their year. We had some of the same friends," he replied. I was unsure what to say, so I said nothing—I knew Jackie was dead, but "Kendra" wouldn't know that. "Remi told you about my sister, I take it," he finally added.

"She did." I latched on to the excuse. "...I was sorry to hear..." My rote sympathies suddenly stuck in my throat.

"Yeah, everyone is."

"I..." That box in my brain threatened to burst. "I'm so sorry, Tom." The words came out of me in a rush, shaky and thick with guilt.

Tom looked up, staring at me oddly—and then I felt him probe at my telepathy wards, blinking as he met resistance. "Did you know her...?"

"I'm sorry—no—I'll leave you alone. Sorry," I blurted out, grabbing my glass and hightailing it out there. I gulped my water as I went.

*I never told him I was sorry*, I realized. Never apologized, never really faced any of this. I never had the chance...no, never gave myself the chance. I gulped the cold water, tried to let it calm the rising panic. *Shit. I am so not prepared for this.* Ten minutes in and I'd barely escaped the Brooke Inquisition and my own guilty conscience. I had to get out of here.

I tried to leave quickly, but the bar had become more crowded. My former classmates were gathering and flitting among little clusters of people like bees to flowers, excitedly greeting one another with hugs and oh-my-gosh-how-are-yous. Once again, the past and the present did and didn't make sense at the same time. I was used to seeing all these people in the same place together, but this was different. Jocks were high-fiving theater kids while academic decathlon team members chatted up former goths, many of whom wore much less raccoon eyeliner than I remembered. Adepts and old power witches were chatting like old friends to the hedges. The humans, the werewolves, and the Fae-blooded were mixing, even the ones who'd been uptight about that kind of thing back in the day.

Like Chris Miller, another old friend and one of Lucca's packmates. Chris had been there that night with Forneus, too, and the price for helping me was losing his leg. But his smile, brilliant white against his dark skin, was as gregarious as ever as he talked—or maybe flirted?—with an Asian man who looked familiar but whose name I couldn't place until I realized that he must be Preston Chang. Then Astrid, a Fae and one of the aforementioned goths, joined them, hugging them both like they were old friends. Astrid had once shaved her head to protest our performance of *Cinderella*. The fact that her hair was now grown into a Mohawk was the most recognizable part of the tableau. The trio was but one of many in the collage of voices and faces around me, memories juxtaposed onto a world that didn't fit.

But the truth was that *I* was the piece that didn't fit.

My water glass slipped from my hand, shattering on the floor. Everyone around me jumped back, staring at me, and I froze, waiting, dreading, hoping that someone would see through my disguise, know who I was, and accuse me of everything I'd done. But no one did. A room full of people I had grown up with looked at me and saw no one. In my head, I could practically hear what Remi would say: *"You wanted to disappear, darling, and so you have. Like any McKenna Ellerbeck plan, you pulled it off flawlessly. If you're having second thoughts now, well, you know how to fix that, don't you?"* My hand clutched at my necklace, feeling the chess figurine hidden beneath the illusion. *"Make the surprise move. Do what they don't expect. Be the black knight."*

No. That's not me anymore.

I mumbled an apology and took the opening to escape, stepping over the mess. My breath was coming in short, shallow gasps, my skin itched, my head pounded. I needed air, I needed to get the hell out of here. Finally, I burst onto the mezzanine balcony, grasped the cool metal railing, and forced myself to take several deep breaths with my eyes closed.

A few minutes passed and I was beginning to calm down when I heard the soft clap of a shoe on the tiles behind me. I turned around, sniffing and wiping at my eyes. Lucca Luppino stood there, staring at me in disbelief, beer glass in hand.

# THE TWICE-SOLD SOUL

His eyes went from my face to my name tag and back. His nose twitched. "...McKenna?"

I'd forgotten Leo's first rule of sneaking around: Avoid the pack like the plague. Sighing, I gave him a shaky, sheepish smile. "Hi, Lucca."

# Chapter 4
# What's in a Name?

In second grade, we played our very own Arcadia version of playground tag called Witches and Wolves. Two teams, two bases. If you got tagged, you could either go to the other team's jail or join their side. The werewolves were just old enough to start developing keen senses, and the young witches could cast some simple charms, including one to mask their scent.

Except me. I was terrible at even the little spells, so no matter how good my hiding spot was, Lucca always sniffed me out. But even when he inevitably found me, he'd grin and ask if I wanted to be a wolf, and I'd smile back and we'd howl and chase after the witches for the rest of recess.

Twenty years later, he was still sniffing me out.

Lucca let out a laugh of disbelief and then wrapped me in a big hug. For a second, it felt alien and unreal, but then I leaned into him, eyes shut, and let his warm welcome carry me back and anchor me to reality with his solid, physical presence. I wasn't a big hugger, but he'd always given great hugs. And

I couldn't remember the last time a friend had hugged me at all.

"Oh, shit, almost spilled my beer on you! Sorry!" He pulled back, letting me go to put his glass down on a cocktail table next to us. Lucca had crested six feet in high school and had gained a few more inches since, as well as the muscle to go with it. There was no such thing as an out-of-shape werewolf, and while Lucca had been in good shape then, he was rocking some Henry Cavill–level physique under the white button-down and gray pants he was wearing now. I laughed when I saw that his navy-blue tie had tiny pizza slices on it. His olive-toned, naturally deep tan complexion was the same, but his all-around shaggy dark hair was now confined to a shaggy patch on top with a neatly-shaved fade on the sides. He had a five o'clock shadow similarly sculpted with neat, sharp edges, though the goatee was more filled in.

He took me in as well, holding me at arm's length. "You're...you're here! Holy shit! Where the hell have you been? Why do you look like this? And why do you smell like Remi?" He was expectedly gruff about Remi, but it made me smile all the same, glad to know some things never changed.

"Sniffed me out, huh?" I confirmed; he nodded. I had already noticed the illusion was only visual, but it was sloppy of Remi to not think of that...then again, maybe she had. Between my rushed and muddled request, and her obvious interest in getting me to this reunion, it wasn't out of the question.

"Yeah, after you dropped that glass back there, I was like, whoa, who's that rando? So I did the standard stalk and sniff, and it was like, hey, wait, I know that smell. Couldn't place it, but it was on the tip of my nose! But I caught the Remi whiff and bam, I knew it had to be you. Except—you're not *you*. What's up with this look?" He gestured at me. I chuckled; it was a classic Lucca breakdown of the situation. He and Brooke really were well suited.

"It's an illusion. And can you keep this on the down-low? No one else can know I'm here," I said. "That's why the disguise. It's from Remi's power. That's why you smelled her on me."

"Has she known where you were this whole time? And she never told anyone?" Lucca growled.

"No! Well, kind of, but it's not like you think. It's complicated," I said.

He rolled his eyes. "When is it *not* with her."

"I hadn't seen her in ten years before tonight," I assured him.

"Okay, but where have you been? Why did you leave? Why are you back? It's great to see you—well, sort of see you—but, seriously, so many questions," Lucca said earnestly. "And that's not even counting the ones Brooke's going to have."

"No! Lucca, come on, she's terrible with secrets. We can't tell her," I stressed. "I love her, I miss her, but we're talking about Babbling Brooke here."

Lucca gave me what I used to call his serious-doggo face. Never *to* his face, of course. "McKenna, she's my wife. We don't keep things from each other."

I weighed my options and offered, "I'll answer your questions, but it has to be just us."

"No deal, *McRemi*," Lucca growled.

"Oh, come on! It's not like that, not since high school."

"One, you're the one who started busting out mean high school nicknames, and two, your name tag *literally* says I'M WITH REMI," Lucca retorted, pointing at my dress.

I scowled and tore the tag off. "Your wife made me write that," I muttered.

"Yeah, well, she didn't make you get in bed with a demon," Lucca retorted.

Now it was my turn for the serious face. "Not that it's any of your business, but I am *not* in bed with her. That ended a long time ago, and it hasn't changed." He looked skeptical. I suppose I couldn't blame him, but it still pissed me off. "Anyway, the point is, you can't tell Brooke or anyone else that I'm here."

Lucca's jaw tightened, and I caught a glimpse of lupine gold in his eyes before he shut them and took a long, deep breath. When he opened his eyes again, they were dark brown and human again, and he had forced some calm into his voice, speaking more slowly. "McKenna, I don't want to argue with you, but if you really can't even give me one good reason not to tell Brooke—"

"She'll be in danger," I interrupted.

That gave him pause. "Are *you* in danger?"

"Yeah. I am." No sense lying; he would know. Werewolves were basically living, breathing lie detectors, and I wasn't anywhere near collected enough to trick him. "Not actively, not right this second, but yeah."

"Is that why you left?"

I sighed. "Look, same deal. I'll answer what I can, but don't tell anyone I'm here, including Brooke."

"What about Leo?"

"Not even Leo."

"Shit." He let out a breath. "Okay, counter-offer: I ask, you answer, and you'll hear me out about why you should tell them yourself. Brooke *can* keep a secret when it's important, you know. I run a security company. The pack's gotten bigger. We've got resources and connections now. Whatever this is, we can help."

"I know you want to, but you can't with this. If anyone could, I wouldn't have left in the first place. So, you won't change my mind, but sure. Deal." I looked back at the bar full of our classmates. "This isn't a good place to talk, though."

"We'll stay out here, out of the crowd. First up, why did you leave?" he asked, picking up his beer again.

I shook my head. "Next."

Lucca rolled his eyes. "Okay, then why are you back?"

"Because I have to be. I'm here for a week, holding up my end of a deal with Remi."

"Thought you were done making deals with demons," he said, eyes narrowing.

"It wasn't that kind of deal. She called in an old debt. I wouldn't be here at all if I could help it, Lucca, believe me. I don't want anyone else to get hurt."

He tilted his head. "Anyone *else*?"

*Well, shit. Now who can't keep a secret?* But before he could push for details, there was a girlish squeal behind us. Turning, we saw Mariposa Perez dash past to throw herself into the arms of a tall blond man who happily embraced and kissed her. When they parted, I saw he was none other than the last person I'd kissed like that in this town and this very building.

# THE TWICE-SOLD SOUL

Bastien Lemaire.

Like Remi, Bastien had the enviable talent of looking at ease and in command of absolutely every situation, but beyond a few more general qualities—intelligent, talented, good looking—that was where their similarities ended. Now almost thirty, Bastien was still well groomed and handsome, and he'd grown into his aristocratic features. Neatly trimmed golden-blond hair; straight nose and a strong jaw, clean of any stubble; alert blue-gray eyes that were no longer hidden behind glasses. *Contacts or did he get surgery? He always hated putting those things in*, I wondered. He looked damn good in a dark-gray suit and maroon shirt, all perfectly tailored, reflecting every dollar spent on them. An equally expensive-looking smartwatch decorated his left wrist.

While his social circle had included some real gems, Mariposa Perez among them, Bastien himself had never been cruel to me, even if we hadn't exactly been friends in our youth. But I'd known he was decent, which was one of the reasons I'd sought his help the night we killed Forneus. Well, that and he'd sort of stumbled into finding out about the situation anyway. Still, after the chaos of being with Remi and the fallout of killing her boss, I found Bastien's reliability, earnestness, and humanity to be exactly what I needed and wanted. He wasn't boring, far from it, but a different kind of challenge, and not without his own way of surprising me. And after you've lived inside the tempest, the safety of the harbor becomes incredibly appealing.

Now here he was, looking so effortlessly happy as he embraced the girl who had gifted me with such memorable nicknames as Hedge Bitch, Hopeless Hedger, World's Worst Witch, Demon's

Whore, *and* Gold-Digging Traitor. My heart ached a little to see that rare, unguarded smile light him up completely. It ached in a very different way to see who it was for.

"Might wanna pick your jaw up before you start catching flies," Lucca whispered. I shut it tightly enough that my teeth clicked as the happy couple parted and went about getting Bastien a name tag. "I'm gonna guess Remi conveniently forgot to mention them, huh? Not like she's been around, though. Maybe she didn't know."

Remi's words echoed in my mind: *Ooh and ahh over Mariposa Perez's big shiny engagement ring?* "She knew."

Lucca winced sympathetically. "Ouch. Well, uh, yeah, they're engaged. Getting married next weekend. It's kind of a huge deal."

"Two of the most promising witches on the East Coast joining their families' magic in marriage? Yeah, I can imagine it's the talk of the damn town. I take it that's the wedding Brooke mentioned earlier."

"Yeah, she and Mari have been besties since college. They work together at the hotel spa now, actually." Ouch. Stealing my old boyfriend *and* one of my best friends?

"Okay, now I'm starting to feel single-white-femaled." My eyes kept wandering to the happy couple.

Lucca frowned as he looked at me. "I recognize that look. You've got no right to judge him or Brooke. Mari's a completely different person now, McKenna. She's changed a lot since high school."

Ouch again. "I know I don't, but that doesn't—shit, perfect couple incoming."

The pair of them had caught sight of Lucca and were walking in our direction. I forced on my best blank, pleasant smile.

"Lucca, sorry I'm late. Looks like the reunion's a rousing success," Bastien greeted, patting Lucca's shoulder in a familiar, friendly fashion. His eyes flicked toward me, clearly going through his mental Rolodex to see if he knew me.

"Hey, no worries, man," Lucca replied genially. "Any and all tardiness apologies are for her, not me!" He grinned and gestured with his thumb to Mariposa, who had her arm hooked through Bastien's.

"I don't believe we've met," Bastien said, turning to me and holding out his hand. "I'm Sebastien Lemaire."

One of only two people I'd ever said *I love you* to was looking at me without any hint of recognition whatsoever. My voice stuck in my throat.

Lucca noticed, thankfully, and jumped in. "This is Kendra," he said, nudging me.

"Uh, right. Yeah, I'm Kendra Moureau. I'm here with a friend who went here," I replied, belatedly taking his hand and shaking it limply. Touching him felt like something I wasn't supposed to do, and not in the fun way.

"Oh? Who's that? Looks like you lost your name tag."

"Yeah, it...fell off. I'm here with Remi Blake."

His brows drew together as he released my hand. "I see. I have to say, I didn't think she would be coming to this."

"She didn't RSVP," Lucca agreed, shrugging.

"And she's left me stranded to boot. Terribly rude of her, but about par for the course, huh?" I said, forcing some humor into my voice. The two men exchanged a knowing look.

"Careful, friends, you know what they say about speaking of the devil."

At the top of the stairs behind them, Remi stood as if she'd just appeared there. In fact, it was more than a little likely the Archdemon had indeed waited for precisely the right moment to make the perfect dramatic entrance. And damn, was she ever pulling it off. Remi had changed into a stunning, clingy red dress with a deep V neckline, no back to speak of, and a hemline that ended well above her knees. Her black hair was longer now, falling to her shoulders in soft and comely waves. She sported the perfect smoky eye and matte-red lips to match the dress. As always, Remi toed the fine line between classy and scandalous with delicate precision. She walked to us, one foot directly in front of the other so her hips swayed in a way designed to inspire bad ideas, slipped her arm through mine, and kissed my cheek. "So sorry I'm late, Kendra. But a dress like this can't be rushed. You know how it is." The others looked at us, plainly trying to determine exactly what our relationship was. Frankly, that dress was almost enough to make me reconsider the matter myself.

"Remi Blake. Aren't you full of surprises tonight," Lucca said flatly.

"She is?" Bastien asked.

"Ah—yeah, you know. Showing up late, bringing a date no one's met before, violating dress code, the usual."

Remi tsk'd. "Please, Lucca, we're not in high school anymore. And when did I ever care about the dress code anyway? I broke that one on a daily basis."

"Come on, even you couldn't manage that," Lucca said.

"Oh? Just how often do you think I was wearing underwear?" Remi smirked, Lucca scowled, and I did my best to hide the color on my cheeks by ducking my head. The demoness turned to the couple. "Mariposa, Bastien, I've been meaning to congratulate you two in person. I'm so glad I caught you together. It's been ages, hasn't it?"

Mariposa smiled and looked unfazed. Like the rest of the supernatural community around here, she knew who and what Remi truly was and had for years. Mari had outright hated Remi in high school, even before Remi's true nature was revealed, and because Mari was from a Catholic family, the whole demon thing was an additional strike against Remi after the fact. Many of Lucca's objections came from a similar place. Of course, *demon* was a very general term, more of a classification than a religious statement. Specifically, she'd been a succubus before the power-up, and as the Archdemon of Desire, her tastes and methods still ran that way. But Remi didn't know the truth about God and the Devil, Heaven and Hell, or what any religion got right or wrong any more than the rest of the world. Most likely her species and where she came from had inspired popular images and beliefs, but whatever sort of deeper truth there might be was still a big question mark.

"Thank you, Remi. And it's nice to meet you, Kendra," Mari said to the two of us.

"You, too. And congratulations," I said, looking down at Mari's finger. It sure was an impressive set of diamonds. "That's a beautiful ring."

"Thank you! It's my something old, Bastien had it made from both our grandmothers' rings," she gushed, gazing up at him.

"Wow. That's incredibly thoughtful." My eyes went to him.

"Thank you," he replied, smiling mostly at his fiancée.

"You know, I never did find out how you two started dating," Remi interrupted. "Did you finally realize it was meant to be after years of traveling in the same circles?"

"Rather more dramatic than that, actually," Bastien said, squeezing Mariposa's waist. "Five years ago, I was a group leader on a service trip Lemaire Hotels sponsored that Mari and Brooke were on. We were building houses in Mexico."

"He's too modest. The whole housing charity effort was his idea in the first place," Mari gushed, squeezing his arm. "And now they sponsor multiple trips per year."

"Really? That's wonderful," I said, impressed.

"Thank you. I'm glad I'm in a position to be able to help people, but the program relies on far more minds and hands than mine. Although it did nearly get shut down that first year." He frowned.

"Why, what happened?" I asked.

"She and Brooke decided to go cliff diving is what," Lucca said gruffly. "By themselves. Mari nearly drowned."

"Hardly, thanks to Brooke. I broke my leg, but she dove right in after me and got me to the shore," Mari said, taking up the tale. "Thank God for her." She crossed herself, but then she smiled, her face brightening as she looked up at her fiancé. "Anyway, Bastien was by my side in the hospital the whole time."

"I felt horrible, and it wasn't only because your safety was my responsibility. We've known each other for most of our lives," Bastien explained to me, the supposed stranger.

"When we got back to the States, we started seeing each other, and... well, here we are, about to have our happily ever after." She beamed at him, and dammit, it was really hard to be bitter after a story like that, no matter who was starring in it.

"That's an incredible story. I..." *I what? I wonder if it ever would've happened if I'd stayed? I wonder if I'd be wearing that ring? Or maybe this was how it was all going to play out no matter what? Ugh, stop playing what-if, Ellerbeck.* I put another smile on my face. "I'd toast to a happy and healthy future for you both, but I seem to be lacking a glass," I said, though my eyes may have lingered more on Bastien than Mari.

"I'll drink for both of us, then," said Remi, lifting a wineglass of her own—where had that come from?—and taking a drink from it. "I can't wait to see the wedding dress," she added, eyes glinting.

The couple exchanged an uncertain glance. "Uh..."

Remi laughed merrily. "Oh, I know I'm not invited! Don't worry yourselves, I'm no crasher," she lied, and they relaxed visibly. "But since I'm in town, I was hoping to get a glimpse. I assume you're having the reception here, after all."

"One of the benefits of my family owning the place," Bastien said.

"The friends-and-family discount ain't bad either," Lucca said. His brow suddenly furrowed, and he turned around a few moments before the rest of us saw why: Tom Harwell stumbling out from the bar, plainly drunk. "Uh-oh."

"Bast! Heey, Bast, there ya are. Whoa, Remi. Nice dress!" the young man said, giving her two thumbs-up. "Hey, we're good, right? I was, like..." He made a zipper motion across his mouth.

"Tommy-boy, we're golden." Remi grinned. Bastien shot her a dark look and released Mariposa to go help Tom.

"You got him drunk?" Bastien accused.

"I did no such thing."

"Not cool, Remi," said Lucca.

Remi turned and addressed me. "Kendra, darling—" I shot her a look for using the pet name again, but, of course, she ignored it. "—shall we go in and say hello? Looks like the party's rocking."

I looked over at Lucca, now busy trying to convince Tom to go home, and was admittedly relieved to not have to answer more questions right now. "Sure, let's go." The werewolf heard me, of course, but I turned away from his disapproving look. I knew our conversation wasn't over.

Back inside, the reunion was in full swing, with animated conversation and laughter. The demoness handed out smiles and complimentary greetings as we went: "So good to see you!" "You look amazing." "I can't wait to catch up and hear all about what you've been up to."

"How much of that do you even mean?" I asked when we reached the bar once more.

Remi shrugged. "Enough to be sincere, not so much that I'm going to look at an overabundance of baby and wedding pictures. I'll sort the wheat from the chaff. More wine? Or are we feeling like a cocktail? I know I am. Two Manhattans, please," she said to the bartender without waiting for my answer.

# THE TWICE-SOLD SOUL

"What's that supposed to mean?" I side-eyed her.

She waved her hand. "Don't be so paranoid. It's not a good look. I mean the interesting ones from the mundane."

"It's Arcadia Commons Academy, Remi, none of them are mundane."

"Not in the non-magical sense of the word. Most of this lot are and always will be distinctly yawn-worthy," Remi said. "Some people, in fact, never change. Others, however, grow more interesting over time. Some of them may even surprise you, for good or ill." She turned to the crowd, leaning against the bar. She ran a finger along my bare upper arm, sweeping it out with a flourish to point farther down the bar. "For example."

Following her finger, I saw Chris and Preston chatting closely. "Yeah, I saw them before. I had no idea Chris was into guys. And Preston... Preston looks great. Happy, confident." I smiled. Beyond just being classmates, Preston and I had taken ballet together for years. His half-Fae nature gave him a natural grace and flair for the arts, and he'd always been so demanding of himself, driven to perfectionism. Now, in retrospect, I could see there'd been more to that than I'd realized at the time.

"Why shouldn't he be? He's found his true self and people embrace him for it."

I glanced back at her. "That reminds me, what are your pronouns these days?"

"Same as before. *She/her* when I'm like this, *he/him* when I'm my male self," Remi replied. "Still defaulting to *she* in general, though."

Nodding acknowledgment, I looked back over at Chris

and Preston, marveling at the unexpected couple. "Chris is so clearly into him. So you knew Chris was attracted to men? And Preston, you knew about him?"

Remi smirked. "Darling, it has been literally my raison d'être for millennia to suss out what humans secretly desire. The deeper they bury the want, the greater their need, the more they are willing to pay to get a taste of it. Of course I knew."

The relish in her voice and her use of present tense were sharp reminders of exactly who and what she was. Of why I had broken up with her. "Did you...?"

Remi's expression softened. "Come on, don't look like that. No, I never made a deal with either of them."

"But you have with others. Since I left, you have, haven't you?"

Remi hesitated, looking less than 100 percent confident for the first time since she'd shown up in Paris. Which already felt like a lifetime ago. "I quite literally need to do these things to thrive, to survive, to stand a chance of holding my own against the other Archdemons. You can't hold it against me for wanting to live, darling."

My gaze narrowed as she continued to use the old pet name. "I told you not to call me darling. Start respecting that or I'll walk out of here, deal or no."

Remi held up her hands. "All right, all right. I'm sorry. It's not as though I can call you by your name, though, is it? To be honest, I'm not a fan of *Kendra*."

"What's wrong with that name?"

"It's not the name. It's the personality." Remi sipped her drink as I tried to figure that one out. "How long has it been since you even cast a spell, hm? How long since you opened that book of yours?"

"I *can't* cast anything, Remi, I locked my power and—"

"How long since you had sex?"

"What? That's none of your—"

"No, you're right, I'm sure you've scratched that itch." She dismissed her own question and leaned into my personal space, her casual façade dropping in favor of something much more intense. "I mean something *real*, something that opened you up the way you opened to me. How long since you even dated? Stayed out too late, drank too much? Talked to someone who looked a little too dangerous? Other than yours truly, of course. Hell, how long has it been since you did so much as open a door that says DO NOT ENTER, *McKenna*?" She hissed my real name in a whisper that, somehow, I knew only I could hear. Her dark eyes began to flicker with flames, with an intensity that made me nervous, especially when I realized that Remi was *angry*.

"I-I've taken plenty of risks, I—"

"Times when you're half dead and delirious from poisoning yourself because you won't use your magic don't count," Remi snapped before I could finish the thought. "*Kendra* is boring. She's mundane. She's buried all the best things about herself, locked them behind a few wards—which is a criminal misuse of tattoos, in my opinion—and forgotten who she really is. But *McKenna*...now, *she* is a woman worth keeping an eye on." The anger passed, the fire in her eyes dimming and her customary smirk reappearing.

I looked away, shaking inside, and quickly sipped my drink,

trying to wash it away with bourbon. "...Was." I tried to sound firm, but my voice came out quiet and fragile.

Remi smiled. "*Is.* She's been missing a long time, sure. But nothing keeps that one down for long. She'll be back. I have faith."

I stared at my glass then at the crowd, feeling more of an outsider than before. Remi was waiting for me to say something, but I had nothing and I was exhausted. How long had I been awake now? How many physically, emotionally, mentally draining shocks had I had tonight already? And now Remi, the one person who knew the truth, the one who had near-limitless power and invulnerability, the Archdemon who'd gotten all her power because of *me*, was judging me for it?

*No. Fuck that.*

"I didn't decide on a whim to leave everything behind me, and you know it. You know *exactly* why I did it and why I can't come back. You know what else? There is zero reason for me to be down here, putting myself through this. I'm going back to my room." I stood up, putting down the half-finished drink. Remi started to rise as well. "Do *not* come with me."

The demoness sat again. "Very well. We'll talk tomorrow. Have a good night." Her voice was neutral, but I saw the hint of an infuriating smirk.

"Don't count on it."

Turning my back on her, I wove once more through the crowd to the balcony. I was angry, I was guilty, and yet I could feel water pricking in the corners of my eyes. Grasping the cool metal once again, I drew in a deep breath of air that was free of bodies and noise and memories.

"Excuse me? Kendra, wasn't it?"

My head jerked up to see Bastien Lemaire standing next to me. "Oh, seven hells, now what?" I said before I could stop myself.

"Excuse me?" His brow furrowed, distrustful and insulted.

I winced. "Sorry. It's been a very long day. But yes, Kendra, that's... that's me." *I think.*

"Right..." He relaxed, but only just. "In any case, I'm Bastien Lemaire, we met earlier."

"I remember. How's your friend? Tom?" I asked.

"He'll be all right." Bastien looked me over, his eyes keen, and I stiffened as I realized he was examining my aura.

"That's a little rude, isn't it?" I snapped.

He arched an eyebrow. "An Archdemon brings an unknown guest to an event in my hotel. Manners aren't my first concern."

"I'm not a thrall."

"Then why do you have Remi's power signature all over you?"

I made a face. "Ugh. Please don't say it like that."

His brow arched again. "I thought you were friends."

"We... are, yes. But we're having a difference of opinion at the moment. As for the aura, she... she loaned me the outfit. Probably she's woven some enchantment into it, but if so, I don't expect it's anything harmful," I said, coming up with a lie that was close enough to the truth.

"I see." Bastien was still looking at me, assessing.

"Don't trust me?" I sighed. "I suppose I can't blame you. I promise you I'm human, and I don't mean anyone here any harm. I'm just in town for a week, that's all." *A week that may yet prove to be the longest of my life at this rate.*

"I see," he said again. "And how do you know Remi?" He asked the question with the air of someone accustomed to being answered.

I rolled my eyes, impatient, tired, and annoyed with all the suspicion and interrogations. "What do you want, a biography?"

His eyes narrowed. "I've had enough trouble from the likes of Remi to—"

"Let me go!"

The yell came from the lobby below us. We both looked down to see two police officers escorting a young man from the direction of the management offices. In a bulky canvas coat, the man struggled despite his hands being cuffed. He had a wool cap on his head, obscuring his face from this angle.

An older man, balding, wearing a sharp suit and a sharper expression, walked out after them. Laurent Lemaire. Bastien's grandfather, owner of the Grand, and a senior member of the Witches Council. "I'd be more compliant if I were you, young man. Caught in the act hardly gives you any basis to plead not guilty," the old man said, with a voice of iron and superiority. "Although a sincere apology might spare you the financial ruin of having charges brought against you."

"Go to hell!"

"As if we wouldn't have noticed someone dressed like this standing out here," Laurent went on, pulling off the cap with disgust, and it took me several seconds to realize that was my little brother.

"*Cameron?*" I gasped audibly.

Bastien looked at me. "You know him?"

I didn't answer, just stared at my brother. *What is he doing here? Why is he in handcuffs?*

Laurent looked up. "Sebastien? Come down here." If Bastien spoke like someone used to being answered, his grandfather spoke as someone used to being unquestioned entirely. Bastien frowned. For a second, I thought he was going to refuse. But then he headed down the stairs with one last distrustful look at me and not another word.

I turned my eyes back on my brother, such a far cry from the sixteen-year-old I'd last seen. His once floppy mop of hair was buzzed close to the scalp. He was taller and leaner, and I spied at least one tattoo peeking out from the collar of his T-shirt. Was it mystical, like mine, or purely decorative? The worn and faded black shirt advertised a place called THE VEIL AND HORN TAVERN. His jeans were of a similar color and condition.

But it was the surly defiance on his face that took me aback. Cameron had been a sweet kid, even when we were younger and constantly fighting like siblings do. I felt like I ought to be rubbing my eyes to clear up this unimaginable scenario. The Cameron I knew would never act out like this against anyone, least of all a powerful family like the Lemaires. That was not to mention that we were in their very own seat of power, in a place that was surely rife with security measures both magical and mundane.

"Cameron, what's going on?" Bastien asked him when he got to the group, ignoring his grandfather and sounding remarkably more patient with my brother than he had with me.

"Trying to rob us from under our own noses," Laurent growled.

"I don't have to justify myself to either of you," Cameron spat angrily.

Bastien sighed. "Actually, you do. I'm trying to help you, Cameron. I'm sure we can settle this civilly. What were you doing here?"

Cameron gave him a grin that had no humor in it. "Yeah, sure. I was bored, I was in town, thought I'd try a little light reading. I hear you guys get the best magazines out here, you know, *Forbes* and *Highlights* and shit. But the real page-turners are in your *private* collection, you know? I didn't think you'd mind if I borrowed one."

Bastien went still. I knew he did because I did, too. Any witch would've picked up on what Cameron was really saying: He'd been after their grimoire.

Reading another family's grimoire without permission and supervision was a crime in our circles. Stealing one? You would have to be desperate or stupid to try that. It wasn't only that you would have access to the family's secrets once you held their tome open in your hands; you could also manipulate their magic. It was even possible to add their magic to your own. When witches married, part of the ceremony was a ritual where the pair shared their magic with each other by adding their names to each other's grimoires. It was a big part of why witch society was so insular and obsessed with marrying other witch families and ensuring that those matches continued their family line, despite the very obvious implications of kissing cousins by this point. But you didn't need a ring for it, just the right ritual spell.

For all that I had barely touched my grimoire since leaving, I still felt something creep down my spine at the very idea of a stranger putting their hands on it. I didn't want to think about what might be done to a person who tried to steal one, but I had a pretty good guess. Especially when that one belonged to the Lemaires.

"Cameron," Bastien began, breaking the silence, but Laurent cut him off.

"Let him sit in jail for the night. See how he feels about this in the morning," the old man said, dismissing my brother and his escort. The cops hauled Cameron out with them; he no longer struggled, but he did glare at the Lemaires until the cops forced his face forward to the doors.

"Frankly, I'm surprised it took this long for him to try," said Remi's voice next to me.

I jumped; she had snuck up on me. Now that I was looking up, I saw that several people had come to watch what was going on, drawn by the commotion.

"This long?" I asked, staring at her. "Remi, did you know Cameron was going to try to steal their grimoire?"

"No, of course not."

Something about her answer was too neat. Too quick and too specific, despite how Remi played it casual. *No...no, she didn't know, of course not. Because humans are chock-full of free will, you can never know what they'll do. Damn demons and their technicalities.* "That's why you brought me back here, isn't it?" Remi's response was to sip her Manhattan and look at me with shadowed eyes. Mine narrowed in response.

"You could've said he needed my help! I would've come willingly, and I wouldn't have wasted my night at this stupid reunion. Dammit, Remi!"

Remi turned to face toward the bar and craned her head over to whisper in my ear. "Watch your volume, *Kendra*. Someone might hear you, and you wouldn't want that, now, would you?"

She started to step away, but I grabbed her arm. "He needs help."

"That he does."

"The Council could sever his magic for something like this," I hissed.

"They might. Maybe you should do something about that."

"Me? Don't you mean *we*? This is why you brought me here, Remi, instead of stepping in yourself or telling me outright. This is your responsibility, too." My grip on her arm tightened, to the point that Remi glared at me and jerked it back easily.

"As I recall, the last time a demon in my position interfered with witches and the order of things, he was killed and yours truly ended up wearing his crown," Remi said. "I have no desire to repeat his mistakes. And as you know, nothing comes for free when it comes to me. But would you look at that? There's a whole host of old friends who are far more altruistic than I am right here in front of you." She gestured at the bar with a sweep of her deceptively delicate hand. Turning back to me, she stepped close. Despite my anger, in that moment I couldn't help but be very conscious of and conflicted about how close her body was to mine. Her eyes held a challenge as they met mine. "If, that is, they knew. And that's a question only you can answer."

"What question?" I asked warily.

"The only one that matters." Remi leaned in, her cheek brushing alongside mine. Her lips stopped a breath away from my ear. *"Who are you?"* She hovered there, then pulled back, planting a light kiss on my cheek. "Let me know when you've figured that one out."

With that, the demoness finished her drink, popping the cherry between her lips as she sauntered down the stairs, leaving me on my own once again.

# Chapter 5
# A Touch of Madness

The sirens whooped once as the red-and-blue lights flicked on, then faded as they pulled away from the hotel. My little brother needed me. But helping him meant revealing myself. Revealing myself meant explaining what happened.

Why I ran. Why I never came back.

I was shaking, inside and out, even though I knew I was standing still. My breath came in short, shallow gasps, and my mind raced in a never-ending circle of indecision and panic.

"Hey." A hand came down on my shoulder. I jerked away, spinning to face my attacker, but it was only Lucca, brown eyes warm with worry. "Whoa. It's me, Mc—Kendra. Are you okay?"

I gave a short, tight shake of my head, trying to slow down my breathing. "No. Cameron's—and I can't—I, I need to get out of here. Back to my room." Lucca put his arm around my shoulders and we hurried toward the elevators. It was empty. I hit the button for the fourteenth floor and leaned my head against the cool metal of the walls.

"Any idea why Cameron just tried to pull off the worst heist ever?"

I shook my head.

"Cameron might not have his shit together, but robbing the Lemaires in their own hotel, at this hour? That's a little far even for him," he said.

"He was after their grimoire," I finally said. "It's stupid. Insane. The Council will strip his magic for it." My fingers wrapped around the chess piece necklace, the dulled edges pressing into my flesh.

"Like they tried to do to you?" he asked. He said something else, but I couldn't hear him over the voice in my head. *This is my fault. It's my fault, I know it is. I left them, I left them weaker than ever. What happened, Cameron? You were supposed to be safe! This isn't like it should be, nothing is . . .*

Suddenly Lucca's face filled my vision and he snapped his fingers in front of my face. "McKenna! Hey—are you in there? Snap out of it!"

I started, pulling back and sitting up. *Sitting? Since when am I sitting? When did we get back to my room?* "What?"

"Oh, good. Sorry, but you were full-on blue screening there. I wasn't sure what to do, so, uh . . ."

"McKenna!"

I looked up and saw bubbly Brooke Bellerieve Luppino standing there, a huge smile on her face. "It's really you? Oh, my gosh! Why didn't you say anything earlier?" Without warning, she bounded over and wrapped me up in a tight hug. I shot Lucca a dark look over her shoulder, loosely returning the hug.

Lucca spread his hands. "I thought you might need medical attention or something."

"And I'm a licensed EMT. It's not my job, but I went through all the training. You did the right thing, Charming," Brooke said. Guess Remi wasn't the only one hanging on to high school pet names. "So why are you in disguise? Can you take it off? I want to see you!"

"Because I didn't want anyone to know," I said in defeat. "No point in that now." I undid the necklace and felt Remi's power tingle as it lifted from my skin. "So...this is me, now."

They both looked me over; Lucca still worried, Brooke still with her bubbly smile. I felt oddly self-conscious and exposed to be seen by my old friends in my own skin. Finally, Brooke clapped her hands together. "You look great! Is your hair darker? Are you thinner? You look a little thinner. But in a good way, not a you-need-to-eat way!"

"Thanks, I think?" I replied. "Brooke, please don't tell anyone else that I'm here. It's temporary."

"But why?"

"And why is it so important for no one to know about it?" Lucca added. "McKenna, what *happened*? Why did you disappear?"

I pulled my hair from the chignon and combed my fingers through it. "I can't tell you."

"Come on! Whatever it was, it's ancient history. Everyone's been wondering if you're dead or not for the last decade!" Lucca snapped. "Do you even give a shit about any of us? Or Leo? Or your mom or your brother, y'know, the one who just got arrested?"

"Lucca, don't yell at her," Brooke said more gently.

"I'm not—!" Lucca stopped, huffed, and continued in a slightly calmer tone. "Sorry. Didn't mean to get loud. But seriously, McKenna. We're your friends, your family. You owe us an explanation. Or do you not trust us anymore?"

"It's not that," I sighed. "I had to leave. It was for everyone's protection."

Lucca sputtered. "What are we, junior varsity? Come on! Werewolf alpha with a badass pack, witches galore, the magical power of friendship! We killed the great Fornholio. What's so bad that you think we couldn't handle it?"

"That fight nearly killed us all, Lucca!" I replied. "Chris lost his leg. Leo nearly sold her soul. We were *lucky*. We had the right weapon, but we barely knew we were doing, and we were going against an Archdemon who didn't see it coming."

"You think I don't remember? But we still *won*. If we had to do it again, we'd be more prepared." A beat, and his jaw dropped. "Holy shit—it was another Archdemon, wasn't it?"

*Shit.* I winced, which was confirmation enough for them. Brooke gasped and stammered, "N-no, no, that's impossible. The barrier keeps demons out. Besides, if an Archdemon were after you, Arcadia Commons would be the safest place to be."

Under normal circumstances, she was right. Generations ago, the founding families of Arcadia Commons created an anti-demon barrier around the town. But these weren't normal circumstances.

"There are ways around the barrier," I replied.

"Yeah, yeah, Remi's a special snowflake with a host body who can get in, but I thought she was the only one," Lucca said.

"She is, but... it's complicated. The point is, I can't stay. It's too dangerous."

But Lucca was resolute. "No. We're older, smarter, and stronger now. Better to fight together than have you fighting alone."

"I'm not fighting alone, Lucca!" I snapped, tired of his obstinance and just plain tired. "I'm not fighting, period! All I'm doing is staying alive and keeping it from what it wants, which is me! And I'm *not* going to let anyone else die for this!" As soon as the words tumbled out of me, I slapped a hand to my mouth. *Shit!*

Brooke's green eyes widened. "Anyone *else*?" she gasped.

Lucca was quicker to piece it together. "Oh, my God... Jackie. It was right before you left." His face fell, the concern for me immediately replaced with a deep, empathetic sadness. I felt my heart tighten. "Is that what really happened to her?"

I fled into the bedroom, pulling the doors closed behind me, yelling "I'm getting changed!" before they could follow. That last, terrible night in Arcadia crawled back into my mind. Ritual lines in the dirt. Blood, salt, and sulfur. I grabbed my head, eyes shut tight, but I could still see Jackie Harwell's lifeless body staring at me.

*I didn't mean to do it, I didn't mean to, I failed, I fucked up, I'm sorry, but I won't let it happen again!*

I forced my eyes open to dispel the ghastly image. *But what good is this secret doing me? Haven't I done this long enough? Cameron's in trouble and trying to steal grimoires...*

*No.* I spun on my heel, pacing the room. *I left for a reason. I bound my magic and hid my grimoire for a reason. I did it to protect them! If I tell them... it will only make things worse.*

My thumb pressed the old scar in the center of my left palm before tracing the tattoos on my wrist, then following the veins up my arm to the injection marks in the crease of my elbow.

*Or is that just what I'm just telling myself?*

I couldn't stay. It wasn't an option. Cameron was in enough trouble without me making it worse. Still, I had to do *something*. Maybe if I told Lucca and Brooke the truth...maybe they'd drop it and we could focus on my brother. Lucca had mentioned having connections; maybe they could do something to help Cameron. Assuming he didn't decide to arrest me as well, of course.

*Okay. Here goes everything.*

I could hear the two of them quietly talking outside the bedroom door as I turned the knob and opened it again. I gestured to the couches. "Sit. I'll tell you what happened."

---

*Ten years ago*

Meet @ Whale's Jaw ASAP

WTF?
No
My grad party's soon

Im not cleaning up your demonic mess by myself
Meet me NOW and I wont tell anyone else about it
Including Bastien

I had no idea what sort of mess Jackie Harwell was talking about, but her threat worked. Was she threatening Remi? The Pit's newest Archdemon hadn't done anything that I knew of to merit this. And even if I was with Bastien now, I didn't want anything to happen to her. Of course, Jackie, being Bastien's best friend, was predisposed to hate my ex no matter what.

Hell, she barely tolerated me. We managed to be civil, for Bastien's sake, but Jackie didn't like the things I'd "gotten away with," and I didn't like her old-school elitist attitude. It was easy for her to think that my family shouldn't rate with witch society when she'd been born into privilege, her magical strength never questioned. She'd never had to prove herself, was never looked down upon because all she could summon was a doll-size pixie or a wind elemental that, at most, could mess up the papers on your desk. Jackie Harwell and her whole family had been telepaths to reckon with for generations now. Sure, we all knew wards against having our minds read, but we also all knew that if a Harwell *really* wanted to know what you were thinking, there wasn't a whole lot you could do about it.

But why this? Why now? My concern and curiosity got the better of me. I suspected it would only further our dislike of each other, though, so whatever Jackie's request or accusation was, I just hoped she made it quick.

I reached the clearing, parked behind her car, and got out. Several yards away, in the shadow of the immense split rock that looked like the parting mouth of a whale—hence the name—Jackie crouched down in the dirt, dressed in the same khakis and blouse I'd seen her in earlier that day at our graduation ceremony. But her shoulder-length copper hair was mussed like she'd been running her hands through it repeatedly, giving her a frantic, troubled look.

"You came alone?" she asked.

"Yes, and you've got five minutes to tell me why I bothered," I replied as I stepped over to her. Something in the air felt off; an uncomfortably familiar tingle moved under my skin. *Demonic power—here?* But Jackie wouldn't be caught dead messing with that kind of stuff, even if it weren't forbidden.

"We need to talk." She stood, dusting off her hands.

I arched an eyebrow at her. "Yeah, well, your choice of venue is questionable."

"It had to be here," Jackie said.

I looked around, still feeling an itch under my skin, but there was nothing to see. That was the giveaway. "What are you hiding? I know you've got an illusion up." I could've tried ripping it off myself, but I wasn't great with illusions.

"I'll get to that, but let me explain first." Jackie paced in front of me. "Look, I know we haven't exactly gotten along, McKenna—"

"Yeah, because you refuse to accept that my past is in the past, and you keep trying to get Bastien to dump me," I said, irritated.

"As long as demons are in this town, it *isn't* in the past."

"Except that demons are *not* in this town. I'm pretty sure we would've all noticed if they were. Look, Jackie, I can't keep Remi from hanging around. She has a human host body, she can come and go, but we all know who she is and she isn't harming anyone. And she knows it's over between us. For the last time, I am not about to cheat on Bastien with her."

Jackie scoffed. "Yeah, then how come you're the one who brought it up and not me?"

I clenched my jaw. "What do you want, Jackie? My graduation party starts in an hour. Which, by the way, I'm officially uninviting you to."

"I wasn't going anyway," she retorted, waving her hand over the ground. "We need to talk about your little gal pal." The air wavered, and what had looked like untouched dirt was revealed to be cluttered with ritual implements: a book, a circle of flickering candles, an athame laid across a silver bowl, and a small circle and runes drawn in chalk, wax, and salt. Some of the sigils were new to me, but some I immediately recognized. I turned and glared at her.

"Why the hell are you trying to summon an *Archdemon*, Jackie?"

"Not summon. Kill." She picked up the black-handled athame, examining the edge of the sharp ritual knife.

"This is insane! How many times do I have to tell you, Remi isn't a threat!"

Jackie shook her head. "Much as I'd love to kick her ass out of town, this isn't about her."

"Then who? Is there some other Archdemon in Arcadia that mysteriously escaped my notice?"

Jackie rolled her eyes at me. "Demons might be your forte, Ellerbeck, but you're not all-knowing."

"I think I'd notice an *Archdemon* poking around, Harwell," I shot back at her, gesturing sharply to the runes. "Even a watchdog doesn't bark at every kid who walks by, but they sure notice when the mailman shows up."

Jackie smirked coldly. "Nice of you to call yourself a bitch so I don't have to."

I tossed her an angry "Fuck you" and started back to my car.

"Wait!" She darted in front of me, holding up her hands. "Sorry. Uncalled for. Don't leave."

I crossed my arms. "You've got ten seconds to give me a good reason not to."

"I need your help. Like I said, this is your specialty, not mine."

"Help with *what*? There's no demon here, I'm not about to summon one for you, and that tiny knife is useless against one anyway!"

But as the words left my mouth, the air shifted and the slithery sensation I'd been feeling jumped up to eleven. I'd thought it was the ritual she'd set up, the sigils that echoed demonic power, but this was more, *much* more. It was like Forneus's power, but different at the same time. An entirely new flavor of corruption.

It's hard to describe how magic feels; it's essentially another sense, but only witches and a few other creatures have it. How do you describe smell or hearing to someone who can't do either? On top of that, it manifests a little differently for different witches. For me, I feel it in my blood. It moves and lives inside of me. When it's clean, it's refreshing, but if it's corrupted, it's like any awful sensation. The same reaction you have to a horrible smell, a screeching noise, a revolting flavor. You recoil, you cringe, it overwhelms you, and all you want is to get away from it. But when it's inside you, pulsing in your veins, saturating your very being, there's no escape.

"You idiot, you already summoned it?" I snapped, turning to see the creature manifesting in the clearing. Before us stood a grotesquely fascinating mockery of the human form. It hurt my eyes and my mind just to look at, yet I couldn't stop myself from taking it in. It was nude and genderless, with mottled skin that kept shifting. Its skull was vaguely human in shape, because it kept changing, too, defying definition: one moment smooth, the next bulbous, the next forming jagged edges. The only consistent features were the empty eye sockets, bottomless and full of dark flames, and two horns that curved back from its forehead. The skeletal, shredded remains of wings sprouted from its back, and each of its two legs split at the backward-bending knees into two clawed limbs that were bony yet slick with ichor at the same time, ending in four feet in total. The long, spindly arms ended in too many fingers, with shadows writhing between them.

"*Demon's witch.* I have been so eager to meet you." Its mouth opened but did not move with the words, showing needle-like teeth as the sound came out. The pain in my head spiked as it spoke. I grabbed at my temples, trying to cover my eyes and ears at once, trying to stop the pounding. Every instinct I had said *run* and I backed up so quickly that Jackie and I both fell into a heap. The clearing felt like it was blurring around the edges of my vision.

Jackie pulled me up. "F-focus! We need to kill it, that's the—*ahh!*" The demon sent the shadows twisting around its fingers to circle her head. She screamed and fell back, trying to grab at her head, trying to fight it off. The athame tumbled to the dirt as blood began to run from her nose, her ears. Of course—she was a telepath. Whatever it was doing to me had to be much worse for her, and now it was attacking her directly.

Trembling, more scared than I'd ever been, I dove for the ground and grabbed up the athame. Everything was spinning around me. *"Ego daemones abicios!"* I screamed, pointing it toward the demon. Magic thrummed through the metal into my hand and out toward the demon in a wild, desperate blast. But without a proper circle, drawn by me, imbued with my power, and designed for this specific Archdemon, I was just throwing raw magic and praying it would work. The only sign that I'd done anything was that the pain in my own head vanished. The demon didn't even flinch; it still held its hand out toward Jackie, who was still screaming and clawing at her head. In desperation, I gripped the knife and lunged forward, grabbing its arm and swinging the blade toward it. But the second I touched it, another mass of shadows rushed at me, sinking into my skin, filling my vision with darkness, and the last things I saw were the flames of its empty eyes looking directly into mine.

Magic and madness coiled and convulsed in a havoc around me.

Someone struggled.

Someone screamed.

A word, an order, a commandment that could not be denied.

"Now."
Metal met flesh.
*Blood.*

I don't know how much time passed—maybe minutes, maybe hours—but when the world began to make sense again, I had the worst migraine of my life. Every sound and every movement, even *thinking* made my head throb. But the worst part of it was that the unclean feeling, that invasive sensation in my veins, was still there. I groaned and cradled my head, trying to make myself as small as possible, trying to make it all go away.

I was sore, cold, and uncomfortable, and the blood-borne aftertaste of madness had sunk into the air all around me. Was it gone? Was it over? I didn't want to look, terrified of seeing the demon again. But then I realized that I wasn't alone. I was curled up next to another body. One that was very still and silent. I cracked open my lids, wincing at the moonlight, the only illumination left in the clearing. Then I screamed all over again.

Jackie lay on the ground next to me, her dead, lifeless eyes locked with mine. The front of her was covered in blood, still trickling out from the neatly sliced gash across her throat.

I scrambled away and threw up on the blood-soaked ground, my head still pounding. Looking down, I saw that I was also covered in blood.

*Her* blood.

And I realized for the first time that in one hand, I was still clutching the athame, and that it, too, was red with Jackie's blood.

I had killed her.

I dropped the knife. The horrible realization sent my senses into another tailspin, or so I thought, until I realized that *thing* was still here. Its inhuman hand stroked my hair like I was a poor, precious pet, and everything twisted, chaos threatening. Whatever, whoever, this demon was, it was clear it commanded madness, wielded it the way Remi and her predecessor did desire. It was an Archdemon and I had no idea why Jackie had summoned it, why it had made me kill her, why it hadn't killed me.

"There now. All will be well. My little demon's witch." Its voice was weirdly soothing and revolting at once. My vision filled with stars, and my head buzzed with the white noise of phantom voices. "Now we won't be interrupted. Such a lovely little prize Forneus found in you. Such a shame he could not keep you. You were wasted in his service. An oversight that I shall not be making."

Despite my headache and spinning senses, things...started to make sense. It was planning something, and I was central to those plans. I didn't know what, or how, but I knew it would bind me as a thrall and drive me to madness until I was useless or soulless. Or both. I stared at my hands in the wet, red dirt. The athame lay on the ground beneath them.

"Get up. We have a long night ahead of us."

I felt the pull to obey it, but as I stood, my finger brushed the blade, pricking it just enough to draw blood. More blood on my hands, but this time it was my own, and with it I felt my senses coming back to me, my magic naturally fighting this thing's hold on me. My eyes fell on Jackie's circle, a few feet away and largely undisturbed. It was still set up for a ritual, albeit a weak one, with runes for an Archdemon—*this* Archdemon.

I couldn't kill it. I was too weak and unprepared to do that, and I had no weapon to wield against something this powerful. But there was something I could do.

I grabbed the knife, wrapping my left hand around the blade so it cut into my fingers. The more my blood and my magic spilled out of me, the more my head began to clear. I deliberately tripped as I stood, stumbling into the circle and letting my hand fall on the lines, pushing my magic into them and activating the runes.

The Archdemon wheeled on me, its shadow-shroud stirring, but this time I had the sense to keep my eyes down and my hands to myself. I squeezed my eyes shut as my mind began to reel again, the white noise getting louder. But I couldn't stop its shadows from surrounding me. "*Ego...*" I coughed on the first word. My throat was raw, my magic already waning as the Archdemon fought against me. On my second try, I started to choke, the whorls of darkness darting into my mouth, my nose, making my body revolt against me. As I fought to breathe, I felt the madness growing inside of me. The world began to grow dark in a different way, shadows and stars creeping into my vision as I asphyxiated, coming dangerously close to blacking out.

*No. I will not be another demon's plaything!*

I stopped fighting for air. I didn't breathe. My vision narrowed to almost nothing, but I didn't need to see for this. Lifting the athame in my right hand, I plunged it straight through my left, blade sinking into the earth, and magic exploded out of me with a rush of blood and pain. It seeped into the blade and the ritual runes, throwing off the Archdemon's hold on me. My throat opened as I coughed, expelling its tendrils from my body. Then I sucked in air, screaming as loud as I could: *"Ego daemones abicio!"*

The runes flared with golden light, filling the clearing, and the next scream was not mine. The Archdemon lunged at me but then it, too, erupted with light. The blinding vortex consumed it, sucking it back to the Pit from whence it came.

Then the light and magic vanished, and I was alone. I slumped against the ground, blinking as my eyes and head slowly cleared, pinned in place by the athame.

I started to cry. I didn't stop for years.

---

Lucca and Brooke were waiting for me when I came out of the bathroom. Retelling the story, reliving the event that still gave me nightmares, had been too much and I'd thrown up all over again. After that, and taking a minute to calm down, rinse my mouth, and splash water on my face, I was startled to see them standing right outside the door.

"Okay, I know my track record may not be great right now, but I wasn't about to vanish while I was in the bathroom," I joked.

Next thing I knew, both of them were hugging me tightly.

"Oof! Okay, guys, I—uh, I appreciate it, but I'm still not much of a hugger," I croaked.

They let go and gave me some space. "Shit, McKenna. Why didn't you say anything? How could you keep something like that to yourself?" Lucca asked.

I cocked an eyebrow. "By immediately leaving town, mostly?"

They both gave me puzzled looks. "Uh, no, you didn't," Lucca said.

"Maybe you blacked it all out. Trauma victims sometimes can't remember things that happened for weeks around the traumatic event, both before and after," Brooke said.

"Okay, one, I wasn't the victim. And two, apart from when I—when that thing made me do that to Jackie, I remember everything a little *too* clearly for my tastes. I left that night. I called Remi once I could manage to talk and...and I made a deal. Not a capital-B Bargain, a deal. I'm not her thrall," I quickly added. "I still don't know how that demon showed up in the first place, but I knew it would be back, I knew it was after me, and it was willing to kill anyone who got in its way. I could *not* let that happen again." I felt another wave of nausea at the very idea.

"Okay, then how do you explain the fact that we all saw you at your party that night and at the funeral, and all the way up through the Fourth?" Lucca replied.

It finally clicked. "Remi. She helped me disappear, but she must've hung around and pretended to be me for a little while after. July Fourth was the last time you saw me? How...how did Remi have me leave?"

Lucca nodded a confirmation. "You kept to yourself a lot. I remember thinking you must be spending a lot of time with

Bastien, but I guess that sneaky bitch didn't want me to sniff her out. You and Bast got into some big fight at the bonfire that night, I don't remember what about. You dumped him, in front of everyone, and stormed off. Next day you were gone—left a note at your house about, like, needing to get away from this town and everyone in it, finding yourself, don't look for me, yadda yadda." He growled in his throat, hands tensed into fists. "I can't believe you went to her instead of us. I can't believe you'd let Remi play us like that!"

Brooke put a hand on his arm. "She fooled all of us, Lucca. Even Bastien. She's a good actress. Besides, she was holding up her end of the deal. If McKenna had gone missing right away, we would've thought she was dead, too. Or that she had something to do with what happened to Jackie."

"She *did* have something to do with it!" Lucca snapped.

I snapped right back. "I left so no one else would be killed! And considering everyone's still alive and sane, I'd say I made the right choice."

"By running away?" Lucca retorted. "We deserved to know what was happening in our own town, McKenna. We could've taken care of it."

"Oh, yeah? You have a lead on another ancient weapon forged by an extinct race of Fae, cooled willingly in the blood of the last member of a dying race, and blessed by an angel?" The sword we'd needed to kill Forneus had been rather unique, to put it mildly.

"Obviously, we don't," Brooke cut in quickly, putting a hand on her husband's arm. "And what's done is done. There's no going back to change it. And maybe no one's been hurt, but I agree you should've come to us about this, McKenna. You know we would've helped you and protected you. We wouldn't have blamed you. I can't imagine what you must've been feeling, but...I wish you'd come to us."

*And who would've protected you?* "I was out of my mind, literally and figuratively. I—" But the words still stuck in my throat. "It was way beyond anything that had happened before. I knew that thing was after *me*, specifically. It kept talking about my power and me being the 'demon's witch.' So I took what it was after, hid it, and led it on a merry goose chase." I held up my wrists, showing them the tattoos. "I looked for a way to fight it, for another weapon, for anything that would do the job. I looked everywhere and followed every lead I could, and you know what I found? *Nothing.*"

Even Lucca was taken aback by my explanation, though he didn't look happy about it. Brooke stepped closer to look. "I thought those looked like runes," she murmured and tapped one in particular. "They're binding wards, aren't they? They hide your power. Can you still detect demons even with them?"

"No, but the ones hunting me aren't exactly subtle," I admitted. "Once I got these, though, they stopped showing up as often. Whenever I had to let off some magic steam, it would be a matter of hours until they did, so...I got used to moving out fast." I rubbed the scar on my left palm again. "But at least no one else has died."

"I can't believe that's what really happened to her. Poor Jackie," Brooke said sadly.

"We thought she died in a car crash," Lucca added. "You

know that curve in Harbor Drive, just after the theater? With that huge oak tree? They said her car must've been going at least seventy when it hit. Whole thing went up in flames on impact. Closed casket. Town finally cut down the tree later that summer."

A fresh wave of guilt hit me. "Remi must've set it up to look like an accident."

"I did not miss demons screwing around in our lives," Lucca growled. "Every time they show up, it's trouble." I caught his sideways glance at me when he said it.

"Don't worry. I'll be gone as soon as I can," I said, not quite able to keep the defensiveness out of my voice.

"Where will you go?" Brooke asked. "Where have you even been all this time?"

I knew that would be coming sooner or later. I ran a hand through my hair, combing it back from my face. "Out of the country. I've been...keeping myself busy."

"With what?"

I sighed. "Does it matter? Look, I know the reunion was everyone acting like they cared what people who aren't their friends have been doing in the last ten years, but we don't need to keep playing up here. We were—are—friends, so we don't need to pretend. I'm not sticking around, so let's not act like I am."

"You're just gonna leave again, really?" Lucca asked.

"This isn't my home, Lucca. Not anymore." It was weird to hear aloud words that I'd said only to myself hundreds of times.

Lucca's eyes hardened. "You didn't even want to come back

here, did you? You didn't want to see any of us or try to fix everything you broke."

"What are you talking about?"

"Did you even notice that neither of us is shocked about Cameron? Did you even hear what I said before?" Lucca asked pointedly.

"You said this seemed a little far, even for him," I recalled.

"Yeah, a *little*! McKenna, come on, do you really think we all shrugged and went on with our lives when Jackie died and you disappeared? Did you think no one cared or tried to find you or figure out what happened? You have no idea what your family went through after that. And apparently, you've got no interest in finding out, either." He crossed his arms, his judgment clear.

*I never should've come back here.* I rubbed at my temples, at the dull pounding of a headache, duly ashamed and unsettled. But what else could I do? Of course I cared. Of course I wondered. Staying, then or now, would only make things worse. They were alive and sane, and I'd take that over the alternative. Knowing anything more would only make it harder. "I'm here for a week and I'll do what I can for Cameron. Let's focus on that. You work security? Do you know any of the local cops? Can you make sure he's okay, find out what's happening to him?"

"Of course. I look after the people I care about," Lucca snapped.

"McKenna, you look exhausted. You should get some sleep," Brooke said more gently. "We'll call you in the morning, okay? What's your number?"

"I don't have a cell phone that works here. Call the hotel and ask for the room," I said. "And thanks."

"Yeah." Lucca still sounded like he was trying to prove his point. I was still certain he didn't understand mine. "Good night, McKenna."

"Welcome home," Brooke said, giving me another quick hug.

I smiled ruefully. "...Lucca, before you go, how's Leo?" I asked. "I didn't see her at the reunion."

Lucca hesitated for a moment. "Leo's fine. Couldn't make it tonight is all," he said gruffly. "Besides, technically not her reunion. If you wanna know more than that, you can ask her yourself. If you decide to stick around."

"Right... well, good night."

The two of them left, leaving me alone again. The way I liked it. The way I was used to. I changed into my pajamas, wishing I'd brought some aspirin with me, and settled for a glass of water instead. I could barely keep my eyes open when I crawled under the covers, but even so old memories mingled with new worries, leading to waking nightmares that kept me up for hours. It was like the early days of my self-imposed exile all over again. Every time sleep came near, it threw horrifying images, half nightmares, half memories, at me.

*My friends are scattered, our plan gone terribly wrong, fools to think this would work. Chris is bleeding out, his leg severed after Forneus threw him into the path of Remi's swing with the sword. Lucca and Brooke try to save him, while Remi herself is slumped on the floor across the room where Forneus threw her into the wall. Forneus's hand wraps around Cameron's throat, my little brother struggling for air while Leo offers up her soul as a thrall to save him, a distraction to buy us a few moments.*

*Across the circle, Bastien's eyes meet mine, and we know we have one last chance. A quick gesture, a few words, and two portals open—one drops the demon-slaying sword into my hand from where Remi dropped it on the floor, and the other, in front of me, leads straight to Forneus. One thrust and he will die. This is how it happens, this is how we win, I grip the blade and stab it into his back—*

*—but it's not him. It's Jackie, the sword in her chest, blood bubbling at her lips. It's not a sword, it's the athame, it's in my hand, I'm on top of her and I see the light go out in her eyes. There's cruel laughter, it's Forneus, it's the Archdemon of Madness, it's Remi with hellfire in her eyes, it's everywhere—*

I jerked awake, a scream on my lips, looking everywhere, in every shadow. No one was there, of course, but me. It didn't stop from turning on every light, opening the curtains, and clutching my athame in my hand until the first rays of dawn crept in and the darkness retreated enough for me to finally fall into a dreamless sleep.

# Chapter 6
# Angry Young Man

The phone ringing woke me up. Groggy, out of it, I rolled over and fumbled to grab it.

"*Allô?*"

"Mc—Kendra?" Lucca said. "Are you awake?"

"*Oui, je viens de me réveiller,*" I replied, yawning audibly. "*Excusez-moi.*"

"Yeah, uh, could you speak English?"

"Huh? Oh!" Right. It all rushed back: where I was and why. "Sorry. Habit. Uh, yeah, I just woke up," I replied, coming a little more awake. "What's going on?"

"Man, you sleep late. It's almost noon. Not a morning person anymore?"

A glance at the clock confirmed the time. "Usually I am. Yesterday was kind of a long one." I cleared my throat. "Did you find out anything about Cameron?"

"Yeah. One of my wolves does some bounty hunting on the side. She stopped by the station this morning. Bastien came down to have him released. They aren't pressing charges, so that's good."

I frowned. "Not necessarily. The Council could still decide to punish him by severing his magic."

"Would they really do that? I remember they threatened to do it to you way back, but for real?"

"For real. Not lightly done, or easily, but trying to steal a grimoire is a big enough deal for them to consider it."

"You guys are way too serious about your books," Lucca said. "I was one day late, one time, returning a book to the Uncommon Collection, and I felt like I had fleas for a freaking week."

I snorted in amusement. "Yeah, waived-late-fee curses was a definite perk of working there. Wait, what did you get out from there? There's hardly any werewolf stuff, it's mostly defunct grimoires, spellbooks, some bestiaries."

"It wasn't really for me. They've got a bunch of old books from Brooke's family—y'know, stuff left over after the flood?"

"Yeah, I've read a few. What about them?"

"When I was getting ready to propose, I signed one out to get a replica of her mom's ring made," Lucca said.

"Seriously? Lucca, that's so thoughtful," I said, impressed and surprised. "She must've loved it."

"Well, she did say yes and all." I could hear him smiling. "So yeah, pretty much best proposal ever. Also the best wedding."

"I'm sure it was." I paused awkwardly. "Anyway, where's Cam now?"

"Bastien's doing paperwork, but it shouldn't be much longer. What's your plan?"

# THE TWICE-SOLD SOUL

I got up from the bed. "I don't know. I need to find out why he was trying to steal the grimoire. I'm gonna shower and get dressed for now. Call again if anything changes."

Half an hour later, I was dressed and guzzling hotel room coffee when there was a knock at my door. Realizing I was undisguised, I looked for my necklace while I called out, "Who is it?"

"Room service, Miss Moureau. You have a package," answered a male voice.

Finding the necklace on the coffee table, I clasped it on and answered the door in my blond disguise. A young man in the Grand's uniform was there with a small rectangular white box in his hand with a red stick-on bow on it. The picture on the outside gave away that it held a phone.

"Who dropped this off?" I asked.

"I don't know, but there's a card attached." He left, and I opened the box and the small card.

> I thought this might make things easier. I've taken the liberty of programming a few numbers into it already. Don't worry, no strings attached to this one. Call it one of many overdue birthday gifts. I'll even throw in a free coffee as a welcome home gift. —Remi

Tucked in with the note was a punch card for Rocket Café, my favorite local café from my teen years, full and ready to be exchanged for a free coffee. I pocketed it, the scent of the place flitting through my memory.

Inside the box, along with some cash, was a smartphone

with Remi's number programmed along with a few others: Lucca, Brooke, Cameron, Leo, the Arcadia Grand, Rocket Café, and a place called the Veil and Horn—the name of the tavern on Cameron's shirt last night.

Then I noticed that Leo's last name wasn't Luppino, but Pallas, and felt the sting of yet another broken promise.

---

*Ten years ago*

Even I knew it was weird to end up crying into your best friend's shoulder after having a good first date. Especially when that date was with someone like Bastien Lemaire, who was basically perfect boyfriend material. "What the hell is wrong with me?" I griped, wiping at my eyes. "Remi and I broke up months ago, I like Bastien, why the hell am I crying?"

Leo gave me a one-armed hug. "Mickey, you're only human. You're only seventeen years old! Yeah, you and Remi had this insane epic roller-coaster first love, but you're allowed to be scared and go on dates and like them and even fall in love with someone else."

I sniffed. "But...that means giving up."

"No. It just means moving on."

I slumped my head on her shoulder. "Nothing looks the way I thought it would anymore."

"Tell me about it," she sighed. "But hey, no matter what happens, one thing is never gonna change: I'm always on your side, no matter what. And I'm your maid of honor no matter who the lucky guy or girl is."

I laughed despite my conflicted heart. "And I'm yours."

———————•———————

I shoved the phone in my pocket and tried to shove away the memory as well. If this town was going to insist on haunting me, it could do it just as well outside this hotel.

The scenery on the cab ride downtown was comfortingly familiar. The coastline gave way to the same New England–style houses that had always been there—the big Victorians leading to the modest Colonials and Capes and then on to the compact single-story ranches. As we got closer to the center of town, we skirted the state forest and the small parking lots that marked hiking trails inward. Every kid who'd been through the Arcadia school system, supernatural and mundane alike, had been on field trips down those trails to see what remained of the original homes in this area, the ones from back before the Revolutionary War when the place was officially called Commons Settlement but better known as Dogtown. After the war, it was nearly abandoned, populated by a handful of widows, pirates, dogs, and formerly enslaved people. But it was saved in the late 1700s when the Lemaire ancestors, along with a few other families, swooped in, bought up and otherwise claimed the land, expanded the borders, and got control of the bay, securing the town for generations to come and renaming it Arcadia Commons.

Another thing supernatural and mundane schools had in

common was that they skipped a lot of the truth, especially when it made the white saviors look bad. The land had originally belonged to the Pawtucket tribe, but contact with European settlers killed them off in huge numbers, from disease, aggressive conflict, and finally King Philip's War. It turns out the tribe never actually lived on much of the land that made up Arcadia Commons, though no one knows why exactly. It was possible the land here had been unsuitable for living on, which was what they taught in the mundane schools. The supernatural community has a different theory, though: The tribe didn't want to establish a community so close to the three leylines, essentially a huge magical hot spot, that lay in what was now a state forest.

Something else they didn't teach outside of the academy was that the rumors about Dogtown's last residents being witches and pirates were true, and a lot of those dogs had been werewolves. The families who saved the town were also all magically inclined: the Lemaires, the Harwells, the Bellerieves, the Blackwoods, the Luppinos, and the Youngers. The latter were my ancestors, specifically Thomasin Younger, the so-called Queen of the Witches of Dogtown.

The founding families had also all known about the leyline crossroads, and in contrast with the Pawtucket tribe, it was exactly the reason they wanted to live here. Classic colonizer behavior, trying to claim and control something that perhaps was better left alone. But for better or worse, in order to both protect and control it, they cast a powerful ritual to raise the invisible barrier around Arcadia Commons that kept evil out. Magically speaking, this meant that demons could not enter unless they were summoned or had a human host body that let them pass undetected, like Remi. Mundanely, our town has enjoyed a notably low crime rate since its founding. It was intended to be a haven for beings both magical and mundane who were of good intent, and thus it was renamed Arcadia Commons.

When I learned Arcadia's true history, it sounded like the witch version of the first Thanksgiving: everyone coming together for the greater good, relying on and trusting one another so we could thrive as a community. Then I grew up, and just like the national holiday, I started to see the hints of the ugly truth behind the pretty picture: stolen land, colonizers, the thirst for power. Whatever had or hadn't happened in the past, the truth of my time was that my family, and other hedgewitches, had been looked down upon and dismissed for generations for our lack of magic. While I grew up privileged and comfortable in the mundane sense, wealth only gets you so far in witch society. If you aren't powerful, you aren't important, and you can't buy magic.

But you can Bargain for it.

Chances are you'll get the raw end of that deal, too.

The cab dropped me in front of Rocket Café. Tourists and residents strolled through the town square, decorated for Halloween, now under a week away. While the outdoor decor hadn't changed much, inside the café I was thrust back into the mix of the familiar and strange. The walls had once been covered in wallpaper featuring a retro rocket-ship-and-coffee-cup design. That signature look was now gone, replaced by a more generic mottled golden-brown paint. Works by local artists still hung on the wall, complete with their names and prices for the pieces. The tables, once a collection of unmatched furniture picked up from yard sales and second-hand stores, were now a uniform fleet of diner-style tabletops with red-cushioned chairs to match.

"Welcome to Rocket Café, what can I get for you?" the college coed behind the counter asked. Her red hair was pulled into a long braid over her shoulder, and her name tag said BREE. I glanced at the menu—the board itself was new, but the selections were mostly the same.

"Large black—no, never mind that. Large cookies-and-cream latte, extra espresso shot," I said, my mouth watering as I changed my order. I didn't generally have a sweet tooth, but when I was stressed, I went all out. The cookies-and-cream latte was both my rainy-day and my celebratory treat, and no one made them like these guys did.

"Whipped cream and cookie on that?"

"Do you still make the whipped cream and cookies in-house?"

"Yep."

"Then absolutely yes."

"You got it. Can I get your name?" Bree asked.

"Kendra. Do you take the punch cards for lattes?"

Bree shook her head. "No, sorry. Just coffee."

I nodded, slipping the card back in my pocket. "*Et un*—uh, and a croissant and a bag of ground coffee, too."

I paid and went to the end of the counter to wait for my drink, my gaze idly trailing over the room, reminded of hundreds of afternoons spent here doing my homework, laughing with my friends, or on a date with Remi or Bastien. There was a seat toward the back that had been my favorite. The layout afforded it a bit of privacy, but there was still light from the last window. I turned to see if it was still there, and unoccupied. I wouldn't mind taking some time to gather my thoughts before trying to track down Cameron...

...who was sitting in that exact spot across from Bastien Lemaire.

"Solomon's bones, I swear this town has only gotten smaller," I muttered under my breath.

Cameron was dressed in the same clothes as last night, and he wore the same surly, sour expression when he wasn't taking large bites of the breakfast sandwich in his hand. Bastien had changed, of course, looking no less well-groomed in charcoal slacks and dark-blue pullover, a pristine white collar peeking out underneath. He was wearing glasses today, however—thin gray rectangular metal frames that worked well on him. He'd always worn glasses back in high school; personally, I thought they suited him. On the table between them sat two cups—one had the top removed, a stirrer sticking out of the black coffee, with some empty sugar packets tossed down next to it. The other had its lid on, and the string of a tea bag hung down the side.

I couldn't hear them, but they had to be talking about the attempted theft. I'd wanted to find Cameron, but now that he was right in front of me, I had no idea what my next move was. Leave? Lurk and eavesdrop? Approach them outright? *Should I talk to him? Can I keep this up around him, this whole Kendra act?* Wait... when had I decided it was an act?

"Latte and croissant for Kendra," a barista called out. I

grabbed my order and looked from the two men to the door, but I couldn't do it. I couldn't leave now.

Of course, that didn't mean I was going to walk up and say hi, either.

Luckily, Bastien was angled such that he couldn't see me. I slipped through the tables and sat near them, safely out of view of my ex but able to see both of them peripherally as well as catch their conversation. I pulled out my phone and pretended to be absorbed by it.

"...if you'd simply tell me what's going on, Cameron," Bastien was saying, clearly not the first time he'd asked this.

"Then what? You'll step down from your pedestal to give a hedger a hand up? Like your granddad's gonna let you do that," Cameron griped stubbornly. I frowned at the term. *Hedger* was a derogatory shortening of *hedgewitch*, the term for the lower-powered witches. The ones with enough magic to keep track of but not enough to worry about. Cameron wasn't that powerless, though... or was he?

"You're not a hedger," Bastien said, echoing my thoughts. "And you know we're not using that term anymore." *We're not?*

"Oh, sorry, *generalist*," Cameron replied with thick sarcasm. "If we're auditioning new labels, I'd rather go with *filthy casual*. Not that I'll even be that once Laurent and his cronies are done with me."

"That might've been something to consider *before* you broke in and tried to steal from us," Bastien pointed out.

"And there it is! So you do think I should be severed."

Bastien sighed through gritted teeth. "I didn't say that. I am *trying* to help you, but again, we both know your family isn't exactly in good favor with the Council. It doesn't help that you keep poking at the laws."

"Hey, technically I haven't broken any of them. Can't hold me guilty for a crime I didn't actually commit." He popped in a bite of the sandwich, wiping his mouth on the back of his hand as he chewed and subsequently making our grandmother roll over in her grave.

"You've come close enough. Look, they are going to call a tribunal about this, and if you don't let me help you or find someone to speak for you, it's not going to go well."

"Finally, their chance to be rid of what's left of the Ellerbecks once and for all!" *What's left of us?* "Y'know, Laurent really oughta thank me for making it so easy."

Bastien leaned back in his chair, rubbing his face with one hand, frustrated. "Dammit, Cameron, why won't you let me *help* you?"

"Because I have no reason to trust you, asshole!" Cameron's eyes burned with an eager anger. "Get it through your head, Lemaire, *we're not friends.*" His hands were fists at his side and his whole body was tensed, coiled like he was about to throw a punch or a hex. This wasn't a spontaneous anger, either; I knew the look of someone who had been itching for a fight to finally happen. Bastien wasn't a brawler—he hadn't been, at least—but he also wasn't the type to just let himself be attacked. Not to mention the obvious, that it would only make things worse for Cameron. If this didn't de-escalate soon, Cameron was going to end up right back in jail.

In the next instant, I was on my feet and interrupting them. "Excuse me!" I said loudly. Two pairs of eyes snapped to me.

"Miss Moureau?" Bastien said with surprise.

"Yes, nice to see you again, Mr. Lemaire," I replied. "And you must be Cameron Ellerbeck?"

"Who're you?" Cameron asked, eyeing me.

I swallowed, my throat going dry as he looked at me and saw a stranger. "Kendra Moureau. I've been retained by Miss Blake to act as your advocate in this... unpleasant scenario."

Two sets of eyebrows raised.

"You're an advocate?" Bastien asked dubiously.

*Time to walk the walk.* Taking a seat on an unoccupied side of the table, I began fixing up my coffee, crumbling the cookie into the whipped cream. Which was simply what I always did, and definitely not to expel any anxious energy. "I'm qualified to act as one, as well as being an adept."

Being an adept—which was where my magic ranked, when it wasn't bound—carried some respect among witches, but what mattered more was being an advocate. If formally brought before the local Witches Council, Cameron had essentially the same right as anyone accused in court: He could represent himself or have someone else do it for him. Laws for witches were a lot like codes for pirates: more like guidelines. But the Council sure did love to stand on ceremony and throw their weight around when they could, and I should know. I'd had to stand before them for judgment as a teenager.

Not long before we killed Forneus, Bastien had learned of my status as a thrall and what my "patron" was putting me through. He agreed to take part in the ritual to end the Archdemon on the condition that once it was done, I would come clean to the Council. I agreed, figuring it was fair enough, little knowing that it would land me in a trial and a ritual circle with a powerful compulsion spell that both prevented me from lying and also made it impossible to hold anything back. I might be stubborn, but I was no match for that. I spilled every dirty detail. More than a few of my strong opinions about how my family had been treated slipped in along the way. I'd barely gotten out of the whole ordeal with my magic intact, not to mention my grimoire unconfiscated. Only my ignorance going into the deal, and the fact that I'd eliminated a dangerous being while securing the alliance of another, had saved me when it came down to it. I came away very unpopular with the Council and with a stern warning to not step out of line again.

The ordeal had stirred my interest—I'd planned to go to law school once upon a time and become a lawyer in both the mundane and magical worlds. Disappearing had thrown that off track, however. While I'd stayed away from running in magical circles, my fear of being caught by demons was followed closely by my fear of being caught by the Council. So I'd learned what I could, just in case. If it came down to it, I wasn't going to go into that room unprepared a second time.

"Remi sent you?" Cameron asked.

I paused, being sure to choose my words carefully. After being forced under a truth spell, you learned that the best lies are the ones that are still true. "Miss Blake directed me to find you and made sure I was aware your situation warranted my attention."

In fact, that rang so true that I made a mental note to reevaluate Remi's motivations later.

Cameron grunted noncommittally, looking me over, while Bastien's gaze more directly took my measure. His eyes dropped to where I was crumbling the last of the cookie into the whipped cream. He frowned, his eyes crinkling in puzzlement.

I stopped and looked as well, brushing the crumbs off on a napkin. "What?"

"Nothing, I..." He shook his head. "Sorry. I used to know someone else who did that."

"Oh." *Shit.* "...The girl at the counter suggested it," I lied.

He looked dubious but seemed to accept that. When he opened his mouth to say something else, Cameron cut him off.

"If you're done interrogating my counsel about her drinking habits, you're dismissed, Mr. Mayor. We need to consult privately," my brother declared.

With a sigh and a look at his watch, Bastien stood up, pulling on his fine wool peacoat. "I have an appointment to get to anyway. Why don't you give me your number, Kendra, and I'll be in touch soon."

"Sure, yeah." I had to pull out my new phone to look up my own number and rattle it off to him then enter his in return, as it wasn't among the ones that had been added before. *Feeling petty, were we, Remi?*

"You may not want my help, Cameron, but you have it nonetheless," Bastien said to my brother, this time with no occlusion or pretense. "I'll do what I can to dissuade my grandfather, but I can't make any promises."

"Didn't expect you to," Cameron said, not looking at him and taking another bite of food. Bastien gave me a look that clearly read *good luck with that* and headed out, and I tried not to stare at my little brother.

How could this be the same sweet, awkward, gangly teenage boy I'd left behind? I used to snicker at his attempt at an angry scowl, but now it was genuinely kind of scary. His soft face, floppy hair, and baby fat had all been chiseled away, leaving behind nothing but attitude, sharp edges, and a shaved head. Even with Bastien gone, he twitched like someone ready to start a fight. His hands were chapped and dry, and the collar and cuffs of his T-shirt were frayed. I still couldn't see what the tattoo on his collarbone was, but I could see that it traveled across his shoulder onto his chest.

Almost the only hint of the boy I knew was, incongruously, another tattoo. Not that he'd had any before, but this one, plainly visible on his left forearm, was a precisely drawn rune. To any other witch, it would be an unfamiliar rune; to a mundane, a vaguely Celtic-looking design. But I knew it as well as he did: the symbol of the Silver Timber pixie swarm.

---

*Twelve years ago*

I crept back into my house after midnight, opening the kitchen door as quietly as possible, fresh from making my deal with Forneus.

I'd done it. I'd changed *everything*. I could feel my new magic tingling inside me, under my skin, in my blood. The same as ever, but so much more. I hadn't yet really tried it out, not since a quick test after shaking on it with the Archdemon, but I was eager to do so.

I grinned as I closed and locked the door behind me. "Try calling me a hedge bitch now, Mari, I dare you," I murmured.

"McKenna?" My younger brother's voice came from the other end of the kitchen. I spun around.

"Cameron? What're you doing up?" Behind him, the hallways were dark. No sign of Mom. I relaxed. "It's past your bedtime."

"It's past *your* bedtime," he retorted. "Where were you?"

"Out with...friends," I said. "You?"

"Playing online with Parker," he said. Parker was his best friend, one of the young werewolves. "I got hungry. What were you saying about hedgers?"

I was going to tell him and Mom eventually, though I hadn't figured out how yet. But I was giddy with magic and success, so I smiled at him. "That we're not going to *be* hedgers anymore."

"What are you talking about?" Cameron asked. "We can't change our magic."

"But we can. I did! It's different now, can you feel it?" I crossed the wide room, meeting him halfway at the island.

He frowned, then his eyes widened. "I...I kinda can. What is that? What'd you do?"

"That's magic, Cam. *Real* magic. The kind that means the Council and all the other witches in town have to stop treating us like we're worthless."

"Are you sure? Something feels different, but...are you drunk? Maybe you're drunk."

I arched an eyebrow at him. "One, I'm not drunk, and two, how would you know what drunk looks like?" I replied. "I'll prove it. Summon something, anything." I was eager to see it work, not just for me but also for him. I had done this for all of us, after all.

"Okay, uh, I'll try Rya," he said. Rya was a pixie friend of his. He picked up the box of sugar on the island and poured a circle of it onto the marble. Usually, we used salt or chalk to make circles, but pixies preferred sugar. "Rya Duskskin, *amicule, voco nomen tuum.*"

With a small *pop!* of air, the six-inch-tall pixie girl appeared, translucent wings beating, her skin a dusky purple, and her hair a bright shock of white against it. She gave off a faint purple glow. She squeaked in high-pitched surprise but then waved at Cameron from inside the circle and gestured to it. "Holy crap, that *was* easier! It was, like, boom, pixie, no waiting! It usually takes a couple minutes. Hey, Rya," he added, breaking the line so she could step out of the circle. She flitted up to his shoulder and sat down, chattering away in her rapid pixie tongue. I couldn't tell if Cameron understood them better than I did because he was better at summoning them or the other way around. They always sounded like the Chipmunks at double speed to me. "Even Rya says it felt different. And I don't even feel tapped out, like, at all. I bet I could summon the whole swarm!"

I smiled back. "What're you waiting for? Do it!"

Cameron hesitated, but Rya squeaked encouragement from his shoulder. He closed the gap in the sugar line, then added some more inside of it, in the shape of the swarm's rune, and then invoked his magic again: "Silver Timber swarm, *amici, nomina vestra voco!*"

A tiny fireworks display went off as a dozen colorful, glowing pixies *popped!* into the room, crammed and contained inside the ring of sugar. Rya fell off Cam's shoulder laughing as their little multicolored faces pressed against the invisible barrier and their rapid chattering filled the air. Cam and I couldn't help but join her as he scattered the sugar to release them. The whole kitchen filled with excitement and arcing lines of pixie-light.

"So, you like?" I asked him as the swarm descended on the fruit bowl.

"Hell yeah! This is next level, McKenna. How'd you do this?" Rya sat on his shoulder with a chunk of apple in her hand while three other pixies chased one another around his head.

I held out my hand for a green-glowing pixie to land on. "I made a deal, Cam. Everything's going to be different now."

---

Seeing my stare, Cameron grabbed his hoodie and pulled it on, covering the tattoo. "Nice of you to help me get rid of the pretty boy, but you can tell Remi no thanks. I don't need her help and I won't be in her debt." He stood. I did the same, hoping to stop him.

"It's not like that," I said. "It's my debt I'm paying off. It's got nothing to do with you having to take anything on."

"She made it pretty damn clear nothing's free, so, sorry,

looks like you're still on the hook," he said. "Good luck with that."

"I'm serious! Remi wouldn't do that to you."

Cameron just snorted. "Yeah, right." He zipped up the hoodie and headed out of the coffee shop. I followed, frowning. *What does that mean? Did she try to get him into a deal? No. No, she would* not *do that, not to my brother... right?*

Outside, walking quickly to keep up, I asked, "Why don't you want anyone's help?"

"Because no one's *really* offering, and I don't need it even if they were."

"You pretty clearly do, Cameron. You know what they might do to you."

He gave me a dark smile. "I'm counting on it."

# Chapter 7
# History Repeating

Cameron *wanted* to lose his magic?

"That's insane!" I blurted out. He glared—he really had gotten good at that—and stalked off. I hurried after him. "Why do you *want* your magic severed?" I asked.

"Why do you care?" he countered. He pulled his knit cap on and stuffed his hands in his pockets.

"I told you, Remi—"

"Let me stop you right there, uh..." He looked at me blankly. I sighed. "Kendra."

"Right. Kendra, I don't give a shit what Remi wants. Remiel Blake, or whatever her true name is, can fuck right off along with Pretty Boy Bastien and everyone else. If they wanted to help, they had their chance." This was more animosity than I had ever seen from him. And I was his older sister, so that was saying something.

"Okay—okay, fine. They had their chance, but I haven't. I want to help. I want my chance," I tried.

He scoffed. "You only want to help because you're in debt."

"I want to help because *I* want to. Because you're in trouble, and living without magic is one of the worst things that can happen to a witch. Trust me, I know." I thrust my wrists up in front of him. He bumped into me and some coffee sloshed out of my cup, dribbling down the side and over my fingers as Cameron studied the runes.

"Why is your magic bound?"

"...Something I had to do. For personal reasons," I evaded. "But I've lived like this for years, and it *sucks*. Magic is...part of me, it's something I had fought for and worked damn hard at, and...without it, I'm..."

"...lost," he finished for me. I looked up. For the first time, his hazel eyes weren't a hard wall keeping everyone and everything out.

"Yeah. Lost. I'm lost, this piece of me is lost, and...and it kills me," I said. *Literally and figuratively.* "I know where it is, but I can't have it, and..." I took a breath, steadied myself. "But at least I *could* get it back if I had to. If the Council severs your magic, you'll *never* get it back. Is that really what you want?"

Cameron rolled his eyes and started walking again; this time I kept pace with him. "Look, I don't trust you. Nothing personal—I don't trust anyone. But if it'll get you off my back, no, that's not what I'm after," he finally said.

Not a lot, but it was something. "Then what are you after?"

"Making those fuckers 'fess up and pay for what they've done," Cameron growled. "Look, around here, the Lemaires have been ruling from on high and getting away with shit for generations. You know they've got two Council seats already? There's Grandpappy Laurent, and then his daughter Adele managed to get one a few years ago. Everyone knows Bastien is getting groomed for whatever spot opens up next, and his fiancée's mother is also on there. They don't give a shit about anyone outside their incestuous little circle of power, and I'm sick of it."

The only Lemaire on the Council when I left had been Laurent, who'd been there as long as I could remember. I didn't know Adele, and while it was unusual for two people from the same family to be on at the same time, it wasn't unheard of. But he wasn't wrong, in general, about how things were around here.

"Okay. Why now?" I asked. "Did something happen?" He shrugged but didn't say anything. I could practically see him rebuilding his wall. "Back inside, you said something to Bastien about getting rid of what's left of the Ellerbecks. What did you mean?"

Another rough shrug. "They drove off my sister and my mom. They'd love to get me outta here, too."

*Wait, what?* I had no idea what had happened to my mom, and while fear of the Lemaires had been a factor in my leaving, it was far from the cause. "What did they do?"

He scoffed. "You wouldn't believe me. No one does. But once I'm in front of that Council, *everyone* will."

I waited for more details, but none came. "Care to elaborate on your incredibly vague and foreboding threats?" He gave me a look. "Right. Trust. Okay, then how can I gain your trust?"

Cameron shrugged. "That's on you to figure out, not me."

We came to a halt at a bus stop off the town center that was also used by the Arcadia Grand shuttle. "You're seriously going back there?" I asked.

"Kinda have to, my car is parked in the garage. You're seriously going to follow me there?"

"Kinda have to. I'm staying at the hotel, and I don't have a car."

After a sullen nod from him, silence ensued. Cameron tucked his hands in his pockets again, looking at me occasionally, but I stayed quiet. He scowled and shoved his hands in farther. I hid a smirk behind my cup, feeling a burst of warmth in my chest. His earlier rage was new and scary, but his petulant silences and scowls were more familiar. *You wanna play the quiet game, Cam, go right ahead. I've never lost to you yet.*

But there were more reasons than my perfect record for waiting for him. He'd pushed back against every offer of help given to him. Ten years ago, I might've silently done something to irk him into speaking first. But if I was going to truly help him and earn his trust, I had to let him open up to me when he was ready.

Besides, I had my own new wounds to lick. Seeing this Cameron, talking to him, being treated like a stranger...it ached in a way I'd never felt before. I couldn't remember my life before him. Carefully holding my tiny baby brother when I was only a toddler myself was one of my first memories. Looking at him now, unrecognizable as he was, brought back a lifetime spent together. When we learned how to ride our bikes together. When he tried to hex me after I broke his red

Power Ranger action figure. When we built a pair of enormous gingerbread houses for the Silver Timber swarm to play in and devour. When we tried to use magic to color my hair, but instead turned the entire bathroom purple and then my hair white when we tried to fix it. We couldn't stop laughing and neither could Mom, no matter how hard she tried to keep a straight face and yell at us. Cameron was the first person I'd told about my Bargain. Yeah, he'd been a pain in the ass sometimes, and we hadn't always gotten along, but he was my little brother. He was Cameron Ellerbeck, awkward skateboarder and friend to pixies.

On top of that, what the hell had happened to my mom?

*If I'd stayed, it could've been worse.* Would've *been. He might be dead, everyone might be dead*, I told myself. But somehow, this time, the words weren't as reassuring.

However, Cameron also looked completely unbothered by how long this quiet game had gone on, while I was getting antsier the longer I was left alone with my thoughts, despite not wanting to push. I sighed. *Goodbye, perfect record.*

"So you live in town?" I asked.

"Yeah."

"...Where about?"

"Near the Gloucester line."

Nowhere near our house. "And your family?"

"Like I said, Lemaires drove 'em off." The shuttle bus arrived.

"But the Younger witches have always lived on Fox Hill!" I blurted out, frustrated with the lack of answers.

He cocked an eyebrow at me. "Remi told you *that* of all things?"

"No, I'm just... familiar with the local history," I replied, following him onto the bus. There were a few other families on the clean, comfortable shuttle. I sat in a cushioned seat across the aisle from him. He slouched back in his chair, eyes closed, and I stared out my window.

The Younger witches. It had been a long time since I'd thought of my family like that. Even after my father, John Ellerbeck, had left us, we'd all kept his name, despite it being a mundane one. Our magical ancestry was solely on my mom's side, stemming from Thomasin Younger. Mundane history does not paint a flattering picture of her: demanding, fear-mongering, sharp-tongued, an all-around mean woman and witch-with-a-b. There's very little left in the history books about her, and even my grimoire didn't have much to say on the past generations of my family.

But when I think about the world Thomasin lived in? A time when so many had gone off to war and died, when her home was dying, when her allies were fewer by the day? I see a woman fighting to hold on to what she had against increasingly desperate odds. I see someone trying to survive. I see someone who took a deal that she probably knew wasn't in her personal best interests but would serve the greater purpose of saving her home.

I like to think I see a little of myself.

It was Thomasin and the Luppinos who brought the other families together to found Arcadia Commons and secure their claim on the leyline crossroads. But after that, things fell apart. Some families grew in power and renown while others dwindled. The Youngers' magic ebbed, fewer werewolves were born into the Luppino family, the Bellerieves split apart. Meanwhile, the Lemaires have always been at the top in Arcadia, with the Harwell and Blackwood families close behind. Over time, notable families like the Perezes, the O'Briens, and others moved here. There are supernatural communities all over the world, and magic makes travel easy, but Arcadia Commons's barrier and the boarding school for supernaturally gifted kids give it a unique draw.

But even though my family languished, we refused to give up. Until now. I'd left, and my mom was gone, too, apparently. Did she have her secret reasons like I did, or was Cameron right about the Lemaires?

The lurching of the bus over the speed bumps on the hotel drive jolted me from my thoughts. The driver pulled up under the canopy at the front entrance. Cameron exited without a word, while I thanked the driver and tossed my empty coffee cup when I got off. My brother was glowering at the doorman when I caught up.

"I'm just here to get my car out of the garage," Cameron said.

"We have clear instructions. You are not allowed on the hotel property. If you don't leave, I'm calling the police," the doorman told him bluntly.

"Happy to oblige. *After* I get my car."

"Excuse me—Nathan?" I said, interrupting and glancing at his name tag. "My name is Kendra Moureau. I'm staying at the hotel and also Mr. Ellerbeck's advocate."

"Advocate?" Nathan grunted.

*Not a witch, then.* "His lawyer in his conflict with the Lemaires."

"Then maybe you can translate for him: Leave. Now."

Truly, Cameron's talent for antagonizing was well honed. "I know you're only doing your job, Nathan," I said, hoping for sympathy to smooth the way. "And I know Cameron here can be kind of a pain in the ass—"

"Hey! is exactly why it would be a huge help if you let ___ in. Because, trust me, he's only going to get worse," us in confidence. "I promise you, I will stay by his side y's off hotel grounds; there will be no interruptions at . Lemaire won't even know he was here."

Nathan's expression softened slightly, but not enough. I sighed inwardly and reached into my purse, pulling out some of the cash Remi had given me. "In and out, no trouble, and we can keep this between us?" I said, offering my hand to shake with the bills held against my palm.

This time he took the bait, shaking my hand and claiming the cash. "No trouble," he reiterated, and waved us in with a nod of his head.

I grabbed Cameron's arm and headed through the automatic doors as they slid open. "Did you just bribe him?"

"See how nice it is when you let people help you?"

As we crossed the lobby, a familiar laugh caught my ear. Over by the stairs, Mari and Bastien were chatting with Preston Chang, who held a large white binder under his arm. But far worse than that, Laurent, the *last* person we needed seeing Cameron back in his hotel, was with them. This must be the appointment Bastien had left the café for. Another blond woman I didn't quite recognize joined them, carrying two wine bottles in a tote. We weren't pas[t the guard]ians yet.

"Shit, Laurent *and* Adele?" Cameron [muttered. I] shushed him, trying to hurry along.

I saw my ex glance up and notice us. My sto[mach] clenched, but then Bastien made a gesture to the stairs, s[ome]thing that the others nodded at. They all started w[alking], their backs turned to Cameron and me. We hurried a[cross the] room. *Thanks, Bast.*

The elevator dinged moments after I hit the button, and [we] got in. Cameron jabbed at the P3 button and down we went.

"So that's Adele Lemaire?" I asked.

"The blond hair and classic evil aristocratic looks didn't give it away?" Cameron snarked. "Look, you already said you don't have a car. You can stop following me now."

"I just spent fifty bucks to get you back to your car. The least you can do is suffer my company for another few minutes," I snapped, frustrated.

He sighed. "Fine. Sorry. I'll pay you back."

"Eh, it was Remi's money anyway."

Cameron gave a satisfied chuckle.

"You don't like her. Why?"

"Because she's selfish," Cameron replied, his humor fading as quickly as it had appeared.

I frowned. He wasn't exactly wrong, but... "How do you mean?"

"I mean I already asked for her help. Over and over. What I said about my sister disappearing?" I nodded. "She and Remi used to date, Remi was basically obsessed with her. After

McKenna disappeared, I couldn't figure out anything about what happened. Remi made herself scarce, but I figured she'd be able to find out. I had to summon her to get her to talk to me, and she was useless. Said she wouldn't tell me anything unless I made a Bargain with her."

I went very still. "Did you?"

Cameron sniffed. "I tried. She turned me down."

A quiet breath escaped me. Remiel was as good as demons got, but she was still a demon, and an Archdemon at that. For a demon, making deals and Bargains meant power. For a human, making a deal meant being in debt, but making a full-on Bargain, becoming a thrall, meant handing over your soul and giving them the keys. Once that happened, an Archdemon could completely control your body and mind. They could plant thoughts, wants, desires, and you wouldn't even realize they hadn't been yours to begin with. They could full-on possess you and all you could do was watch, helpless, locked in your own mind, while they did as they pleased with your body. It was terrifying, even if it wasn't permanent. Death was no escape either—selling your soul meant you became one of their demon minions once you died. Killing Forneus had not been easy, but it had been absolutely worth it.

"That's what you meant when you said she had her chance," I concluded.

"Yep." He stuffed his hands in his pockets.

"And why you won't trust me. Because she sent me."

"Yep."

*But she didn't. I'm your sister. You can trust me, Cam. There's no conspiracy here with the Lemaires, at least not with me.* I rolled the chain of my necklace between my fingers. What if I took it off, told him the truth?

The scene from my nightmare flashed before me. Cameron being choked, Jackie's dead and bloodied body, mad laughter ringing in my ears.

*No.* I let go of the chain. The plan hadn't changed. I would try to help him while I was here, but any amount of guilt and hurt was better than seeing him dead. I was just more danger he didn't need in his life.

The elevator dinged, the doors opened, and as we stepped out, my decision was made.

Then the hellhound attacked us.

# Chapter 8
# Internal Damage

The hellhound slammed into Cameron, knocking him into me and sending us both to the concrete. Pain spasmed in my shoulder as I saw the grotesque, mottled thing crouched and snarling atop my brother's chest. Shadows writhed around its muzzle and feet, filling the air with sulfur and rot.

*No, no, not here, not now! How did they find me again?*

I wanted to run, to scream, but the air was too thin and panic held me in place. Once again, I hadn't been prepared, hadn't expected this. I didn't know how they'd found me and...and something was different. A slithering uncleanness in my blood, my vision narrowing, the world threatening to go sideways. The hellhound growled, but all I heard was the maniacal laugh of the Archdemon that haunted my nightmares.

I could do nothing as it raised a foot, shadows coalescing around its sharp claws. It slashed downward, but Cameron thrust his forearm up to block it at the last second. The two struggled, the claws inching closer to Cameron's face. But the demon was so focused that it didn't notice my brother's other hand until it planted flat against its chest. "*Repello!*" Cameron yelled, blasting it off him with magical force.

He jumped to his feet, ready, unfazed. "Get out of here!"

But I couldn't move. He grabbed me, hauled me to my feet with surprising strength. "Look at me!" My eyes snapped to his. "You can't help me, so get the hell out of here!"

He shoved me toward the elevators; I caught myself against the wall and saw that the doors had closed already. Trembling, I reached for the panel, but a new set of claws slashed at it, tearing it apart and sending sparks into the air. This time I did scream as I backpedaled away, falling against a car and setting off its alarm. The second hellhound crept closer, snarling things that almost sounded like words, but words that made my head spin. Out from the shadows stepped the figure that haunted my nightmares: the Archdemon of Madness itself. But instead of the usual vague darkness that came with these memories, this time, I was there. Back at the Whale's Jaw, straddling Jackie's still-living body, a knife in my hand.

"*Carve the runes, demon's witch...*"

"No! No, I won't! You can't make me!"

"*Can't I?*"

"No!"

"Hey, ugly!" Cameron yelled. My eyes snapped open. I was still in the garage, my brother standing between me and the demon. His hand thrust out—"*Repello!*"—and the thing slammed into the wall with a wet sound. The shadows fell away, revealing it to be another hellhound, rather than my nightmares made real.

*But I saw... what was that?*

"Get outta here!" Cameron snapped at me. "Stairs, that way, go!" He pointed before turning his attention back to the demons.

"Are you insane? We can't get away from those things!" I screamed.

"Not yet I'm not," Cameron said, facing our attackers.

I cowered behind the car, eyes shut, trying to breathe, trying to clear my mind, but it refused to comply. Around me were thuds, growls, words of power, a chaotic mix of magic and shadows in the air. My blood pounded, filth crawling in my veins and under my skin. My hand hurt and I didn't understand why until I opened my eyes and my clenched fist. I'd clenched it so tightly that the cuts from the shattered vial, when I'd faced these things last night in Paris, were bleeding anew. Most of it was caught by the bandages, but a small trickle of blood oozed down my wrist, past my wards...

*My wards! They're still up—it's all in my mind!* The sick, dirty feeling in my skin vanished, nothing more than a hallucination of my own making. My head reeled, but only from panic and hyperventilating.

My brother yelled in pain.

I leaned out and saw him on the ground and bleeding from his forehead. "Cameron!"

He jerked his head to look at me, but the moment he did, the hellhound pounced on him, its shadow-claws sinking into his temple. He screamed and so did I, this time flinging my hand out with a cry of *"Repello!"* Inside me, my magic jumped, startled by the command, rushing to comply, only to be stopped by the wards, the walls I had put up.

But my brother didn't die. He didn't even bleed. The hellhound pulled back its paw and left not a wound but three black marks, one for each claw. Cameron's eyes rolled back as he began twitching and convulsing beneath it. I started to activate the ward to release my power, disguise be damned, but at the last second I stopped myself, feeling the immense surge of magic behind my wards. It was too much to control. Banishing the demons wouldn't help if I brought the hotel down on top of us.

The two hellhounds looked at me, and I started to pull back in on myself again. *Stupid useless excuse for a witch, can't cast, can't kill, can't banish—*

*Wait.*

*Yes I can.*

Frantic, I dumped my purse out on the ground, eyes flicking between items until I saw the circular red compact with the rune on its lid. My insurance policy.

I clawed at the clasp, nearly dropping it as the two demons growled and came closer. Just as one started to leap, I felt the catch click under my finger, the prick of the hidden pin as it fell open, and the garage was filled with a burst of light and magic. The stored banishing spell blasted the hellhounds' physical forms to dust, there one moment and banished back to the Pit the next.

Who says paranoia doesn't pay off?

I slumped against a concrete pillar, the blaring car alarm now the only sound. My breath came in shuddering, shallow gasps that weren't sobs but weren't far from them, either, and tears slid down my cheeks.

"McKenna...you're here..."

I froze as my brother spoke my name.

"You almost missed your party." Cameron gave a nervous, fluttering laugh.

*What?*

I opened my eyes. My brother was starting to sit up, arms hugged around himself, rocking slightly and staring at empty air.

"...Cameron?" I asked.

"Y-yeah, I think I...I think I fell off my skateboard," he said to the air.

"Cameron, who are you talking to?" I asked more loudly.

"My sister," he said. "Where's Tom? I was supposed to meet Tom."

"Tom?"

"McKenna, you almost missed your party..."

I squeezed my eyes shut, taking a deep, long breath. Panic wanted to set in, panic and sobs and crawling into bed to shake for hours on end. *My brother needs me. I need to help him. I need to fix this. Focus, Ellerbeck, focus on the here and now.*

Cameron was rambling, mumbling to himself or, more accurately, to some imagined image of me. Was it the head wound? His forehead was still bleeding, but then my gaze went to the black marks on his temple. Black marks left by a minion of the Archdemon of Madness.

It had done something to his mind. Instead of wounding him physically, it had wounded him mentally. I had no idea how to help him.

First things first. We had to get out of here. I shoved the

contents of my purse back inside it, then pulled Cameron to his feet. "Cam, I need your keys," I told him. He looked at me for the first time and recoiled.

"Who are you?" he demanded.

"I'm Kendra, remember? Cameron, I need your keys so we can get out of here."

"I don't know you and I'm not going anywhere with you." He looked around, panicked. "Where'd she go? Where's McKenna? What did you do with my sister?"

I pulled my hands back, hoping he would calm down. "Cameron, I'm Kendra. We met this morning, remember?" *Please...*

"No! I don't know you, get away from me!" He stepped several feet away from me, searching the garage for, well, me.

There was no time to talk him down. More demons could show up, or security, or Laurent Lemaire, and I wasn't entirely sure which one was worse. With a deep breath, I reached back, unclasped the necklace, and looked at my brother with my own face.

"I'm here, Cameron."

He looked at me, his bloodied and bruised face lighting up, and for the first time, I saw the brother I'd left behind. "McKenna!" He hugged me. I hugged him. I bit my lip to keep from crying. "You disappeared."

"Yeah, I...I know. I'm sorry," I told him, sniffing despite my efforts. "Cam, we need to get out of here. Where are the car keys?"

"I dunno. I can't drive, duh," he replied.

"Uh, right, yeah. But where are the keys? You took them,

remember?" I said, playing along. Was it still playing along if I was playing myself?

He looked confused, then reached into his pocket. "Oh, yeah. Here you go." He dropped them in my hand. I hit the LOCK button on the key fob until the car beeped, then steered us a few rows over to yet another familiar sight: my old car. The red hybrid was worn and faded, with some new scratches and dents, but it was mine all the same.

"Shotgun!" Cameron glibly called out, almost tripping on the way there. Whatever was going on had not left his motor skills untouched.

I got in, adjusted the seat and mirrors, turned the key in the ignition, and nearly jumped out of my seat at the blast of hard rock from the radio. Flicking it off, I pulled out of the space, but realized I had no idea where to go. Who could help him? Remi? Probably not without a deal. For him, I'd make one, but he'd hate it, and maybe things weren't that bad yet. *I wish someone could tell me what to do to help him, to make this right...*

"Cameron, maybe we should call Mom," I suggested tentatively. Wherever she was, maybe we could go to her.

"Mom? Nooo, no, she's not home," he said, dragging out the sound and shaking his head. "Are we going to Tom's? We should go to see Tom."

"Tom Harwell?" I asked. He nodded. He'd mentioned him twice now. I didn't remember them being friends, but maybe that had changed. "I need his address."

"It's in my phone," Cameron said, pulling it from his pocket. "Call Tom," he instructed it before I could stop him and handed it to me.

"Cameron? Are you okay? I know I fucked up, I'm sorry—" Tom said in a rush when he picked up.

"This isn't Cameron," I interrupted. "It's Kendra—we met last night?"

"Oh." Pause. "Remi's friend. What are you doing with Cameron's phone?"

"It's...complicated. Cameron needs help. Something hurt him bad and he's not doing great. He's seeing things."

"Shit. Okay, yeah, I can help, but can you bring him back here?"

"Where's here?"

"Our apartment. Head toward the highway, we're on Commons Avenue. I'll text the address." *They live together?*

"Okay. We're at the Grand, be there in about twenty minutes." I was on the other end of town here; I'd have to drive around the forest to get there.

"Anything you can tell me about what did this to him?" Tom asked.

"I know this sounds impossible, but it was a demon. Hellhound. It left these black marks on his temple—"

"Got it. Just hurry. If he's seeing things, go with it to keep him calm," Tom interrupted. "See you soon."

With that, he hung up and left me wondering why this information was in no way shocking for him to hear. But I didn't have time for that right now. Once I had the address, I got moving.

Getting out of the parking garage was easy enough, thanks to Remi's supply of petty cash. In the interest of keeping Cameron from freaking out, I kept my disguise off and continued to humor him as we drove across town. I was halfway there when a male voice spoke up from behind me without warning.

"Leaving so soon?"

"Fuck!" I cursed, slamming on the brakes. The car jerked to a stop, a weight thudding into my seat from behind.

"Whoa!" Cameron exclaimed.

Panic turned to irritation when I saw Remi sitting in the back, now wearing a male form.

"Dammit, Remi, you scared the shit out of me!" I snapped at him. "I could've crashed! What are you doing here?" I pulled over to the side of the road and turned in my seat to face him.

Like his female form, the male one was the same he'd worn back in the day, when the mood struck. It was similar enough to his female form to pass as a sibling or cousin—which is what he (or she) told people when asked. His dark hair was longish, in a fashionable, carefully styled way, and he sported a neatly trimmed goatee, complete with a sculpted shadow of stubble along his jaw. His outfit was somewhere between hipster and metro—dark-blue jeans, a spotless white V-neck T-shirt, and a maroon blazer with the sleeves rolled up, all fitted to take advantage of his lean physique.

"I thought you'd last at least twenty-four hours before trying to make a break for it." Remi smirked, but his face fell as he took us in. "What happened to you two?"

"Hellhounds attacked us in the parking garage."

"In the Grand?" he asked, brows rising in surprise.

"They found me again. I don't know how they're doing

this, especially here. We managed to get rid of them, but they did something to him. He's acting like he's a kid again, he's seeing things... taking off my disguise was the only way to calm him down."

"That explains that at least. Are you hurt?" Remi asked.

"Just some bruises. He wasn't so lucky. Hey, Cam, turn your head?"

"Hm?" Cameron looked up, noticing the demon for the first time. "Oh—Remi! You're a dude today. Why're you here? McKenna, does Bastien know you're driving around with your ex-girl... boy... with your ex?"

"Yeah, they're on a break right now, Cam," Remi said off-handedly, looking at the marks. "This isn't good."

"No shit. I'm taking him to Tom. He said he could help."

"Aha, and that explains why you're so close to the edge of town. I was afraid we were going to have a problem, but that will be fine."

I arched a brow at him. "Excuse me? I don't need your permission to help my brother."

Remi held up his hands. "Far from it, but if you leave town before the week is out, you'll be in violation of the terms of our deal. Things might get a little... sticky," Remi said. "Focus on helping Cameron. I'll look into the hellhounds, but... I'm not sure they were here for you."

"... Wait, you and Bastien are on a break? What happened?" Cameron asked belatedly. We both ignored him.

"What do you mean, not here for me?"

"You've done no magic, your wards are intact, and I assume you were still in disguise at the time."

"Most of which was the case back in Paris, but they still found me there."

"Fair. But it sounds like Cameron wasn't surprised by them?"

I frowned, shaking my head. "No, he wasn't. He knew what they were and how to get rid of them. Tried to tell me to run so he could deal with it, even."

"Were he in his right mind right now, I suspect he could tell you why. So take a deep breath. There's no need to run off. But while you're in the area..." Remi checked something on his phone. "Excellent. This will work out perfectly."

"Huh? What will?"

"The small favor you owe me for that disguise. To repay your debt, I will require you to go to the Veil and Horn and repay a favor I owe the owner, Trevan Stonehill, on my behalf," Remi told me.

I glanced at Cameron's shirt. "Veil and Horn—does Cameron work there?"

"Indeed," Remi replied. "Ask for Trevan and explain you're there to fulfill the favor I owe, and that I expect you to be released from service by sunrise tomorrow at the latest. He's Fae, so watch what you say."

I raised a brow. "You got in debt to a Fae? Since when are you that careless?"

"Careless nothing. We came to a very equitable agreement."

I gave Remi a dubious look. Fae and demons both made deals, but in different ways, and neither carried the guarantee of being equitable without intense and careful negotiation. With demons, you had to knowingly agree to a deal, and both sides had to be getting something out of it. They always went for the soul first, of course. A demon would offer you a piece of gum for your soul, but you didn't actually *have* to agree in order to take it. If you did, that's when a deal became a Bargain, you became a thrall, and when you died, you became one of their demon minions. The only time something *had* to be a Bargain from the get-go was when the request was something that couldn't be achieved by magical or mundane means. If you broke a deal or Bargain, you had to repay with something equivalent to the severity of the break. Maybe they'd kill you, maybe they'd pull you into the Pit for a while, maybe you owed them ten bucks, maybe they would be free to possess your body for an hour. I had no idea what would happen if a demon broke the Bargain, as I'd never heard of that happening.

With full-blooded Fae, any spoken or written oath witnessed by them was a binding Promise, whether or not you knew it was happening. It didn't matter if you got anything out of it. Unlike demons, the Fae couldn't lie, but that didn't mean they weren't just as tricky with their words. And while a Fae couldn't steal your soul or possess you, a broken Promise on either side would be revisited upon the guilty party threefold.

"Fine, I'll go, but not until I know Cameron's going to be okay," I insisted.

Cameron's wandering attention came back at hearing his name. "Hey, what does being on a break mean, anyway?"

"He lives down the street from the bar. You can get him to Tom and then go take care of this business for me," Remi explained.

Well, at least I'd be rid of the smaller debt. Besides, yet again, I didn't have much of a choice. "Fine." I held out my hand to Remi to shake. He pouted. I gave him the eyebrow. "The best you're getting for this is a handshake, Remi. Take it or leave it."

"Oh, very well." We shook on it.

"Okay, Veil and Horn, here we come." I faced the front again.

"Here you come. I have other business to attend to," Remi said.

"Like what?"

"Like poking around in the parking garage of the Arcadia Grand, apparently." He scooted over to open the door, pausing to smirk and pat the back seat. "Nice seeing you again, old friend. Remind me to get you a proper detailing. McKenna kept you much cleaner than Cameron does." He lifted his eyes to meet mine in the rearview mirror. "I hope Cameron is all right. If there's something I can do for him, let me know." With that, he got out.

Based on Cameron's reaction simply to hearing Remi's name before, that kind of help was the last thing he wanted. Speaking of... I unbuckled and hopped out, catching Remi's arm before he walked away. On foot, he was half a head taller than me in his male form. "Cameron said he asked for your help to find me, but you refused, even when he was willing to Bargain. Is that true?"

Remi sighed. "It is. He wasn't happy about it, but our arrangement"—he gestured between the two of us—"would've been negated. Plus, I knew you'd kill me if I ever made a

Bargain with your brother. Or any of your friends or family, for that matter."

"You're not wrong. So other people tried, too?"

"Of course they did. Cameron, your mother, Leo, Lucca, Brooke, even Bastien tried to knock on my proverbial door," Remi said, holding up a finger for each on his free hand. "Not all of them would've made a Bargain; some just wanted to shake me down for information."

That sounded like Lucca. "What did you tell them?"

He shrugged. "I avoided them, told them I didn't know anything. Then I told them I couldn't find out unless they were willing to pony up for it. Cameron's the only one who tried at that point."

"...That was hard for you, wasn't it?" I asked, watching him.

"Well, it's not the easiest thing to ignore someone begging to give you exactly what you need and say no to them over and over again, no." He shrugged again, eyes cast aside, tugging at his lapel.

"Remi."

"I didn't deal with them, McKenna. I'll swear it in front of a Fae if you don't believe me," he said curtly.

"Look at me, Remi."

He obliged. Sure enough, his dark eyes flickered with flames and shadows, and I found myself standing very, very still. He stared at me, taking a deep, slow breath. The fires dimmed to embers before disappearing.

The mere memory of turning down my brother begging for a Bargain brought Remi's darkest nature out. Brought him to the edge of his control, that border between incorrigible flirt and terrifyingly powerful Archdemon.

But he controlled it. Then and now. *Isn't that what I've always wanted? What I was always afraid he couldn't do?*

I caught his hand in mine. "Thank you for not taking advantage of them."

Remi's fingers tangled with mine for a moment. "You're welcome," he said with forced lightness. "Drive safe, McKenna. Call me later."

"I will. And watch your back," I replied. Our hands released, and by the time I got back into the car, he was gone from sight.

———— • ————

Half an hour and a huge helping of stress later, I finally parked by Cameron and Tom's apartment. My brother's vacillation among being spaced out, talking to me like we were still teenagers, and muttering under his breath proved highly distracting. Which led to me missing a turn, ignoring the GPS because I was certain I knew how to get back on track, learning a popular pass-through street from my youth was now a one-way, and getting lost in an unfamiliar, newly developed neighborhood before relenting and letting technology guide me.

All the while trying to keep Cameron calm. I was worrying about him, about the demon attack, and also about that new addition to my memory of Jackie's death I'd had.

I'd always been aware that the details about that night were lacking in my mind. While I had imagined and dreamed plenty of nightmare scenarios, I only knew with certainty that I had been the one to slit her throat. I was equally certain that not recalling the details was one of very few blessings I had going for me.

But now there was this new slice of memory—of arguing with the Archdemon. I didn't know what to make of it. Or even if I could trust it. It felt real, but was it? What runes would the demon have wanted me to carve? Worse yet, had I done it?

As I parked, my nerves turned to seeing Tom again. The Harwells specialized in mental magic, so fixing Cameron must be something Tom could do. Maybe it was even something he was personally good at. I still felt strange about interacting with him, knowing what I'd done, but I reassured myself that my mind was still shielded as I put my necklace back on. Luckily, Cameron didn't notice.

I helped him out of the car and into the foyer of a two-story brick building. Shortly after pressing the buzzer for their apartment, the glass door opened and Tom came out. He was dressed in jeans and a gray Henley shirt, his hair unstyled, light-red stubble on his cheeks. He strode over and set himself under Cameron's other arm. "I got it from here, thanks."

"Tom! Hey, l-let's play video games," Cameron said, smiling wanly.

"I'll help," I said. "I need to make sure he's okay."

"He will be, but I've got it," Tom insisted. "You got him here, thanks, but you can go now."

I narrowed my eyes. "I'm not leaving until I know Cameron is okay."

Tom stared back, unmoved. "I have no idea who you are,

Kendra, and I'm pretty sure he doesn't, either. This is no longer your concern."

Cameron looked at me and suddenly pulled away, finally noticing my changed appearance. "You're not my sister!"

I winced, but I wasn't giving up. "You can't stop me from staying here until he's recovered," I pointed out, following them.

Tom moved Cameron through the doorway and into the building proper. "Actually, I can," he replied, tapping his knuckles on the inside of the doorframe as he passed through it. When I tried to follow, I found the way blocked, the doorway as impassable to me as it would be to an uninvited vampire.

"Hey! Oh, come on. Tom! Please, let me in!" I called out, suddenly desperate as the distance between us grew. "I just want to know he's going to be okay!"

Tom paused on the stairs, glancing at me over his shoulder. He sighed and relented at last. "This is gonna take a while. Meet me at the Veil and Horn in an hour if you want an update." With that, he brought Cameron up to the first landing and into the apartment on the right, slamming the door behind them. The thunk of a dead bolt sliding into place followed.

"Yeah, a drink sounds pretty good right about now," I said to myself, and headed for the bar.

# Chapter 9
# The Veil and Horn

There's something about Irish pubs that makes them all feel familiar: lived-in, homey, welcoming. They're like family in that way, all siblings or cousins, so much alike you know they're related as soon as you meet them. The Veil and Horn was no exception.

It looked larger and much nicer inside than out, with an L-shaped bar taking up a good half of the entire establishment. Stylized lighting fixtures illuminated the hardwood, textured to look old while still having a polished sheen. The tables and chairs would've been as at home in an ancient mead hall as they were here. On the walls were signs advertising different ways to imbibe along with long mirrors and—more unusual—large woven tapestries. While some displayed intricate knotwork à la the Book of Kells, others depicted people and creatures of Celtic legends. They looked old but well cared for, especially considering they were hanging in a bar. Irish music played over the speakers at a subtle volume, enough to add ambience without overpowering conversation. There were about a dozen people inside, the kind of crowd you'd expect for a Sunday afternoon. Too late for lunch, too early for dinner.

Two people tended the bar, both wearing black T-shirts with the bar's name on them, the same as the one my brother had. One was the tallest woman I'd ever seen, easily over six feet, placing glasses on a high shelf with no trouble at all. Her skin was a deep brown and the rest of her was bright green—dyed green hair, eyes, and nails painted green as well. This woman was all in on verdancy. The other was a handsome man with spiky red hair, a few inches shorter than her and with a stockier build, in contrast with the woman's long leanness. Freckles liberally dotted his pale skin, and he had a short red beard along his jaw.

"Hey there, have a seat. What can I get you?" the man asked in an Irish brogue when I approached.

"What do you recommend? I'm not usually a beer drinker," I replied, sliding onto a barstool. "And I've kind of had a day."

"So I see. Are you all right, luv?" he asked, nodding at my shoulder. Following his gaze, I realized that Cameron had bled onto my shoulder and stained my blouse at some point.

"Dammit. Yeah, it's not mine. Hells, that sounds bad," I winced. "I mean, I'm not hurt, but a friend of mine was. Could I get some seltzer to try and clean this off?"

"Of course." He filled a glass from the tap and handed me that along with a stack of napkins and a shaker of salt. "Bathroom's that way. Pour the salt on first, trust me."

"Thanks."

His directions led to a hallway past the bar, which also led to a darkened back room and into the ladies' room. Since it was empty, I pulled the shirt off and started working on the stain. It was bigger than I'd thought at first, but even small head wounds were always bleeders. *Not even a full day back and I've literally got someone else's blood on my hands.* "Out damn spot, out I say," I joked under my breath, but a sob caught in my throat as I tried to laugh it off. I pressed my hand to my face, the scents of quinine and salt in my nose as tears spilled over my fingers. How was this all going to hell so quickly and thoroughly?

There was a knock at the door. "Miss? You still in there?" It was the bartender.

I sniffed, wiping my eyes. "Yeah...yeah, I am."

"Here." The door pushed open a crack, and he held out a black T-shirt with the bar's name on it. "Had to guess for the size, but I figured you wouldn't want the other one back on."

Putting my shirt down, I gratefully grabbed the new one and pulled it on. "It's great, thank you," I said with relief. "How much is it?"

"Ah, don't worry about it. On the house. Looks like you could stand to depend on the kindness of strangers," he said. "Speaking of, you got a name?"

"I'm Mc—you can call me Kendra." I winced at my near-slip, grateful he couldn't see my face. "You?"

"Trevan, nice to meet you."

"Trevan Stonehill? Bar owner?"

"That's me."

"That's the first luck I've had all day. Remi sent me here to fulfill her debt to you," I told him.

# THE TWICE-SOLD SOUL

"Is that so? Well, get yourself together and then come talk to me, Call-Me-Kendra."

"I will. Thanks again."

The door closed and I buried my head in my hands. So my slip had not gone unnoticed. Why was it suddenly so hard to keep my shit together? I ran my hands through my hair, looking at my unfamiliar reflection in the mirror. My face might be an illusion, but I'd been using the name Kendra for a decade with no such mistakes. But where once that had been the only thing I had to lie about, now I had to lie about *everything*. Gone was the luxury of being able to wear my own face, of not having to second-guess everything from what I was wearing to how I drank my damn coffee, of not telling lies-that-weren't-lies to my brother when all I wanted was to comfort and protect him.

I grabbed my necklace, the rounded edges of the knight pressing into my palm, the chain tight against the back of my neck. One sharp tug was all it would take.

But while the bar may have been full of strangers, Cameron worked here, and he and Tom could be here any minute. I let go; the black wood thumped against my chest. This was armor I had to keep wearing.

Instead, I touched up my makeup and headed back out to reclaim my barstool, tucking my stained shirt into my purse and putting in an order for a veggie burger and the brewed-on-site cider.

With that done, Trevan turned to me, leaning on the bar. "So how do you know Remi?"

"Old friend. You?"

"The same," he answered enigmatically.

"Why does she owe you?"

"Ah, that's between her and me. Wasn't anything big, I'll not be asking you to scale mountains and return with sacred artifacts or anything," Trevan said, waving a hand.

"That's good. I definitely left my climbing gear at home." I sipped the cider. "Mm. This is really good."

"Darn right it is!" said the tall bartender from the other end of the bar.

"Pip's our brewer," Trevan explained. "So, Kendra, what have you to offer?"

"I'm great at research, even obscure topics. I'm a library assistant," I offered.

Trevan shook his head. "I know too much about the things I know as it is. What else?"

"Okay. I'm sort of an amateur advocate, if you've got any negotiations or supernatural disputes to deal with?"

"Nothing right now. Are you a witch yourself? I saw the runes," he asked, nodding at my wrists.

"I am, but not currently practicing." He looked at me quizzically. "Long story. Let's see, I can balance books; are you behind on any receipts?" He shook his head. "Minor house repairs? I can ground an outlet, patch a wall, fix a leaky faucet… organize closets?" Again, nothing. "Drive stick? No? Okay, I'm also fluent in French, conversational in Italian and Spanish, I can edit, transcribe… seriously? Nothing?"

"There's not much I need right now," Trevan said apologetically. "Sorry if it puts you in a tight spot with Remi. I've been where you are, even if there are worse types to be in debt to."

I sighed. "Honestly, if there's nothing you need, I'm happy for you. I don't know why she sent me here without something in mind, though."

There was a buzzing sound, and he pulled out an old-school flip phone. "I'll think on it. I've got to take this, excuse me." He stepped away.

The anxiety of an unsettled debt set in as I ate. I hadn't made a full-on Bargain, so I wasn't in forfeit-your-soul territory, and besides, this was Remi. Any other Archdemon might've jumped on the chance to claim a soul or throw me into their demonic version of debtors' prison (which was *not* an experience I wanted to relive). Remi was different, but one way or another, I had to balance that ledger. And the question of why she'd sent me here to settle a non-urgent debt lingered.

I'd just finished my meal when Tom walked in, alone and even more mussed and tired than earlier. Spotting me at the bar, he jerked his head toward the door. I pulled my coat on and followed him outside.

He was leaning against the corner of the building and lighting up a cigarette when I caught up. "Where's Cameron?"

"Resting."

"Still? And by himself? You said you could help him!"

"I did," Tom replied, inhaling. As he held the puff and exhaled, I realized it was a joint. "He's better, but he needs to sleep it off now."

"What about the demons? What if they come after him?"

Tom waved a hand. "Our place is warded AF. Kept you out, didn't I?

"I'm not a demon." He shrugged as if this made no

difference, and I scowled. "Been a while since I checked, but isn't it illegal to smoke that out in public?"

"Helps to have an illusion spell worked into the leaves." He offered it to me. I declined.

"I can see it."

"You're a witch," Tom replied, releasing a plume of smoke. "It only works on normies in a fifty-yard range. What's your deal, anyway? I can't read you." He tapped his head, then his chest. "But I can feel you."

"What do you mean?" I asked guardedly.

"Dunno if Cam explained, but mental magic's my thing. Decent at telepathy, but I'm better with empathy—reading emotions." I waited while he took another hit. "Your thoughts are blocked. It's like trying to listen through a thick door. I know someone's talking, but I can't make out the words. But your emotions I can get. And you're like a big old murky rainbow." He waved his hands in an arc shape in my direction.

"I'm a what now?" I asked, half laughing at the unexpected metaphor.

"You ever see Rainbow Brite?" He took in and held another puff off the joint, exhaling through his nose. "Okay, so Rainbow Land is all full of color, right? Rainbow Brite, the Color Kids, Sprites, the whole gay gang. But then over in the Pits, you've got Murky Dismal, and he's always trying to get rid of all the color. Sometimes he pulls it off—he'll suck out all the color. Your emotions are like that. There's supposed to be color, and there kinda is, but most of it's been sucked out. A murky rainbow."

"So I suck the color and fun out of everything. Gee, thanks," I replied flatly.

"No, no, you're getting it all wrong. You sure you don't want this?" He held out the joint again. "You might need it more than I do."

"I get more silly than relaxed when I'm high, and I'm not up for that right now." He snorted like this was funny. "Could we please talk about how Cameron's doing?"

"Yeah, just a sec. It's not that *you* suck out all the fun and color. It's that something sucked it all out of you." Tom gestured like he was pulling something out of me and tossing it away into the air.

"Oh. Well... I can't say you're wrong." I looked away from him as visions of his dead sister loomed in my mind.

"You should try to get your color back," Tom advised.

"So I can be Rainbow Brite again?" I asked, cocking an eyebrow. "I say with confidence that I have never been a Rainbow Brite."

"Yeah, I'm getting that. You're more of a Stormy. Yeah!" He snapped his fingers and pointed at me. "Stormy."

I cleared my throat. "Cameron?" I prompted.

"Cameron." He puffed out one last cloud of smoke, then snuffed out the joint with his fingers and pocketed it. "He'll be okay, but he'll be out till morning."

"That long? What did that thing do to him?"

"You got attacked by hellhounds, right?"

"Yeah. In the Grand parking garage, the second we got off the elevator. It was... I think they were expecting us. Somehow."

"Mm. Yeah, they probably were. Hellhounds are relentless hunters." He tilted his head at me. "And... you feel guilty about that. Why?"

"Because he got hurt protecting me. Who wouldn't? But back up. Cameron wasn't surprised to see them, and neither were you. Now you're saying... what, that they were hunting him? Why?" *Why him and not me?*

It was Tom's turn to get cagey. He scratched at his lower lip. "Let's just say it's not the first time we've had to deal with them around here."

"Key words being 'around here.' How did demons get inside Arcadia Commons even once, much less multiple times?" I asked. "They didn't have human host bodies. That means someone summoned them and let them loose. Who?"

"Beats me. Some people might start asking about the strange new witch who came out unscathed, though."

I did a double take. "You think *I* did this?" I snapped. Even if they were after me, I certainly hadn't brought them on purpose.

"I think it doesn't look good," Tom said. "We don't know a lot about you, and you *are* blocking anyone from reading your thoughts."

"Like I'm the only one using a telepathy ward in Arcadia Commons." I crossed my arms.

"You're the only one who has it inked onto her skin." Tom pointed at my wrists. "Along with a few other things..." I adjusted my arms so the runes were blocked from view.

"I want to keep my thoughts to myself. That isn't a crime," I said, more defensively than I wanted. "Anyway, I would never do that. And you said it's happened before, but I got here yesterday."

"I'm just saying, people hiding something usually have

something to hide. But as long as you're not hurting Cameron, it doesn't matter to me what you hide from anyone else."

If he'd known what I was hiding, I somehow doubted he would say that. "Well, if you wanna read my emotions, read this one: I didn't summon those things and I don't want to hurt Cameron. I don't want anyone or anything to hurt him."

Tom watched, nodding slowly, scratching at his lip again. "Yeah... yeah, you really don't. You mean it, you feel very... protective of him." He sounded mystified. "But you barely know him. What's your deal?"

I rubbed at my shoulder, the one I'd landed on in the parking lot earlier. "Like I said, I feel responsible for what happened today. For not being able to stop them. I owe it to him to make sure he's okay."

"Hmm." Tom kept running his nail over his lip.

"Do you need some lip balm?"

He pulled his hand away from his mouth. "Bad habit. No, thanks, I've got some." He patted his pockets and frowned. "Somewhere. Anyway, I'm going inside. If you wanna know anything else about Cameron, take it up with him tomorrow." With that, Tom turned and headed inside.

I did the same, settling up my tab with Pip. I was about to text Remi when Trevan walked over, trailed by Tom. "How're you at bartending?" the Irishman asked.

I put down my phone. "Pretty good. I don't have a license in the States for it, but I did some bartending stints overseas," I replied. "And if booze isn't an international language, what is?"

Trevan grinned. "Truer words. Good, then I know how

you can pay off that debt. One of my guys called out sick, we've got some bands playing tonight, and I need someone to cover his shift."

"Cameron was supposed to work tonight?" I asked, looking between the two of them. Tom nodded. "Okay. But Cameron gets any tips I earn." It was the least I could do.

The corner of Trevan's mouth turned up as we negotiated, and I remembered Remi warning me he was Fae. "Tips only if you get no complaints."

"None?"

"Cam's good at his job. I expect the same from you."

"Okay. I'll cover Cameron's shift tonight, no complaints, and Remi's debt to you will be fulfilled. Deal." We shook on it, and an invisible weight settled on me, as if someone had dropped a light blanket on my shoulders. The sensation of negotiating with the Fae.

Trevan went behind the bar, motioning for me to follow. "How do you know Cameron?"

"It's...complicated," I replied, glancing sidelong at Tom. He was now nursing a gin and tonic provided by Pip.

Trevan quirked an eyebrow at me. "Is it now?" To my relief, his eyes twinkling, all he said after that was, "You are a curious one, Call-Me-Kendra."

He opened the register and pulled out a green glass bottle with a dropper. "This will let you see through glamour. Always better if you know who you're dealing with when you're working. Two in each eye will be enough for the night. Try not to stare, though, yeah?"

Unscrewing the eyedropper and tipping back my head, I

did as instructed. The drops tingled as they hit, and silver stars danced in the corners of my vision for a moment. "How long will it take to—whoa!"

When I looked at him again, I saw exactly what kind of Fae the bar owner was: a full-blooded satyr. A pair of goat horns curled back from his forehead, his ears had pointed tips, and under the kilt he wore were two goat legs ending in hooves. His eyes were now amber, with black rectangular irises.

After a minute, Trevan cleared his throat. "Remember what I said about staring?" Abashed, I looked away. "Take a look around, get used to it."

I did, and saw that about half of the customers weren't human, though most could've passed at a Ren faire. Others were much more obvious, like Trevan. Pip was actually a dryad; I could now see the barklike texture to her brown skin and the leaves naturally growing in her hair, including the woven crown. The green color was indeed all natural. I also saw, for the first time, patrons I hadn't seen at all before—a handful of pixies flitted through the air, coming and going from one of the rafters, where I could just make out their colorful glows. I smiled, reminded of the Silver Timber swarm. *I bet Cameron always treats them well*, I thought, and I determined to do the same.

"We set some dollhouse furniture up there for them," Trevan told me. "Don't worry, Pip will take care of them for tonight."

"It's okay, I like pixies," I replied. "Give me a minute to text a friend, and I'll be ready to go." I pulled my phone out, sending Remi an update. Next, I sent one to Lucca as well.

## Katie Hallahan

*Back TF up, demons?! How??*

*Beats me. Cam's out till the morning and*
*Tom won't tell me anything more.*

*Lets check the garage.*
*Meet me there in 30.*

*Can't. Gotta cover Cam's shift at the*
*Veil and Horn tonight.*

*What? Why?*

*Repaying a favor for Remi.*
*Gotta go, let me know if you find anything.*
*Going offline.*

With that, I tucked away my phone and got to work.

The next few hours were a crash course on how Trevan ran things, where everything was kept, and how to make their specialty cocktails, which varied in weirdness. "Titania's Tonic" was a gin and tonic with cranberry juice, whereas the "Slutty Mermaid" was a super-sugary concoction that could've killed a diabetic but had a salt rim. It tasted gross to me, but Trevan assured me some of the regulars loved it. After that, I warmed up my cocktail-slinging skills on the dinner crowd, which kept me from dwelling on the roller coaster that had been the past twenty-four hours, Cameron's well-being, or the many unanswered questions I had. Throwing myself into a task felt good, and staying busy actually had me feeling refreshed.

Before I knew it, it was dark outside and the diners began to dwindle. Trevan called for me to follow him. "What's up?" I asked.

"You're taking to this pretty well," Trevan complimented. "Even looks like you're enjoying yourself."

I smiled and shrugged. "It feels good to focus on something more straightforward for a while."

"If you're looking for something more regular, let me know. One of my staff gave notice a few days ago, so we've got an opening."

I shook my head. "Thanks, but I'm not in town for long."

We arrived at the back room I'd glimpsed earlier. With the lights on, I could see it opened up considerably and included a stage where four human women were setting up and tuning instruments, a few high-top tables, and another bar. "You'll be working back here the rest of the night, wanted to introduce you to the first band. Ladies, this is Kendra," Trevan said.

He started to gesture to the women, but my eyes snapped to the guitar in the stand by the lead mic. "That's Edie with the violin—" There were three tombstones drawn on it, each with a band name and the years they had existed. "Kida on the bass—" Two were unfamiliar, but the first one on it was THE WHATNOTS, a band from my first two years in high school. "Tansy's back there on the drums—" They broke up when their lead guitarist and singer had been forced to drop out of Arcadia Commons Academy to attend public school instead. I'd helped her memorialize them on this exact guitar: She'd drawn the tombstone in Sharpie, and I'd cast a spell to ensure it would never fade from the wood.

"And this is Leo."

Her short, dark hair was streaked with blue highlights and swished as she turned and hopped down off the stage, a painfully familiar crooked smile on her face. "Hey," my best friend said, holding out her hand, and my heart stuck in my throat. "We're Sass and Malarkey."

# Chapter 10
# I'm with the Band

*Twelve years ago*

"Happy birthday!" Leo Luppino jumped in front of my locker, a cardboard jewelry box in her hand with a purple bow stuck to it.

"Thank you? My birthday's not for three weeks," I said, taking it with a confused smile. It was the first day of our junior year.

"Duh. But this gift is way too important to wait that long, so for the next five minutes, your birthday is today," Leo declared. "C'mon, open it!"

"Okay, okay!" Dropping my backpack, I lifted the lid to reveal two silver cuff bracelets.

"One for each of us!"

"Best-friend bracelets?" I chuckled. "Leo, I love you, and we are totally BFFs for life, but I'm turning sixteen, not eight."

"Look a little closer, Mickey! These are leveled up. For the mature, sophisticated young women that we are," Leo replied in her faux-snotty voice.

I examined one to find that the outside of the band was inscribed www and burst out laughing. "Official WWW club merch, at long last!"

"We are long overdue for official recognition," Leo said, plucking up the other one. "But wait, there's more!" She tapped the inside of the bracelet. I turned it around to find another inscription.

"BEST BITCHES?" I laughed again. "Where did you get these?"

"The internet!" Leo crowed with a delighted cackle. "Go ahead, tell me how amazing and perfect they are."

"They are amazing and perfect," I agreed, slipping it on, admiring the light glinting off the metal and inscribed letters. "World's Worst Witch and Werewolf Who Wasn't. We sound like animated sidekicks."

Leo's grin had an edge to it. "Pssh, please. We are no one's sidekicks. We're A-list, full-season regular material, Mickey."

"Damn straight," I agreed. "Wait, is this real silver? The school won't let us wear them if it is."

"No. I tried. Way too expensive," she said, wrinkling her nose. "Won't stop me from telling Lucca it is so he keeps his paws off it."

"Are you ever going to not enjoy taunting him about his 'allergy'?"

"Nope. He got to be a lycanthrope and I didn't, the least he can do is put up with it. Plus it's my prerogative as his twin sister." Her grin sobered then. "Besides, I think you mean *your* school won't let *you* wear it."

"Is that why you're giving me this now? This is about the testing today, isn't it?" I asked more seriously. "You know it doesn't matter if we're both at the academy or not, we're still best friends."

Leo huffed. "I know, just...look, it might only be a little, but you've got magic. I've got nothing and it's pretty obvious I never will. They're going to boot me to public school, and I'm gonna miss you like crazy, so, y'know. I wanted us to have these."

I hugged her tight. "It won't be the same without you, Leo," I said, wishing I could tell her somehow that they wouldn't kick her out. But she wasn't supernatural—if you hadn't shown any signs by sixteen, it was pretty much a guarantee you never would. "It doesn't matter if you're on the other side of town or the other side of the world, you will *always* be my best friend."

"Damn right I will," Leo said, her voice gruff as she hugged me back. "Happy birthday, my best bitch," she said, arm over my shoulders.

I slung my arm around her waist in return. "Thanks, best bitch." We laughed again.

---

I wanted to hug her and laugh and cry and tell her absolutely everything. All I actually did was stare at her. On her wrist was the www silver cuff bracelet. A gold ring and a dog tag hung on a chain around her neck.

"Uh, hello?" Leo said again, louder.

*Right. Act normal!*

"Hi!" I forced out cheerfully, shaking her hand, fighting

the urge to pull her into a hug. "Kida, Tansy, Edie, Leo Luppino," I pointed to each in turn as though associating each name with a face. "Nice to meet you all!"

"Leo Pallas," Leo corrected.

"Right! Sorry!" Why was I yelling? I cleared my throat. "Leo Pallas," I repeated, at a normal volume. That felt weird to say.

"First night?" asked the drummer, Tansy. She was naturally tan, with long hair dyed in multiple shades of blond and bright pink, and several ear piercings. Edie, who was tuning some kind of very modern-looking electric violin, was brown-skinned with a dash of freckles and bouncy, curly dark-red hair. The glamour drops also revealed some iridescent scales along her face and arms and snake-like eyes that I assumed were hidden from the view of most.

"Yeah. Well, only night." I fiddled with my necklace.

"She's filling in for Cameron," Trevan said.

Leo frowned. "What's wrong with Cameron?"

"Another migraine, according to Tom," said the satyr, nodding his horned head toward the front room. *Another?* "Kendra's covering his shift."

I filed that away for later. "Can I get you anything?" I asked the group, though my eyes kept landing back on Leo.

While I was filling their orders behind the bar, Leo came over to Tom, who had wandered into the back room and sat in front of the taps.

"Tom, is Cameron okay?" she asked him.

"Leo! Hey, wassup," Tom greeted. How much had he already had? "Yeah, yeah, y'know, he'll be fine. Got a bad headache, 's all."

"Jesus, Tom, are you drunk? It's eight o'clock on a Sunday!"

Tom waved a hand at her. "I'm fine. Stormy's watching out for me, right, Stormy?" He leaned his head back to look at me.

Leo looked as well. "Stormy? I thought it was Kendra."

I shrugged. "It's some Rainbow Brite thing."

"Sure. You two know each other?"

"Yeah, we go way back to last night! And this afternoon. Right, Stormy?" Tom said, winking at me.

I gave him a look. "Okay, *that* makes it sound like we—"

Leo shook her head. "Relax, I know you didn't sleep with him. But what does he mean?" She focused on me, apparently deciding the sober one would give her real answers. Next to her, Tom shook his head at me. "Tom, I can see you doing that," Leo snapped without turning her head. He slunk down in his seat like a scolded puppy.

"I...met Tom at the reunion last night," I started.

"You didn't go to Arcadia Academy, and it wasn't Tom's reunion," Leo said flatly.

"Right. I know. I mean, obviously. I was there with Remi Blake. I was her date." Leo arched an eyebrow. "She's an old friend. Tom was at the bar."

"I'm sure he was." This was said with a disapproving sigh. Yep, time to cut him off.

"And this afternoon, Cameron needed a ride back to his place. Because of the migraine. So I drove him back," I went on.

"Where was Cameron and what was he doing that he needed a ride from a stranger?" Leo pressed.

I handed her the water she'd ordered to buy myself a breath from her rapid-fire interrogation and put together the truth with as little falsehood as I could manage. "I—I met him last night and ran into him again this afternoon at a coffee shop. His migraine was coming on, so I offered to drive him."

"There are at least a dozen people he could've called who would've driven him back," Leo pointed out. I shrugged and spread my hands, hoping responsibility for that would fall on my absent brother. "So you met him at the reunion at the Lemaires' hotel? Yeah, 'cause that sounds like something he'd do." Yikes. Leo was burning through my cover story in no time, but I wasn't sure what else to tell her, or what she already knew. Hell, I barely knew what Cameron and Tom knew. On the flip side, it was nice knowing she was looking out for him.

Leo turned to Tom. "What were you two *really* doing at the Grand last night?"

Tom groaned, not looking at her. "Leo, c'mon, stop playing nosy ex-girlfriend." *Wait, what? Whose ex?*

"Don't trivialize me, Tom. None of this adds up. What, you trust some strange friend of Remi's more than me now?"

"Call Cameron in the morning if you wanna know so bad," Tom said. "If you're so interested in his life again, you can ask him."

Leo glared at him, but Tom persisted in not meeting her eyes. Finally, frustrated, she grabbed her water and stalked off.

"She and Cameron dated?" I asked as soon as she was gone.

"Yeah. Our senior year, it was a whole messy thing," Tom replied, peeking in her direction now that it was safe.

*My best friend and my little brother?* "... Was it serious?"

"Kinda? It was, like, high school serious. Bad breakup, she moved on, he's still in love with her," Tom rambled, then jolted upright and leaned over the bar, so quick and close he nearly headbutted me. "Oh, shit, I'm not supposed to tell anyone that! Don't tell her, okay? Or anyone. Ever."

"Uh, yeah, no problem. I won't say anything."

"Promise?"

"Not using that word inside a Fae-owned bar. But I won't," I replied.

"Right. Sorry. I forgot. Hey, can I get another drink?" he asked, sitting back down.

"You can have water. Or something to eat. I am not serving you more alcohol."

Tom pouted. I was unmoved. He rolled his eyes and slumped against the bar. "Fine. But hey, if you're so interested, maybe you can help him get over Leo."

"Ew! Gross, no!"

"On his behalf, *ouch*. What gives? He's a good-looking guy."

"Just—no. Ugh!"

I brought the rest of the band their drinks and got back to work, but before the band even began their set, Brooke Luppino of all people appeared at the bar.

"Hey, Kendra!"

"Brooke, hey. What're you doing here?" I asked, glad she remembered to use my pseudonym.

"I came to see the band! Well, okay, also Lucca asked me to check in on you."

I rolled my eyes. "Of course he did. You want a drink?"

"Ginger ale, thanks," Brooke requested. "So how do you like the place?"

I started filling a glass for her. "It's pretty cool, grungy in a good way. I like the pixie setup. Do you all hang out here a lot?"

"I guess, yeah. It's nice having a supernaturals bar in town instead of having to go to Boston. And they've got great karaoke nights," Brooke replied, fingers playing with the ends of her hair. I passed her soda to her, and she started tracing shapes in the condensation instead.

"I'm not trying to lean too hard into bartender clichés, but—something on your mind?"

Brooke looked up, her big green eyes blinking. "I'm fine! It's—well—can we go talk in the bathroom?"

Uh-oh. Emergency conference in the girls' room was a classic Brooke move. Anything heavy *had* to be discussed in the girls' bathroom. And I really did not want to add to my pile of heavy.

"I'm kind of in the middle of a shift here," I said, "and I haven't seen Leo perform in ten years. I don't want to miss any of it."

Brooke pouted, turning on the sad, pleading anime eyes. "Please? It's important."

I sighed, looking at the stage. I hated missing this, but... "Okay, okay. They haven't started yet, but make it fast."

Pip cleared me to take five, and Brooke followed me to the bathroom after saying hello to Leo and her bandmates. Once we were inside, Brooke checked the stalls. Seeing they were empty, she locked the door behind us.

"Brooke! What the hell? We can't lock the door to the women's room while the bar's open!"

"I know, I'm sorry, but... McKenna, you need to leave," Brooke said, turning back to me and biting her lip.

"I made a Promise to cover Cam's shift, Brooke, I can't just take off."

"No, I mean...you need to leave Arcadia. Now. Or when your shift is up, I guess, but as soon as possible."

I scowled. "Did Lucca put you up to this? Let me guess, he doesn't want me talking to Leo? Because the way I remember it, she hated it when he tried to tell her what she could and couldn't do."

"It's not. I mean, he did tell me to say that, but this isn't from him. It's from me," Brooke admitted, looking at her hands.

That actually stung. "But...why?"

"Because it's better for everyone if you do." Brooke, bubbly, happy-go-lucky Brooke, lifted a quivering chin, her eyes brimming with tears. "I'm sorry. I really am, but...things were bad after you left, okay? Lucca doesn't want to tell you, but Cameron, Leo, and Bastien were heartbroken. We all missed you, but for them it was worse. Bastien didn't date anyone until he and Mari got together, and they're finally about to get their happily ever after."

"I'm *not* trying mess up that for them—"

Brooke cut me off and pressed on. "Cameron barely graduated, he never went to college, and he's been this awful, angry person ever since. And did you know your mom sold the house and moved, like, five years ago? I don't think she even talks to anyone from Arcadia anymore."

I dropped my eyes, running a hand through my hair. "Cameron mentioned something about that."

"And Leo's life, it's been a roller coaster, McKenna. She was angry and hurt, she shut everyone out for a long time. It got better when she and Cam were together. I thought maybe they'd both be okay. That ended badly, but she met someone else." I looked up as Brooke's voice lifted a little and saw a small smile. "Alex. They were so good together from the start. They got married, they had a son! His name's Griffin, he's four, and he's so great. But..." The smile faded. "Alex had cancer. He died two years ago."

Every word punched me in the gut, the ache of the truth immediate and sharp. "No...oh, no, Leo..."

"She's just starting to get her life back together. I, I don't want to make you feel bad, McKenna. I know I am, and I'm sorry for that. But I can't watch any of them get hurt again and not try to stop it. You said you're not staying past a week anyway. Isn't it better if you leave now before anyone else finds out? And now, with this attack, demons following you here..."

Someone knocked on the door. "Hello? Is anyone in there? The door's locked!"

"Occupied!" Brooke called back, and turned to me. "McKenna, I really am sorry. It's not that I don't wish you could stay, it's just—"

"It's just all I do is break things. Yeah. I got it." I pushed past her, unlocking the door, letting the line of anxious ladies outside pour in. I shoved my way back to the bar without waiting for her, fighting back my own tears.

"You okay?" Pip asked when I returned, looking me over.

"Am I gonna get in trouble if I have a drink?"

"Nah, one's fine, Trev's not a hard-ass," she said. "What'll it be?"

"Whiskey." She poured out a shot for me and I threw it back, letting it burn down my throat and cauterize the invisible wound left by Brooke's words.

Leave. Leave before I made things any worse. Before I broke anyone else. Really, why should that be so hard or hurt so much? I'd been gone ten years and back for barely a day. And it wasn't like I hadn't left behind other would-be friends and temporary lovers in over a dozen other cities in the last decade.

But these people were different. These were *my* people. The ones I'd done this for in the first place. And maybe worst of all was that she wasn't wrong, either. I'd been noticing that about a lot of people in the last day. But if none of us were wrong, then what was the right answer? What was the right thing to do?

*Whatever hurts the fewest and protects the most.* That's what I had to believe. Whatever had happened to Cameron before now, my being here would only make it worse. And I couldn't stand the idea of doing that to Leo, Bastien, Lucca, or Tom, either.

Or Leo's kid.

A kid. Shit. Leo had a freaking *kid*.

I'd talk to Remi. Convince her to let me out of the deal. She and Lucca and the others would look out for Cameron, help him now that we knew something was up.

"Oy! Eyes and ears up here, fairies and folk!" Trevan's voice through the speakers brought all attention to the stage, where he stood at the lead mic. "That's more like it. Now, it's my pleasure to introduce this evening's entertainment—Sass and Malarkey!"

Trevan stepped aside to give the stage to the band, who

were greeted with some applause. Leo stepped up to the lead microphone, guitar strapped on. "Hello Veil and Horn!" Leo shouted with a big showwoman's grin. "We're Sass and Malarkey, and we're gonna put some local flavor in the first song for you! You might know it by another name, but we like to call this one 'The Devil Came Up to Boston.'"

I wiped my eyes and couldn't help but smile up at her. For now, I still had a Promise to keep. So for one night and one night only, I could watch my best friend be a rock star.

Tansy rapped her drumsticks together to count off. "One, two, three, four!"

They launched into a fast-paced song that I recognized as soon as Edie jumped in with her violin, with a little less country and a lot more punk rock than the original. Leo started singing:

*The Devil came up to Boston, he was lookin' for a soul to steal*
*He was in a bind 'cause he was way behind, he was willing to make a deal*
*When he came across this young miss sawin' on a fiddle and playin' it hot*
*And the Devil jumped up on a busted T stop and said, "Girl, let me tell you what"*

I couldn't keep the smile from my face, even if the story in the song was a little close to home. Leo's joy was infectious and fierce, eyes sparkling, fingers flying over her guitar, short hair flipping as she got into it. Energy filled the room, heads nodding, feet tapping, people singing along, myself among them. Whatever she'd been through, Leo had clearly channeled at least some of it into this. She had always been good and had only gotten better with time.

The room exploded as they finished, and a hurried rush of drink orders between songs kept me busy. Brooke had returned to the bar in that time, looking like a scolded puppy, and I ignored her well into the next song when things finally slowed down.

"Shouldn't I be the one looking like that?" I said, irritated.

"I didn't like saying any of that," Brooke replied.

Grabbing a towel, I focused on wiping down the bar. "I didn't do any of it to hurt them, you know. I did it to protect them, to keep them safe. I...I did the right thing." *Didn't I?*

"You did what you had to do. The only thing you could."

For a moment, I wasn't sure if she'd said it or I'd thought it; when I looked at Brooke, her gaze was unexpectedly sympathetic.

A sympathy I didn't deserve. "What, did you get telepathic while I was gone?" I said, falling back on sarcasm.

Brooke cracked a small smile. "No, that's still a Harwell thing. I'm still just a hedger."

"Thought the term was *generalist* now."

"It is, I keep forgetting," Brooke said, shaking her head. "I'm so used to hearing the old word. *Generalist* is much nicer, though. I'm glad Mari's been pushing for it."

My brows lifted in surprise. "Mari's behind that? Mariposa 'Ellerbeck-You're-More-Like-Hedgebitch' Perez?"

Brooke nodded. "Yeah. She's changed a lot since then, you know."

"She must have, if Bastien's marrying her," I remarked.

The mean girl I'd known would never have had the emotional capacity to heal anyone's broken heart.

The next wave of orders hit, and Brooke wandered into the crowd to listen as Leo announced their next song. The stage light dimmed, a spotlight focusing on her. She spoke and it felt like we were alone in the room. "This one's for anyone else who's ever had to rebuild themselves." Her fingers strummed a slower, sadder melody, and when she sang, her voice held me like a siren.

*Broken doesn't mean not whole*
*My pieces are what make me beautiful*
*If I were always smooth, unbroken, and unstained*
*Maybe there would be no pain*
*But there'd be nothing, nothing, nothing there to see*

*Staying fragile, clear, and in one piece*
*It's a state of mind that just won't keep*
*Perfection is a nightmare, not a dream*
*No one can hold to that extreme*
*And it will never, never, never make you free*

*Life shattered me and left me a mess*
*But I am not debris, I am stained glass*
*A mosaic of my scars*
*Strong as these iron bars*
*More beautiful and more complete*
*Tempered, tried, and this is me*
*I am stained glass*

The song was a sledgehammer. Tearing down my walls, shattering me and picking up the pieces all at once. I rubbed at the scar in my hand as she finished and the room burst into applause, though I didn't join in. I couldn't move at all.

Pip had to snap her fingers in my face to get my attention back on my customers. But as I worked, Leo's song haunted me, lingering in my mind. I kept looking up at her on stage, wondering if somehow she knew even though it was impossible. Wondering who had the right of it—Brooke, trying to keep anyone else from being broken? Leo, singing her anthem to rebuilding and growing stronger? I didn't know anymore. At this point, I felt so spun around I just wanted an easy answer, but I knew none was coming.

Eventually, Sass and Malarkey wrapped up their set, and by the time they came back to the bar for a celebratory round, I had my fake smile firmly in place.

"Rum and Cokes all around!" Kida, the bassist with pale-bronze skin and sleek shoulder-length dark hair shaved on one side, declared. I got out four glasses.

"You were amazing!" Brooke said, hugging her sister-in-law and the rest of them.

"Oh, go on. No really, do," Leo said, grinning crookedly.

"She's right, you were fantastic," I said as she took a seat at the bar. "That song 'Stained Glass' was really moving."

Leo gave me a pleased smile. "Yeah? Thanks. Doesn't come off as too rah-rah, Kelly Clarkson–esque?"

"Nah, Kelly's got nothing on you," I replied, grinning—right before Leo gave me a very weird look and I realized that was something I used to say to her all the time. "Ah, you want anything else with the rum and Coke?" I quickly asked, hoping she'd chalk it up to coincidence.

"...No, that's all," Leo said after a long pause. I busied myself making their drinks and going about the standard business of bartending. I could feel Leo's eyes on me for a while after that, but I kept my distance as I served other customers. Eventually she seemed to shrug it off and go back to hanging out with her bandmates and Brooke, whom I could swear was making an extra effort to keep her away from me. Eventually Tom, who had somehow gotten his hands on another cocktail, joined them.

But as the hour grew late and the crowd thinned, my buffer shrank, and Leo returned to the bar for a drink on her own.

"What can I get for you?" I asked, trying to play it cool.

"Tequila blanco."

"Rocks?"

"Straight."

I poured out her drink. I knew I should serve it and move away, but... it might be the last chance I ever had to talk with her. A little conversation couldn't hurt, right? "How long has your band been together?"

"Three years, but we've been friends since college," Leo said. "Been through a lot together. It's nice having friends who really know you, you know?" She looked at me over the rim of the glass as she drank.

I cleared my throat, which suddenly felt very dry. "Yeah, it... it is." I poured myself some water. "I kind of have trouble hanging on to people," I found myself saying.

"Yeah? Why's that?"

My brow furrowed as I considered the matter. "I...have trouble making the right decisions."

Leo tilted her head. "What do you mean?"

"It's nothing, never mind," I said, suddenly uncomfortable. "Did you serve?" I asked, nodding at the dog tags on her necklace along with a gold ring. She stared at me and tossed back her drink. I immediately regretted the question.

"Another." I silently refilled the glass. She lifted it back to her lips as soon as I pulled the bottle away, but paused before drinking. "No. Alex did. My husband. He died two years ago." Her fingers ran over the metal bead chain.

Even having known this, hearing it from her was heartbreaking. "I'm so sorry," I said. *I'm sorry it happened. I'm sorry I wasn't here for you.*

"It wasn't your fault," Leo said. "I appreciate it, but you don't have to sound so guilty."

"Sorry—I didn't—I just—" *Want to apologize for being the world's worst friend.*

This time she chuckled a little and sipped her tequila slowly. "Relax. It sucks and it still hurts like hell, but we got to say goodbye at least. Prepare for it as best we could. It's more than most people get."

The corner of my mouth tugged up, ruefully. "But not as much as you wanted."

"God, no," she agreed.

"What was he like?" I asked, leaning on the bar.

She ran her fingers over the letters on the tag. "He was the best man I've ever known," she finally said, slowly smiling. "Joined the army out of high school, did two tours overseas before getting stationed in Boston. He was incredible. Brave, funny. Hottest guy I'd ever seen, too," she added, eyes glinting.

I smiled back. "Got a picture?"

"Oh, tons. Lemme find my favorite..." She pulled out her phone to search for it.

"How'd you meet? Through Lucca?" I asked. She gave me a curious look. "Remi mentioned he'd been in the military."

This answer seemed acceptable. "He was, but no. Lucca was a marine, Alex was army. No, it was the classic 'drunk boy meets drunk girl in a bar in Southie and a would-be one-night stand turns into a whole lot more.' Here we go, that's us."

It was a picturesque family moment, taken on the Fourth of July. I knew because it was at the same parade route spot on Washington Street downtown where the Luppino family always sat to watch, right before the judges' booth and the town hall. I'd sat there with them every year for as long as I could remember, until I left. In the photo, Leo was standing next to a tall, handsome young man with a deep tan, short-cropped dark hair, and a goatee. Both of them had sunglasses on, as did the tiny baby they held up between them.

"That's our son, Griffin. He's two months old here," Leo said.

"He's beautiful," I said, fixated on the picture.

"The kid or the guy?" she joked.

I laughed. "Both?"

"Good answer!" She turned the phone around and looked at the picture, smiling with affection. "Those are my boys," she sighed, then scrolled to another picture. "This is Griff now. He's four." In this one, the newborn had become a little boy with a messy mop of dark hair in *Star Wars* pajamas, sitting on the faded flower-patterned couch of the Luppino family living room. He had his mom's smile, a nose I assumed was his dad's, and ears that he would hopefully grow into.

"Still beautiful," I said sincerely, handing it back. "Looks like a really happy kid."

"He is, he's really great," Leo said. "He's got a lot of people who love him."

"It sounds like you do, too," I added.

She smiled, though it was again touched by melancholy. "I've lost more of them than I'd like, but, I do."

The lump crept back up in my throat. "I'm sorry to hear that," I said, looking away. When I did, I saw that there was a buildup of customers I'd been neglecting. "Excuse me," I said, and stepped away to take care of them.

When I returned, Brooke, Edie, and Tom had rejoined Leo. Tom was leaning heavily on the bar, and his eyes had an unfocused look. I hung back, wiping down some glasses and eavesdropping.

Leo was trying to get him to drink some water. "Look at him, he can't get up there by himself. He'll probably fall down the stairs trying!"

"I can help get him up there, but not by myself," Edie said. Brooke saw me watching. "Could you help her, Leo?"

"Don't do that to her, her ex lives up there!" Edie chastised.

"From, like, forever ago! He's probably asleep anyway," Brooke tried to argue. The other two gave her a look. "Okay! Okay. I'll help, it's fine."

"Text me if you need more help, though, okay? I'll wait here," Leo said. Brooke obviously wasn't thrilled. I kept my eyes elsewhere but I could feel her giving me a worried look. "See you soon. And Tom, I hope your headache in the morning teaches you something," Leo said to the drunk witch.

Tom slurred something that vaguely sounded like good night at her as Brooke and Edie helped him stumble out. He tossed a "Stormy!" at me as he went, and I gave him a wave in return.

Leo sat back down in front of me. "He's got a problem, doesn't he?" I asked.

She sighed, nodding. "Yeah. It's not exactly surprising, but I wish he'd get help. He's a good kid, but he's had a rough time."

No thanks to me. "I heard his sister died?"

Leo nodded. "Night of graduation—different schools, but Jackie was in my year. Died in a car crash. Tom's never really been the same."

Yet another person I'd broken. The centerpiece of my nightmares, Jackie's cut throat and lifeless body, swam before me. From far away, someone was speaking.

"Kendra!" I jerked my head up. Leo was snapping her fingers at me. "Are you okay? You went all fugue-state there."

"Sorry, I..."

Leo waited for me to finish, but I didn't. "Sorry, did that trigger you or something?"

"...Something like that," I replied slowly, rubbing at the scar in my hand again. "That sounds awful. I...I can't imagine what that must've been like for his family."

"Yeah, it wasn't great." Her eyes drifted to my hands. "What are those tattoos?"

"Some wards—it's a witch thing," I said absently.

"You're a witch? Is that why you're doing this advocate thing for Cameron?" Raising an eyebrow, I nodded. "Tom's drunken ramblings," she explained.

"Remi asked me to help him out," I said.

"Uh-huh. You two must be pretty tight. You know her well?"

"Sometimes I think I do," I said, shaking my head. "Other times, well, you know how she is."

Leo chuckled. "I sure do. You've got some experience with this kind of stuff then? Witch tribunals? I mean, practical experience. I've never seen one myself, but I've heard they can be tough."

"They can," I agreed, leaning back, a hand on one hip. I hadn't had much time to think about it yet, but now that she mentioned it... "The Council will show up with a plan in mind for how things are going to go, and how they're going to punish Cameron."

"And what's your plan?"

"I don't have one yet. Cameron hasn't exactly agreed to let me represent him. But if he goes in there with nothing but a surly look, he's screwed, Laurent will drive right over him. The only thing he's said is that he *wants* the tribunal to happen, which doesn't make any sense," I said, thinking aloud, and remembering now that he'd be alone in there if I did leave early after all. And Brooke's worry aside, I wasn't so certain that would leave him better off. *Maybe I* should *stick around for the whole week...* "I mean, he knows what this is going to be like, he's seen it before. He knows what kind of people he has to convince. Some of them might be sympathetic, but if Laurent says jump, they're going ask what spell he'd like them to use." My lips pressed together, remembering how he'd tried to do that with my tribunal. "If Cameron would stop being so stubborn, I'm just trying to help..." I trailed off as I noticed that Leo was laughing. "Did I say something funny?"

Leo shook her head, her hand over her mouth to stifle the sound. "No, no, it's just..." It was then I saw the tears pricking in the corners of her eyes.

"He'll be okay, I'm going to make sure of it," I promised her.

"I know you will. You'll do better than anyone else ever could." Leo looked at me, lowering her hand, and I saw that despite the tears, she was smiling. "How could you not? You're his big sister."

The world froze. The sound fell out. I should've been denying it, shutting down the very idea. But all I could do was stare at the only person who'd seen right through me. The only person to see *me*.

So I did the only thing I could. I undid my necklace and took off my armor.

"Yeah. Yeah, it's me."

# Chapter 11
# Since You've Been Gone

We hugged, we laughed, we cried, and I told her absolutely everything. Eventually.

From the night I left to everything that had happened since I'd come back, once I started telling Leo the truth, I couldn't stop. For the better part of an hour, we drove around Arcadia Commons in her car. Exactly like we used to, though the beat-up tan sedan she and Lucca once shared had been upgraded to a newer-model blue sedan with a child seat in the back.

"Is that all-night Stop-and-Gas still open?" I asked as we passed near the highway without getting on it. I was still restricted to the town borders, after all.

"Kinda. It's a Cumberland Farms now," Leo answered, turning right to head that way.

"Whatever, as long as they still sell ice cream sandwiches and grape soda," I said, grinning.

We went inside, laughing like a couple of high schoolers out past curfew. Remodeling had been kind to the place, with tan carpet replacing linoleum and diffuse lighting instead of bare fluorescent bulbs above us.

Leo loped ahead to the coolers, grabbing two purple bottles. "Geez, I feel like a teenager buying this sugary crap! Last time I did this, I was with...uh..." She shot me an awkward sidelong look.

"With Cameron," I said, taking one from her. "Because you dated my little brother."

Leo winced. "Yeeeaaah, I dated your little brother," she confirmed. "...Welp. This is awkward."

"Little bit!" I cleared my throat. "But that was a while ago, from what I hear?"

"Yeah, years ago. Feels like another lifetime, honestly. But if you need to get in, like, an obligatory big-sister beatdown, you can have a few swings before I'll fight back."

She might've been serious, but I laughed. "Nah. I'm assuming you didn't cheat on him or something like that—"

"Of course not!"

"—and I hurt both of you, so we're good," I finished. "I'm sorry it ended badly, though."

Leo nodded. "Yeah. Things started off great, but then we fought about everything. He was mad at everyone but me and Tom, but he didn't want to leave Arcadia even though he hated it here. When I found out he lied about even applying to colleges and called him on it, he called me a traitor for forgetting about you."

"He *what?*" I exclaimed. "Leo, you weren't. You know that, right?"

"I know. Felt like shit at the time, but I know." Her smile softened. "Anyway, Cam and I didn't talk for years, but we're okay now."

Except that according to Tom, Cam was still in love with her... "Tell me more about Alex and Griffin."

This time, she fairly beamed, but there was still some sadness in it. "Both amazing. And they both snuck up on me. Like I said, I wasn't looking for anything serious when Alex and I met, but turns out something serious was looking for me. I know, super cheesy," she said when I chuckled. "That's how Alex liked to put it. He was kind of a goofball."

I smiled. "Must've gotten along great with Lucca."

"Yeah, they were good friends, too. Lucca offered to let him in the pack, but it wasn't what Alex wanted," Leo said.

"Not even when he got sick?"

"No. It wouldn't have helped, anyway, or I might've hated him forever for saying no." She sniffed. "Werewolves heal faster and don't get sick, but since he already had cancer, it probably would've made it spread faster."

I shook my head. "That's so unfair. All this power and magic and shit like that still happens."

Leo smiled crookedly. "Alex liked being human. He said being human is what all the monsters really want, when you got down to it, so it must be pretty damn special."

"Sounds like a smart guy."

"Best guy ever," she agreed.

"Does that mean you're more okay with it now, too?" I asked.

She scoffed. "I was always fine with being the token human, thank you very much."

I gave her a dubious look. "Aren't we kinda past hiding behind teenage bravado?"

"Hmph. Speak for yourself. That was something Alex and I both believed," she insisted.

I shrugged, letting it drop, and ran my finger along the ridged edge of my bottle cap. "I'm so sorry I missed meeting him, Leo. I'm sorry I wasn't here. For the good stuff or the bad stuff or the weird, you-dated-my-brother stuff...all of it."

Leo nodded but was otherwise silent, cracking her knuckles as we headed to the freezer section. We pulled some ice cream sandwiches, and she grabbed a box of Popsicles, too. "Griff loves the lime ones and we're out," Leo said when I asked, starting to smile again. "They are excellent bribery for good behavior."

"Didn't your mom used to do that with you and Lucca?" I recalled.

"Oh, yeah. I did not realize how much of a manipulative genius my mom was until I had Griff," Leo said. "I have no idea how she dealt with three of us. One's a handful as it is, and he's a great kid."

"So nothing like Teddy the Terror?"

"No, thank God! He is nothing like his uncle," Leo confirmed. "Who, by the way, is getting his bachelor's in business this spring."

"What? No! He was supposed to be an irritating tween for all eternity," I protested. "I guess the natural progression from there *would* be to slimy salesman."

"Yeah, he's still a pain in the ass, but he's one who's good at math," Leo said. We paid and headed back out to her car, busting out the ice cream sandwiches as we sat on the hood.

The bottles hissed as we opened them and drank. I lay back, closing my eyes, and I was sixteen again, celebrating Leo getting her license, planning road trips we'd never take, talking for hours about boyfriends and girlfriends, homework and school plays. So much future in front of us.

But I opened them again and we were adults. With pasts and scars and, in her case, a kid. "Tell me about being a mom. I still can't quite get my head around that one."

"Took me a while, too. Everything happened so fast. We had an 'oops,' five seconds later we were getting married, ten minutes after that we were parents," Leo replied. "I've never been more scared or clueless in my life. He's amazing. I don't know how he's my kid. I'm still waiting for everyone to realize I'm just making this shit up as I go."

"You always were good at improvising," I noted.

"Ha, true! But it's hard to put words to it. It's great and it's the hardest damn thing in the world, but I wouldn't change it." Leo paused and sighed. "Well. Except for the one thing."

I turned my head, looking at her as she gazed upward. "Alex."

"Yeah." Her voice shook a little. I set my ice cream sandwich in its wrapper on the hood and reached over to take her hand. "He healed me, you know? I don't know how or who's going to do that now. It's been two years and it's still...And people say, oh, you've got a son, let him be the light of your life and crap. But he's just a kid, I can't put that on him."

I didn't know what to say. No, that's not true. I knew exactly what to say: *I'll do it, I'll be here, I'll help you heal this time*. But the words stuck in my throat. I didn't know if they were true, if I could make that kind of promise.

Leo reclaimed her hand to wipe at her face, sniffing. "Okay, we need a pick-me-up." She shoved the rest of her ice cream sandwich into her mouth as she looked for something on her phone. "Yes! Here we go!"

Tapping the screen and setting the phone on the hood, she hopped in front of the car, dancing dramatically at me to some goofy pop song from our high school days.

I laughed so hard I almost snorted soda out of my nose as Leo belted out some ridiculous lyrics about "fire" and "desire." She pulled me down to join her and soon the two of us were dancing to choreography we'd made up in sixth grade, singing and twirling and smiling until we were breathless, a scene right out of another lifetime.

"Nailed it!" I exclaimed afterward, high-fiving her.

"Hell yeah!" She laughed. "I can't remember what's on my grocery list, but middle school talent show dance choreography is written in permanent marker on my brain."

I was smiling wider and feeling lighter than I had in years. Feeling like I was home. Or at least like I could be. Feeling like maybe there was a way to fix all of this, to finally have the one thing that I knew I'd always wanted, to come home.

Feeling *hope*. For the first time in years.

*Get real, Ellerbeck. One silly dance with Leo doesn't change what you've done*, my inner cynic sniped.

But it wasn't that. It was that I was finally telling my friends what I had done, why I had left, and despite what I had expected, what I deserved... they were accepting it.

# THE TWICE-SOLD SOUL

Accepting *me*. Well, Leo was anyway.

"We should get going. We've officially gone from Brooke's worried texts to Lucca's angry ones," Leo said, rolling her eyes at her phone.

"When has that ever stopped you?" I asked, arching an eyebrow.

"Never, but he's likely to send the pack to find me soon at this rate, and that's a pain in the ass for everyone involved," Leo said, getting in and buckling up. She sent a reply to one or both of them.

"Sure, yeah," I said, joining her in the car and sighing wistfully. "I wish this night didn't have to end."

"If only we could be teenagers again forever, right?" She started the engine and headed out to the streets of town. "Can't believe you went and set up shop in Paris to live some glamorous expat lifestyle without me. Junior year abroad together! We had a plan!"

"I know. I thought about that so many times. Or about calling you or emailing and telling you everything. I missed you so much, Leo," I confessed.

"What stopped you, Mickey?" she asked, looking at me sidelong. "You've been recapping nonstop since we left the bar. Why didn't you do it before?"

"Because I couldn't put you in danger."

"Okay, *that* is crap," Leo said bluntly. "One, I live in Arcadia Commons, where yellow alert is the default. Two, we went through plenty of tough, dangerous, potentially fatal shit in high school, and we all survived that. Three, hello, my brother is the local werewolf alpha, on top of your witch badassery, and the rest of our little Scooby Gang to boot. Maybe you didn't *want* me to be in danger, but you knew I could handle it. We all could. What made this so different?" Lucca had said as much the night before, and I grasped for the same excuses I'd given him.

"We didn't have anything capable of killing this demon—"

"We would have found something."

"What do you think I've been trying to do for the last ten years?" I said, exasperated.

"You *just* told me you tried to stay away from magic this whole time," Leo pointed out.

I ran a hand through my hair. "I stayed away from *using* magic. I could never stay in one place too long because of it. And I still tried to find out who the demon was, or if there was any other way to kill one. And there isn't. There's no information, and no way to kill it."

"Remi doesn't know who it is?" Leo asked, dubious.

"No. I showed her the rune for the name. She hadn't seen it before, and demons aren't big on sharing their true names. With the rune, I *could* summon it, but that would be insanely stupid without a plan or knowing what I'd be up against."

"Having more people working on that could've uncovered something, you know. Strength in numbers. And you're getting off-topic," Leo said. She turned to take the long, meandering road that went around the state forest instead of driving through town. The long way home.

"Seems pretty on-topic to me."

"Why didn't you call, McKenna?" Leo pushed. "Even to just say, *Hey, FYI, I'm still alive and well*?"

"...I left a note," I said in my own defense.

Leo scoffed. "Hell of a note. 'I have to go. I'm sorry, I'm okay, I love you, don't look for me.' And then nothing for ten years."

I rubbed at the scar in my palm. "You would've looked for me. I couldn't let you."

She scowled. "We could've helped you, but you wouldn't let us. Again! Why do you keep doing that? When has that ever worked out for you?"

"What are you talking about?" I looked up in surprise.

"I love you, McKenna, but you are and always have been terrible about letting people help you," Leo sighed. "Which must be genetic—Cam's the same way. You make all your problems yours and yours alone. You were pissed about how the witches treated you, so you went off on your own and made a deal with Forneus."

"Hey, I admit that was stupid. I had *no* idea what I was really getting into! And I *did* get help to get rid of him."

"Eventually. But when Remi got that power, you freaked out and pulled away again. You shut us out and tried to find another solution for her on your own. Don't try telling me you didn't, I know you. Maybe you stopped eventually, but I'd bet it wasn't until after you started seeing Bastien, and that's part of why you felt so guilty about it. I miss anything so far?"

There was no use denying any of it, but at the same time, I couldn't help smiling. "I missed having someone around who knows me better than I do."

Leo smiled back. "Damn right I do. You take everything on yourself, you can't keep a secret when you don't want to, and you go way too far to protect the people you love. And since I know you've always believed forewarned is forearmed, one more time: *Why?*"

I stared at my hand. I wanted to speak, wanted to tell her, but the words stuck in my mouth, as though my tongue were too thick to form them.

"McKenna." She held up her wrist, shaking the engraved bracelet. "Whatever it is, you can tell me. Best bitches, remember? Always, even from the other side of the world."

"But we shouldn't be!" I finally blurted out. "I *killed someone*! Why aren't you getting as far away from me as you can? You've got a kid, Leo! It's not like I can just come back and everything goes back to the way it was, all of us getting in way over our heads with magic and demons and werewolves, oh my!" The air tightened around me. My head spun. I couldn't breathe. I fumbled at the window controls, and a blast of cool air greeted me, carrying the scent of the woods and the distant ocean, and I sucked it in.

"Hey—hey, McKenna! Look at me!" Reluctantly, I did; Leo's eyes met mine with earnestness, and she grabbed my hand. "I might be the Werewolf Who Wasn't, but that doesn't mean I don't have a pack. And you're in it. Whatever kept you away, it's killing you. And I don't mean that whole magic blood poisoning shit; I mean in here." She tapped her hand over my heart, thudding in my chest while tears spilled down my cheeks. "I know you've changed. We all have. But in case it wasn't obvious, I am *not* letting you get away again. So stop carrying this by yourself already and *come home*."

My cold hand trembled in hers, but she squeezed it gently, her warmth seeping in, bringing hope with it. *She's right. Dammit. But...*

"I don't *deserve* you. I don't deserve any of you, not your love or trust or forgiveness, not after what I did." I sniffed and wiped at my eyes. "I'm a *murderer*, Leo, I—" I stopped and sniffed again. A rotting, sulfuric stench carried on the breeze. I jerked my eyes to the road in front of us. "Leo, look out!"

The headlights lit up the hairless flesh of the hellhound charging straight at us. Leo swerved and the car careened off the road, pitching into the forest. We clipped a tree and the world spun, glass and metal smashing again and again. Something punched me in the face, and everything went dark.

---

The blaring car alarm woke me up. I coughed, choking on the blood pouring down—no, *up* my face. With the only light being a single headlight and the dashboard, it took a few moments for my eyes to adjust and register that the car was upside down.

"Leo?" I asked in a clogged voice, turning to look her way. Why was my nose so stuffed up? I touched it gingerly and yelled at the flare of pain. Not stuffed up. Broken. That explained the blood. "You okay? Are you awake?"

There was no answer. "Leo? Leo!" I blinked and squinted, wiping blood from my eyes and reaching over to shake her.

"McKenna?" she groaned after a moment.

"Thank the goddess. Are you okay?"

"I've been better." There was a dull click. "My belt's stuck. There's a Leatherman in the glove box, can you reach it?"

"Working on it." I pushed at my buckle a few times before it released me, dropping me onto the ceiling of the car. "Ow!"

Pinpricks of pain erupted all over from the shards of glass I landed on. I patted my pockets, trying to find my phone for some more light, but it was gone. It could be in the car or anywhere between here and the road.

I did find the glove box, though. It opened easily, raining papers, manuals, the Leatherman, and the contents of an open bag of M&M's out on top of me. Muttering an apology for the mess, I grabbed the multi-tool, flipping it open and starting to cut at her seat belt.

"Stupid suicidal deer," she griped as I worked.

The image of the creature in the lights came back to me just as the stench drifted back in on the air. "That wasn't a deer. That was a hellhound. Call Lucca, now." I scrambled backward out of the broken car window and got to my feet as I heard a growl. The hellhound stepped out from between the trees, entering the beam from the headlight. Shadows already writhed around its claws. The pocketknife was utterly insufficient but better than nothing. I brandished it before me.

"What? Only one of you this time?" I said with forced bravado. The second the words left my mouth, I heard a low growl and a second stepped out next to it. I groaned. "I just *had* to ask..."

Behind me, from Leo's side of the car, came a third bestial growl. "Okay, that's overkill," I croaked, my throat tightening up. My heart raced erratically as they came closer. I cringed away from the darkness they brought with them—

*I screamed—how long had I been screaming? Why couldn't anyone hear me?*

"*CARVE.*" *My hand was white-knuckled as it clutched the knife* and dragged it across my enemy's skin. Forneus trembled beneath me, his black eyes wide, and I felt a surge of satisfaction at being the one to terrify him for once.

No—not Forneus. The false image shifted, changed, out of focus, and I saw the true face before me. Jackie! Her eyes were so wide, so dilated, it was nothing but white and blue and hardly any black. I felt her shaking beneath me.

"McKenna!"

Was the scream real or in my mind?

"McKenna Ellerbeck, get me out of this fucking car!"

Definitely real.

The two hellhounds on my side of the car were almost on me when I snapped out of it. One slashed at me with a shadowed set of claws before I could dodge. The shadow-claws marked my hand with black lines. There was no blood, but a burst of pain as my hand spasmed, muscles twitching out of control. The knife fell to the dirt. Grabbing my one hand with the other, I watched in terror as the shadows sank into my skin and started to flow as if traveling up through my veins. *No!* The poison, the madness that had driven me to kill was in me again, and Leo was right there, trapped. What if it made me hurt her this time—

But when they hit my wards, they stopped dead, dissipating back into the air. Harmless, useless. The wards had worked. The demons couldn't drive me mad. They *worked*.

The forest was silent. The growling had ceased. I looked at them. The hellhounds were as shocked as me.

I gave the demons a dark grin. "So that's what it looks like when you cut a demon's balls off."

One of them barked and dropped back on its haunches, ready to lunge at me.

Right, they could still kill me the old-fashioned way.

I dropped down under its leap; it landed on the car with a crunch and groan of metal, the frame starting to buckle under its weight. Leo yelled from inside, "Could we hurry up with getting me out of here!"

"Working on it!" I saw the knife in the dirt, grabbed it, and tossed it inside. "Here!"

"Gah! Do not throw open switchblades at me, thank you very much!" The earsplitting sound of nails through metal filled the air as the hellhounds began ripping at the car, but the one still in front of me had resumed growling and circling, and I was out of weapons. It let out a nasty bark, the sound itself making the air around me waver and shudder and spin—but while I felt it, once again, it didn't affect me. *I was the only thing that could shut me down*, if I let the panic get to me. I was sure as hell scared, my heart racing and my legs itching to run, but no. I refused to let it control me again.

*Not this time. I let Cameron down, I let him get hurt. I won't let it happen to Leo.*

"What the fuck was that?" Leo half yelled, half groaned, from inside the car.

The maddening barks became growls. It prowled closer, forcing me away from the car, away from Leo. I held up my hands, a useless, instinctive gesture, and my eyes fell on my wrists, my tattooed wards. The only things protecting me, and yet... *I could open them... just for a minute, just long enough to banish them...* The power roiled and rushed within me, eager to be free, to be wielded. But hope fell as quickly as it flared. I couldn't attack without hurting Leo if I opened them now. The hellhounds couldn't drive me crazy, sure, but that didn't mean I could do anything to them, and they were smart enough to know it. They were herding me, keeping me away from her. Panic rose again as the beast crouched, ragged, rotting muscles flexing as it leapt—

—and collided with an enormous black wolf in midair!

"Lucca!" I fell back against a tree as two more wolves joined the fray: a she-wolf, smaller and leaner, brown with a white belly, and Chris, golden-furred, as big as Lucca, and—wearing a prosthetic leg? I did a double take. "Okay, now I've seen everything." But I grinned as Chris grabbed a hellhound by the neck and tossed it away from the car. Clearly, the prosthetic wasn't slowing him down in the slightest.

The she-wolf wrestled with the third hellhound, tearing out its neck, but the thing swiped back at her, claws scoring down her side. She yelped, then let out a strange howl, tossing her head around and scraping at her nose with her paws as though there was something on it. They might be a match physically, but they could still be infected by the madness in those shadow-claws. And the last thing we needed was an insane werewolf.

"Get them away from the car!" I yelled, circling to stand in front of the upturned vehicle. "I need a clear shot!"

Lucca howled. Chris herded his opponent back, but the she-wolf turned a circle and threw herself on the ground, yelping. Chris then leapt over her at her attacker. His powerful jaws ripped the ragged, skeletal wing from the hound's back. But the enemy he'd left rallied and leapt on his back, tearing at him with dark, vicious teeth. Shadows swirled around its mouth as it pulled back, and Chris began bucking and howling.

"The shadows will drive you mad! Don't get hit by them!" I warned them belatedly. I looked around and grabbed a rock, throwing it at the demon attacking Chris. "Hey! C'mon, ugly, I'm the one you're here for! Come and get me!" The hellhound turned toward me, snarling. *Hurry, Lucca!*

Seizing his current opponent in his teeth, Lucca threw him back and into a tree near where the one-winged hellhound was regaining its balance. Not losing a second, the alpha slammed into the side of the one coming at me. He wrestled with it, both of them snapping at each other, neither scoring a hit. Lucca was thrown on his back, but it was a ploy—as the hellhound went for him, he gathered his back legs and thrust them at the demon, throwing it back with its fellows.

*Yes!* I lifted my hands, crossing my wrists to align the runes and release the power, but then Chris and the female wolf tumbled into my line of fire, fighting each other. Before I could even curse at the luck, Lucca loomed over them and let out a single, booming bark of command that echoed supernaturally. *Alpha voice for the win!* Despite the madness poisoning them, this broke through enough to make them both scramble back like they'd been smacked with a newspaper.

I had my shot.

*"RESERA!"*

My blood sang, my body woke up, every sense sharp as my magic exploded out of me in a torrent of golden light that had both physical and mystical force. Trees snapped and crashed, ripping up the forest floor, dirt and stones launching into the air. The wretched, rotting flesh of the demons was blasted from their grotesque forms, their skeletal remains splintering before the light faded, leaving nothing but foul, bloody stains where they'd once stood.

"Holy shit!" Leo had finally escaped the car wreck, cradling one arm, and stared at the destruction I'd wrought. I saw her grin out of the corner of my eye.

Three shadows lingered, the true forms of these demons now that their bodies were destroyed. The wolves circled, growling at what remained of these trespassers. With time or help, the demons might be able to rebuild their bodies before they were forced back to the Pit, but I did not intend to give them that chance. I opened my hand again, and this time thin golden strands of magic shot out, latching onto each of the demons. Another two snapped to Chris and the she-wolf, attaching to the shadowy madness infecting them. Whatever my magic was doing now was entirely new to me, but it felt as natural as breathing. It felt *good*.

"I've got a message for your boss." The demons tried to flee, struggling against the strands of my magic, making no progress. They didn't stand a chance. "Tell them McKenna Ellerbeck is *done* running."

My hand snapped shut. I felt their essence, their darkness, and I *pulled*. They came reeling to me, caught in my power. It wasn't just them, either. Chris and the other wolf yelped, and, to my amazement, the shadowy energy in their wounds answered my call as well. The shadows began to extract themselves from the wolves and twist up along the filaments of my magic, twining together with it. Maybe it was the backload of power I was sitting on, but it wasn't until that moment that I realized I hadn't spoken a word of a spell since unlocking my magic, much less drawn any runes. I had blood, yes, plenty of it from the accident, but with nothing more than that, I wasn't just binding or banishing their power. I was *controlling* it as easily as my own. I closed my eyes, and it struck me that the two didn't feel all that different. My intent had been to banish the demons, but I suddenly knew that I could do anything I wanted with their power. Banish it, disperse it, direct it... *claim it.*

"McKenna!" Leo yelled, breaking my trance, looking at me with wide eyes. "What're you doing?"

I opened my eyes and saw that the shadowy forms of the demons were no longer held in place in front of me. The shadows surrounded me, hanging over me like a mist, centered on my clenched fist. I slowly opened it, and the shadows swirled around my fingers, sliding against my skin like a lover's touch.

I was entranced. I was tempted.

I was disgusted.

"*Ego daemones abicio!*" I screamed, thrusting my hand outward again. Light burst from my palm, banishing the darkness. Without waiting, I pressed my wards together again. "*Claude,*" I commanded, my heart pounding. The switch flipped, the power was gone, my magic locked up. I collapsed against the car, feeling weak and empty as the world became a little duller once again.

Leo ran over and hugged me with one arm, the other

# THE TWICE-SOLD SOUL

cradled against her chest. "Holy shit, Mickey. So much for World's Worst Witch! What was that?"

I held on to her, staring at the destruction my magic had wrought, the dark forest of natural shadows that felt no less foreboding. "I have no idea."

# Chapter 12
# Family Matters

Once again, I was awakened by the damn phone ringing. Cell phone this time. I reached over and declined the call, but it rang again moments later, so I declined again and turned the thing off entirely without even looking at the screen. I began slipping back into the loopy half-dreaming state of the truly exhausted—

"Sleeping in again?" Remi asked from the foot of my bed.

"Nngh!" I jumped up, startled, my head woozy with adrenaline and sudden wakefulness. "Wh' th'—what the *fuck*, Remi?"

Remi's smile was unapologetic. She shrugged. "Hey, I tried calling twice, but you didn't answer. All things considered, I wanted to be sure you were all right." I rubbed my face, wincing at the bruises, and pushed my hair back. She straightened as she saw my black eyes and the tiny cuts all over my face and arms from the car crash. "Which you clearly are not! Seven hells, McKenna, what happened?"

"You'd sleep in, too, if you'd ended the night fighting demons after they drove your car off the road," I replied groggily.

"I'll kill whoever did this," Remi swore as she sat beside me, eyes flickering with fire. Her hands hovered at my face and my bruised shoulder—visible since I'd worn a tank top to bed. Her fingertips lightly touched my cheek, as though afraid I might shatter. I reached up and took her hands, gently lowering them.

"They're as dead as they're gonna get, and as far as their boss goes, you can take a number. I'm fine. No one died, and we'll all recover soon enough. Well, except Leo's car. That's done for. And she's worse off than me with that broken arm." This time I winced with guilt. Barely a few hours around me, and both my brother and my best friend were nearly killed. Not for the first time since the night before, I wondered if I was making the right call in deciding to stay.

But when I had dared ask that aloud at the ER the night before, Leo had sternly grabbed my chin with her good arm to force me to look her in the eye. "Not another *word* about ditching us again, Mickey. You're home and you're staying home and we are figuring this out together, end of story. And Lucca, whatever you're about to say, don't," she'd added, almost preternaturally sensing her twin was about to share some opinions on recent events. Lucca and I were both successfully cowed into agreement.

But as much as I loved having my best friend on my side again, it didn't mean all my guilt was gone. Not by a long shot.

"How about I get you some coffee and painkillers, and you catch me up on what happened?" Remi suggested.

"Sounds good. Right, so, I got Cameron to his apartment..." I went on to fill Remi in. She brewed the coffee and got the pills, which together did wonders for my state of being. Enough that I caught the little smirk she tried to hide when I told her how Leo had figured out who I was. "You knew she was playing last night, didn't you? You were hoping this would happen."

The smirk broadened. "Well...I like to keep an eye on the local talent. And tabs on friends. And I *may* have been of the opinion that you were long past due to catch up with your BFF. And that she *may* have been able to talk some sense into you about extending your stay." I narrowed my eyes at her. "Oh, come on! I know you're happy about it. I saw you smiling. You missed her, you needed her, all I did was give you a little push in the right direction."

"Yeah, yeah. Maybe. But that doesn't mean I liked being manipulated into it."

"Would you have gone if you'd known?" I made a face, sipping my coffee, and she took that as confirmation. "Didn't think so. Your determination is admirable, McKenna, but it also means sometimes you need help getting out of your own way. You don't need to be an army of one, you know."

"So people keep telling me." Maybe it was time I considered that they might be on to something. "Anyway, we got out of there before Brooke got back. We drove around town for a while, catching up and ignoring our phones, which is why Brooke called Lucca to tell him what happened when we didn't answer her texts. Turns out he had Chris and the other wolf, Elle, patrolling around town because of what happened to Cameron, and he remembered Leo and I used to circle the woods back in high school, so they were all pretty close by when the hellhound drove us off the road..."

Remi grinned fiercely as I talked about unleashing my magic and sending the hellhounds packing—though I skipped the weirdness of feeling like I could've claimed their power as my own. I didn't know what it meant, and this wasn't me trying to answer that by myself so much as not being sure how to tell the person I'd dumped for taking on demonic power that I had almost done the same.

"I would have loved to have seen that. You in all your magic glory, kicking ass and taking names." She looked at me with heat in her eyes, and not the Hellfire kind this time. "It's been far too long since I got to see you at work."

I smiled back, my skin warming at that look and inwardly preening a bit. "It did feel pretty awesome. Though I still don't have the one name I actually need if I'm going to put an end to all this and get my life back." The true name of the Archdemon of Madness yet eluded me.

Remi's brows went up in surprise. "Get your life back? Are you saying what I think you're saying?"

This time my smile was softer. "Yeah. I want to stay. I want to come home."

She practically beamed with happiness. "Yes! That's fantastic—okay, put your mug down so I can hug you!" I laughed as we both set our mugs aside and Remi wrapped me in a warm embrace that for once had nothing suggestive to it. It was friendly, joyful.

A welcome-home hug. One I gladly leaned into. When we pulled back, her dark eyes were full of fond affection. "I don't think I can tell you how truly happy I am to hear that, McKenna. I'm... this place isn't the same without you."

She brushed some hair back from my face, fingertips grazing over my cheek as she did, and I was suddenly aware of how physically close we were. Something in me felt a pull toward her, so long dormant and so damn familiar at the same time.

*What if home isn't the only thing I come back to...?*

Unspoken words swirled in the air between us. Her lips parted to speak, and a bolt of fear went through me. Too much was already going on; I couldn't handle unpacking my romantic history on top of everything else.

I pulled away and occupied my hands with my coffee mug, speaking before she could. "But I need to figure out how these demons are getting here in the first place. Figure out how they found me, or *if* they did," I said. Remi took the hint and sat back, still sitting on the bed but no longer touching me. "Three times in two days they found me when I hadn't done any magic and had my wards up, even with me changing continents in between. Cameron and Leo both got hurt. I *cannot* let that happen again."

"So, what's your next move?" she asked.

"Talking to Cameron. He knows more than he's saying. But if I'm going to get any answers out of him, I need to let him know I'm me." I blew out a breath. "I don't think he's going to be too happy to hear it."

She placed her hand near me on the comforter. "He'll be

glad you're okay, alive, and home. Just like I am. Just like we all are."

I didn't dare meet her gaze. "And then there are these flashes I keep getting from that night," I went on. "Something else happened at the Whale's Jaw, something important, but I can't remember it."

"Something like...?"

I shrugged. "Nothing good. The Archdemon wanted me to carve some kind of rune, and it made me think Jackie was Forneus? That might be how it got me to...anyway, I can't remember anything else. And so far the triggers have been nearly lethal, panic-attack-inducing encounters with its minions, and I'm *not* looking to have more of those."

Remi nodded. "What about hypnosis? Or a memory spell?"

"Maybe..." But those spells weren't my forte, and while I wanted to know, I also very much didn't want to know. "First things first: I need to know how they're tracking me. The two attacks here in Arcadia are probably connected. I don't know how they found me, or Cameron, but he wasn't surprised by it for some reason. And once they ran into me there, they could've tracked me from the hotel to the bar and followed me and Leo out. It's the attack in Paris that makes less sense. I don't know how I slipped up there."

"Maybe they got lucky? If the Archdemon of Madness has been trying this long to find you, it had to happen eventually," Remi said. "Perhaps they caught on to your alias?"

"No. The people who knew about that before I came back are all in this room right now, so unless you've got something to confess, it's not that," I said with a faux-stern expression.

Remi chuckled. "No, I can assure you I've broken neither our deal nor your confidence to sell you out to an Archdemon even I can't identify," she replied. "That said, while I'm good at what I do, I admit I'm not infallible."

"Wouldn't it technically mean you broke our deal if the Archdemon found out somehow?" I asked.

She shrugged. "It depends on how exactly it happened, and unless we know for certain that I messed up, then no, it's not broken," Remi said. "For what it's worth, I haven't picked up any mystical trackers on you. Your wards are very effective against that."

I sighed. "So it all comes back down to needing to talk to Cameron."

"Do you want some company for that?"

"He'd be even less happy to see you than me," I pointed out, finally getting up from the bed. My various injuries ached and protested as I did.

Remi nodded. "True, but the offer stands. There is one thing I can do for you, however." She stood up, setting down her mug and mine. "Keeping other demons out of Arcadia Commons is certainly helpful for me, so we can say I owe you for that one, and in exchange I'll heal you up. If that's all right with you?"

"Since when do demons deal retroactively?" I asked, surprised by the offer.

"Since always, but we rarely do because it's hardly ever in our best interests. I'll ask that you keep that tidbit to yourself, if you don't mind. So, what'll it be?"

I glanced in a mirror on the closet door, getting a good

look at the raccoon eyes I had from the airbag and dozens of tiny cuts from the glass. "Yeah, I'm not loving this look. But! This means you owe Leo, too. She helped and she's in even worse shape."

"Are you sure she'll be willing to accept that kind of offer from me?" Remi asked.

"Will the newly carless single mom who's a graphic designer by day and musician by night take a free pass on not having a broken arm for six weeks?" I replied. "Yeah, pretty sure she's gonna be fine with that."

"Good point. All right, then, I'll heal her up and handwave the medical records away. But no telling her the retroactive thing, please," Remi said.

"Fair enough. Deal." I offered my hand. Instead of shaking it, she lifted it to her lips and kissed my fingertips, sending a trickle of her power over my skin. The scrapes on my body healed and disappeared as it traveled up, and the pressure and soreness of my bruises lifted. Checking my reflection again and gently prodding a few spots, I found myself whole and hale, though also a bit redder in my cheeks. I smiled. "Much better. Thanks."

"My pleasure," Remi purred. Her fingers lingered along the underside of my palm for a moment, lips hovering so near that her breath brushed the back of my hand, sending a different kind of tingle along my nerves.

I awkwardly extracted my hand, still not ready for that. "Okay, well, I need to shower, and you need to take care of Leo, so..."

"Say no more." She stood up. "I'll see myself out. Good

luck, McKenna, and try not to get attacked by any other demons in the meantime, would you please?"

I laughed. "One of my top priorities, believe me."

---

After showering and getting dressed, I went back to the Rocket Café and got another cookies-and-cream latte and some breakfast before calling Cameron. I was going to need the sugar boost. Sitting down on a bench in the town square, I finally called.

"Cameron, it's Kendra Moureau," I said when he answered. "How are you feeling?"

"Oh. Hi." Pause. "Better. Tom helped. Thanks for getting me back to my place yesterday. And for covering my shift." His tone was grudging but genuine.

I smiled. "You're welcome."

"How about you? Were you hurt?"

*Not anymore...* "I'm okay, but there was another demon attack last night."

"What? Where, when? What happened?"

"Leo gave me a ride home last night, and a hellhound—"

"Is Leo okay?" he interrupted me.

"Her car's totaled, but she'll be okay, yeah. Three of them came at us in the woods, but Lucca and some of the pack helped us out."

"What about the hellhounds? Where are they now?" I could hear him moving around as he spoke.

"... They're gone. I banished them," I said, hesitating.

"How? Your magic is bound."

"I unbound it. Emergencies only."

"And us getting jumped in the garage didn't count?"

"It wouldn't have helped then, but I'm sorry, Cam. I can't tell you how sorry I am," I said, the apology practically tumbling out of me. "I was scared. But after what they did to you, I wasn't going to risk that happening to anyone else."

He was silent, then, "Okay. Sorry about that, just...forget it. Thanks for taking care of Leo."

*Maybe Tom was right.* "Of course." I sighed again. "Could we talk in person? Today, somewhere in Arcadia?"

"About the Council? Let me reiterate: hard pass." Quickly as it had appeared, the tenderness in his tone was gone.

"It's not. There are other things we need to talk about. Like why and how demons are in Arcadia. And why they're coming after me."

"They're not after you." I heard a door close over the phone.

"What do you mean?"

"I'll deal with them. Sorry to get you caught up in this, but I'm on it."

"Cameron, has this happened before?" I asked. "How long has this been going on?"

"I've got it handled," he insisted. Another door, and the sound of an engine turning on.

"Cameron, where are you going? Please, hear me out—"

"Kendra. I appreciate it, but this shit isn't your concern. Go back to hiding behind your wards and minding your own business, if that's something you actually do." I bristled at his tone. "Might wanna change hotels. Or get the hell out of town."

"I'm not going anywhere. You need my help, and we need to talk," I pushed.

"Yeah, well, you're not my mom and you can't tell me what to do, either," he retorted.

"If I were, you can be damn sure I'd—"

"You don't know *anything* about my mom, or about me, so fuck off!" He hung up on me.

"Dammit!" *Doesn't matter how old we are, you're still an annoying little brother!*

A few minutes passed while I collected myself. This had to happen now, before anyone else got hurt, and I knew one thing that he wouldn't be able to ignore.

I called again. It went to voicemail. Sighing, I called a third time, and he picked up.

"Give me one reason not to block your number," Cameron growled.

"I know where your sister is."

Silence. Followed by a lot of loud honking. "Shit—fuck! Fuck!"

I winced away from the phone. "Are you okay?"

"Yeah, I'm—yeah, I know, asshole!" he yelled, laying on the horn again. "Geez. A little warning next time?"

"Me or the asshole?"

"Both!"

"You weren't exactly interested in hearing me out," I pointed out.

"Where is she?" he asked.

"I'll tell you, but we have to meet in person."

"Fine. Meet me at, uh—"

I jumped in with, "Mill Pond?"
"Yeah, okay. Mill Pond. One hour."

---

Mill Pond was quintessential New England. Reflections of autumn leaves and afternoon sun rippled on the water's surface. The smell of cold in the air welcomed me with hints of pumpkins, apples, and cider spice. But it was memories of summer days that lurked in my mind. My comeback tour of Arcadia Commons had largely been highlights of high school drama. But this place belonged to the Ellerbeck siblings.

Before my dad's midlife crisis yacht moved our water play to the marina, this was where we'd come with our mom on too-hot summer days. Wendy Ellerbeck would lie out in a beach chair on the small excuse for a beach with sunglasses and a pinup-style two-piece, hair spritzed with Sun-In, while her two kids splashed, fed the ducks, dug for worms to fish with, threw sand at each other, and went swimming, which wasn't exactly encouraged—there was now a sign warning against it, in fact—but everyone always did anyway.

Up until that one time, that is.

We had been diving for pearls after seeing it in some cartoon, too young at only five and seven to know we'd never find anything of the sort here. But it was fun, and we had new scuba flippers and goggles to try. We had contests to see who could stay under longer. I usually won, but this time I stayed until I saw stars before kicking up to gasp for air—and Cameron didn't come up after me. I ducked under and I saw him, but he was stuck on seaweed or something. I tried to pull him, but I couldn't, and I came up screaming for my mom.

My mother gestured sharply, shouted words I didn't understand, and my brother's small body was pulled to the surface by unseen hands, dragged to the shore. It was the first magic I'd ever seen. Mom held Cameron tight, soothing him as he coughed up water and tears, though her nose was bleeding by the time I got back to shore. Cameron recovered fairly quickly, as kids that age often do, but we went home right away and Mom collapsed in bed for the better part of two days. When she finally got up, I asked her what had happened.

"That was magic, McKenna," my mother had said. "It'll be yours someday, too."

The crunch of tires on gravel broke my reverie. Cameron parked and slammed the door closed as I turned to watch. He wore the same jacket, knit cap, and surly expression he'd had on in the Grand the night I arrived. The rest of his outfit was new but interchangeable with what I'd seen him in before. I felt too clean by comparison. Especially with what I had to say.

"What do you know about my sister?" he said, stopping in front of the bench, hands shoved in pockets.

My palms itched. "Can—can we talk about this demon problem first?" He glared at me and started to walk away; I leapt up, grabbing his sleeve. "Wait! I'll tell you what I know, I promise. But once I do, I know that's all we're going to talk about."

"You're pushing it, Moureau."

*Oh, that is IT.* "Actually, *you* are, Ellerbeck," I snapped.

"I helped save your ass in the garage, I got you home and got you help, I covered your shift, *without* pay, and I banished three demons last night while your ass was laid up. I think I've earned a few answers without the attitude."

Cameron puffed out a breath, letting his scowl slip a little. "Fine. But you are telling me before either of us leaves here." He sat on the metal arm.

I arched a brow. "Comfortable?"

"What do you wanna know?"

*Okay then.* "How long have demons been getting into Arcadia? And how are they doing it?"

"Ten years, give or take." He shrugged. "Might've started before that. But someone is summoning them. My money's on a Lemaire."

"Ten *years*?" The whole time I'd been gone? "Why would the Lemaires want or need to summon demons?"

"To stay in power. One of them could've made a deal, and cracking the door open is their end of it. And no, I don't have hard proof. But they've got portal magic, they have the most to lose, and the pattern of demons I've banished centers on that hotel," Cam said.

"That's circumstantial evidence and conjecture," I pointed out. "Plus, no probable cause. Laurent and Adele have secure spots on the Council. And Bastien would never work with a demon."

"Okay, Miss New-in-Town, how do you know what he would or wouldn't do?" Cameron asked.

"Remi caught me up on their history," I said. Close enough to the truth. More important, if the demons had been coming for ten years, that meant they *hadn't* shown up yesterday because of me. It still left the attack in Paris a question mark, though. "Do you have any idea why the demons are being summoned? Is there something they're after, something they try to do when they're here?"

He shrugged, leaning forward, elbows on knees. "I've got theories. None of them do any real damage, just enough to get my attention. They make some noise, I banish them, rinse, repeat. But the ones getting in lately have been bigger, stronger."

"Ever find any summoning sites?"

He shook his head. "Nope. And I've looked. Probably they're doing it from their home or some other private property. I checked as many as I could—"

"You've been breaking into other witches' houses?"

"—but I've never found anything," Cameron went on, ignoring my question. "It's like..."

"Like what?" I asked when he hesitated.

"You're gonna call me crazy." He shook his head again.

"Cameron, I would never do that," I said. He looked at me sidelong, dubious. "I'm serious. I've had my brushes with crazy. Actual, real crazy, and it's not a term I'm about to throw around. What's your theory?"

He gave me a hard look, then finally spoke. "All right. I tell you this, and then you tell me where my sister is. Got it?"

I nodded, clenching my hands anxiously. "Got it."

Cameron nodded. "I think they're walking in on their own."

I blinked a few times. "But that's impossible. The barrier keeps them out."

"The barrier *should* keep them out. I don't have the right kind of power or spells to do an in-depth check on it, but my theory is that the barrier is getting weaker, and some Archdemon out there knows it. They're sending their minions to test it, or maybe they're the ones weakening it. If I can't figure out what's causing it and how to fix it, eventually it's gonna fail completely, and then it's open season for demons in Arcadia Commons." Cameron's face was grim, but he spoke with utter determination. This was his mission, and nothing was going to stop him from seeing it through.

Even if it killed him. The thought made me colder than the chill off the pond.

*Shit. This lone-wolf thing really is genetic.*

"If that's what's going on, that's not all on you, Cam. Nor should it be," I told him after a moment. "The Council needs to know about this. They can pull in the power and the numbers needed to fix the barrier. Not to mention finding whoever's helping the demons get in. If the barrier is breaking down, there has to be a reason. The demons wouldn't have just wandered in by accident and found out that way. Someone must have helped the first one get in."

He gave me a wry, humorless grin. "Yeah, sure, if they believed me. If they didn't think I was a crazy conspiracy nut from an upstart hedger family who had it out for their biggest bankrollers. Remi's been filling you in on so much, she must've mentioned that."

I started to deny it, which was at least true this time, but stopped as everything everyone else had been saying started to click. Lucca saying how Cameron didn't have his shit together, implying that my family had gone through hell after I left; Leo describing how fixated he'd been on blaming everyone for my disappearance; his own overwhelming anger at Bastien the day before, accusing the Lemaires of trying to get rid of our whole family. He'd even gone so far as to try to make a deal with Remi. I looked up at him, not sure what to say now.

"Having second thoughts about throwing in with the town pariah, huh?"

"No, I'm not, but…look, if you went to them with evidence—"

"I don't *have* any evidence. I've got my word and Tom's, and they don't trust either of us. He's my best friend, but even I know he's a mess and a drunk."

Something else clicked. "That's why you tried to steal the grimoire. Why you wanted to get caught!" The satisfied gleam in his eyes told me I was right. "You'd either find proof it was the Lemaires, or you'd get caught and go through a tribunal, where you'd be forced to tell the truth. They'd have to believe you."

"All I have to do is keep my shit together till then," he replied cryptically.

I frowned. "What does that mean?"

"Nuh-uh. Your turn." He crossed his arms. "Where's my sister?"

I knew I couldn't keep putting it off, but I couldn't let this go, either. I stood, looking him in the eyes. "I'll tell you—but, Cameron, it's *not* just your word anymore. I saw the hellhounds yesterday. So did Leo, Lucca, and members of his pack. You don't have to do this to yourself. You don't have to do this alone." *You don't have to make the same mistakes I did.*

Cameron squinted, confused almost, as if what I was saying made no sense at all—or maybe it did, but the logic somehow didn't apply here. He stared at me almost the way Leo had the night before, and for a second I thought he might see through me as clearly as she had.

But he looked away, shaking his head, breaking the moment. "You're not my advocate, remember? Now stop dodging the question. Where's McKenna?" The surliness was back.

*No more running.* I ran a hand through my hair. "It'll be easier to show you."

"Tell me, show me, print out directions, I don't care, just answer the question."

The nervous lump in my throat refused to go away as I faced him. "Okay. Before I do, though, I..." I'd run a hundred different versions of this through my head. I'd thought I was prepared. But now, in the moment, there was only one thing I could think to say. "I'm sorry, Cameron."

That look of confusion was back as I unclasped the necklace and let it drop into my hand. The illusion tingled as it disappeared, leaving me standing before him in my own skin.

He stared at me, unblinking, his lips moving like he was trying to speak, but he remained dead silent. Then he looked away, then back. Rubbed at his temples. He dropped his head down, nearly between his knees, whispering something. I couldn't make out what it was, but there was a rhythm to it, the same words over and over, and I finally couldn't stay quiet.

"Cameron? Are you okay?"

He looked up; he looked *afraid*. "Are you real?"

*What?* "Yeah, I'm real. Why wouldn't I be real?"

Cameron stood up, hands reaching partway toward me, then stopping, hovering. "Were you real yesterday? After the attack?"

I nodded. "I was, yeah. I'm sorry I didn't come clean then, but it was a weird situation. I didn't know what else to do." I wanted to hug him, but I didn't want to push him, either.

He reached forward enough to touch my arm, to feel I was a solid presence, but then he pulled back, expression hardening. "No. No, this is some kind of trick, an illusion. Whoever you are, the Council sent you to fuck with me!"

"Cameron, I swear, I'm real. It's me, McKenna. Your sister. I know I've screwed up. I left you, and I'm so sorry. But I can explain. Ask Remi, or call up Trevan and have me Promise, if that's what it takes," I offered.

He laughed in response, a short, clipped noise. "Yeah, right. Like I can trust Remi? Or like the Council wouldn't make sure you could make a Promise. Probably even changed your name legally, right? I'm not an idiot!"

Now I was the one staring at him in disbelief. "Cameron, please—what can I do to prove it? I'll show you my magic, I'll tell you something only you and I would know. Whatever you want, just tell me!"

But he was shaking his head, backing away. "I'm not gonna fall for it. You're either an illusion or an imposter, but you are *not* my sister!" He yanked his car keys from his pocket with enough force to send some coins out onto the dirt. "*Don't* call me again, and don't come anywhere near me—or my mother!"

*Mom?* I started to follow him. "What do you mean? What's going on with Mom? Please, Cam, don't go! I swear, it's me! I know about Rya, your tattoo—the time Mom saved your life, right here, when we were kids—"

"*Repello!*" The blast of force knocked me on my back and drove the breath from me. I pulled myself up, gasping for air that wouldn't come as he peeled out of the parking lot, fleeing the scene. When my breath finally returned, it came in a shuddering sob.

I thought I'd felt every kind of grief I could by now. I'd even resigned myself to never seeing my friends and family again. I knew I deserved nothing but their anger, and certainly not their help or their acceptance, but...

Last night, I'd been so sure. So hopeful. I finally wanted to come home, I'd started to believe I could. But for all my years of self-exile, I'd never truly felt what it was to know that home didn't want me back.

# Chapter 13
# Friends and Former Lovers

Eventually, I picked myself up and reclasped my necklace. That had been disastrous, no doubt about that, but I couldn't stay still. I'd spent ten years staying still while running away. No more. Even if I hurt in every way possible.

As I got to my feet, I noticed two small, round white pills mixed in with the coins that had fallen from Cameron's pocket. I frowned and pocketed them. Maybe he needed them. Maybe he'd thank me for returning them. Maybe he'd slam the door in my face and never speak to me again, but the pills gave me a chance at least.

With that, I walked. Away from the pond, away from the parking lot. Down suburban streets until they became main thoroughfares of Arcadia Commons. Past houses, schools, parks. Over the bridge at Goose Cove, past the docks at Lobster Cove. Stores, restaurants, and businesses; parents, children, tourists, office workers, dockworkers, sailors, retirees. I expected it all to be the same, but I found that it both was and wasn't. I'd looked at this town through the eyes of a child and a teenager, but now I looked at it as an adult. It was smaller in a lot of ways, sure, but also more real. I saw where the homes got bigger more clearly than before, where the stores with chipping paint ended and the town-funded storefronts began. I saw the cars get shinier, the cracking pavement turn to fancy cobblestone paths. I could practically draw the lines of the different school districts in chalk without a map to guide me.

Halfway to the hotel, because such was my luck, storm clouds gathered and unleashed themselves on the town. Waves tossed restlessly as I walked along the docks and beaches leading up the hotel. My feet ached and squished inside my shoes, and I couldn't remember if I'd even brought another pair aside from the heels I'd worn to the reunion.

All told, it was more than an hour later when I came to the top of the Arcadia Grand Hotel's long driveway completely soaked. I considered it part of my penance for all the shitty things I'd done. I wrung myself out under the awning before heading inside, getting some sympathetic looks from the employees. One of them was kind enough to get me a towel to dry off the worst of it. Sighing and looking forward to a long, hot shower, I trudged through the automatic doors, carrying my wet boots wrapped in the towel to the elevators. The two going down to the garage were roped off with an OUT OF SERVICE sign, and some men in well-worn jeans and T-shirts were talking to Bastien Lemaire. *Fantastic.* Making myself as inconspicuous as a wet, dirty rag in the middle of a pristine room can be, I sidled over to hit the UP button on the regular elevators.

"...gotta rewire the whole thing and repair the box down there. Be at least a day," one man was saying to Bastien in a thick Boston accent.

"It's already been out for an entire day," Bastien said.

"Yeah, took us that long to figure out the extent of the damage. Look, the panel and the wall around it were all fucked up. Looked like Wolverine went at the thing. Bad, but doable, y'know? Then it turns out a shitload of the wires and circuits were fried, too. It's pretty fucking bad in there, and that's why it's gonna take longer," the man explained.

Bastien paused, and without even looking, I knew he was pinching the bridge of his nose in aggravation. "Fine. I understand you're doing the best you can, but do whatever you must to repair this quickly. Letting the guests use the freight elevator isn't an ideal situation," he said with forced patience.

"Will do."

"Thank you. And if you could refrain from swearing around our guests, please, I would also appreciate it."

The man grunted a vague affirmative to that, then the whole work crew headed down the garage stairs. Meanwhile, I contemplated the idea that the hellhound claws had damaged the electrical circuits and what that might mean. *Is that how their claws work? They caused some kind of temporary insanity in Cameron and the wolves. Does it boil down to an electrical malfunction on the neuron level? What would that mean if you got a bad hit, or more than one?* Trying to puzzle it out was giving me a headache—or maybe that was just the one I already had.

"Kendra?" Bastien asked, doing a double take. "Caught out without an umbrella?"

"What gave it away?" I replied with tired sarcasm. He was completely put together, of course. Hair combed, suit tailored, face shaved. Dry. No glasses today.

"If you need to borrow an umbrella, we have some spares at the front doors, or the concierge can send one to your room. Or we sell them in the gift shop," he said.

"I'll keep it in mind," I said, pushing the button again. Was this elevator ever coming?

He started to leave, but then paused and turned back to me. "You were in the garage yesterday, weren't you? With Cameron?"

*Shit.* "Yeah, I walked him to his car down there. Why?"

"We're having a problem with the elevators. One of the garage panels was... damaged." He gestured to the ropes, and I acted like I was seeing them for the first time. "I was wondering if you saw anything?"

I shrugged. "Sorry, they worked fine when we went down."

"And when you came back up?"

"Yeah. I had no problems with them," I lied, nodding.

"I see. Thanks." *Good, please go away now.* But he didn't. "How are things going with him, by the way?"

"About as good as you'd imagine," I grumbled, taking a deep breath so I wouldn't start crying again. Thankfully, the elevators dinged and opened then. "Look, no offense, but I'm soaked and I've got a bitch of a headache. I just want to get to my room and collapse for a while."

"Of course. Sorry to impose. I hope Cameron comes around," Bastien replied. "Take care."

I forced a smile. "Thanks. You, too."

He lingered as I got into the elevator, a crease in his brow. Thoughtful, like he was figuring out a puzzle. I gave him an awkward wave as the doors closed, which jolted him back to the present, and he looked briefly embarrassed to have been caught in the moment as he nodded back and walked away.

There were, thankfully, no more interruptions as I got back to my room, showered purely for the warmth, and collapsed. Before passing out, I texted with Leo, confirming that Remi had healed her as promised and she was doing okay, and that my meeting with Cameron had gone horribly. She offered to talk to him, but I declined; my relationship with my brother was my mess to clean up. But a mess I'd worry about after some sleep.

———•———

I woke to the sound of knocking. It was a nice change from the phone ringing, at least.

Remi was in the hall when I answered. "I knocked this time. See? I can learn," she said cheerfully as she came in. "Catching up on beauty sleep? Not that you need to."

"Regular sleep, mostly." I yawned and went about setting up the coffeemaker. "You want a cup?"

She perched herself on the couch and crossed her legs. "No thanks. So how did it go with Cameron?"

I groaned. "An absolute disaster. He didn't believe me."

Remi cocked her head. "About what?"

"About *me*." I recapped our conversation while the coffee

brewed, eventually sitting down with the warm mug in my hands. "He didn't believe that I'm actually me. He thinks I'm either some imposter trying to trick him or that I'm not even real! That hellhound must've really done a number on him," I said. "He was raving and acting paranoid, like I was out to get him or working against him with the Council? I'm worried, Remi. People told me he'd gotten obsessive and was acting out, but I had no idea it was like this. He drove off after telling me to stay away from him and Mom. Not that I even know where to find her. Apparently she moved out of town. Did you know about that?"

"I did. I'm sorry, I knew it would be stressful to hear on top of everything else," Remi said.

"That's fair, I guess." I slumped forward, head in my hands, placing the mug on the table. I felt Remi's weight shift closer on the couch and the warmth of her hand on my back, rubbing in gentle circles.

"It'll be all right, McKenna. We'll get through to him," she assured me quietly. "Come on, when has an argument with your little brother ever stopped you?"

I almost laughed. "This is different. What if something's really wrong with him? He thought I would call him crazy, and I found some pills he dropped. I don't know what they are, but I'm worried."

"If he needs help, he'll have it. We'll help him."

"What if he won't let us?" I pointed out.

"Again, like that's ever stopped you?" This time I did crack a very small smile. "Ah, there's my girl," Remi said at the triumph.

"Still, that's only one problem. Demons getting into town, someone helping them, the barrier weakening? Did you know about that?" I asked.

Remi shook her head, her hand still resting on my back. "No. I haven't ever had trouble getting in and out, since I have a host body."

"What about your minions? Can they come and go?"

"I haven't asked anyone to try."

"Well, is there one you trust that you could ask, so we can see for ourselves?" I asked.

"No one's available," she replied.

I arched a brow. "They're *all* too busy doing your bidding and recruiting souls or whatever?"

"Anyone I trust, which is precious few, is otherwise engaged right now," Remi replied. "Surely there are other ways to test the barrier and find out. But I am at least certain the barrier will hold until tomorrow, because what you need right now is a night off."

This time both my brows went up. "A night off? Three demon attacks in two days, and you think a night *off* is the solution?"

"But note that nothing has happened *today*," Remi countered. "Last night you proved to be more than capable of taking on our mysterious opponent. They underestimated you, and they've pulled back to reconsider their approach."

"Which is why we should be pursuing them more than ever," I said.

"Sure, if you were at your best, which you're not. No offense. Now is our time to lick our wounds and recover, so we can go in fresh for the next round."

It was hard to argue given my emotional exhaustion. At least I was finally adjusting to the time zone and felt more well rested after the nap and the coffee. "I suppose you have a point," I admitted.

Remi smiled brightly. "I knew you'd come around. So finish this coffee and go slip into something nice. I'm taking you out."

———————•———————

From my limited wardrobe, I pulled out a nice pair of black slacks and a red blouse with off-white pinstripes. My boots were still drying out, and while I could have used magic to speed that along, I was reluctant to invite another demon attack for something so trivial, and my heels worked better with the ensemble anyway.

When we pulled out of the hotel drive onto the main road, Remi said, "I love the outfit, but I'd like it much better on McKenna Ellerbeck than Kendra Moureau."

I couldn't help chuckling. "I really thought you were about to say *in a pile on my floor in the morning*."

She smirked. "That, too, for the record. But we're going to a new place, very exclusive, and I asked for a more private table. No one there will know or bother us unless they're being paid to."

I arched an eyebrow at her. "You're certain?"

"I promise." She touched my hand for emphasis. "The only thing you'll be in danger of tonight is falling for my irresistible charms."

I chuckled again. "I'll ready my shields. If you're sure, though... yeah, it'd be nice to be me for a stretch." I removed the necklace, the illusion falling away and taking some of the weight on my shoulders with it. "Where are we going?"

"Eden's Table. The latest in cutting-edge cuisine, with a twist. Their seafood menu is unique, even for this area, and the cocktails are divine," Remi gushed.

"How are their vegetarian meals? I don't eat meat anymore," I told her, hoping I wouldn't be stuck with pasta or salad.

"Also excellent. All food allergies and dietary preferences are catered to. There are several vegetarian, vegan, and gluten-free options."

"Sounds like you know the place well. Are you a regular?"

"You could say that."

On the northern edge of town, toward the peak of Cape Ann, we parked in front of a rustic building on the water's edge. Despite being newer construction, it blended in well with the local aesthetic, looking more like a small coastal mansion than a commercial building, complete with a wraparound porch and benches. Past a velvet rope on the porch area that overlooked the bay was an outdoor bar with some high tables and a small crowd getting drinks. Large bay windows offered a somewhat voyeuristic view into the dining area, and a healthy array of greenery highlighted the exterior: small, unique-looking trees, succulents, and flowering plants. Above the door, a carved wooden sign bore the name EDEN'S TABLE, along with a three-dimensional carving of an apple with a bite taken out of it. Sea salt blew in on the breeze, mingling with the aroma of good food as we went up the stairs to the front door. A waft of sweetness drew my attention to a single young apple tree at the edge of the parking lot, in a grassy section to one side of the entrance. A few late-blooming fruits hung on its branches, with more gathered in wooden boxes on the ground below.

The warmth of an active kitchen and a full set of tables welcomed us inside. The large interior was mostly dark wood, with strategic LEDs adding enough light to be friendly, enough shadow to be romantic. The room was open to the second story, with a staircase leading to some seating on a balcony level that overlooked the lower dining room. Closed doors behind those led to what I imagined were function rooms for private events; I'd seen a large outside area on the second story from the parking lot.

Remi spoke to the host, a well-dressed young man in a dark-red shirt and dark slacks. "Blake, reservation for two."

"Miss Blake, welcome! Wonderful to see you again. We have your usual table ready for you. Please follow me," he replied, beaming a well-practiced smile at her.

She took my arm, and we followed him toward a set of stairs leading up. "Usual table?" I asked.

"I've got some cachet in this town yet," Remi replied, enjoying her mystery.

"So it would seem. Please tell me you didn't set aside a whole function room for us."

"No, just a nice upper-level table. Less foot traffic up here," she said.

The host seated us, going so far as to pull out the chairs for both of us. "Bread and apple butter will be out soon. Can I get any drinks for you?"

"No, thank you, Allan, we'll look over the cocktail list first."

"Very well. Here are your menus—our specials for the night are here. Your server will be with you shortly. Enjoy!" After handing over menus, Allan departed, and I was able to appreciate both the table and my companion at it.

Remi's hair was longer again tonight, brushing past her shoulders in large, loose curls. The V neck of her sleeveless black dress was more suggestive than daring, but the way it hugged her form was filling in plenty of details. It did leave her legs largely bare, however, so I needed neither my imagination nor my old memories to know how lovely they were, especially with that slit on the side that went a little scandalously high. Her smoky eyes and dark-red lips completed the femme fatale look quite nicely. She caught me staring with a smile, and I turned my attention to the more inanimate objects in the room.

On one end of our small, round table were lit wax candles in glass holders, flanking a display of more richly colored flowers and greens. The menus had the same bitten-apple iconography, and a pattern quickly emerged from the drink list.

"Poisoned Apple, Forbidden Fruit, Snake Bite. Oh, hey, True Knowledge was just vodka and fruit juice this whole time, who knew?" I read aloud and arched an amused brow at her this time. "You own this place, don't you?"

Remi smiled. "Guilty as charged. I never could hide anything from you for long. So, what do you think of my little side project?"

I looked around again. "It's really nice, actually. Classy, romantic, well put together...kinda sexy." *Am I describing the restaurant or Remi?*

Remi snorted. "Only you would consider 'well put together' part of sexy."

"I'm not the *only* one," I said in my own defense, though I returned her smile. "And yes, organization and order: very sexy. Chaos: highly overrated."

"Hmm, I don't know about that. A little chaos keeps things interesting, and, as I recall, you've been known to enjoy that," she returned, her eyes sparkling with mischief. "Not to mention having caused quite a bit of it."

"I didn't say it was bad, just overrated," I pointed out. "A little's okay, but I've grown to appreciate moderation."

"You know me, I've always been one to revel in indulgence," Remi said with a happy shrug of one bare shoulder.

"What inspired you to open a restaurant of all things?" I asked, looking at the wine list.

"Turn that over and look at the bottom," Remi replied.

Giving her a curious look, I did so, trailing down to the last item among the cocktails: Black Knight.

I thought instantly of the necklace sitting in my purse. My dinner companion was smiling fondly at me when I looked at her. "I told the bartender I wanted something bittersweet and strong, complex, with a taste that lingers and leaves you wanting more," she said. "Whatever else you experience, nothing else will ever be quite like her."

My throat was dry. "Don't you mean *it*?"

"You know who I mean." Remi's fingers covered mine on

the table, curling around them. "You've always been my black knight. My inspiration."

Heat crept up over my face. "And how does that translate to this?" I asked, gesturing around us with my other hand, not sure what to do with this attention.

"You always wanted me to be invested in the human world beyond the parts directly connected to you." Her fingers traced looping lines along my hand. "I found myself wanting to forge a deeper connection to Arcadia Commons in your absence. To be invested in it literally and figuratively. The only fancy place to get a good drink around here is the Grand, and we all know I'm not terribly welcome there. So I came up with this."

When we'd been together, I was worried that the sole reason Remi was "good" was that we were together. When we broke up, I'd been afraid of what she might do. And now, ten years later, ten years without me around, she was doing it.

*She's in control. She's connected to the world and...okay, maybe it's because of me, sort of, but it also had nothing to do with me. She's...good.*

"It's...impressive. Really impressive, Remi," I replied, looking around us. "Consider me impressed." My gaze returned to her, and my hand turned in her grasp, my fingers curling around hers in return.

The turn of her lips was hopeful. Suggestive. "Just impressed?"

Saved by the waitstaff. Our waitress delivered a basket of bread and apple butter to the table along with glasses of water, and asked for our drink orders.

"I'll try the Black Knight," I said.

"Forbidden Fruit martini for me, Jessica. Thank you," Remi ordered. I busied myself looking over the menu and gushing over the bread and butter (which were amazing) until our drinks arrived a few minutes later. We put in our dinner orders and were once again alone.

"What shall we toast to?" she asked, glass delicately balanced between two fingers.

I lifted mine, a martini glass filled with cool, dark liquor. "To... friends?"

"To friends," she replied, clinking my glass, then winked and added, "and former lovers."

I rolled my eyes, smiling, and sipped. Oh. Damn. This was a *really* good drink.

"You like?" she asked.

"Your mixologist deserves a raise," I said after another sip.

"I'll pass along the compliment. Would you like a sip of Forbidden Fruit?" She slid the glass across the red tablecloth to me.

"I see what you did there," I remarked, taking the glass. It looked and smelled like mulled cider, complete with an apple slice garnish, but it had a smoky, spicy kick when it washed over my tongue, followed by some unexpected effervescence. "That's good. Different, but I like it."

"Glad to hear it." She made sure our hands made contact again as I returned her drink, then nodded at mine. "May I? It's been a while since I tasted this one." The double entendre wasn't lost on me.

I knew this game. It was Remi's preferred method of

seduction, sneaking in as many teasing touches, suggestive sayings, and lingering looks as she could. Seeing how much she could get away with, how much she could build up anticipation. It took me back to one of our very first dates, in fact.

*"What are you doing?"* I asked when she slid her hand along my leg under the table, my whole body blushing at this new sensation.

*"Whatever you'll let me,"* Remi whispered in my ear. *"Whatever you want of me."*

Said the immortal demon to the sixteen-year-old girl. Yeah, in retrospect, a *lot* of my early sexual experiences were highly inappropriate. Between my age and Remi being the first girl—or at least being that wasn't strictly male—I'd been attracted to, she'd been ahead of me in quite a few ways. I got comfortable with that, but after we broke up, I was back to awkwardly dodging her flirtations. Then I was dating Bastien and dodging them for entirely different reasons. Then I was just gone entirely. Still, as Remi had once said to me, she may have had more physical experience, but she had none when it came to genuine emotions; in that regard, I'd been the experienced one who'd had to teach her.

But "then" was a long time ago. I didn't regret it, even if I wouldn't exactly recommend it. This was now, where we stood on more equal footing. I wasn't an inexperienced teenager still trying to figure out my own sexuality anymore, and she wasn't a demon with no idea what love or goodness meant.

I nodded, meeting her gaze. "Be my guest." She slid her chair around next to mine then plucked up the glass, her leg brushing against mine, and sipped, dark eyes on me until they closed in pleasure.

# THE TWICE-SOLD SOUL

"Mmm...even better than I remembered."

The rest of dinner played out much like that. An unspoken agreement naturally fell into place to avoid the weighty and worrisome issues of the present as we ate. Remi stayed next to me, and we talked about our lives like it was any other day, any other date between a witch and a surprisingly decent Archdemon. I told her about finding refuge and resources in the supernatural black market known as the Crossroads, finding ways to hide my identity, and getting my ward tattoos. My various odd jobs and stuttered education, the places I'd lived, the handful of friends in passing I'd had. She told me about her ventures in human business beyond Eden's Table, and some colorful stories and developments of note in Arcadia Commons since I'd been gone. Movies we'd seen, books we'd read. If I was still doing ballet (yes, whenever I could manage); if she was fencing (she had a collection of new rapiers she'd love to show me); if her black cat, Mr. Mephistopheles, was still around (despite his advanced age, he was, though Bargains between felines and demons were not *entirely* uninvolved). That was one of very few direct comments she made on her doings as an Archdemon, however, a topic I noticed more and more that she deftly danced around.

There was almost constant touching throughout: a lingering hand, a mischievous nudge of a foot, legs brushing against each other. Remi would reach over to tuck a hair behind my ear and trace a path down my cheek to my shoulder. I would playfully tap her arm in jest then let my hand run over her skin to her wrist and rest on hers. When our food arrived, we shared bites. It was as delicious as the cocktails, of which we had another round. For dessert, we ordered a slice of a rich, velvety dark chocolate cake with raspberry filling (dubbed Dark as Sin on the menu) with two forks and two cappuccinos.

Remi held up her fork to me, a bite perched on the end, as soon as we were alone again. "Taste," she directed.

I closed my mouth over the offering. "Mmm. Salt and chalk, that's the best cake I've ever had. And I've been living in Paris," I gushed. "This cake might be better than sex."

Remi arched her brow. "Is that a challenge?"

This time I was the one smirking. "Maybe." I offered her a bite from my fork. "Might wanna know what you're up against, though."

She took the bite, relishing the flavor. "Mmm. It is divine, but I'm not sure I'm convinced."

I knew her flirtation bait when I saw it, but there was something else on my mind. "You know," I said, setting down the fork. "You've been avoiding something."

Remi blinked, looking mildly surprised. "I have?"

"Mm-hm."

"I see. And what exactly is it I'm avoiding?"

"You've barely said anything about what it's been like being an Archdemon for the last ten years," I replied. Her playful demeanor slipped away, and she said nothing. *Okay, maybe something more specific.* "Come on, tell me. What are your minions like?"

"You're asking about my underlings." Her tone was deadpan. "You, McKenna 'I-Never-Want-to-Hear-About-That-and-I-Wish-It-Had-Never-Happened' Ellerbeck, are asking about the demons sworn to my service and…what, if any of them are my new besties? Yeah, right. What's this really about?"

I sighed a little, staring at the cake as she called me out. "I'm...trying. You've changed—or, more accurately, you haven't. You're in control, you've made a life in this world for yourself, you've grown into your role without letting it corrupt you. And I'm trying to be more than the teenager who was too scared to face what she'd done. With you, with Jackie...with this whole town. I was terrified, Remi. The world was barely done being black and white for me, and I...I didn't understand that a person could be more than one thing. I knew people wore false faces, pretended to be something they weren't, but I didn't know it was possible, deep down, for *both* those faces to be true, to be real." I lifted my eyes to hers. "I didn't know you could be an Archdemon *and* a good person. I didn't know *I* could be a..." Even now, the words stuck.

"A victim *and* the strongest person I know?" Remi supplied. Her voice was an open door, offering refuge.

I wasn't quite ready to step inside. "I was thinking more like a killer and a coward and...forgivable, maybe."

She gently touched my hand. "There's nothing to forgive. Whatever happened that night, you weren't in control."

"But I still did it. I did it, and I ran, and I broke everything. Everyone. My family, my friends. And yet they *have* forgiven me. Well, most of them."

"Cameron will come around."

"Cameron's the only one treating me like I deserve," I said, my dark mood from earlier edging back in. "Even you, I... I don't even know why you helped me that night. Especially without asking a higher price after I broke your heart."

Remi was both shocked and affronted. "What? McKenna, I—do you really think I would ever—no, it doesn't matter. Listen to me." She cupped my cheek, lifting my face until I met her eyes. "I don't blame you for ending things. And I should've been better about accepting it, about understanding what you were going through. Forneus put you through hell, sometimes literally. You had to be away from that. It hurt, but it was what you needed. In retrospect, we both did. I needed time to adjust as well. I didn't understand that then, but believe it or not I've also learned a few things over time. So, truly, *I* am the one who's sorry for making you feel bad for it."

I stared at her. While she hadn't been happy about our breakup, she hadn't been awful about it, either—mostly just deeply hurt, and she hadn't tried to hide it. I hadn't realized until that moment it was a piece of guilt I had still been holding on to. "Apology accepted," I finally said quietly. "And thank you."

She, too, suddenly seemed a little lighter. "Thank *you*. And you are more than one thing, too, you know. You're...everything." She smiled warmly at me. "Fact."

The space between us, on either side of that threshold, between her eyes, her lips, her body and mine, suddenly felt too close and too far all at once, like I could cover it in an instant and still never be close enough.

But damned if I wasn't going to try. I let myself step inside and kiss her.

She tasted of chocolate and cocktails and delicious ideas. Her naturally smoky scent coupled with coffee and sweet things surrounded me as her soft lips pushed and parted against mine, her hands in my hair and pulling me closer. I pulled her in by the small of her back as sensation spread from my lips down the rest of my body.

We parted, at some point, breathless, wordless, staring at each other.

"McKenna..." she finally sighed, but she didn't know how to finish saying whatever else was on her mind or in her heart.

I did. I knew what I wanted. Knew what she wanted. And it was so much more beautifully simple than everything else right now.

"Get that dessert to go."

---

Much faster than the speed limits would've liked, we tumbled into my hotel room, kissing, grasping, desperate to be closer. Her dress fell to the floor along with my shirt and slacks, and only then did we pause, taking each other in for the first time in years. Remi held my hand aloft. "Turn around. I want to look at you." I slowly spun under her arm, but halfway around she grew impatient, her arms sliding up my back and gently pushing me back onto the bed under her and kissing me again.

"Seven hells, you're gorgeous," she murmured, her lips moving downward from mine toward my collarbone.

"What," I panted, "I don't get to take a look at you?"

"Not much has changed," Remi said, but she did lift herself up, straddling me. "But I encourage full-body inspections. And plan on conducting one of my own, of course." I sat up and kissed her smirk as I undid her bra, letting my hands roam over her skin as she hastened to do the same. In a moment, she was the one on the bed as I set to exploring, her moans and hot whispers urging me on. But I did pause when I saw above her breast, in a spot that must've been barely hidden by her clothing before, a small tattoo of a knight chess piece.

My fingers traced over it. "Did you put this here just now for my benefit?"

"No. I've had that there for more than ten years, no matter what form I've worn." Remi took my other hand, kissing my fingers. "Ever since we broke up. I've always kept you in my heart, McKenna. Or"—she smirked again—"as near to it as I could."

My eyes flicked up to hers. Dark and smoldering, they always hid something; Remi always knew more than she let on. But not right now. Not this time. She wasn't playing a game right now.

I kissed the tattoo and then her lips, and for the next long while, we let our bodies do the talking.

———•———

Later, when we were a sated tangle of limbs and perspiration, we retrieved that to-go box and fed each other the rest of the cake on the bed.

"It's a near thing, but, having done the comparison, and considered all the factors, I can definitively say: This cake is almost but *not quite* as good as sex," I declared.

Remi laughed and bowed, waving to an imaginary audience. "Thank you, thank you. I'd like to dedicate this win to everyone who voted for me, all my fans, admirers, and stalkers, and I'd like you all to know that I never doubted myself for a second."

"And so modest, too!" I took a sip of water from a glass on the nightstand. "You really don't ever doubt yourself, though, do you? That's something I've always admired about you. And envied, sometimes," I added, leaning back against the pillows.

"Me? Not a chance, darling." Remi scooted over to lay next to me, an arm around my shoulders. "I'm nothing more than a remarkable actor who's mastered fake it till you make it."

"Oh? And what do you doubt yourself about?"

"Real answer?"

"Of course." I turned my head, resting it on her arm as I looked at her.

"I doubt myself about you. About doing what would make you proud, doing the 'right thing.'" She made air quotes. "I've let you down in the past, and I don't want to be the one who lets you down ever again."

I kissed her cheek. "The very fact that you worry about that means you're more than halfway there already."

Remi smiled softly, a real smile and not a smirk at all. "What about you?"

"Only all the time." I smeared some frosting around in the container with my fork. "Especially lately. With everything going on..."

"Now, now, there's a strict no-pouting-in-bed-after-amazing-sex-with-Remi clause," she chided, lifting my chin with a finger. "I know it's been hard since you got back. Maybe even since you left—"

"I'm starting to think it's *always* been hard when it comes to this town and me." I sighed, and Remi pressed her finger to my lips.

"No interruptions. Award winner talking here. We *can* get through this, McKenna. I firmly believe there's nothing you're incapable of. You've proven every assumption anyone ever made about you wrong before. You'll do it again. It's only a matter of time. Fact." She moved her hand to hold mine. "And on that glorious day, I'd be very happy to be at your side, holding your hand." Her lips quirked with mischief again. "Or stealing a victory kiss, one of the two."

I laughed lightly. "Knowing you, both." My gaze lingered on her. "You really never did stop believing in me, did you?"

"Not for a second." She kissed my knuckles. I kissed her lips and held her close.

"I missed you, Remi," I confessed, my voice a whisper against her ear.

"I missed you, McKenna," she replied. "It's good to have you back where you belong." Her words brought a warmth with them, a contentment I hadn't known in years, and for a stretch, we held each other quietly. Eventually, she kissed me again and with another smirk said, "But of course, I have to ask—how *much* did you miss me?"

Her voice deepened as she spoke, her body blurring and changing, then sharpening into focus when the shift into her male form was complete. He wore the same playful expression, eyebrow cocked, and, sure enough, the same tattoo over his heart.

Moving the empty container and forks to the nightstand, I swung my leg over his lap to straddle him. "I think I'd rather show you than tell you."

# Chapter 14
# Too Good to Be True

For once, I didn't wake up to a phone ringing.

Instead, I slowly came to wakefulness as pleasant memories of the night before returned. I stretched luxuriously, my hand grazing the body next to me, and I opened my eyes to see Remi was already awake, sitting up and looking at her phone. She smiled at me.

"Morning, gorgeous." She greeted me with a kiss, putting down the phone.

"Morning." I checked the clock. Only half past nine; I was finally adjusting to the eastern time zone. "How long have you been awake? I don't recall you being a morning person."

"You know how it goes, no rest for the wicked," she quipped.

"Am I keeping you from your busy schedule?" I teased.

"There is nothing on my schedule that can't be put aside for seeing you wake up naked and next to me," Remi answered, running a finger along my bare shoulder. I leaned over and caught it gently between my teeth. "*Especially* when you're waking in this kind of mood." She bent down to kiss my neck, sending shivers down my spine.

"Mmm...much as I'd love more of that, there's a lot we need to do," I said, though my protests were weak.

"The only thing *I* need to do is right here," she murmured as her hands got in on the action. "Everything else can wait at least half an hour."

I moaned, but there were at least a few things that had to come first. "Fine, but give me a minute to brush my teeth, et cetera?"

"Mm, okay, that's fair," Remi agreed reluctantly.

Slipping on a hotel robe, I went about a few morning necessities, brushing my teeth while Remi did the same, although she had no issue doing so naked. As I was about to get back in bed to wait for her to finish brushing, there was a knock at the door. "Oo, breakfast in bed, good idea," I called out as I went to answer.

I was already pulling open the door when I heard, "I didn't order anything," and found myself, with no disguise and nothing but a bathrobe on, faced with none other than Bastien Lemaire.

The two of us stared at each other in a stunned silence that was starting to feel familiar.

"McKenna," he breathed, "it really *is* you."

"...You knew?" I blurted out.

Bastien started to reply, but then his eyes flicked up over my shoulder and his soft, stunned expression grew cold. *The society mask.* "Remiel." I turned; Remi had put on a robe as well and stepped into the room. He looked between the two of us, at last night's clothes still piled on the floor just inside the door. "...Of course." His voice was quiet, but it carried the note of disappointment with perfect clarity. I tugged at my robe, trying to will it into something larger, or possibly turn into a hole I could climb into.

"Bastien," Remi greeted, unperturbed and natural as ever.

"How long?" Bastien asked us bluntly.

"That's rather personal, don't you think?" Remi replied, smirking.

He scowled. "How long have you known where she was? How long have you had her hidden right in front of us?"

"Hey!" I interrupted, waving my hand between them. "'She' is right here and can answer for herself!"

Bastien nodded brusquely, turning his attention back to me. "Apologies. I suppose I've gotten too used to not having any answers from you directly, McKenna. But please, feel free to answer for yourself."

I winced. "Okay, I deserve that. But Remi hasn't been hiding me, *I've* been hiding me. From everyone, including her." At least as far as I'd known, until the other night. "I've only been in town since the reunion."

"All right, that fills in between now and Saturday. Any details you care to add to cover the decade prior to that?" Bastien said sharply. His posture, already straight as an arrow, was stiffening, and I caught the twitch in his jaw. The mask was slipping.

"Bastien, please. I-I know you're angry, you've got every right to be, but I..." *I can explain? Explain how I killed your best friend and went on the run?* "...it's a long story, but I had to leave."

"Without a word of explanation? Without so much as a goodbye?" Bastien demanded.

"Yeah, actually, without any of that," I replied, starting to get angry myself. "Do you really think I'd do that for the hell of it? Without any reason at all? You know me better than that!"

"I don't know you *at all*, McKenna," he replied coldly. His eyes flicked to Remi again. "Or maybe I do. Maybe you're exactly who everyone always said you were, and I'm the one who's been foolish enough to believe otherwise."

I narrowed my eyes. "And what is *that* supposed to mean?"

"Consorting and keeping counsel with demons, putting them and their interests above the rest of us," Bastien listed.

Remi scoffed. "You were right the first time, golden boy. You don't know her at all."

"And I suppose that means this is who you are and always were, too? Following in the family footsteps, spouting Granddad's rhetoric without forming your own opinions?" I retorted.

His eyes flashed back to me. "I am *not*—"

"And neither am I." I raised my chin, meeting his bitter, stubborn gaze with my own.

His nostrils flared as he took in a long breath, his shoulders coming down as he exhaled. "I didn't come here to yell at you or throw around accusations," he said more calmly.

"Then what *did* you come for?" I asked.

"To talk. I didn't expect to find you...indisposed." He gestured at Remi.

I cleared my throat. "Right. Okay, I'm going to change.

Have a seat, and I'll be back in a few minutes." Bastien nodded, slowly walking over to the couch. I scooped up our clothes once his back was turned and gestured for Remi to retreat to the bedroom with me. She closed the doors behind us.

"So much for morning sex," she grumbled. "I'd really hoped the days of Mr. Mayor boxing me out were over."

"Hey, immortal demon, could you stop acting like a teenager, please?" I snapped, keeping my voice down as I grabbed some fresh clothes. "I know you don't like him, but I owe him an explanation at least."

"Do you plan on telling him the truth?" she asked as she got dressed.

"I...I have to." Jeans and a sweater on, I ran a brush through my hair. "Maybe not right away, but eventually. I know he wants to help Cameron out, and when he hears about the barrier, he'll want to help."

"A theory that's still only a theory," she reminded me.

"One thing at a time." I pulled on my now dry boots and tucked my necklace in my pocket. With both of us dressed, I opened the French doors, and we went back out to the sitting room. Bastien was seated on the edge of one of the chairs. He was dressed in gray slacks and a button-down dark-blue shirt that set off the lighter blue of his eyes and the blond hair he was finger-combing back into order. He wasn't wearing glasses today.

I broke the silence as we reached the couch. "You got contacts."

"Yeah, a few years ago. Mari convinced me," he said, absently rubbing at the bridge of his nose. "I'm sorry about before. I didn't mean to accuse you of anything. I'm sure you understand that your appearance is unexpected."

"I know." I sat down on the couch; Remi sat next to me, casually crossing her legs. "How did you figure it out?"

"Security cameras, actually. After we spoke the other day by the elevators, I knew there was something you weren't telling me, and I thought to check the cameras for the garage exit. I wasn't sure what I might find, but you driving Cameron out wasn't even on the list."

*And here I thought I got out unnoticed.* "I didn't even think to check for security cameras," I said. "Here's hoping no one needs to check any traffic cams I went past."

"So Cameron knows?" Bastien asked.

"He does now. He didn't then. Not really. You're still trying to find out what broke your elevator?" Bastien nodded. "Two hellhounds attacked us when we got off the elevator yesterday. One of them hit Cameron with some kind of psychic attack; afterward he was hallucinating and acting strangely. He only calmed down when I let him see me as me."

Bastien was taken aback, questions clearly flying through his head. "Let's put a pin in that—are you all right? Is he?"

"I'm okay. Cameron's better now, but when I told him I really *am* me yesterday, he refused to believe it. I don't know what's going on with him," I admitted.

"I see. Well, I'm glad you're not hurt."

"Not for lack of trying. Two of them attacked me in Paris on Saturday before I came here, and then on Sunday night, they attacked again. Three of them drove Leo and me off the road. Totaled her car and nearly did the same to two of Lucca's wolves," I added.

"Psychic damage? Hallucinating, nonsensical?" he asked. I

nodded, and he rocked back in his chair. His eyes were distracted as he calculated something, then snapped to Remi like a target. "And what do you know about this?"

"Oh, am I part of this conversation now?" Remi asked, looking up from her nails. "Calling the resident Archdemon expert to the stand?"

I gave her a look. "Remi..."

She rolled her eyes and sat forward. "Not much more than what McKenna knows and what you can easily conclude yourself. Demons with an affinity for madness are getting into Arcadia Commons, and it looks like they have inside help."

When she stopped there, I added, "Cameron thinks the barrier is weakening, but I haven't been able to test that yet."

But Bastien was still glaring at Remi. "Care to share the 'more' with the rest of us, Remiel?"

Her dark eyes flicked to him, her tone irreverent. "No, Sebastien, I have no further relevant information."

I looked from one of them to the other. "Okay, why do I feel like I'm the one who's missing something now?"

"Because Remi has left out some *very* relevant information," Bastien replied evenly.

Remi's confused expression changed then into one of alarm. "No. Bastien, that is *not* relevant. There is no need to—"

"To tell her the truth?" Bastien cut her off.

"Truth about what?" I asked.

"That's not going to help. There's nothing she can do about it," Remi said sharply.

"She deserves to know," he replied.

"Stop talking about me like I'm not here!" I snapped,

getting to my feet. They both shut up, still glaring at each other. "Whatever the hell it is, someone better fucking tell me, *right now*." Bastien simply gestured at Remi, so I turned to her. "Remi? What is he talking about?"

Remi stood up, her face softening with guilt as she reached for my hands. "I didn't tell you this because there's nothing that you can do. That anyone can do. Once this was over, I was going to tell you, but—"

"Get to the point, Remi," I said with an edge in my voice, pulling my hands away.

Remi sighed. "... It's your mother."

My whole body stilled. "What about her? Is she okay? Seven hells, is she dead?"

"No! No, she's not dead," Remi quickly assured me. "But... she's sick."

It was Bastien who finally told me. "She's in a mental institution. She was admitted five years ago for schizophrenia. Her condition has since worsened."

The world fell out from under me. I knew I was sitting; I knew people were talking, but all I could hear were Bastien's last words on repeat: *Schizophrenia. Her condition has since worsened. Schizophrenia. Her condition has since worsened.*

*Schizophrenia. My mother has schizophrenia.*

My mother, trying to scold us for turning the bathroom purple, failing utterly and laughing until there were tears in her eyes.

*"Finally, their chance to be rid of what's left of the Ellerbecks once and for all!"*

My mother, hugging me and saying she loves me when I tell her I'm bisexual.

*"And your family?"*

*"Like I said, Lemaires drove 'em off."*

My mother, using magic to save my brother's life.

*"But the Youngers have always lived on Fox Hill."*

My mother, smiling in beautiful disbelief and wonder when our magic grew stronger. Then crying with me when I admitted what I'd done to get it.

*"You're gonna call me crazy."*

My mother, her eyes red and trying to hide the shake in her voice on the news clip about her missing daughter from ten years ago. The last time I'd seen her face outside of a picture.

*"You're either an imposter or an illusion, but you are not my sister! Don't call me again, don't come anywhere near me—or my mother!"*

"Cameron," I gasped.

"McKenna?" Remi's face filled my vision. "Are you okay?"

I slapped her.

She fell back on her ass and I rose to my feet, my fists and voice shaking with fury. "Five years. You kept this from me for *five years.*"

"There was nothing you could've done—"

"I could've been here!" I roared. She flinched. "I could've been here for her, for Cameron! You could've found me, you could've told me—"

"You didn't want to be told!" Remi threw back at me; it stung as much as my slap probably had. She got back to her feet. "You wanted to disappear, so I helped you disappear. You didn't want to know anything happening here, so I did what you asked of me. I did the only thing I could to protect you."

"Protect me? You think that was *protecting* me?" I retorted.

"What could possibly make you think that's what you were doing?"

"Because I love you!" Remi's eyes flared with fire. "And the last thing I wanted was to see you broken and in pain, again, when I could do nothing about it and neither could you."

I stared at her, wordless. Tears fell down my cheeks. "I guess you still have a lot to learn about what love means," I rasped.

"As everyone likes to constantly remind me, I am a demon. You'll have to forgive me if I'm bad at it," Remiel said bitterly.

*I don't have to forgive you for anything.* I closed my eyes. "Get out."

"As you wish." I felt a change in the air pressure around me, a hint of sulfur wafting.

"She's gone," Bastien said. I opened my eyes; I'd nearly forgotten he was even here. "I'm sorry, McKenna. Truly."

I sniffed and gave a single, firm nod. "Take me to see my mom."

He nodded. "I can. I will. But you should know: It won't be easy," Bastien forewarned. "She's not who you remember."

I nodded again, wiping my eyes. "I understand. Let's go."

"Right. We can use the circle in my office. You should probably put your disguise back on, if you can," he advised.

Touching that necklace and making use of Remi's power again bothered me, but it was necessary. Bastien's brow furrowed again as he looked at my blond disguise, and he held the door open for me. I spent the elevator ride trying to sort myself out and stop thinking about how thoroughly Remi had played me to get exactly what she wanted. Bastien led the way to the offices on the ground floor. The plaque on his door read SEBASTIEN LEMAIRE, HOTEL MANAGER.

# THE TWICE-SOLD SOUL

Inside was the nicest office I'd ever seen—a huge window overlooking the bay, plush couches and chairs surrounding a gorgeous dark wood coffee table, large artwork adorning the walls. The expensive desk at the other end had a fancy ergonomic chair; a sleek laptop was plugged into multiple monitors. The shelves behind it were filled with binders and books on management and tourism, as well as a number of framed photos with faces I recognized: his family, his sisters, his friends, his fiancée. One was a group shot in front of some small, newly built houses—when I saw that Brooke and Mari were also in it, I realized that must be one of the charity trips Brooke had told me about. Near it was a professional-looking photo of him and Mari, smiling and posed to show off her engagement ring.

On another shelf was an older picture of Bastien and Jackie as gangly teens, sitting in a sailboat together.

I swallowed and turned away to see Bastien pulling up a rug, revealing a ritual circle etched into the floor. "What do you tell your normie clients when someone accidentally kicks over the rug?"

"Nothing. I dispelled an illusion when we came in that makes it look like the rest of the floor," he said, standing upright.

"Oh. Right, duh." I rubbed my head. "Actually, can I get some coffee before we do this? I kinda forgot I hadn't had any yet."

"If I'd known that, I would've stopped on the way. Nothing as dangerous as an under-caffeinated McKenna," he replied, with a touch of humor. "I'll get something brought up from the café. Are you hungry?"

"Yes, please, I'd kill for a croissant right now," I said, my stomach growling at the mere suggestion. I dropped onto the couch and undid my necklace while he put in an order with his secretary, then crossed to sit in a chair opposite me and waited quietly.

"You probably have a lot of questions," I said after a pause.

"I do. But I've waited this long, I can wait a little longer," he replied.

I had to smile. "Still have the patience of a spider, huh?"

He laughed. "Now, that I haven't heard in years."

I shrugged and gestured around us. "You *are* sitting in the middle of the biggest Lemaire web there is," I pointed out.

"You've got me there. But I'd hesitate to call this place a trap."

"Well, yeah. *You* haven't been attacked, arrested, betrayed, or driven mad in here."

"McKenna, what *happened*?" Bastien asked, searching my face with such concern that I found myself fighting back tears again. He noticed that, too. "I'm sorry, I'm trying not to push, but..."

"No, it's not that, it's... you're supposed to be *mad* at me." *I killed your best friend.* I sniffed, wiping my eyes again. "Why isn't anyone other than Cameron mad at me?" I asked, bewildered and rhetorical.

A knock at the door saved me from the answer. He brought over my breakfast, handing me a coffee cup and setting the pastry in front of me along with a fruit cup, all of which I gratefully dug into.

"I'm sorry about earlier, yelling at you like that, accusing you of... I don't even know what. I don't think that of you. I just didn't expect to find you like that. I was angry and hurt for a long time, yes, but I also moved past it. Some of it's bound to be coming back to the fore now. You did always manage to stir things up." He gave me a melancholy smile. "But to answer your question—"

"You don't have to."

"—I'm sure the answer is that everyone, including myself, is relieved to see you and wondering why you left. I'm far more worried about you and your family than about a decade-old bad breakup."

"That's more than I deserve, but thanks," I said, returning the smile. "But... some of it I'm not ready to talk about. I know I should be, I've had ten years. But, honestly, I didn't think I'd ever be coming back to Arcadia."

He swallowed his questions as he took a sip of his coffee. "Where did you expect to be, then? Where were you?" he asked. "You mentioned Paris earlier?"

"Yeah. Been there about a year."

"I studied abroad there junior year. Guess we wouldn't have crossed paths, then," Bastien said, again with a touch of melancholy.

"I remember you wanted to. I was in... the London area for most of that year. I've moved around a lot. But it was amazing to finally see Paris," I said.

"I know what you mean. My semester there was unforgettable," he agreed. He seemed about to add to that but stopped himself. I could guess why. Though we were going to different colleges, we had planned on staying together and talked about studying abroad in Paris at the same time, maybe even the same school. Who knew if we would've made it that long, but we'd been serious enough to talk about it.

Speaking of... "So, Mariposa Perez, huh? Have to admit I'm a little surprised," I said, changing the topic.

"I can imagine, but she's changed since you knew her. A lot. I think you'd get along now, actually," Bastien said.

I arched a dubious eyebrow. "How do you figure that?"

"Mari's done a lot of advocating for witches with less power. She's the one who suggested we stop calling them hedgewitches and use the term *generalists*, and she's been working to connect them to the larger community," he said.

So Brooke had told me. "That's good, albeit unexpected. Why the change of heart? I mean, we're talking about the girl who loved throwing that in my face for years."

"That accident, on the charity trip, when she almost drowned? She didn't just almost lose her life; she lost her magic."

I froze.

"That's... possible without severing? How?"

"Her family's power is connected most strongly to the brain," Bastien explained. The Perez family specialized in oneiromancy, the fancy word for dreamwalking. "When her brain went without oxygen for too long, there was damage. She survived and recovered in the mundane sense, but her magic is almost entirely gone. Going through all of that changed her outlook and attitude considerably."

"Wow. Yeah, I can imagine, it's... an adjustment." That was putting it mildly. I looked at my wrists, rubbing one.

"...Do you think she'll be able to use your magic after the wedding ritual?"

Bastien sat back in his chair. "We hope so. Since portaling is more about hands and feet, it follows that she should be able to, but we won't know until the ceremony on Saturday." He looked at my wrists as well. "Why did you willingly cut off your magic?"

"Long story short: I didn't want to be found," I replied. "I can unlock it if I have to. Had to do that the other night to banish the demons who crashed Leo's car."

Bastien hm'd. "Demons. Salt and chalk, all this time and it was true." He sighed. "I'm so sorry we didn't listen to them."

"'We'? You're not on the Council."

"No, but my grandfather and my aunt are. I could've done more, at least tried to convince them. Instead, I took them at their word about your family." He sighed. "After Wendy was committed and Cameron started spouting the same lines, it seemed sad but inevitable that he was falling to the same illness."

"What's kept them from committing him, too?" I asked, hesitantly.

"Cameron still has his own authority, and after your mother's health declined, he knows how to keep it. He agreed to send her to the Harwell Institute when the Council forced the issue; he knows what they're looking for in him. But with this tribunal coming up..." Bastien looked at me.

*And she's at Jackie's dad's institute at that. How poetic.* "They'll try to do the same to him," I concluded. "That's why he was so convinced your family is involved with what happened to me, isn't it?"

"It is," he said. "And on top of everything else, before she was committed, the Council severed Wendy's magic. With it, she was a danger to herself and others. Cameron believes this only made things worse and is part of why she's declined since."

I wanted to be shocked, but given everything else I'd learned, it made perfect, cold, logical sense. "Let me guess—Laurent's idea to start?"

Bastien nodded.

My heart was pounding. My mom loved magic. She was first and foremost worried about me when she learned why we had more of it, but when the danger of Forneus was gone, she'd been so happy. She'd cast silly spells to entertain us or even to take care of practical matters in the house. Things she'd had to work so hard at her whole life were suddenly effortless. Severing was the harshest punishment witches had, a permanent removal of one's magic. It was so severe, it took seven adept-level or master-level witches to cast the spell to make it happen. To imagine her cut off from that... Well, I sure was discovering new depths to my well of guilt by the hour.

"I'm ready. Let's go see her," I said, standing up.

Bastien stood and went to the circle. "You might want to put your disguise back on. I'm not sure how well seeing the real you would go over."

That made sense. As much as I felt like I owed it to her to face her myself, I didn't want to make things even worse. I quietly fixed the necklace back in place, my appearance changing with it.

He wove his hands through the air, precise, sharp

movements, his eyes focused on a place far from here. "*Ouvre la porte à Harwell Institute.*" The Lemaires preferred French for their magic.

A shimmering portal appeared, shaped like a door. He turned the not-quite-real doorknob and opened it, holding it open for me. *Always the gentleman.* "Final boarding call for Lemaire Airways," I joked as I approached.

He grinned. "Please keep your extremities inside the portal at all times." *Just like old times.* I stepped through, feeling an incongruous tingling warmth pass over my body as I did. I couldn't recall Bastien's portals feeling like that before, but it had been a while.

We came out on the other side into a plain, empty, windowless room. A ritual circle was drawn on the linoleum floor, and the lights went on from motion detection as I stepped in. Bastien entered behind me and closed the doorway. "They've got a permanent circle here, too?"

"For general use, yes," Bastien said. "It's handy for traveling in and out, and any other magic the Harwells might need to cast. They use some spells in their treatment of some patients."

"Makes sense," I said. Telepathy, empathy—if I remembered right, Dr. Douglas Harwell, Jackie and Tom's father, was a bit more specialized in mental manipulations. A talent that served him well in his chosen field.

"You know an awful lot about this place and Dr. Harwell's practices," I observed.

"I stay informed," Bastien said.

"And I imagine you tried to get help for Mari from him, too?"

"We tried, but there was nothing he could do," he said ruefully.

I followed him out into the main hallway to an elevator; inside, he hit the button for the third floor.

My brow lifted. "You know what floor to go to?"

"I've been here before."

A middle-aged woman at the check-in desk with graying dark hair peeking out from under a hijab greeted Bastien with a smile. "Bastien, hello! Wasn't expecting you today. Oh!" She looked at me and smiled slyly. "Did you finally bring your fiancée? Sweetie, it's such a pleasure to meet you at last," she said.

Eyes wide, I looked at him. "Uh—"

"Yes, finally," Bastien said smoothly, putting his arm around my shoulders. *What the hell?* Also, damn, his arm was much stronger than I remembered. I smiled and leaned in, going along with it. "Naheed, this is Mari. Mari, this is Naheed Awan, head nurse for the unit."

"So nice to meet you, Naheed," I said, holding out a hand to shake hers.

"And about time, too! So glad I get to congratulate you two in person. It's this weekend, right?" Naheed said.

"Yes, Saturday afternoon," Bastien confirmed.

"And I can finally see this ring in person—oh!" She was surprised to see my bare finger.

"Oh, it's—it's getting cleaned," I said quickly. "Want to make sure it's gleaming for the big day!"

"Naturally!" She accepted this answer without pause. "You're in luck, sweetie, Wendy's having one of her good days. Let me get you some passes and you can go ahead to the common room."

Once we had VISITOR tags clipped to our shirts, she buzzed us through the door, where we consciously uncoupled. "Sorry about that. It seemed easiest to roll with it," he apologized.

"Bastien, three questions." I stopped in the hallway to face him. "One, I thought you said Mari was treated here?"

"Different departments, and Naheed started well after Mari stopped coming here."

"Okay. Two, how often do you come to see my mother? Naheed doesn't just know you, she knows you *well*."

He let out a breath. "About once a month. Sometimes more than that."

"Why?"

"Because she's a good person. And she was good to me. Supportive in ways my family wasn't," Bastien said, eyes meeting mine. The steady blue-gray of them reminded me, as ever, of the sky over the sea after the storm had passed. "My parents aren't like my grandfather, but they're also less involved in our world, in the politics of it. When I took an interest, it was under his wing, not theirs."

"I remember," I said, nodding.

"You opened up my eyes to things that he would never have told or shown me; things he didn't consider worth the bother. And after you were gone, Wendy continued to do that. For a while, at least," he told me. "She was there for me when I lost not just my best friend but my... my first love." He turned a bit pink, and judging by the warmth on my face, I did, too. "It's the least I can do to be here for her now, and

I'm happy to do it." He puffed out another breath. "Not that your brother agrees with that, of course."

I hugged him. Strong arms wrapped around me in return. He smelled of aftershave and magic and clean ocean air. Of home. Of things that were no longer mine. "Thank you," I whispered, my voice shaking.

"As I said, I'm happy to do it," he whispered in return, but he did hug me closer for a moment.

"You're way too good for me," I said, something I'd often half joked with in the past, but this time I knew it was entirely true. I kissed his cheek, then immediately thought better of it and ended the embrace. Bastien was not Remi and not available, and these were old habits that needed to die. "Sorry."

I caught a glimpse of him briefly stroking his cheek with his thumb. "What was the third question?"

"Huh? Oh! Right." *Awkward.* "Ah—you been working out?" I jokingly tapped his biceps with my fist, trying to reclaim the innocent, friendly intent I'd been going for.

He chuckled. "CrossFit. And a blue belt in jiu jitsu."

"Nice work." I flashed a thumbs-up, felt awkward, and pointed down the hall. "So...?"

"Yes, this way." He gave a quick nod and we continued down the hall toward my mother.

# Chapter 15
# How I Re-Met My Mother

"What can you tell me about her? How did she end up here?" I asked Bastien as we walked.

"I don't know her specific medical details since I'm not family," he said. "But here's what I do know. After you disappeared, Wendy put everything into trying to find you. The police eventually stopped looking; there was no evidence of a crime, and with the note you left, signs pointed to you having left voluntarily if abruptly. You weren't a minor, so there was only so much they could do. Wendy kept trying, but when they stopped listening, she brought her theories to the Council instead."

"I'm sure they loved that," I sighed.

"Exactly as much as you'd expect," Bastien confirmed. "The theories steadily went from the mundane, to involving the supernatural, to claiming that demons had taken you by force, then insisting demons were overrunning the town, and finally accusing the Council of being in league with them."

"Did anyone even hear her out?" I asked.

"At first. But when they looked into it, there was nothing there. No demons, no signs of them, nothing," he said, spreading his hands. "And Wendy was...coming unhinged. She would go wandering in the woods for days, alone, claiming she was hunting demons. She lost her job at the paper when she kept missing days and declared that the editors were all part of a demon-worshipping coven who were out to get her."

"Okay...none of that is *good*, but it's not sever-someone's-magic-and-send-them-to-a-mental-hospital bad," I said.

We had reached a solid wood door. A windowpane in the wall next to it showed a common room of sorts with a few people sitting or walking around. Before we went in, though, Bastien turned to face me.

"She started a forest fire," he said grimly. "She went out into the woods—that's where she claimed she found demons most often—and she started a fire. One that could only be put out by magic."

"Seven hells," I gasped. "How did they stop it? Was anyone hurt? Was she?"

"Cameron stopped her. He was with her but didn't realize what she planned. They both had some burns but nothing too bad. He told the Council that she claimed they were surrounded by demons when no one was there at all. After that, she was severed and taken in here."

Cameron's anger made even more sense now. He'd had

to turn her in to authorities both mundane and magical. I knew without a doubt that he saw her fate as his fault, that he blamed himself for not being able to help her on his own and for having done what was, no doubt, the right thing for her at the time. No wonder he was angry and obsessed, especially knowing as he did that she wasn't entirely wrong.

All things that I, yet again, had left him—both of them—to deal with alone. *Daughter and sister of the fucking year.*

"I know this is a lot to take in," Bastien said when I gave no response. "If you need a minute..."

I shook my head, sniffing. "No. I mean, yeah, later, several of them. But let's do this. I need to see her."

We were buzzed in. The room was a good size, decorated with warm and neutral tones. There were comfortable-looking couches and chairs, a TV mounted high on a wall, tables. Some books and games were on a bookshelf to one side. A handful of patients were in here along with some nurses.

One of them, at a table and shuffling cards, was a grayscale version of my mother.

Wendy Ellerbeck was a full-color person. Dark-chocolate-brown hair, glossy and styled, bright-red or pink lips, nails lacquered in an ever-changing rotation of colors. Full-figured and always wearing something yellow, her favorite color, whether it was the focal point of her outfit or just a pair of earrings. I used to think she didn't smile often, but it turned out that was a side effect of being married to my philandering father. I was twelve when he took off and never returned. That was when Mom started smiling a whole lot more and, as she would say, living her best life.

The woman before me had dull, faded brown hair that was gray at the roots, air-dried into uninspired, uneven waves. Her clothes hung on her unimpressively. Black leggings around calves that no longer jogged or swam every day. A slouchy gray sweater that once only got pulled out of the closet on the coldest of winter days. Her nude mouth set in a line as her hazel eyes focused on the one truly familiar thing about her: the Tarot deck she expertly shuffled in her hands.

---

*Sixteen years ago*

"So, what, do I like pick a character or something?" I asked my mom when she insisted I let her do a reading for me. She shuffled the cards on the table between our poolside lounge chairs.

Mom laughed. "Pick a character? Goddess forgive me that I let you almost get to thirteen without knowing how Tarot cards work! What happens is we do a reading to guide you and give you insight on something. Any big questions looming in that brilliant head of yours?"

"Yeah, whether Chris Miller thinks she's cute!" Leo yelled from the pool, where she and Cameron were swimming.

"Ohmygod, Leo! Shut up!"

"Chris is a nice boy, but are you sure he's your type?" Mom asked, arching an eyebrow at me.

"Anyway! Okay, then who are all these people on the cards? I know they have names," I asked, ignoring the question and pulling a card from the top. "Like the...Knight of Swords? Okay, maybe they don't all have names."

"They're more like personas or archetypes. Symbols and extended metaphors. No one's ever just one of them; we all change as we go through life. Although the Knight of Swords isn't a bad fit for you. He's ambitious, driven, determined."

"He?"

Mom shrugged. "Masculine and feminine in the cards aren't about gender, really. Just like in real life. The point is, there's no stopping you when you've made up your mind. For better or for worse. You're determined to face any challenge."

"A challenge like Chrriiiiss," Leo singsonged, having swum to the edge of the pool to listen in.

"Leo! Shut up or I'll throw your towel in the pool!"

"Hey, what about me, Mrs. E?" Leo asked. "Which one am I?"

Mom chuckled and shook her head again. "Again, not how it works, but I see this is what we're doing now. Hmm...you remind me of the Page of Cups, Leo. Creative energy, open-minded, all about dreaming your big dreams."

"What about me?" Cameron called, pulling up next to Leo.

Mom grinned. "You, little man, are still the Fool," she said, and Leo and I both cracked up at his protests.

---

"Hello, Wendy," Bastien said as we approached.

My mother looked up and smiled at him so warmly that she almost looked like herself again. She stood and hugged him. "Bastien! So good to see you."

"You, too," he replied, returning the embrace. She let go and saw me behind him; her smile vanished and she threw a suspicious expression my way, reminding me exactly who I'd learned the art of the eyebrow from.

"You brought another witch." Her voice was full of suspicion as she looked at me. "Not one I know." The by-now-familiar pain of being a stranger in my own skin made itself known.

"This is a friend of mine, Wendy. Her name's Kendra Moureau," Bastien introduced.

"It—it's nice to meet you," I managed to force out, extending my hand. She eyed it and sat down without touching me. Bastien gave me a sympathetic look, and we sat down at the table as well. Mom began shuffling again, this time darting her eyes to different corners of the room and muttering indistinctly under her breath. The gold foil edges on her Tarot deck glinted as they caught the lights in the room. Her nails were short, with chipped golden-yellow polish on them.

"This stinks of your grandfather," she said to him, ignoring me entirely.

"It's nothing at all to do with him, Wendy. Kendra's an old friend, in town for the wedding," Bastien explained patiently.

"And why's she here?"

Bastien looked at me, giving me a chance to answer for myself. My mind raced, then I looked at her shuffling. "The cards. Bastien told me how good you are with them." She'd insisted on reading for him once while we were dating, at least.

"Not that the King of Pentacles listens to them," she muttered, giving him a look.

*Interesting.* "Well, I'm at something of a crossroads. I was hoping you'd do a reading for me?"

She narrowed her gaze at me, then thrust the deck out. "Cut."

I did as asked. "What spread?"

"Three cards. Past, present, and future."

I restacked the halves of the deck. Her hand hovered above it, her eyes looking hard to the right for several long moments. Then she finally flipped the top card: a knight on a white charger, sword drawn and ready, staring straight ahead, red tabard over his gleaming armor.

"Your past is the Knight of Swords. Well. Weren't you just a clever little one?" My fingers clutched the knight hanging from my necklace. The cards themselves weren't magic, and neither was she, not now. But could it really be a coincidence? "Smart, proactive. Impulsive. You faced a challenge and won, but let's see where that got you, hmm?"

She flipped another. Upside down, this one showed a man, face down on the ground, ten swords in his back. A clouded sky behind him, but a calm sea at his unmoving fingertips. "The present: Ten of Swords, reversed. Maybe that challenge didn't go so well after all. But time has come to face the matter, Kendra. You've been running too long from it."

*How is she doing this?*

"And last but not least, the future." Mom flipped a final card: a figure with a crown upon their head, scepter in hand, and the cosmos above rode in a chariot drawn by two sphinxes, one white, one black. "The Chariot. There's that strength of will of yours again. Big things afoot for you. Another test ahead, and no more running. It's time for action." Her voice had become intense. "Which path will you take this time?"

I stared at the cards, then at her. Her gaze was as sharp and intense as her voice, boring into me. What do you say at any age when your mom catches you in a lie? "I...I don't want to run anymore."

She stared at me, eyes boring into mine, and then she suddenly threw the cards in my face with a scream and lunged for my necklace. "Demon! *Demon!*" she screamed. Her short nails dug into the skin of the hand I already had around the charm, and I stumbled forward off the chair, both of us tumbling to the ground as I tried to keep the chain from breaking.

"Stop! Mom, stop!"

Her hand went slack at my slip, suddenly filled with fear instead of wrath, and she echoed Cameron's response. "...Are you real?"

I was spared answering when an orderly pulled her off me, holding her arms to keep her from attacking anyone else, while a second one dug her hand into the pocket of the sweater. She pulled out a handful of little white pills, identical to the ones Cameron had dropped at Mill Pond. "She's been skipping her meds again," the woman said. "I'm sorry, Bastien, we need to get her back to her room."

"Of course. I'm sorry we upset you, Wendy," Bastien said calmly to my mother as he helped me up. Mom said nothing, just stared at me as she was walked out of the room by the two of them.

Like mother, like daughter. I was similarly numb and silent as Bastien led me out. I was only vaguely aware of returning to the ritual room and walking through the portal back to Bastien's office.

"How are you?" he asked after closing the portal.

"This is all my fault," I mumbled. "I...I left and, and now she...she's like this..." My skin felt hot, and my breath came in short, shallow gasps.

"McKenna." Bastien grabbed my arms, forcing me to look him in the eyes. "Stop. Breathe with me. Deep breaths, come on." He took an exaggerated inhale and exhale, not breaking eye contact until I did the same, making sure I took several breaths with him before he spoke again. "This is not your fault. No, hear me out. Despite her condition, what Wendy was saying all those years was true. Demons were here, *are* here, and we *all* left her and Cameron to fight them on their own. We dismissed all of it as hallucinations and told ourselves that what we were doing was for the best for her. Her condition may have been inevitable, but that surely didn't help. So if you consider yourself at fault for leaving, then the rest of us are as culpable for not believing her. And for that, *I'm* sorry." His whole body loosened, slumping, his eyes falling to the floor and his hands from my arms. When he spoke again, it was almost to himself, shame written in each word. "I called myself her friend. But I ignored every warning she gave and took my grandfather's word over hers."

"Bastien, you had no way of knowing." I touched his shoulder.

"I had more ways of knowing than you did," he replied. "I was here."

I tried to swallow my guilt, but instead a confession tumbled out of me. "And I *wasn't*. I ran away. I ran away because the Archdemon of Madness attacked me and Jackie, and I thought it would follow me if I left. Instead it drove her mad and it's driving Cameron mad and I...I thought I was protecting you. I thought it was *all* I could do to protect you."

Bastien looked up once again, blue eyes wide with shock as the truth came out. "What?"

But before I could say anything more, a voice in my head that wasn't mine said, *Forgive me, darling, but you did break the rules.*

I blacked out.

# Chapter 16
# The Scene of the Crime

It was probably inevitable that someday I'd be back at the scene of the crime, but I would've hoped I'd go there knowingly and of my own volition. Instead, one second I was in Bastien's office and the next I found myself there, no choice, no warning.

When my eyes opened, the immense Whale's Jaw rock formation loomed before me. A fire flickered, throwing ever-shifting shadows onto the stone, hiding the inconstant face of my nightmares. Corruption and magical filth slithered over my skin, and I didn't know if the screaming was in my mind or in my throat.

I turned so hard to run that I flung myself onto the dirt and began tearing the grass as I scrambled to flee. Hands grabbed me, hauling me to my feet, and with a panic-fueled surge of adrenaline, I swung my fist at my attacker, connecting with a loud and painful *smack!*

"Ow! Dammit!"

I didn't look, just planted my foot to turn and run—

"*Prohibere!*"

—and stopped precisely there. *No no no, it has me, no, not again!* But try as I might, I could not move, could only watch, my pulse and every instinct in me fighting uselessly as the footsteps came closer. I squeezed my eyes shut and prayed for it to kill me before it made me kill anyone else.

"McKenna, open your eyes." *Cameron?*

"No! It's a trick. I won't let you do this again!" I yelled.

"Shit, Cam, she sounds like you."

"Seriously, Tom?" Cameron snapped.

"*Froid apaisant,*" Bastien groaned in French.

*Wait, what?* Hearing myriad voices, I cautiously cracked one eyelid and saw three young men before me: Cameron, Bastien, and Tom. The phantom sensation of foul magic along my skin faded.

"It's us, McKenna. We're real," Cameron said.

"Remi wasn't kidding when she said she wouldn't like this," Tom remarked.

"Remi? What's going on?" I asked. "Cam, let me go, please." He waved a hand, and I rocked back onto both feet, arms wheeling. Bastien caught me and kept me from falling again. His hands were tentative, gone as soon as I had balance. I went to thank him and saw that one eye was bright red and puffy. "Oh, shit, did I—?"

"You've still got a hell of a right hook," Bastien said, wincing as he nodded. He brought one hand, which was glowing faintly blue with his magic, back over it. Right, he'd cast some kind of magical ice pack spell a moment ago.

"I'm sorry, I thought you were—" I stopped, aghast. "I just gave you a black eye and you're getting married in a few days!"

"Nothing a little magic can't fix or an illusion won't hide, if need be," Bastien replied, though he still kept out of arm's reach.

I looked back at the others then, slowly, at the split boulder of the Whale's Jaw behind us. I swallowed and rubbed my arms against a shiver from within.

"Adrenaline wearing off?" Cameron asked.

"Something like that." I turned to him and realized that I wasn't wearing my disguise, and he wasn't accusing me of being a hallucination. "Cam..."

"Tom, can you finish up the circle?" Tom nodded and got to work on the large ritual circle I now saw they'd been drawing. My brother and I walked over to the car, and he pulled out a spare sweatshirt for me. "Sorry for freaking out yesterday."

I pulled it on. "It's okay. Sorry for going AWOL for ten years. You don't need to say that's okay."

"Wasn't gonna."

"I know we've got a lot to talk about, but can we start with what the hell is going on right now? How and why are we all here?"

"According to Remi, you're the one who knows why," Cameron said. "The how: Remi said you broke the terms of your deal with her, so she got to drive for a while. Said the nature of the deal let her override your wards."

This time the shudder brought a wave of nausea, and I had to grit my teeth against it. "No. She wouldn't do that, she *knows* what I've been through."

"Yeah, trust me, we gave her hell for it. About the one thing Mr. Mayor and I agree on. Here, she left a message for you." Cameron unlocked his phone and handed it to me, queued up to a video. When I hit PLAY, I was greeted by myself.

"Hello, McKenna," Remiel said in my voice. "First things first: I'm sorry. I'm sorry about taking over like this, but you broke the deal by going outside the town limits for a time, and this is the most mild way I have of rebalancing that. I'm not pretending to be you to anyone, though I am arranging for something you won't like. But it's something that has to be done.

"And I'm sorry for... everything else. For keeping things from you, for everything that's happened. I thought it was for the best..." She trailed off and sighed. "No. I told myself that, and I believed it, but the truth is I didn't want to be the one to bring you pain by telling you. I even told myself that I could fix everything here for you, until it became clear things were beyond my ability to remedy or control. But you don't need a white knight, and you never have. As usual, the only one who can rescue you is you. Lucky for us all, you are generally adept at that." Her mouth—my mouth—quirked into an unusually rueful smirk, and I found my lips twitching to mimic it. *Stop that.* I forced them back to neutral. *And what exactly does "fix everything" mean?*

"And so, my next confession: Yes, I know more than I've let on. Much more. But my situation renders me unable to directly interfere with or even advise you. However, you have all the tools you need to find that information. But you need a push. I realize this is the last place you ever wanted to come back to, especially with these people, but you need to. You need to remember that night, and Tom, Cameron, and Bastien need to know what happened. *And* they need to hear it from you."

*Dammit. She's right.*

"You know I'm right."

"Oh, shut up," I muttered to the screen.

"All right, you're surely telling me to shut up about now, so just one more thing." She adjusted the phone so she was looking directly at me, and despite what was on the screen, this time I saw Remi's face, heard her voice. "I believe in you, McKenna. You've done the impossible from the moment I met you, and though you've tried to bury that, to play it safe, to be someone else, I know you still have it in you. My black knight." She smiled, and I heard the words she wasn't saying. "I've let you down, but you've never let me down. I know you never will. Fact."

The video ended there. I sniffed, handing it back to Cameron, and ran my hands through my hair.

"What's this other information she won't tell us herself?" my brother asked.

I rolled my eyes. "Right to business, huh? Gee, thanks."

"What, you want me to pretend it's all good 'cause we're family?" he scoffed. "You ditched me and Mom, and you only came back because of Remi. You made it pretty clear you don't want any part of this family."

"I *do* still want to be a part of this family, Cameron. I can't say I'm sorry enough for not being here for you and Mom, but—"

"Everything before 'but' doesn't count," Cam interrupted. "That's what you always used to say."

"Okay, you got me there. Look, I *am* sorry, Cam. And I deserve your anger, I deserve you never even speaking to me again, and I'm going to do everything I can to make it right, and—and fucking hell, I sound like Dad!" I ran my hands through my hair again, taking a moment to tamp down all my gut reactions and think first. "Whatever it takes, I promise you, I am never going to run away from our family again. You need time to trust me, I get it. I won't rush you. But right now, I desperately need your help. And in time, I hope we can find a way to *be* a family again." I lifted my chin, meeting his stubborn look with one of my own, crossed my arms, and waited. He characteristically shoved his hands into his pockets and scowled.

"How long do you think they're gonna do this?" Tom asked after a long stretch of silence.

"I saw them go for ten minutes once," Bastien said. "And McKenna claims their peak was a half-hour standoff."

"Oh yeah, she finally gave in when Pretty Paisley Ponies came on or something, right?" Tom said. *I did no such thing!* My mouth twitched and I almost broke, but I refused. I saw Cameron smirk.

"Her? Ha, no, that was him," Bastien said. His eye was looking much less puffy and red now, though it was coloring up nicely. "You didn't know he was a pony bro?"

Cameron's scowl made a swift return, and now I was smirking.

"His favorite was...oh, who was it...Bedtime Shine or something?" Bastien said.

"Her name was Dreamtime Shimmer, I was eight, it was a phase, and I hate both of you!" Cameron exclaimed, rounding on Bastien and Tom.

Bastien chuckled and I flashed him a thumbs-up from behind Cameron, dropping it as my brother turned back around.

Cameron rolled his eyes. "Fine. I'll hear you out. Where do we start?"

I reviewed the events of the last few days to decide that myself. "Our family's magic. Mine's been acting weird since I came back. Two nights ago, I banished the hellhounds without a circle, but before that, it felt like...like I could've absorbed their power. Has that ever happened to you?"

Cameron shook his head. "Nope. Only absorbing I've done from them is when they've shoved their claws in me. Same for Mom, far as I know."

"Yeah, Bastien took me to see her. I...I don't know what to say. She's so different, but the same?" I shook my head as if that could put my thoughts on my mom in order. It didn't. "It made your reaction at the pond make more sense, at least. You dropped this, by the way." I pulled the pills from my pocket. "Are you okay, Cam?"

He quickly snatched them from me and shoved them in his jeans. "I'm managing. For now. But yeah, eventually I'm gonna end up like Mom. The demons make it worse, but... guess maybe you lucked out."

"I...I don't think the demons make it worse, at least not for you and Mom. I think they're the reason it's happening entirely," I told him. "The thing that's been hunting me all this time, and sending its minions after you and Mom? It's the Archdemon of Madness."

All three of them stared at me with wide eyes this time, and it was Tom who spoke first. "That actually...makes a lot of sense given what we've been going through. But why would this Archdemon be targeting your family?"

I shrugged. "I'm not totally sure. The first time I ran into it, it seemed pretty clear it was interested in me and my magic. That's why I ran away—I thought it would follow me and stay away from here. And since the hellhounds kept showing up, I thought it was, but somehow it's here, too."

"And you couldn't have told us all that then?" Bastien asked.

Instead of answering, I looked over the lines on the ground. "What spell is this for?"

"Remi said you were going to need help remembering something and that we needed to see it, too," Tom said. "You'll need to take those wards down, but this will bring out the memory and let us see it with you."

And there went my stomach. "You mean, we're all going to tromp around in my head together?"

"Sort of. We'll be limited to whatever you let us see, but we will all experience it from your point of view," Bastien said.

"Fucking hell." I bent over, hands on my knees, taking deep breaths.

"McKenna?" Bastien asked, stepping closer.

"No." I held out a hand, holding him off. "I have to do this. But first, you all need to know what you're going to see." The three of them stood a few feet away, but it felt much farther. Still, I forced myself to look at them all in turn as I spoke. "I should've told you when it happened. I should've, but I was scared and... and I thought I was making the right call, that it would be the best thing for everyone, but it wasn't. So many more people got hurt, and I wish I could change it. I wish I could change everything about this."

Cameron's hands were still shoved in his hoodie pockets, and he was wearing the surly look that I was coming to accept as his default. I caught a glimpse of worry from Bastien before he slipped on his serious, neutral, society mask. And Tom, poor Tom, looked mildly confused and completely unprepared for what was about to happen.

Those were their faces the moment before everything changed.

"Jackie didn't die in a car crash. She died here. And I killed her."

———————●———————

I told them everything I remembered about that night, from Jackie's text to the demon's appearance to waking up to her dead body to banishing the demon to calling Remi to help me cover it up.

For a long time, they said nothing. Then Tom went to his car and got a flask out of the glove box, which he chugged down before lighting up a joint and taking an impressively long drag off it. Cameron joined him after a moment. Leaving me with Bastien, who stared at me in a way I couldn't read at all.

"Please say something," I finally begged, my voice hoarse.

"I don't know what to say," he replied. "You're not a killer.

Whatever happened, I know you couldn't have consciously done this. I don't blame you for Jackie's death, McKenna."

"Then why is your jaw twitching?"

"I'm angry. I'm not angry at you." He exhaled through his nose.

"You sure about that?" I asked meekly.

"Yes, but I don't recommend poking at it."

I flung out an arm at the circle around us. "Bast, we're about to do nothing *but* poke at it. You're about to watch the whole fucking thing go down in high definition with surround sound, and believe me, it is *not* pretty."

He took a few deep breaths in and out, trying to stay steady. Cameron approached again, clearing his throat to get our attention. "Tom's kinda busy self-medicating and I'm not about to stop him this time. The three of us can handle the spell."

"I'm still sitting on more power than I know what to do with, so yeah, sure. Literally the least I can do is spare Tom from seeing this," I said. "Bastien? What about you?"

"Of course. The circle is already drawn. All we need to do is activate it," Bastien said.

"I meant are you sure you want to see this?"

"I most certainly don't. But I need to know what happened and what we're up against if we're going to stop it." He looked at me and nodded once, resolute.

We stood along the circle's edge, much as we'd done eleven years ago when we summoned Forneus to kill him. Brooke had been our fourth that night. This time we might not be summoning an Archdemon, but we would be seeing one nonetheless, and it would be even bloodier than that night had turned out.

I crossed my wrists, preparing to release my magic away from the others. "Fair warning: When I did this the other night, I uprooted several trees. *Resera*."

Once again, there was a burst of magic rushing out of me, but I was both prepared for it and not quite as maxed out. Some branches snapped and trees groaned, but that was all. That combined with not being in a life-or-death situation meant I could actually enjoy the moment, the sensation of power running through my veins, the way it made my entire body alert and ready for anything. When I turned back, Bastien and Cameron were both blinking and rubbing at their eyes.

"You weren't joking about having a buildup," Cameron said.

"The only power source brighter that I've ever seen is the barrier itself," Bastien added.

"Hm. I've never actually looked at that." I turned my attention upward. With this much magic coursing through me, it only took a moment of focus to see the barrier swirling around my hometown, a brilliant, blazing sphere of golden light, moving like something living. "It's beautiful."

"It's not blinding you?" Bastien asked.

I shook my head. "It's bright, but no."

"I don't even know *how* to look at the barrier, and you just did it without even casting a spell," Cameron said.

"I did tell you my magic was acting weird," I reminded him, still looking up. I reached out a hand; the barrier was over a mile away, but it felt closer. It felt... familiar. Curious, I sent a pulse of magic at it, a sort of formless ping. To my surprise, it reacted, flaring even more brightly where my magic touched it, and the pulse that came back was more than familiar. It was *mine*.

"It's a binding spell," I said in awe.

"Well, yes," said Bastien. "Our ancestors bound the town to keep demons away from the leylines."

"No, I mean, it's like one of my binding spells. The magic looks and feels like mine. I pinged it and I can feel the whole thing, Bastien. The barrier..." My brows went up. "The barrier was made with my family's magic."

"McKenna, your eyes..." He was staring.

"Huh? What?" I lifted my hand near them, but they felt perfectly fine.

"They're glowing. Gold. Like your magic," Bastien said, taking a look. "Has that ever happened before?"

"Not that anyone's told me," I said, growing concerned. "How do I turn it off?"

Bastien murmured some words and squinted at me. "It's the barrier. You're connected to it—I can see the energy flowing between you." He turned to look at my brother. "And there's one to Cameron as well. Fainter, but still there. It *is* your magic. But how? And how did no one ever see this before?"

"It's not like you or anyone else could've made an extensive comparison of our magic and the barrier until about twelve years ago," I pointed out. "And I'm pretty sure no one has since. Who studies the barrier anymore, much less compares it with some hedgewitch family's magic?"

Cameron spoke up. "I'm getting a theory here. McKenna, cast a spell, doesn't matter what. Lemaire, keep an eye on the connection when she does it."

Shrugging, I cast a simple elemental spell, a gust of wind. It came easily and was stronger than I had intended, but nothing damaging.

"The barrier changed. Some of the power moved from it to you," Bastien reported.

"That's not good." I quickly ended the spell that was letting me see the golden cage sitting over Arcadia.

"Your eyes aren't glowing anymore, but the connection is still there," Bastien said.

"Shit." Cameron cursed. "I was right. The barrier *is* weakening."

"Because it *is* our family's magic," I said, putting it together. "When we cast spells, we pull magic from the barrier. The weak points are letting demons in."

"And for every one of them that you banish, the barrier gets even weaker, continuing the cycle," Bastien concluded. "But how? It's been up for hundreds of years, and your family has lived here that whole time. Why now?"

"Not *just* now. It's been getting weaker for ten years. Like I've been saying," Cameron argued.

Then it clicked.

"Not ten years," I said. "*Twelve.* Ever since my deal with Forneus. *That's* where the power came from. That's why it stayed after he was dead! The barrier is made from our family's magic. Magic that dwindled after the thing was made, magic *we* didn't have until I made my deal. Demons can't make something from nothing. When I made that deal, when I asked for our magic to be stronger, it broke whatever spell they used to make the barrier. And every time we use our magic, every single spell since then has made it weaker, and it's all my stupid fault!"

"McKenna, it's not—" Bastien started to say.

"Yes it is! One stupid, bad, selfish choice that I keep having to pay for and now everyone else does, too! Chris lost his leg and we all nearly died killing Forneus to get me out of it, and that wasn't even the end of it! My mom, Cameron, Jackie, all of you, the whole damn town!" I kicked the enormous boulder, sending a jolt of pain up my leg. "Fuck! Ow! Solomon's bones, I couldn't just get a bad haircut or get knocked up, nope, no standard fuckups for McKenna Ellerbeck! I had to be the one to open the floodgates to demons, and now they're overrunning this place and ruining everyone's lives!"

I slumped against the Whale's Jaw, hiding my face. *How in seven hells am I ever going to fix this?*

I felt a hand on my shoulder. "If you're quite done," Bastien said gently, "may I point out how this is not all your fault?" I turned my head only enough to spy his face from the corner of my eye.

"I appreciate the effort, Bast, but it's pretty damn clear that it is."

"Why? Because a sixteen-year-old girl who had been left completely uninformed made a bad decision? Because you were taken advantage of by a master of manipulation with millennia of experience?" he replied. "It's not as though the rest of the families were any help, either. Your family was shut out. I don't mean just kids being cruel, but the adults, too. I'm not sure if anyone knew about this connection, but if they did, they never shared that information."

"And it wasn't selfish." I turned around to see Cameron behind me, his hands out of his pockets for once. "You didn't do it for you. I know you did it for me."

"Cameron..."

"You think I didn't notice the timing? I'd just started high school. Hugo Phillips hexed me in gym class and I ended up with a black eye and sprained ankle. Danielle O'Brien couldn't stop laughing when a pipe *happened* to burst over my locker and soaked all my books and my homework. And since one hex wasn't enough, Hugo hit me again in the cafeteria, and your sweet little fiancée"—he shot Bastien a dark look—"sent me nightmares for a week for spilling pizza on her bag."

"Mari's not like that anymore—"

"Whatever." Cameron focused back on me. "Point is, I tried to hide it, but you knew, and you were pissed. Next thing I know, one night you come home late, telling me everything's gonna be different now, and we summoned enough pixies to empty out the pantry." He actually smiled for a second. "You did it for me. So if it's your fault, it's mine, too. And Hugo and Danielle and Mari and everyone else who put you in that position in the first place, sis."

"Sis?" Warmth burst in my chest again.

Cameron rolled his eyes, but he was smiling again. "Get it over with."

I threw my arms around my brother. He hugged me back. One tiny piece of my life clicked back into the place where it belonged. "You got taller," I mumbled into his shoulder. We pulled back and I wiped my eyes. "Thanks," I told the two of them.

"I've got your back no matter what. Besides, if we're right, our family's been protecting this place for a few hundred years while the rest of them got fat and rich, so you know what? It's about damn time they chipped in," Cameron said.

Bastien was wearing another unreadable look. "There's surely a way to fix this so that protecting the town and the leylines doesn't rest entirely on your family. It's unfair to say the least. Once we deal with this current situation, we'll figure out a solution."

"Your grandfather won't like that," I said.

Bastien shrugged. "No. But that's his problem. For now, however, we'd best get to this spell so we can deal with said current situation."

"Right. How do we do this?"

"You sit in the center, and we sit around you. Focus on the thing you want to remember, and when you activate the circle, anyone inside it will see the memory from your point of view," Cameron said.

"Has to be my magic?" I asked.

"Yeah. But I don't think one spell is going to bring the barrier down around us just yet," Cameron confirmed.

I still hated doing this. But I knew I had to. My hands tightened until my nails dug into my palms, but I nodded and we all took our places.

The golden light of my magic spread outward along the lines and runes, encircling each of them until it filled along the outer edge of the circle, then gleamed and shot back toward me, blindingly bright—

—and then I was eighteen again, walking toward Jackie, irritated at her untimely summons. It was viscerally real—a phrase that would be too literal far too soon—but at the same time, I was aware that it was only a memory and not the real thing. Like a lucid dream, I was both participant and observer. And I wasn't the only one.

It wasn't telepathy, I couldn't hear anyone's thoughts, but I sensed their presence, and I knew they could sense me, too. I knew they were seeing through my eyes, feeling what I had felt as the memory played out. I expected to panic at the sensation of other people in my consciousness, reminded of the corrupt and alien feel of Forneus and the Madness demon, but this was different. Like grabbing someone's hand during a scary movie. It doesn't make the movie any less scary, but it helps to know you aren't alone. Goddess knows I needed to not be alone reliving this.

Things played out as I recalled. Jackie and I bickered; I saw the summoning circle and tried to leave. My knot of panic tightened as we reached the moment when I looked up at the Archdemon, the moment when I ceased knowing what happened until I woke to the aftermath.

I fell to my knees, blankly staring at the object of my nightmares. For a long time there was nothing else. The Archdemon stared at me like a curious child, tilting its head this way and that.

Then a third car pulled up and parked behind mine.

It felt like all of us were leaning forward, eager and afraid at once to see who would step out. Despite everything, I half expected my brother to be right, and to see Laurent Lemaire.

But it wasn't Bastien's grandfather who got out of the car. Instead, a familiar and utterly unexpected blonde stepped out.

Brooke Bellerieve.

# Chapter 17
# The Things We Do for Love

*Ten years ago*

"McKenna! Jackie! What's going on?" Brooke hurried over to us.

"How fortuitously timed," the Archdemon hissed.

"Are they okay?" Brooke asked, peering down to look at me, waving a hand in front of my face.

"They are rendered insensible. How did you know to come here?"

"Jackie texted me. Said to meet here, that she had to talk to me about something important. What are you doing here?" Brooke replied. "This isn't what we talked about."

"How did this one—" The demon pointed to the prone, whimpering Jackie. "—learn the rune for my name?"

With a gasp, Brooke fell to her knees next to the circle

Jackie had drawn, looking at the runes. "I didn't tell her, I-I have no idea."

"Isn't this one the telepath?"

Brooke's hands halted, fingers hesitating above the dirt. "She must've read my mind. That's why she wanted to meet. And McKenna..."

"To summon me forth and kill me, as she did Forneus," it concluded. "You have grown careless, Brooke! You have put me in danger, put *us* in danger! After what I have done for you, this is how you repay me, *this* is the kind of friendship you offer?"

Now, at last, Brooke trembled before it, cowering with tears on her face. "No! No, Saranthiel, please, don't be angry! I, I just need to work on my wards, make them better. You know how hard it is for me."

"Mm. Perhaps if this one weren't an issue, your lack of talent wouldn't be a concern any longer," Saranthiel said, circling Jackie.

"What do you mean?" Brooke's voice was wary but intrigued.

Saranthiel's too-long fingers stroked Brooke's cheek, gently wiping away her tears. "Brooke, we have an opportunity here. A chance for me to be by your side every day. I could protect you—from danger and other demons and false friends alike. What do you think they were about to do to you?" It spoke smoothly, convincingly, and gestured at the ritual circle and knife. "You've told me what the telepath thinks of the demon's witch, how she distrusts her. She would have killed me. Killed me and left *you* alone."

Brooke's face trembled, tears falling. "No, I...I have Lucca and my friends, and... can't we find another way, Sara?"

"You've seen how quickly human love fades, how it can be taken from you. Like your parents, like your old friends. You're about to leave this town. I know you care for them, but do you really think you'll all be as close once they've found new friends, new homes? Do you think Lucca's love will last forever?"

Brooke whimpered.

Saranthiel knelt, hands on Brooke's shoulders, lifting her chin with a gentle touch. "I am immortal, Brooke, and we are bound to each other forever. I will always love you, and will never leave you. We have a chance now to be together. All we need to do is remove this threat, and then I can always keep you safe." There was a smile in its voice that it was physically incapable of showing. "Isn't that what you want?"

Brooke bowed her head, falling into the Archdemon's embrace, shaking with tears while it cooed and comforted her for several minutes. Finally, she lifted her head.

"Tell me what to do."

Saranthiel stood, brushing hair from the teenager's face. "Set up a circle. A clean one, around the telepath. The demon's witch will take it from there. It's in her blood, after all."

Brooke nodded and quickly got to work, drawing a perfect circle around Jackie's prone body. Once she was finished, she dusted her hands off in the grass. Saranthiel nodded in satisfaction.

"Go. Your other friends are waiting. When we meet again, I will finally be with you in body and not merely in spirit, Brooke." The demon wrapped its inhuman arms around her, a jarringly maternal gesture that Brooke accepted without any hint that she found it unnatural.

"Finally," Brooke said in a sigh of relief. "I love you, Sara. I'll see you soon." She was starting to sound excited, almost giddy, about the prospect as she headed back to her car and left.

Saranthiel turned back to me, every trace of warmth gone. By now, senseless and ignored for so long, I was drooling on myself. "We have work to do, demon's witch. Take the knife." Its voice was smooth and compelling again. I looked at the knife, and it made all the sense in the world to pick it up.

"Good. Now cut your hands."

I cut a line across one palm, then turned the knife on the other. Blood welled forth and I began wondering, *Why am I doing this?*

"Summon your grimoire."

Tracing a small circle on the ground, dripping my blood onto it, I summoned my grimoire with no more than a thought, and it appeared before me. How had it never occurred to me that I could do this? It was so simple.

"Such a smart girl. Now find the runes to create the host."

I flipped the pages. Drops of blood dripped from my hands, becoming ink as spells appeared on the once blank pages. *It's in my blood... that's how it works... how does it know all this?* I stopped at a page titled CORPORIBUS DAEMONUM: the Demon's Body.

*I can make a host for a demon.* How? Why hadn't I known that before?

Wait. Why would I *want* to?

Saranthiel loomed eagerly over my shoulder. "Carve the runes, demon's witch. Prepare my host. *Now.*"

My mind moved sluggishly, a fogginess obscuring any thoughts not immediately in front of me. It wasn't until Jackie screamed that it even registered that I was already straddling her, holding her down with one hand and dragging the athame over her skin, drawing runes in her flesh, letting my magic seep into her skin to prepare it for its new owner.

*What am I doing?*

"No." It took everything to get out that one word. "No, I won't. You can't make me."

"Can't I?" Saranthiel seized my hand, licking my bloody palm, its words slick and coated in corruption that crawled over my skin and into my mind, grabbing and breaking and twisting.

Someone was screaming—*I* was screaming! My throat was on fire, how long had I been screaming? Why couldn't anyone hear me? Why was I screaming?

I looked down and knew why. Beneath me was Forneus, that bastard, he was here, he was alive, but I had the upper hand!

*CARVE.*

My hand was white-knuckled as I clutched the knife and dragged it across my enemy's skin. Forneus shook beneath me, his black eyes wide, and I felt a surge of satisfaction that he was trembling beneath me this time, at being the one to scare him for once.

Then the false image shifted, changed, lost focus, and I saw the true face before me. Jackie! Her mouth was moving but I couldn't hear her. Then she changed again and again, from Jackie to Forneus and around and around and I had no idea what was real but I knew I had to do something. I flung the knife away. "Stop—stop, I won't! I won't do this! Jackie, we—we need to run—we need to—"

"I lose my patience, demon's witch!" Something hit me and I went flying across the clearing, my back smacking into the boulder. Saranthiel lunged at me, seething, anger and darkness that I couldn't look at without feeling pain erupt through every nerve. I shut my eyes and waited to die.

Then, just as suddenly, it pulled away. There was an explosion of noise, bursts of demonic power in the air, and then there was silence. The corrupted presence withdrew from my mind and the clearing. I dared not open my eyes, fearing a trick, then I heard coughing, heard my name.

"McKenna..."

Remi?

Slowly I opened one eye, and then another. Remi Blake knelt on the ground a few feet from me, clutching her stomach. Blood seeped into her clothes, dripped from her mouth.

"Remi!" I lurched forward, grabbing her. "What happened? There was a demon—it wanted me to—"

"Saranthiel. I know. I felt its presence, followed it here—drove it off. That asshole will think twice about showing its face in Arcadia again anytime soon." Remi smirked cockily but it was ruined by a coughing fit, and her hand came away bloody from her mouth. Her face was pale and her skin cool as she straightened up, leaning heavily on me.

"Remi, you're *dying*." Hysteria threatened to take me over.

"It's okay. You're safe, McKenna, that's all that matters," Remi said, brushing her cool fingers over my cheek. "This body might die, but I won't. And I'll always watch over you."

Tears spilled down my face. "No...no, you won't be able to come back. I'll never see you again, I...this can't be happening..." My body shuddered with grief, anger, fear, and my next words were a whimper. "I don't want to say goodbye."

"It's not goodbye," Remi said, but we both heard the lie in her words. I lifted my eyes to hers, cupping her face, and then I was kissing her. Her lips were cold, slick from blood, weirdly fluid and uncertain on mine.

I pulled back and laughed with gallows humor. "You can't even kiss properly. Now I really know we're fucked."

"Sorry, my love. I...I wish it were another way, but..." Her eyes drifted away. "But...maybe there is..."

I followed her gaze to where Jackie's body lay, still and unmoving. "You mean...? No...no, Remi, I can't. I might be able to save her."

Remi shook her head. "I'm sorry, McKenna, but she's already gone. Whatever you did...I think you killed her." Her words hit like a stone. I buried my face in her hair, stricken.

"No! No, I didn't mean to, I thought—that thing played tricks with my mind—oh, seven hells, Jackie, no..." I sobbed into Remi's arms. She held me, stroking my hair.

"I know you'd never do this otherwise, but..." She was overwhelmed by a coughing fit, her hand and lips coming away bloody once again. "No one has to know. You could still save me. That is, if you...if you think I'm worth saving."

Her voice grew weaker, her words broken up by more coughing fits.

It was now or never. I was already a killer. I couldn't lose Remi, too.

"I'll do it." My voice was a hoarse whisper, as guilty as it was certain.

I half carried Remi over to Jackie's body, wiping my tears, focusing on the task at hand. Any emotions were shoved behind a wall of practicality. I gripped the athame and completed the runes on Jackie's body. Remi held the dead girl's hair back and instructed me as I carved the rune for her name onto Jackie's scalp. It looked strange to me, but Remi assured me it was correct.

"Now slice her across the throat," Remi said, "and cast the spell."

"What? That's not in the book," I said, creeped out.

"It's symbolic, to make sure the vessel is empty," Remi said, before being overcome by coughing, so bad this time that she collapsed onto the ground.

"Remi!"

"Do it!" she gasped between coughs that sprayed blood onto the dirt, barely able to breathe at all.

I sat astride Jackie, knife shaking in my hand as I looked at her empty gaze. "I'm sorry, Jackie." Steeling myself, I slashed the knife across her throat and yelled the final words of the spell.

Golden light and bright-red blood erupted at the same moment. A scream hit my ears, starting in the middle, ending too soon. Jackie's body bucked beneath me as her life gushed out of her.

*No! What? How? Jackie!*

Then I was screaming, too, dropping the knife and trying in vain to put my hands to her neck to stop what I had done. But it was too late, and a horrible laughter shook me, crawling over my skin. Remi's body floated up from the ground, rippled and twisting itself, turning into its true shape as the Archdemon Saranthiel.

"You are strong, demon's witch, but as easily manipulated as any in the end. You will be an excellent tool," it said, the words scrambling my senses once again. I screamed, grabbing my head, the pain in my mind, the corruption along my skin, my nerves, spiking to a crescendo until I collapsed, the world given over to darkness.

———————•———————

The rest of the memory played out as I remembered. I came to, banished Saranthiel, and called the real Remi to get me out of there. As she teleported us away, it ended, and the memory spell released us all back into the present day. I collapsed onto the ground, shaking, screaming, sobbing. Someone grabbed me but I shoved them off, scrambling over the dirt to get to my feet.

I faced the three of them, hands thrust out and glowing with golden light, magic rippling through me. "Don't touch me! I-it could be anyone—it could be either of you!" My whole body shook as I tried to determine who they really were. "Don't come near me!"

Cameron and Bastien—if that's who any of them really

were—kept their distance, exchanging glances. Finally, Bastien spoke, his hands held out in front of him. "McKenna. Please, we all saw what happened. We know what you went through, how you feel, but none of us are the demon."

"How can I believe you?" I shouted back at him. "Host bodies are undetectable. It could literally be anyone! There's no way to know!"

Cameron stepped forward. "There's one way to know."

I jerked, holding a hand up to block him. "Stop moving!"

"If you kill the host body, the demon goes back to the Pit," Cameron went on. "So come on. Do it. Let's find out."

Was I hearing him right? "What?"

"It could be anyone, like you said. Whoever this demon is, they're fucking with our town. They killed once and they'll do it again, if they haven't already. We need to know who it is, and there's only one way to do that: Kill the host body. So c'mon, sis, let's get started." Cameron stared me down, hands at his sides.

"But I—no, if you're not, then—I could kill you!" I squeezed my eyes shut, shook my head. "Stop playing games with me, stop, st—"

A finger tapped me on the tip of the nose. "Boop!"

A silver spray of magic burst over my face. My body immediately went slack. The last thing I saw as I slumped off to sleep was Tom's goofy grin as he caught me.

---

The room was dim, the sheets were soft, the comforter was extremely fluffy and warm, and I was reluctant to rouse myself. I'd been having a pleasant dream about being on a baking show with polite British people and woke with a craving for jam-filled pastries. When I didn't recognize the room, I bolted upright, and a piece of paper sitting on the nightstand caught my eye:

McKenna,

Morning. You're in my room, don't freak. You're okay. I'll be in the TV room when you get up.

—Cameron

I relaxed and looked around. Though the room was unfamiliar, some of the contents were not: pictures of our family and of his friends, some books I dimly recalled Cameron reading, the same digital alarm clock he'd had in high school.

Slipping out of bed, I saw I was still dressed in the jeans and shirt I'd had on at Whale's Jaw, though my shoes, coat, and purse were nowhere around. I opened the curtain on the windows, taking in more of the room. A cluttered desk held spellbooks and implements, along with an open notebook filled with scrawled runes and notes about demon attacks. A map of the town on one wall was filled with dozens of pushpins of different colors. Spotting red pins at the Grand, the woods where Leo and I were attacked, and a black one at Whale's Jaw, I realized it was a map of demon attacks; the colors were probably denoting types of demons. Taking a step back, I saw that the top was labeled with the current year. Next to it was another one, labeled for last year, and on the floor were five more rolled-up maps.

By-now-familiar guilt stirred, but this time it hardened me. This was going to stop, even if I had to summon Saranthiel and choke the demonic life out of it with my bare hands. I clenched my fists and felt an unexpected sting—looking at them, there were bandages across my palms. Cuts from my own nails. Considering my state of mind before Tom sleep-spelled me, that wasn't shocking.

That was fine. It hurt, but this was the least of the pain caused by Saranthiel. And Brooke.

*Brooke. All this time. She was my friend, and the whole time she was...* I tightened my fists again. I was so sick of hurting. But I was done running away from it.

Out in the hallway, I saw a bathroom at one end and a closed door to, I assumed, another bedroom. The other end opened into a living room plucked out of my youth: Cameron sitting on the couch from the basement den in our house, playing video games. He had more scruff on his jaw now, though.

"Morning," I said.

"Hey. I mean, morning. I'll be off in a minute, okay?" Cameron said, turning to respond while trying to keep one eye on the screen. I waved him off and smiled to myself. It was pleasantly normal and nostalgic.

While Cameron finished his game, I crossed the living room to their kitchen and found myself some coffee and cereal, then returned to sit in a plush chair that had likewise been part of the basement set. He finished up, set down his controller and headset, and looked at me. "So..."

"So." I nodded at the TV. "Is this how you kill time between bartending, breaking and entering, and demon hunting?"

Cameron chuckled. "Yeah, I guess."

"At least some things never change," I replied, tucking my legs under me. "What'd I miss?"

"Sure you can trust me?" Cam asked.

"Yeah," I replied.

"Seriously? Why? I wouldn't."

"Because no demon could perfectly capture you the way I know you. I saw your demon-hunting command center just now, I know you're too smart and too paranoid to leave yourself open to possession, and I'm not in the middle of a panic attack," I replied. "Do you trust me?"

"After what we saw? Yeah." He leaned forward, elbows on knees. "And I get why you left."

"Thank you. I'm still sorry, though."

"Yeah, well, I'm still angry. But I get it," Cameron said. "After you conked out, we decided you needed rest somewhere safe, and here is the safest place. We agreed we'd wait till you were awake to make a plan. Lemaire said he'd see what he could find on Sara. That's what we're calling it to be safe. Avoid the full name, don't wanna draw attention."

"Smart. You know, when Brooke first moved here, she'd talk a lot about her best friend from home named Sara," I recalled, slowly shaking my head. "She's been a thrall this whole time. Since before she even moved here."

"Yeah. She's in real deep." He shook his head. "How're you doing with that?"

I shook my head again. "I don't know yet. It doesn't make sense, but we saw what we saw. But she's *Brooke*. She was one of my best friends, she married her high school sweetheart, she goes on charity trips. She was homecoming queen because everyone genuinely *likes* her. How could *she* be a thrall to the Archdemon of Madness?"

Cameron shrugged. "People do shit you'd never expect all the time, McKenna. Case in point."

I gave him a look. "Kind of a low blow there, Cam."

"I'm not trying to make you feel bad, I'm just saying," he said. "And does it matter? Find out why later, we need to figure out how to kill that thing first."

"We can't." I sighed. "No demon-killing sword, and I've been trying to find another way for ten years. There's isn't one."

"Then we bind it or banish it till we find one," Cameron replied. "Get our little dream team working on it. Tom's still sleeping it off, but I said I'd tell Lemaire when you were awake."

"You willing to text Bastien—this really is serious," I joked without much humor. "So no word from him yet, but maybe we can do our own research. The grimoire's in my hotel room, and apparently it's possible for me to just summon it."

"Yeah, from what we saw, that looked kind of easy for you," Cameron said, a little less comfortably. An alarm on his phone went off; he turned it off, then pulled one of those little white pills out of his pocket, swallowing it with the last of his coffee. I watched uneasily.

"Maybe now that we know it's magical, not medical, we can do something about that," I said when he was done.

Cameron shook his head. "Tom and I talked about it while you were out. I've had tests done. So has Mom. Maybe it started off magical, but it's physical now. Irreversible. Mom—Mom fought until she couldn't. Until they took her magic and shoved her in that place. And I'll do it until I kick the demons out for good or I lose my mind trying. But there's no magical or medical way to fix this; the damage is done." His mouth was a bitter line across his face. He stood, grabbing an empty coffee mug of his own and taking it to the kitchen.

"No. No, there has to be *something*, Cameron," I said, turning in my chair as he passed. "I'm here, we've got the grimoire, we can find something to help you and Mom."

"Maybe if you wanna turn thrall again, you can bargain for one of us," Cameron threw back over his shoulder. "You know how it works. Anything that you can't possibly do yourself means you gotta pay full price. Not even Remi can give you a pass on that."

"Yeah, I know," I muttered. "Well, I'm not giving up on this, on you or her. I'm going to find a way to help you both. I promise."

He made a noncommittal grunt. That was fair; I still had to prove myself, and I would, no matter how long it took. "Okay. Time to summon a grimoire." I looked at my wards. "And weaken the barrier that much more," I sighed.

"Might not be such a bad thing," Cameron said. "There're some spell supplies in the end table."

"Letting demons have access to a major leyline junction? Yeah, what possible repercussions could that have," I replied sarcastically. I got the salted chalk out of the drawer and began setting up a circle on the floor of the den. There were traces of this having been done many times in the past.

"It's not like ours is the only junction in the world," he pointed out. "Or like we'd let just anyone walk in and use it. Do you even know where it is exactly? I sure don't."

I shook my head. "I think only the Council does."

"And we both know *they've* got everyone's best interests at heart," Cameron said with his own sarcasm. I smiled to myself, hearing the same intonation in his voice that I would've used.

"What, if they had to do some actual fighting, get their hands dirty, you think that'd change their minds?" I asked, dubious that he had that much faith in change.

Sure enough, Cameron scoffed. "Hell no. But it'd take the burden off us and put it on everyone. Why should we be their super soldiers and pay the price for it without so much as a thanks? Or a paycheck. Or a free trip to the loony bin."

"I know you're mad about Mom, but don't call it that," I replied.

I heard him sigh over the sound of the coffeemaker starting up. "Yeah, I know. Sorry. It's easier to be a jerk about it sometimes." I could understand that. "I had to sell the house to afford that place for her, you know. Got a good price for it, and Tom's dad did what he could to reduce the cost for me, but that money's pretty much gone now."

I looked down and squeezed my hand once again. "I'm sorry. But I'm here to help now, too."

Cameron appeared in the doorway again. "Yeah? Your years on the run led to a nice fat savings account and a sleek résumé?"

"Not so much. But I've managed and I will again. Point is, it's not just on you anymore. We'll take care of her together."

For all his cynicism, Cameron's expression did soften a bit. "Okay. That'll help." It wasn't much, but I'd take it. The coffeemaker beeped, and he shortly returned with a fresh mug.

"Let's do this thing," he said. "Though I kinda wonder if you even need the circle. You did it without one before, plus you're all supercharged."

"That's why I'd rather use one. I can't fully control all this power. The circle will help contain and direct it." I sat in the middle of it, unlocked my wards, and took a stab at what I thought would be the appropriate words for this. *"Liber mei, ad me te voco."*

Nothing happened. *"Liber mei de magia, huc veni."* Still nothing. I scowled. *"Liber, terga tua move!"*

"'Book, get your ass over here'? Really?" Cameron snickered.

"If you've got a better idea, I'm all ears," I retorted. "I'm getting nothing. Maybe Sara's the one who did it and not me."

"No way. Okay, think back. What did you do?" Cameron asked me.

"I don't know, I just... *did* it and it made perfect sense. But that shouldn't be possible. You don't summon non-living physical objects like that. You use telekinesis, but not from across town."

He frowned. "Are we sure a grimoire isn't living?" The look I gave him must have spoken volumes, because he scowled and said, "*No*, I have not hallucinated books talking to me. Grimoires aren't normal books, though. They're full of magic, and they can even give a witch more magic if you add their name."

I slowly nodded. "True. Grimoires are made from magic. Our magic."

He snorted. "Just like the barrier."

*Just like the barrier. Just like the demons.*

The way the barrier felt so familiar. The way the hellhounds' power called to me. The way the grimoire's magic slipped over my skin when all I did was touch it.

They were all the same. They were all mine.

*The demon's witch.*

The title was far more than Forneus's disgusting little pet name for me. Saranthiel had used it, too. It's why she wanted me, though I still didn't understand more than that. My magic, somehow, was the same as their power. For all that the terms were often used interchangeably, and they meant much the same, magic was a witch's domain, and power was a demon's or a Fae's. Magic was a force we could manipulate, while power was something inherently belonging to a supernatural creature. There was a level of minutiae to it that I didn't fully understand, but if I was right, then... then what did that mean about me? About Cameron, about our family?

New and unsettling questions whirled in my head, but I clenched my hands again, letting the sting of pain clear them away. They'd still be there later. For now, I knew what I needed to do to call my grimoire.

I didn't need to search for a thing. I needed to search for a power.

My power.

Eyes closed, I searched for those connections and sent a

pulse out along them. Three things pinged me back—my brother, the barrier, and the book. *I guess there are no demons in town right now. That or they know how to hide from me.* I reached toward the grimoire and pulled with my magic. There was a subtle shift in the air, and when I opened my eyes, the book sat before me on the floor.

"That was awesome!" Cam exclaimed. "You have got to show me how to do that"

"Later." *Much later, please.* "Right now, let's see if this thing feels like talking."

I picked it up, the worn leather, the uneven, gold-edged pages, the five indentations on the cover that only Cameron, Mom, or I could unlock. Unlike when I'd packed it, with my wards up, this time the whispers slid over me and connected with the magic living inside me for the first time in a decade. The intertwining of its power and mine was so sudden and intense I gasped, warmed from head to toe. It felt a lot like the hellhounds' power had the other night. The magic of my grimoire was as eager to get "intimate" with me as Remi had been. That memory combined with the feel of the magic of my skin right now brought a flush to my face.

"You two need a minute alone?" Cameron interrupted, clearing his throat.

Now I flushed in embarrassment. "Sorry. It's, uh, intense. Haven't held this thing with my wards down since I left." My brow furrowed. "I think it *missed* me."

He gave me an incredulous look. "Missed you?"

"I know, it sounds weird as hell, but I can't think of another word for it," I replied. "Let's file this under stuff to look into later, but, Cam, I'm starting to wonder just how alive our grimoire really is."

He looked at it warily; I could see the anticipation of having renewed access to it on his face. I put it on the floor between us and opened it to a random page in the middle. It was, of course, blank. The words in this tome had always been temperamental.

Cameron ran his fingers over the paper. "You're right. It does feel... like it *feels*."

"Maybe it's ready to be a little more forthcoming, too," I said. I touched the opposite page and, not sure what would happen, addressed it directly. "Tell us about Saranthiel."

Gold light flared over the page, then faded fast to reveal black ink. Saranthiel's rune, the one that had haunted my nightmares, sat right in the middle.

"It knew! It knew the whole time!" I exclaimed. "I tried for months to get answers from this thing, I drew that rune dozens of times, and it never showed me anything before!"

At the bottom of the page, a new line wrote itself:
*You were not ready before.*

# Chapter 18
# Knowledge Is Power

"You saw that, too, right?" Cameron asked. "I'm not hallucinating a book that talks?"

I nodded, eyes wide. "I did. You're not."

"Good. In that case"—he turned back to the grimoire—"how do we find that demon and how do we kill it?"

Once again, golden light flared across the page to reveal freshly inked letters:

*Kill the host body and remove the demon's power.*

"Yeah, that's a little easier said than done," I pointed out, shaking my head. "I can't believe I'm talking to a book. How is this happening?"

*Not strong enough before. As your power grows, so, too, does the knowledge of the Codex.*

"And now our grimoire has a name," Cameron said. "That's not creepy at all."

"A name that means 'book.' It's not like it asked us to call it Norman P. Mander or something," I pointed out. "Still, we'd better not have to stab this thing with a basilisk fang later."

Cameron snorted. "Nerd."

I elbowed him, then turned my attention to the words again and frowned. "Sounds like its magic, or its contents at least, are connected to the barrier, too."

"That explains why the writing in this thing was always coming and going, but we still don't know how or why," Cameron said.

"Maybe now's our chance to find out." I addressed the book again. "Do you know why the barrier is connected to us?"

There was a longer pause this time, and the light that preceded the words was slower. Almost like it suddenly had a longer load time.

*Your family's magic was the primary one used to create the barrier and continued to power it thereafter. With each generation, the barrier grew stronger as the Younger family magic grew weaker. The Codex spell, too, weakened over time to the point that physical manifestation was no longer possible. Until the uplink between the barrier and the bloodline was severed.*

"You mean, until my Bargain with Forneus," I sighed.

"How did this thing learn the term *uplink*?"

*Correct. The deal allowed Forneus to break the spell that bound your power to the barrier.* A line break, and it added, *The Codex's knowledge evolves with time and the witches of the family.*

My brow furrowed. "Forneus must have known. How did he know?"

"And how does Sara know?" Cam added.

"Maybe they were allies? Remi says it's pretty literally

cutthroat in the Pit, but think about what must've been at stake."

Cam rubbed at the stubble on his chin. Still weird to see, considering he'd barely started shaving when I left. "A barrier that keeps demons out, but it has a few very specific weak points. Demons in human hosts can get in—"

"Which are extremely rare."

"—or, if the power source for it could be cut, it could fall. Slowly, but who cares when you're immortal, right?"

I nodded. "So, somehow two Archdemons know about this. It's not gonna be easy to break it down so they start... cooperating? No, even just saying that sounds wrong."

Cameron snapped his fingers. "Not cooperating. Competing. Think about it. They both had thralls here, you and Brooke."

"True, but, what does Brooke's family have to do with it? Most of the Bellerieves were dead and Brooke's barely got any power. Sara kind of ended up with a lemon if that was her plan."

"So did Brooke. Whatever their deal was, she didn't get any more magic out of it," Cameron replied.

"Good point. So what *did* she get out of it?" I drummed my fingers on the Codex's page, which was blank again. "Sara talked a lot about protecting her that night at the Whale's Jaw."

"Right, yeah, and about losing her friends and family," Cameron recalled.

I held up a finger. "She was the sole survivor when her family died in that hurricane. That's gotta be it: She made a Bargain to survive."

"Maybe," Cameron agreed. "Although I kinda always

wondered how a family of water witches died in a flood. You think her deal had something to do with that?"

I shrugged. "It is weird, and we can't trust anything we think we know about Brooke at this point. But we know she was bound to Sara before she moved to Arcadia. Long before I was a thrall to Forneus." I rubbed my eyes. "We don't have enough information to keep conjecturing. What else do we know for certain?"

"Our family's magic is tied to the barrier. Your deal broke the connection. Every spell we cast weakens it," Cameron said, counting off on his fingers.

"Sara wants us to bring it down. Presumably to get to the leylines," I added. "Brooke is her thrall. She got me to kill Jackie and make her into a human host—wait a second." I spread my hands on the book and addressed it again. "The spell for making human hosts—why is it so rare? Why is it in this book?"

*The spell requires a mastery of binding magics. Few know it, fewer can cast it.*

I gulped. "Lucky me. That makes sense, though."

*The copy in the Codex is the only known written copy of the ritual.*

My hands went still, hovering over the pages, suddenly feeling very cold. "Are you saying that this ritual is one our family created? That it's a Younger family spell and we're the only ones who can cast it?"

*Correct.*

"Does that mean... did an ancestor of ours... bind Remi to her body?"

*Unknown, but likely.*

"Holy shit..." Cameron read the words at an angle. "McKenna, that means—"

"That Remi knew exactly who and what I was even before we ever met." I could taste my own bitterness.

"It means both Sara and Forneus *didn't* know about the connection to the barrier! *This* is why they went after you. I think the barrier thing must be a backup plan. They wanted you for the human hosts you could make."

Taking a deep breath, I focused on my brother's words instead of my latest emotional turmoil. "If I'd still been Forneus's thrall—or under Sara's control—"

Cameron looked at me, realization sinking for him, too. "If you hadn't killed him, or if you hadn't left and bound your powers..." He swallowed, looking pained. "Maybe you weren't totally wrong about that."

"I wasn't totally right, either," I said with a tight and joyless smile. "But thanks for saying it."

He returned the smile for a second, then looked at the grimoire. "We've gotta keep this quiet. Assuming Sara and Forneus didn't tell every demon around."

"They didn't. Forneus would've known from Remi, from when she first got her body. I'm not sure how but Sara learned it, too, and she used Brooke to get closer to me, I guess? Doesn't change the fact that now she's trying to bring down the barrier."

"But she also knows you're back. She'll come after you now, too."

"The wards will hide me, mostly," I said, still unsure about how I was found in Paris, "but I'm done running. We need to figure out who she is now and take her out. And that means confronting Brooke."

"And how are we gonna get her to tell us something she's been keeping a secret for more than half her life?" Cameron said.

A new voice suggested, "Good old-fashioned emotional manipulation."

Leaning against the wide living room doorframe was Tom. He looked pale and haggard—dark circles under his eyes, unkempt hair, uneven coppery stubble on his cheeks, and yesterday's rumpled clothes. "Cameron. Stormy. Morning," he said, his voice rough from the kind of sleep you get from whiskey before bed.

For a second, his eyes met mine, but he visibly winced and looked away. I dropped my gaze to the grimoire. There were things I owed him, things I could never repay or replace, things he deserved to hear from me, yet there was absolutely nothing I could say.

"Hey, man," Cameron greeted after clearing his throat. "How're you feeling?"

"Hung over as hell," Tom grunted. "Gimme a minute."

He trudged past us into the kitchen; I heard the sounds of water in a mug and the microwave whirring to life. Cameron and I sat in awkward silence until his roommate came back, steaming mug in one hand with a tea bag tassel hanging over the side and a granola bar in the other. He sat down on the far side of the couch. "You want info out of Brooke, you're going to have to convince her. Or guilt-trip her."

"How?" Cameron asked. "If she doesn't know or care that her demon master is an evil bitch by now—"

"Shut up and let the empath talk," Tom interrupted. "I don't know Brooke too well, but I do know she's all emotions. Kinda gives me a headache to be around her for too long. Brooke's smart, but she doesn't lead with logic."

"Sara was definitely manipulating her," I said, glancing at Tom, who was focused on his mug. "Telling her she'd be alone without her, she was the only one Brooke could rely on, et cetera." My brow furrowed. "Basically the abusive gaslighter's handbook."

"So, what, we tell her we're gonna be there for her instead? After what she's done?" Cameron said, surly again.

Tom shrugged. "Basically. Be open, appeal to her, relate to her. Have empathy. Don't get angry. People dig in when confronted with anger and being told they're wrong, especially when they already think they're alone."

"In other words, hide exactly what we're really feeling to get what we want?" I surmised.

"Yeah. Well. You're pretty good at lying." Tom stood up. "Play to your strengths." He walked back to his bedroom, slamming the door shut as we watched.

Cameron started to talk, but I held up my hand. "No. He means it, and I deserve it. Besides." I let out a breath. "He's not wrong."

We both got up and went to the kitchen for more coffee. "I cannot keep my cool around her at this point," Cameron said.

"Then I'll talk to her," I said as he poured.

"Alone? And get your ass immediately kicked when she calls for her Archdemon guardian angel?" Cameron said.

"I didn't say alone. You stay nearby as backup. But you have a point about Sara." I sipped as I thought out the problem. "What if we make sure the conversation is just her and me? Set up a safe space circle. Nothing in, nothing out. Make sure her evil overlord isn't listening. I used one a few times to keep Forneus out. It doesn't last long, but it's something."

He considered it. "That's our best bet, then. Maybe the Codex has a spell to help boost it."

We asked the grimoire, and sure enough, it displayed a ritual circle that was surprisingly simple but more robust than the one I knew.

"I've got all the stuff you'd need for this. How are you gonna get her alone, though?" Cameron asked.

I grinned. "I'm going to get a massage."

---

I was happy to see that the DO NOT DISTURB sign had been acknowledged when I returned to my room at the Grand. On the other hand, that meant the sheets were still in disarray from my wild night with Remi. I straightened it up and took an overdue shower before heading down to the midafternoon appointment I'd set up with Brooke at the Pasithea Spa. She'd had an open slot that day, and thanks to a gift card that had been left with the front desk for me, it was even affordable. No doubt Remi's attempt to make things up to me, but it was going to take a whole lot more than that.

Once our plans were made, Cameron and I had updated Bastien. Though he had a meeting he couldn't miss without bringing too many questions his way, he would be able to sneak my brother into the hotel despite his persona non grata status.

I went down to Pasithea early, back in my Kendra disguise. It was a nice place, smelling of lavender and lemongrass in the lobby, with soothing soft music and a trickling fountain display on one wall. I was given a complimentary cucumber water upon checking in and waited in one of the comfortable chairs to be let into my massage room.

While I waited, Mari Perez came by to talk with the receptionist and spotted me flipping through a magazine. "Kendra, right? Nice to see you again. Are you getting a treatment today?" she greeted, smiling as she walked over.

*Okay, Ellerbeck, give her a chance. She's marrying Bastien.* "Yeah, I've got a massage in a few minutes. This place is lovely, by the way," I replied, making the effort.

"Thank you! I put a lot of work into it." Mari beamed, then leaned over and spoke in a whisper. "I heard you were in an accident with Leo the other night. I hope everyone's okay?" she asked, the picture of concern.

"Oh—uh, yeah, thanks. She had to swerve to avoid a deer. The car got totaled, but thankfully, we're both okay," I said, surprised she cared.

"That's a relief," she said, tucking her dark hair behind one ear. "You must need a back massage after that! Whiplash is no joke, you know."

I managed a small laugh and rubbed my neck. "No kidding! I'm looking forward to it."

"Who are you seeing?"

"Kendra!" Brooke gushed as she walked in, wearing a top with the spa logo on it, her hair pulled back into a ponytail. "I'm so glad you decided to come! These hands are magic, you're going to feel *amazing* after." She waggled her fingers at me.

Mari smiled. "If you're with Brooke, you're literally in good hands. I'll let you get to it. Enjoy and let your worries melt away!" It was the spa's slogan, but it still sounded weird spoken aloud.

"Will do," I said, glad to be done with that. "Hi, Brooke." I turned to the other witch, having to force my smile. I shoved my hands in my pockets and clenched them to fight my instincts as my reclaimed memories roared to the surface.

"The room's right down here, follow me." I followed her down the hallway as she prattled on. "I'm so glad you're here! I talked with Leo, she's doing okay, but I'm trying to convince her that a massage would be perfect to get rid of all that tension. She's borrowing our second car for now, actually, until she can figure out what she'll be doing about getting a new one. Elle—you met her the other night, right?—she has some connections, but Leo needs to find out what insurance will give her first. I'm so relieved I called Lucca and that he went out to find you two." She dropped her voice to a whisper. "He told me all about what happened. I can't believe it! Thank the tides you're all okay. How do you think those things even got inside the barrier?"

She lied like it was breathing; there wasn't even the barest hint of a hidden truth. I stared at her, searching for any tic or tell, any sign she was holding back. Was she blinking more than usual, or was that her normal rate? Was her friendly smile any different than usual? What about how she adjusted her ponytail as she held the door open? I couldn't find anything, but then, I'd known her for years. Were all her tells things I had long since filed away as standard Brooke-isms? Or was she just that good at it by now?

"...McKenna?" Brooke whispered my name.

"Huh?" I shook myself.

"This is the room," she said, probably not for the first time.

"Oh, right. Sorry." I stepped inside and looked around the cozy room. A handful of white candles in glass jars lit the room dimly, a diffuser sprayed pleasant herbal scents into the humid air, and a massage table lay ready for me to lie on it. I gauged the space on the floor, covered by a dark rug. This would do.

"I'll give you a few minutes to get ready," Brooke said, and closed the door behind me.

As soon as she did, I opened up my purse, grabbed a salt-infused stick of chalk, and got to drawing the circle and runes around the table. I'd packed two of Cameron's chalks, one light and one dark, and thankfully the dark-brown one was nearly invisible on the rug. Once I was done, I quietly unlocked my wards as I heard a knock on the door.

"Hang on! Not ready yet," I called out to Brooke. I hurriedly pulled off my shirt, shoes, and socks, leaving my bra on along with everything from the waist down. Brooke needed to think everything was normal, but I didn't intend to go into this conversation literally exposed. I fired off a text to Cameron, concealed a silver pin in my hand, and lay down on the table, face down. "Okay!"

The door opened and Brooke stepped in. "Did you have any trouble?" she asked.

"Stubborn shoelace," I replied. "All set now."

"Great. First, I've got a few different oils to choose from..."

I had to go through the process of selecting my essential oils and then waiting as she got herself set up before she actually began. Her hands started on my shoulders. I was caught between the fact that I was very knotted up and she actually was very good at this, and the fact that she'd betrayed and sold out every one of us. Thankfully, I didn't have to deal with it for long. The rune I needed to activate the spell was directly under the hole where my face rested. I pricked my finger with the silver pin and let a drop of blood fall onto it as I whispered, "*Secretum.*"

Golden light flared all along the lines of the circle as it came to life. My ears popped as the air pressure changed. Brooke gasped and I sat up, facing her.

"McKenna, what's going on? What did you do?" she asked, confused.

"I made sure your friend can't hear us." My voice was cold and hard. I couldn't help it.

"My friend? Who—"

"I know what you've done, Brooke. I know what you are." I gripped the edge of the table, anger rushing through me despite my best intentions.

"I-I don't know what you—" she stammered, eyes darting.

She was afraid. Good. It was her turn.

"*Thrall.*" The word hit her like a weapon. Brooke stared wordlessly at me. "Nothing to say, Babbling Brooke? Because now's the time. Saranthiel can't hear us right now. No one can." I got to my feet, gesturing at the circle.

"How—how do you know?" she gasped.

"I finally remembered. You probably shouldn't have shown your face in front of me, even if your boss did fuck with my head," I replied. "You know, that night? The night Saranthiel forced me to kill Jackie and make her into a host and you *helped*?"

"McKenna—no, I—I didn't have a choice! I can explain—"

"I don't want an explanation!" I roared at her. "I want a name. Who is she? She didn't take over Jackie's life, so who is she?" I demanded, stepping closer.

"I can't tell you!"

"Like hell you can't!" My hand were fists, my arm stiff against my side.

She whimpered but turned away, arms wrapping around herself. "Wh-whatever you've done, it won't last forever. She'll find me, she'll protect me. She always does."

Shit. Tom had been right. All I was doing was making her shut down. I closed my eyes, took a deep breath. *Have empathy.*

"Brooke. I know what it's like, serving as a thrall. I know how they act, how they make you think there's no choice," I tried, keeping my voice calm this time. "I know Sara's made you think she's your only friend, but she isn't. You have people in your life who love you."

She sniffed, her shoulders shaking. It was working.

"People like Lucca." Assuming the demon wasn't posing as him, that is.

She choked on a sob. "He would *hate* me if he knew."

"No, Brooke. He loves you. He married you; he made a vow. For better or worse. He'll still love you." I didn't know if that was true, but I had to hope she believed it. "Tell me who she is and we can end this."

"I *can't*. It's part of my Bargain." Brooke turned toward me with tears streaming down her face. "She saved my life. I can't tell you anything about her, or—or my soul..."

*Bam.* My anger hit a wall and shattered. Her Bargain. Her soul. Her very humanity, whatever state that was in, and it hinged on keeping her master's secrets. I knew that fear. That desperation.

"Tell me what happened," I said, resting a hand on her arm.

She sniffed, speaking between gasps as she fought tears. "The hurricane, the one that wrecked my family's house, down in New Orleans. It flooded, there was no power, they were all dead, and, and no one was coming. I was alone, in the attic. I couldn't get out. I knew I was going to die, too. There was no food. The water wasn't safe to drink. It was just me and... and a lot of old books. I was only twelve, McKenna, I didn't want to die! So I started casting spells. But I was weak and starving and dehydrated and none of them worked, until Sara answered." Even in her distress, Brooke's eyes shone as she spoke the name. "She answered my call. I made a Bargain and she saved me. She brought me food and water and kept me safe. It was two weeks until anyone else got to the house and found me." She wiped her face. She *smiled*.

Anger and disgust returned but this time, they weren't at Brooke. The whole picture fell into place: a scared young girl on the edge of death, grief-stricken and alone. A powerful demon swooping in as her last chance to live. Who better to brainwash and manipulate? Hell, she'd even left Brooke in the house instead of taking her away from the danger and isolation after the deal was struck.

Brooke went on as I pieced it together. "I know she's done bad things, horrible things, but she's not like that all the time. She's still learning! She's like Remi. She can love, she does love, she's just...she hasn't always been great at it, McKenna, that's all," Brooke pleaded, grabbing my hands. "She's saved my life more than once. She's good, deep down, I know she is."

"Bad things? Brooke, she made me kill Jackie and turn her into a host. She's trying to tear down the barrier. She's sending demons into the town. She's been doing it for years—that's why my mom has schizophrenia, why my brother's developing it. She's lied to you, used you. We have to stop her, Brooke, you must see that."

"What? No, she...why would she try to bring down the barrier?"

"To get to the leylines, same reason the barrier exists in the first place," I replied.

Her brow furrowed. "What do you mean about your mom and brother? What happened to them?"

She didn't know? "Saranthiel is the Archdemon of *Madness*. You can't tell me you didn't know that," I replied. "Her minions have been getting in and attacking them, and every time they do, it gets worse. You seriously didn't make the connection between what happened to my mom and her presence here?"

"I didn't know anything happened to your mom. Cameron said she moved to Connecticut, to be near some friends or something! When did she get sick?"

*Things that would've been good to know, Cameron!* "Of course he kept it quiet. Dammit! She's been in an institution for the last five years," I told her.

"But...that was before..." Brooke's brow furrowed in thought, but then she quickly looked guarded again.

"What? What is it?"

"I'm sorry. I can't. I didn't know about your mother, or these other demons, or..." Brooke trailed off, but I heard the uncertainty in her voice.

"Brooke, please. There has to be a way around your deal. We need to stop her before—" Something pounded against the walls of the spell with the force of a sledgehammer, rocking me back into the table. Time was up. I grabbed her by the shoulders. "She's here. Brooke, you have to give me something before she hurts anyone else!"

Her green eyes locked on mine, wide and stunned and silent. Then the spell shattered and the door exploded inward.

We were both knocked to the floor as corruption filled the air, the wrongness seeping into my blood. My heart slammed in my chest, and my eyes clenched shut as the demon of my nightmares stepped into the room. Everything in me screamed *run!* But there was nowhere to go, and my muscles refused to move.

"Don't hurt her, please!" Brooke cried out.

*"Demon's witch..."* The voice filled my ears, and my senses began to spin. "Escaped my minions twice, but now you are

*mine.*" I pushed the heels of my hands into my eyes, gasping in breaths that were too short. Razor-sharp nails raked along the skin of my exposed back, and I screamed, remembering perfectly the too-long fingers, the extra joints, the mottled, rotted flesh. The tendrils of dark madness slithered along my skin, eager to seep inside me—

"Your wards!" The command came from the doorway. From my brother, seconds before he threw a spell at Saranthiel.

"*Claude!*" I rasped, pressing my wrists together. Saranthiel hissed in anger as my magic was yanked back inside, sealed up, leaving me feeling weak but protected. I was still terrified, still panicked, but the demon's madness couldn't breach my protections.

"*Ego daemon*—" Cameron began to yell, but his spell ended in a choke.

"No!" Brooke cried.

I dared to look, careful not to meet the eyes of our adversary. The demon's back, with its gross skin and decayed, skeletal wings, was turned to me as it held my brother by the throat in one hand, lifting him from the ground. He kicked and grabbed at its hand, as effective as a fly against it. Just like Forneus had done. But this time, I had no magic sword, no way to save him.

"You have outlived your usefulness," it hissed at him, lifting its other hand. Terror pierced my heart, but my voice was stuck in my throat and I still couldn't move.

With one quick thrust, its claws sank into Cameron's skull and a mass of shadows writhed around his head, obscuring his face entirely. He screamed with fear and pain so raw I felt it in every nerve in my own body. Then it dumped him like a used, empty piece of refuse onto the ground.

"Surrender or stay out of my way, demon's witch. Or share your family's fate," the demon seethed at me over its shoulder. The shadows surrounded it and it disappeared.

Cameron was convulsing, shaking with seizure. I wanted to go to him, but I may as well have been bolted to the floor. Brooke shoved me aside, rolled him on his side, and called for help. Dimly, I registered that there was smoke in the air, people were shouting and running past the room, and a fire alarm was blaring. But all I could do was sit and stare.

# Chapter 19
# Nothing Left to Lose

A psychotic break. That's what the doctor called it. Or something like that. The long, droning speech he gave me I largely tuned out as I stared at my brother, sedated and restrained in his hospital bed.

It was Thursday morning by the time I could see him. The entire Arcadia Commons Grand Hotel had been evacuated as a result of the small fire that had started in the massage room when the door was kicked in by Cameron Ellerbeck in the midst of his "psychotic break," which led him to trespass and attack an innocent spa employee and her client. At least, that's what the story was to the public. I'd been nearly catatonic myself, but someone—an EMT or a fireman, I was told, I couldn't remember anything—carried me out. Physically, I was fine, and eventually Bastien found me and ushered me away from the emergency responders and the crowds. Later that night, he was the one who filled me in on everything. I'd called the hospital and even admitted I was Cameron's sister to get information, but the best I got was that he couldn't be seen until the next day.

So that's where I was the moment they'd let me in. Tom and Leo were there, too.

"McKenna!" Leo hugged me tightly. "Are you okay?"

"Not really. I mean, I'm not hurt, but..." I hugged her back. Tom gave me a nod but didn't look at me.

"They're saying he snapped. Snuck into the hotel and attacked you and Brooke?"

My jaw clenched and I glowered as I looked at my brother lying there helpless and confined. "That's not what happened."

"It was the same demon, wasn't it? The one that killed Jackie?" Tom asked.

I nodded. "Yeah."

Leo held up her hands. "Okay, can we back up for the uninformed here? What are you talking about? Same one as Jackie, you mean a demon did this? *The* demon?"

"Yeah. Turns out it's—she's got a host body." I realized Brooke had called the demon a "she" as well. "I don't want to say the full name. We've been calling it Sara for short. She's been trying to get the barrier to come down by forcing my family to use our magic. Turns out it was used to make the barrier, so every time we cast a spell, it gets weaker. Sara's been doing it for years. The attacks gave my mom schizophrenia and now she's done it to Cameron, too. And Brooke is her thrall."

"Brooke is *what*?" Leo gaped at me.

"Keep it down!" I hushed her. "Yeah. She has been since

she was twelve. She's basically brainwashed, and thanks to her deal, she can't tell anyone who the demon is. I confronted her to get a name and that's how this happened." I stepped over to my brother's bedside, taking his limp hand in mine. "Has he been awake at all?"

"A few times. All he did was struggle and scream at the doctors. They're keeping him sedated until he can be transferred," Tom said dully from the chair in the corner.

"Transferred?"

"To the Harwell Institute."

I squeezed Cameron's hand, picturing him and my mother sitting together at that table with her Tarot cards, whispering to each other about demons and monsters that only they could see. For the rest of their lives.

Desperate, I looked to Tom. "There's nothing you can do? You helped him recover before."

He shook his head. "I wish. That was damage control; it was never a cure-all. We thought he had a few years at least, but a direct attack from an Archdemon is a whole other level. Far beyond me or even my father's ability to fix. This..." He looked at Cameron, and tears spilled down his face. "...this is permanent." The regret in his voice was palpable. "He's gone."

As I saw Tom cry, my own tears weren't far behind, and suddenly he and I were holding each other. I had no idea how or who moved first, but the brother of the girl I'd killed and whose body I had desecrated, however unknowingly, and I clung to one another as we sobbed over the loss of my brother.

Leo had to leave an hour or so later, but Tom and I remained. Trevan and Pip from the bar came by at one point, and a lot more nurses and doctors. Including Dr. Douglas Harwell himself, Tom's father and head of the Harwell Institute, who performed a brief, subtle magical diagnosis. Dr. Harwell was about my height, soft from late middle age and a sedentary profession, with glasses over the same blue eyes as his children. His strawberry-blond hair was now gray and thin. He was surprised to see me, to say the least.

"It's complicated, but I came back as soon as I heard Cameron was in trouble," I said when asked. "I didn't know about my mom until I was in town. Cameron kept that information mostly to himself."

"Some prefer to do so in these circumstances," Dr. Harwell said with sympathy. "And a tragic set of circumstances it is to come home to. I assure you, we've been treating Wendy with the utmost care, and we will do the same for Cameron."

"Of course. Thank you, Dr. Harwell, for everything you've done for her. And for coming to see Cameron so soon," I replied. Accepting sympathy from this man, from whom I'd taken so much, felt cruel.

"Cameron has been there for Tom over the years. He's practically family. It's the least I can do."

Tom, who was also still there, made a face. "Dad, I've told you how weird that sounds."

Dr. Harwell smiled at what was apparently a familiar response. "And I've told you there's no shame in loving your friends or expressing it. Just say no to toxic masculinity and gendered stereotypes, Tommy!"

Tom turned red. "Seven hells. Please stop."

I couldn't help smirking, though I had begun to suspect that Tom's feelings for Cameron went further than just friendship.

There was another knock at the door. "I'll look over the information and be in touch soon," I said as I went to answer it. "I'm sure I'll have questions."

"My staff or I will be happy to answer them. However, without the proper health care power of attorney, there will be limits as to what we can tell you and what you can decide at this point. I recommend talking with a lawyer as soon as possible," Dr. Harwell said, gathering his things.

"Of course. I'll get right on it." But all thoughts of that fled when I opened the door and found Remiel Blake standing on the other side.

"McKenna, I'm so sorry. I—" Remi stopped short as she glanced behind me and saw Tom's father. "—I came as soon as I could. I hope you don't mind my being here."

Dr. Harwell stepped up. "McKenna, again, welcome home. We'll talk soon," he said.

"Right. Thank you, Dr. Harwell. Take care," I replied, shaking his hand.

The man had a subtle look of skepticism when he saw Remi but merely said, "Ms. Blake," as he went past.

"May I come in?" Remi asked.

"Yeah, sure. I guess so." I closed the door behind her again. She walked over to Cameron's bed, frowning.

"I wish there was something I could do," she said. "He didn't deserve this."

"No one deserves the things Sara's done," I said darkly.

"Sara?" Remi raised an eyebrow.

"Saranthiel," I said quietly, still paranoid about saying the name. "The Archdemon who did this. The one who's been doing all of this, with Brooke's help to boot."

"Couldn't you heal him?" Tom cut in, his eyes intense.

Remi hesitated. "I could, but something like this, beyond the ability of both magic and science to heal? That's a thrall-level deal."

"Then I'll be your thrall, just heal him," Tom said without hesitation.

"Whoa, slow down, Tom!" I interrupted, stepping between them, hands held up. "Remi, don't you dare accept that offer!"

Remi sighed. "I wasn't about to, but do me a favor and don't tempt me, hm?"

"Why not?" Tom railed. "I'm here, I'm willing, I know what it means. If it'll save him, then I'll do it. I don't care about the cost."

I set my hands on his shoulders. "Tom. I know Cameron means a lot to you. But you know he wouldn't want you to do this."

"I can live with that if it means he's saved," Tom insisted.

"But can you live with what it would do to him?" I asked. "With him being as obsessed with saving you as he's been with defending the town, with finding me, with defeating this demon? With how much he'd hate himself for putting you in this position? If you do this, he won't be saved. He'll be even more tormented than he already is."

Tom's gaze dropped, the fire gone out of him, and he

numbly shook his head. "I just..." He looked at my brother helplessly.

"I know," I said quietly.

Remi watched us. "If there were another way, I'd do it."

"But there isn't, so why did you come here?" I asked, releasing Tom.

She looked taken aback, then defensive. "Because I care about Cameron and you. All of you, believe it or not. Have you been asking everyone who comes in what their ulterior motives are? Or is that reserved for friendly demons only?"

"It's reserved for people who've pissed me off and withheld important information so they could manipulate me lately. Not to mention ones who've taken uninvited rides in my head," I returned.

"You broke the agreement. You didn't leave me much choice," Remi said evenly.

"You didn't tell me my mom was mentally ill!" I yelled at her. "Or severed from her magic or in an institution!"

"I was going to tell you once the week was up—" Remi started to say.

"And what was your excuse for the five years before that?"

"Stop it!" Tom snapped. "You're upsetting Cameron." He gestured to the bed; sure enough, Cameron was starting to toss.

I hurried to his side. "The sedatives are wearing off. Cameron? Can you hear me?"

Cameron's eyes blinked and he mumbled as he tried to sit up, only to discover the restraints that held him down. "Wh-what? What's going on?"

"You're in the hospital, Cam. You had a—well, there was an incident at the hotel—"

Drowsiness flipped to frenzy as I said the word. "I have to be there! The demons have my sister there, the Lemaires are in on it! I need to get her out of here! I have the words, the words, the ... words ... they're gone! The words are gone!" He bucked, teeth gritted, repeatedly trying to jerk his hands out of the cuffs and yelling. "That thing took the words, give them back!"

"Cameron, please, calm down! I'm here, I'm safe, so are you, please!" I begged, but then he looked at me, his eyes as sharp as a knife, and screamed. A wordless shriek that sent me backpedaling into the wall.

He didn't stop, not even as the nurses rushed in, one holding him down as the other injected another sedative into the IV. My heart pounded as I watched, detached from what was being done to him. They asked me something, but I didn't hear the question and just stared at them, at him. Tom stepped in, and Remi took me by the arm, gently guiding me out into the hallway.

"I should stay," I finally said a few steps past the door.

"No, what you should do is take a breather. You've been in there all morning, haven't you? It's already afternoon," Remi said, nodding at a clock as we passed the nurses' station. "Let's get you some lunch."

My stomach grumbled at me. "Yeah, sure, let's find a vending machine or something."

"I was thinking more along the lines of a meal that requires utensils and plates," Remi said.

I shot her a glare. "I am not setting foot out of this building, never mind going back to your restaurant."

"I was talking about the cafeteria," she replied grumpily.

"Oh... sure."

We took the elevator to the cafeteria, got some lunch, and sat down at a table near a window. The world looked bright, full of sunlight and fall colors. One of those autumn days in New England that almost felt like summer. It was all wrong.

As was Remi being quiet, for once. But I needed the food and the quiet and to think about the many things that were bothering me. So it wasn't until several minutes later that I finally spoke.

"You sent the hellhounds after me in Paris, didn't you?"

Remi's dark eyes lifted to mine. "How'd you figure it out?" she asked, not denying it.

"You're the only person who knew both who I was and where," I said. "When Sara attacked at the spa, she said her minions had come at me twice and failed. She was only counting since I'd been back in Arcadia, because before that, the last time I saw her minions was over a year ago."

Remi nodded. "They never would've actually hurt you, you know. I wasn't about to risk that."

"No, but they did give you a chance to be all heroic and convince me I had to leave, so why not come here?" I said, and sighed. "Why not talk to me? Tell me the truth?"

"The truth isn't as easy for me as it is for you, McKenna," Remi said.

I laughed mirthlessly. "If you think the truth is easy for me, you have not been paying attention," I replied. "Time for some practice. You said you knew more in the video. I take it that means you knew about the Archdemon—that she has a human host—and about the barrier?"

Remi nodded. "I did. I don't know who it is, not for lack of trying, or what plan it has beyond bringing the barrier down."

"Did you know it was in Jackie's body?" She hesitated but then nodded. "And that I made that host for her?" Another nod. My jaw tightened. "And did you know my family could make hosts before we even met?"

Remi sighed heavily. "I did. The more I came to know you, the more sure I was. But I swear by everything, McKenna, that had no effect on how I felt about you, or what happened between us. I never expected to fall for you, or to help you kill Forneus."

I looked at my plate full of sad raviolis lost in a sea of too much marinara. "I want to believe you. But you know I can't take you at your word on that."

Once again, she nodded miserably. "I know. But if I may tell you something you don't know about me?"

I lifted my gaze, waiting for her to go on.

"I don't know how I got this body. I don't know who it belonged to, who gave it to me, whether it was one of your ancestors or not," Remi told me. "My memories of that time are incomplete. I know Forneus told me to secure him a human host, but it ended up being mine instead. For that betrayal, he tortured me in the Pit for nearly a century. I can't fully recall all of that time, either. But when he released me, he told me I had finally had a chance to repay him, and he sent me to keep an eye on you, his newest thrall." She spread her hands, smiling. "Little did the old bastard know, that was the moment he signed his own death warrant."

My breath trembled. My heart did, too, the traitor. I was mad at her, but I couldn't stop myself from caring about her, either. She stared back at me, her own feelings plain to see.

"If I could've finished this fight for you, McKenna, I would have. I tried for a long time. But I'm afraid my resources are rather limited, being the new Archdemon on the block," Remi told me.

I took a breath and said, "The fact you won't take any thralls probably doesn't help, either."

She smiled ruefully. "Clever girl."

"I had my suspicions, but you turning Tom down confirmed it," I said. "So that's why you brought me back. To finish this?"

She drew her head back sharply. "No! No, it wasn't. Yes, we needed you for this, and yes, your debt was due. But the real reason I brought you back was because *you* needed it." She set down her fork, her eyes traveling the room as she gathered her thoughts. "I kept tabs on you, yes. But it was more than just what I could sense because of the unsettled debt between us. I could always find you, and at times I went myself in one disguise or another. Other times I sent one of the few followers I have."

I blinked in surprise. "Wow. Stalker much?"

She shrugged, not bothered. "You think it's creepy. I suppose you're not wrong, but it's what demons do. We keep tabs on debtors."

"That doesn't excuse—"

"It's not an excuse. It's an explanation. Let me finish." She waited until I gestured for her to go on. "We never interacted directly. I never spoke to you and neither did anyone I sent to check up on you." I imagined, as she spoke, her face in the background of my memories of the last ten years. Her eyes hiding behind the random faces of people I'd never met but passed on the street, ridden a train with, sat next to in a class or a café, drinking at the same bar. It was strange, but knowing this, I felt both like Remi had once again overstepped and violated my privacy, but at the same time relieved that she had been watching out for me. I wasn't sure how to reconcile the two feelings. Leave it to Remi to be everything I wanted, maybe even needed, but go about it in entirely the wrong way.

"I hoped you'd find a new home, new friends, a new love, even. Every time, I told myself that if you were happy, I would stop and let the debt lapse indefinitely. Now"—she smirked, at herself this time—"who's to say if I could have ever held to that. But it never came up, because you were never truly happy." The stubborn part of me wanted to protest this, but that would've been a lie. I frowned and let her go on. "It took me a long time, because what do I know about home and family? But I finally put it together. It wasn't just your locked-up magic that was killing you. Staying away to keep them safe, and hating yourself for leaving at the same time? Changing your name, denying who you are after you fought so hard to define yourself on your terms? Never settling in, never truly connecting with anyone, never letting yourself move on or know peace? All because of something that wasn't your fault. It was *all* killing you."

I ran a hand through my hair, face warm, feeling like someone had been reading my nonexistent diary. "When did you get to be the expert on all this?" I tried to joke.

"When I asked myself the same question I've been asking myself since we met," Remi said, smiling kindly this time. "*What would McKenna do?* Except this time, I didn't apply it to me. I applied it to you. And what you would do is tell yourself to get your ass home and find a way to be with your friends and family. But since you clearly were not telling yourself that, I pulled another classic McKenna move and meddled." She made a pyramid of her fingers and smirked at me, her mischief creeping back in.

I laughed, lightly, seeing it all fall into place now. "And then you had to wait for the perfect time, when everyone would be together for the reunion and the wedding."

Remi nodded. "A few hints and fortuitous run-ins, and all your natural instincts took over from there."

"So you meddled with a meddler, knowing she wouldn't be able to resist meddling herself." I had to laugh. "Am I really that predictable?"

Remi grinned. "I'd say reliable. You have to admit, it worked perfectly." She sobered. "Well...almost."

I sighed. "Almost." I pushed around my food on the plate. "Remi, if I offered myself as a thrall, in exchange for curing my mom and my brother, would you do it?"

"No," she said without hesitating.

"I figured," I replied. "But I had to ask."

"I know. Besides, I could only cure one of them. A life for a life. And you'd hate yourself for making that choice."

"Right. Maintaining the balance, blah, blah, blah." I speared and ate the last bite, then stood. "I'll grab something for Tom. If we're gonna figure out how to make this bitch pay, we should all be operating on full stomachs."

———•———

Tom wolfed down the sandwich, chips, and soda, and we got to work on a battle plan. Unfortunately, it was hard to make one when we had no idea who our enemy actually was.

"If it were me," Remi said, "I'd have taken on some entirely new persona. Blended into the group over the years. It's the path of least resistance. Why do you think I pulled the new-girl-in-town schtick when I first came here?"

"By now, she'd be thoroughly blended. No one seems new if you've known them for ten years," Tom said. "Even college friends are old news."

"I think we can narrow it down to females, at least. Brooke called her 'she' before I did," I said.

Tom looked at Cameron. "Sorry, Cam, I know you were hoping for Laurent. Guess he's just a run-of-the-mill angry old rich, cishet white man."

"One down, the rest of the town to go," Remi remarked.

"No kidding. I want to say someone close to Brooke, but who knows." I rubbed my scar as I searched for possibilities. "Maybe Cameron was close, though. What about Adele Lemaire? She's new in town since I left, even if she is a Lemaire. What do we know about her?"

"She's Bastien's aunt, his dad's youngest sister. She used to live down in Hingham, but she bought a place up here after joining the Council," Tom supplied. "No spouse, no kids. And that's officially everything I know about her."

I arched an eyebrow. "No family would've made it easy for Sara to step in and take over her life."

Before we could explore that further, there was a knock, and the door was pushed open.

"Hey, McKenna, you in here?" Lucca Luppino's form filled the doorway, his dark hair less shaggy than when I'd last seen him, his goatee neatly trimmed, his smile broad if also a little awkward.

"Lucca!" I smiled back for a second before remembering that it was his wife who'd betrayed us. How the hell was I going to tell him about Brooke?

"Hey, McKenna—you look like you! Is it okay if we come in, is now a good time?" Lucca asked, stepping into the room. Behind him lurked a timid blond head. The sight of Brooke, even with an innocuous bouquet of flowers in her hands, made me go cold and still. She practically hid behind her husband as they walked in.

Remi stood, looking at my face and Tom's, and addressed them. "No, I don't think now is a good time."

"Never's a good time," Tom muttered under his breath.

I got to my feet as well. "Lucca, there's something you need to know—"

He cut me off. "Brooke's a thrall. Yeah, I know."

I did a double take. "You—you *know*? What the hell, Lucca!"

He narrowed his dark eyes at us. "I know *now*. Brooke told me last night." He put an arm around her as though shielding her. "And we need to talk to you before you do something stupid."

"*Excuse me?*" I glared right back. "Whatever she's told you, it's half the story at best. She isn't even *allowed* to tell you most of it."

"Yeah, well, it wasn't exactly an easy conversation for a lot of reasons, but we managed," Lucca said, planting his feet, unmoved by my words.

"You realize that she's part of this, then? She's why Jackie is dead, why my brother and my mom have both lost their sanity, why the barrier is breaking down? Why demons got in here and nearly killed Leo the other night?" I said, anger growing with each accusation.

"I *know*, McKenna." His eyes flashed the golden color of the wolf, and there was a growl behind his words. "And those things are not Brooke's fault. No more than what you did as a thrall to Forneus was your fault."

My teeth ground against one another, my jaw clenched so tight it hurt. "Don't you *dare* compare what I did to what she's done!"

"She was a child!" Lucca roared.

"She lost that excuse the second she turned her back on me and Jackie," I growled right back.

Lucca took a half step forward, starting to loom over me. "She was alone and dying and desperate and a demon took advantage of her. It's better than your excuse was for making a deal."

"Lucca!" Brooke finally spoke, chastising her husband. "You can't say that to her, that isn't fair."

"Oh, come on! She did it for power. You were trying not to die," Lucca replied, turning to her.

"She wanted to protect her family. Power was a means to an end," Brooke said, looking past him to meet my eyes.

I looked away. I don't know how she knew that, but she was right, and we were the only two people here who knew what it was like. To make that choice, and then have all other choices taken away from you. She knew, and I knew, and I hated that because I wanted to hate her for it.

Brooke stepped out from behind Lucca and into the light, setting the flowers down on a chair. "McKenna, I didn't call her to me yesterday. I didn't ask her to do this, I didn't want her to. I didn't know about your mom, and..." She bit her lip, her voice wavering as she looked at Cameron. Tears slipped down her cheeks, and Lucca put his arm around her shoulders. "I'm sorry. For both of them, f-for Jackie..."

"Sorry won't bring them back," Tom said gruffly.

"I know." Brooke looked down. "I wish I could change that, but..."

"But you can't," I said flatly, arms crossed over my chest.

She looked up at me, her green eyes rimmed with red. "I can't. I made a vow. And I can't break it."

"You know you're putting your soul above their lives," Tom said.

Lucca and Brooke exchanged a look. I furrowed my brow. "Something else you want to tell us?" I prompted.

"It's not just her soul, or her life," Lucca said. "We just found out the other day. Brooke is pregnant." Despite their tears, despite the whole messed up situation, the two of them looked at each other with joy in their eyes at this long-awaited news.

Well, shit. That was awfully convenient.

"You're sure? A real doctor confirmed this and it's not some trick of your BFF?" I asked.

Lucca's eyes flashed at me again, but I was focused on Brooke. She nodded. "I went to my OB to confirm it. It's real. Sara has nothing to do with this."

"Mazel tov and all, but I wouldn't be so sure about that," Remi said. All eyes turned to her. "By saving your life, physically, she essentially has dominion over your body. It's entirely possible your difficulty conceiving was at her discretion and that your success at this point is as well."

Lucca growled while Brooke gasped.

"Thrall-level deals are not a simple one-off. Brooke belongs to Sara, body *and* soul," Remi reminded them. "It's *possible* she never interfered, but unlikely. Brooke has proven she loves Sara more than perhaps anyone. Why risk letting her bring a child into the world who might rival that devotion?"

"N-no...no, she wouldn't..." Brooke stammered.

"Wouldn't she?" Remi countered.

Lucca stepped between them, his large frame tense. "Shut up, Remi."

Remi shrugged, stepping back and leaning against the windowsill. "Don't gut the messenger, Big Bad. It's hardly my fault if she loves Sara more than—"

"I said *shut up!*" Lucca grabbed her by the shirt, newly sprouted claws tearing the material, lifting her off the ground, his eyes an angry, blazing, molten gold.

"Lucca, stop! Let her go!" Brooke grabbed his arm and his face, forcing him to look at her. "I love you more than anything or anyone, you know that! You come first, you and our child, I swear!"

Lucca finally lowered Remi to the ground. Brooke forced him to back away, and I grabbed Remi's arm, pushing her partly behind me, mirroring the werewolf's own protective stance from earlier. "You two need to leave."

Lucca took a slow, deliberate breath. When he spoke, his voice was thicker than usual, and the movement of his lips showed a mouth full of fangs. "None of us like this situation, McKenna. We're on the same side. But if *anyone* hurts Brooke, or the baby, they'll answer to me and my pack."

"Understood."

Brooke turned back to us one last time. "I'm sorry. I made a vow," she said again, her eyes locking onto mine. "I made a vow."

None of us spoke as they walked out and left. Not until the door closed and Remi slumped against the window with a relieved sigh, rubbing at her sternum. "That was closer than I'd have liked."

"I know it's a long shot after several millennia of doing the opposite, but do you think you could maybe learn when to shut up for once?" I advised, looking her over. Other than a ruined shirt, she appeared unharmed.

She grunted. "I told him the truth that Brooke won't, or can't, tell him. Now, if we could point him at the proper target..."

"He'd end up like Cameron," Tom said. "He might be bigger and stronger, but his brain is just as vulnerable."

I nodded. "Werewolves aren't immune. I've already seen it."

"Meaning our situation has only gotten worse. Any move against Sara could bring her to threaten Brooke or the baby, and that will bring Lucca's ire down on us since he can't act against her directly, either," Remi pointed out. "Our adversary has effectively gained a werewolf pack to her list of weapons."

"Dammit!" I hit my fist against the wall. "Ow. But dammit, I am done with this. I am not losing anyone else to that bitch. We need to take her down, and it needs to be as soon as possible."

"Agreed, but nothing's changed. We still don't know who she is, and finding out could take days, weeks, even months," Tom replied. "Sorry, Stormy, but I don't know how we can speed that up."

I paced, my hands on my hips. "There has to be *something*."

"The odds aren't exactly in our favor. Could you put a ward on the Grand to keep out Sara specifically?" Remi suggested.

"Like the Lemaires would let that happen," Tom said.

"If Bastien made himself useful and backed her claims, perhaps."

Tom shook his head. "The second McKenna shows her face and we start explaining this, the Council will launch a whole investigation to verify it. That'll take weeks at best, and it's not like they'd even start until after the wedding. Probably not until Bastien's back from his honeymoon."

*Of course.*

"Tom, you're a genius." I spun around to face them.

"I am?"

I turned to Remi. "You've got an open tab at Titan. I assume that means the bartender owes you?"

"You assume correctly," she said, looking at me curiously.

"Good." I smiled at my co-conspirators. "I know how to find our demon."

# Chapter 20
# The Best-Laid Plans

"Stop twitching."

"I can't help it, you're right on top of my eye."

"Duh, it's eyeliner. You didn't used to be this bad about this. Deep breath, exhale slowly, don't blink!" Leo deftly swept liquid eyeliner across my lid. "There! I am a neurosurgeon with this stuff. Was that so bad?" she said, grinning at her handiwork.

I smiled back. "Not so bad at all, Doc. Now the left one?"

"We'll give it a sec. Have you, like, not used eyeliner in ten years? After all those dance recitals and school plays, you used to be able to put this on yourself one-handed while chugging a venti latte."

"Wasn't much call for it." I sat back on the chair in front of the vanity in her hotel room.

It was Saturday afternoon. I'd checked out of my room that morning and, to all appearances, left the Grand entirely. In truth, I'd slipped back in with Bastien's help and was crashing in Leo's hotel room now. As a wedding guest, she was staying there for the night while her parents watched Griffin. Meanwhile, I needed to be in the Grand but somewhere more secure than my previous room. And if Sara and Brooke believed that I'd given up and run again, so much the better.

"Oh, c'mon, you must have gone out, had some dates, something," Leo said. "Please don't tell me you traveled all over Europe and never got any. That would be way too depressing."

"Leo!" I laughed and hit her arm. "If you must know, yes, I did find time to get laid a few times while on the run."

"Nice," Leo said, grinning and giving me a fist bump. "Now tell me about your illicit European affairs so I can live vicariously."

"Vicariously, huh?" I asked gently.

Leo gestured for me to prepare for the next eye. "I'm not ready for that, but that doesn't mean I can't appreciate a good tale about getting some tail. So." She lifted her hand as I lowered my lids. "Who was your latest conquest? Sexy French dame? Charming English chap? Stoic but soulful German?"

"Um, actually it was...Remi," I admitted.

"What?" Her hand jerked, sending a black smear across my temple.

"Hey! What happened to the neurosurgeon of eyeliner?" I exclaimed, grabbing a face wipe.

"What happened to *not* sleeping with your demon ex?" Leo retorted.

"I—we—Cameron had just completely shut me out, I felt like crap, she took me out to her fancy restaurant, we talked and ate and drank and flirted and...and it felt good," I said, shrugging, trying to figure it out myself.

"I should hope so. She is a succubus."

"Not that part! Well—okay, yeah, that part." Leo rolled her eyes, but smirked. "I meant it felt good to be myself and be with someone who really knew *me*, for the first time in a really long time. When I saw how in control she was of her power, how she'd been making her own life here...." I sighed.

Leo rubbed my shoulder. "I know how big a deal that was to you, back in the day."

"Yeah. Of course, then she had to go and *not* tell me about my mom or Cameron or anything," I added.

"Not telling someone something important in order to spare their feelings and also because you feel guilty. Hmm, where have I heard that one before?" Leo tapped her chin while giving me a look.

I winced. "Fair, but ouch." I tossed the face wipe in the trash bin. "I hadn't thought about it like that."

"She's pretty much always followed your lead on how to deal with the big stuff, it's not exactly surprising. I'm not saying it was the right thing to do or that you haven't got every right to be angry, but..."

"But it is a little hypocritical of me at the same time, yeah." I sighed. Leo lifted the eyeliner again and I obediently held still. "I've known her for twelve years and she's changed so much, yet somehow Remi is still everything I do and don't want her to be, and I don't know what to do with that."

Leo finished and nodded in satisfaction at her work. "Can I offer some old-married-lady advice?"

I snorted, amused. "Sure, go for it."

"In a lot of ways, you and Remi haven't really changed that much. Hear me out," she said when I gave her a look. "You obviously still have chemistry and meddlesome feelings for each other. On some level, you're still hoping for the miraculous happy ending to your against-all-odds, until-the-world-burns-down, epic love. You challenge each other, you're passionate for each other, it drives you crazy in the best and worst ways."

"Where's the *but*?"

"But: You're not a teenager anymore. That's all great, yeah, but in the end, if you can't trust each other and give each other some stability, it's going to fall apart. Considering what she is, even if she's on the side of the angels, that relationship is always going to be fraught," Leo said. "Doesn't mean it can't work, but it'll never be easy."

I forced a crooked, rueful grin. "No one ever said love was easy," I pointed out.

"No one said it had to be that hard, either."

"But isn't love worth fighting for? Worth changing for?" I asked.

"If you're both willing to do it. Look, I'm not saying do it or don't, just that you don't *have* to. Maybe you didn't have any serious relationships while you were gone; you fell for Bastien, and that alone means you know you can have passion without so many complications," she replied.

"Man, you married ladies really tell it like it is," I half joked.

She grinned and hugged me with one arm. "You know me. On your side no matter what, and bluntly honest no matter what, too."

I hugged her back, leaning my head on her shoulder. "I know. Both reasons why I love you."

"Damn right you do."

"Thanks, Leo. And thanks for the makeup, although I still don't think it's necessary. I'm a wedding crasher, not a guest."

"This is your big return to Arcadia Commons in front of the who's who of the witching world. Might as well look like a rock star doing it." She opened her eye shadow palette with flourish.

"That's what else I love about you, Leo: You have your priorities in order."

She went about her work for a few minutes, focused on the task. In the quiet, my mind wandered to what lay ahead of us.

"You're fidgeting again," she said.

"Sorry. I'm nervous. Not about Remi, about everything else."

"Makes sense. Do you want to talk about it?"

I swallowed, though my throat still felt dry. "Every time I get close to Sara, or even a whiff of her power, I freeze up. In the garage, in the woods, in the spa. I had a full-on panic attack after the memory spell. I don't know what's gonna happen when I see her again, but signs point to someone getting hurt."

"Not that I'm a psychiatrist, but, Mickey, has it occurred to you that you are almost certainly suffering from PTSD?" Leo asked as gently as one can ask that kind of question. When I awkwardly didn't answer, she set down the eye shadow. "Alex was in the army. He didn't suffer from it, but he had some good friends who did. What they went through sounds a lot like what you described. And you definitely went through some really traumatic stuff."

What would it mean if I agreed? "...We all did."

"Not the same way you did. And people can handle the same experience in different ways; there's no right or wrong," Leo said. "Look, as far as tonight goes, I believe in you. You know it's coming, but she doesn't. And you're not alone. Whatever happens, you've got people in your corner."

I grabbed her hand, squeezing it more tightly than I had intended. "Thank you," I said, taking a deep breath to steady myself. "And...maybe after this...would you help me find someone to talk to?"

"Absolutely." Leo hugged me, and I took another moment to hug her back and take a few more breaths. Finally, she pulled back and handed me a dusky rose-colored lipstick. "For now, let's get the rest of your battle armor on."

"Good plan." I lifted the lipstick to apply it but paused, my gaze falling on my nails, which I'd painted golden-yellow earlier. "Actually, got any good reds?"

Leo grinned. She knew why I was asking. "Hell yeah I do." She grabbed that lipstick back and passed me another. It was exactly the kind of bright red my mom would love. "And hey, half of psyching myself up to play a show is getting ready for it, looking and feeling the part. Think of it like being a sexy demon assassin. By the time she knows what's going on, it'll be way too late."

"In theory. She could still do some damage. Promise you'll get the hell out of there if shit starts going down?" I asked her.

"I'd say yes, but also we both remember how I totally did not do that when we killed Forneus," Leo pointed out.

Did I ever. Everything had gone to hell. Remi had accidentally severed Chris's leg—leaving her unable to wield the demon-slaying sword because she'd harmed an innocent with it—and been knocked out, Forneus had Cameron by the throat, and Leo jumped in offering to become a thrall. Buying Bastien and me time to get the sword into my hands and, thereafter, Forneus's gut.

"True, and probably none of us would be here if you hadn't, so maybe I ought to stop asking that," I said.

"Mm-hm. Regardless, yeah, I'll be careful." Leo's eyes met mine in the mirror. "Hey. You got this."

I forced a smile that looked confident and applied the lipstick, then handed it back. "Let's hope so."

I stepped back into the main room and pulled on the rest of my outfit for the night—black shoes to go with my black pants, and a black vest over the white button-down shirt. Then I pulled my hair back and tucked it up under a wig of a short red bob, slid on a pair of non-prescription glasses, and fastened my necklace around my neck once again. Since Sara and a number of others already knew about my "Kendra" disguise as it was, and I couldn't risk using my magic and giving myself away too soon, I was adding to it the old-fashioned way. There should be no chance of being recognized before I was ready. The one risk factor was Lucca's wolfish sense of smell, but borrowing Leo's clothes and her perfume and blending in with the staff would buy me time.

"Got everything?" Leo asked. She was wearing a red halter-style dress with a knee-length skirt that was very swingy and full, and a pair of red heels to match.

I patted my pockets to be sure. "Yep. Ready as I'll ever be." We hugged one last time. "Kick ass down there."

"Right back to hell," I replied.

I waited five minutes after Leo left, spending the time doing some deep, slow breathing to calm my racing heart and sweating palms, before also heading out. My nerves were still on edge as I stepped into the hall. No turning back now.

---

I spotted the bartender from Titan, Remi's contact, in the hotel kitchens. "Dale?" I said as I approached.

He was startled. "Yeah. You're, um, Remi's friend? Tina?" The fake name we'd agreed upon.

"That's me."

"Cool. Look, this isn't going to get me in trouble is it? I know I owe her a favor, but I really like this job," Dale asked.

"You're not going to get in trouble, Dale, everything'll be fine," I said. It was only half a lie. No one was going to come looking for him. "All I'm here to do is serve drinks and apps."

"Right, yeah." He didn't believe me, but I didn't need his belief, just his cooperation. "This way."

I followed as he gave me a quick tour and explanation of what to do, but I was only interested in one thing: where they kept the drinks.

"Down here's the wine cellar, you need an employee ID to get in—"

"Great, swipe me in," I interrupted him.

"What? But—I can't—"

"Remi told you that if you helped me, your debt was clear, right? All I need is access to the wine cellar. Do that, tell whoever that the champagne will be up soon, and your slate is cleared."

"Okay..." He took out his employee ID and held it up to the pad next to the door. The light went from red to green and the door clicked as it unlocked. I grabbed the handle and pulled it open.

"Thanks. And do yourself a favor, don't get in debt again," I advised as I headed in.

The stone stairway that led downward made it feel like I was walking into a modern dungeon. They must've dressed this area up for when they had to show off to investors or business partners or something. Money well spent; the way the stairway opened into a large and rustic wine cellar, with stone walls, smooth tile floors, and countless bottles, was impressive. Racks taller than me were filled with wine floor-to-ceiling. In the center, a space was cleared out to make room for a tall counter with chairs and glasses, a private tasting station. Behind that was a glassed-off, temperature-controlled room-within-the-room that held more bottles, including the champagne. I slipped inside; the air was chill but not cold. Here, metal racks were set into two of the walls, while stand-up metal racks held the rest of the bottles. There was another, smaller tasting table toward the back. Conveniently, someone had set a box with four magnums of bubbly on it, complete with LEMAIRE/PEREZ written on the side.

"McKenna? Is that you?"

I jumped in surprise, both at having company and the use of my real name, then sagged with relief to see it was Bastien. Who looked frankly fantastic in his sleekly tailored black suit.

"Hey, Bastien. You look, uh..." I fumbled, then smiled in a way I hoped wasn't awkward. "Well, like someone who's about to get married."

"Thank you," he replied, congenial as ever. "Nice wig. How's it going?"

I'd explained the plan to him beforehand. "Almost all set. How are you?" I asked. "I mean, you're the one who's about to find out who among your closest friends and family has been lying to and betraying you. *At* your wedding."

"It won't be easy, but it's better that this whole situation is taken care of as soon as possible," he replied.

"A practical but efficient way of looking at it," I agreed. "Still, I'm sorry this has to kind of ruin your wedding reception. And that...that I'm going to be causing you pain once again."

"What do you mean?" Bastien asked.

"I mean what I did to Jackie and then ditching you with no explanation," I said. "You've been incredibly patient and even kind to me, and I know I don't deserve it. And I promise, I'm not going to do it again. I know you've got your life sorted out now, obviously"—I gestured at his suit—"but I want you to know, I'm sorry for hurting you before, I'm happy for you now, and I'm done running away. Thank you for helping to show me I didn't have to." I smiled wryly. "Basically, thanks for being my friend even when you had every right not to be."

I held his gaze, wanting him to know I was serious, that I was sincere. Wanting, I suppose, to feel worthy of how well he'd treated me. And then, out of nowhere, he kissed me.

One second Bastien was standing there, eyeing me

thoughtfully, and the next he was cupping my face, bringing his lips to mine in a shockingly hungry kiss. His lips were warm and inviting as they moved against mine, his tongue darting across them, one of his hands sliding down my arm to grasp my hand as the other went to my hip, wine bottles rattling as he pressed me back against the wall rack behind me. For a second I started to kiss him back, my lips parting, a flush of heat rushing over my body. But then my senses quickly asserted themselves and I jerked away, breaking contact with his lips.

"What the hell are you doing?" I gasped.

Bastien looked at me with a curious tilt of his head. "Wanted to see what all the fuss was about. Honestly? I was expecting better."

*Huh?*

Cold metal clicked and tightened around my wrist before I could process that, and I looked down to see that my right hand was now handcuffed to the metal rack that was bolted into the stone wall. "What—"

Oh, shit.

This wasn't Bastien at all.

"No!"

His fist slammed into my face. My head ricocheted off the metal wine rack, senses spinning. The fake glasses went clattering over the floor, and I was only dimly aware of a second handcuff roughly securing my left hand to another part of the wine rack, leaving me facing the open room, arms locked far from each other. I felt blood spilling down my cheek.

"S-Saranthiel..." I slurred. Everything still spun, but I

latched onto anger and the focus it offered. "You...bitch. You bitch! What did you do to him?" Bastien was one of the best people I'd ever known. But she was him and that meant he was dead. Probably had been for years. And it was, once again, my fault.

Saranthiel smiled smugly. "Did you think this would work?" The demon taunted me with Bastien's voice as he pulled off my wig. "Did you think I don't know the name and face of every single person who works in this hotel? In this town?" He grabbed my necklace and yanked. The chain snapped against my neck, stripping me of my last disguise.

I struggled, pulling at the cuffs as hard as I could. They clanged against the wine rack behind me and bit into my wrists. "I'm gonna kill you!" I screamed. "You're gonna pay for this, Saranthiel! I am going to *kill you*!"

"Please. You and your little cadre of misfits?" Saranthiel scoffed. "Remiel has no army. You have no weapons, no power..." He looked at my wrists, smiling, and I realized the full extent of what he had done. I had no way of unlocking my magic with my wrists this far apart. The thought drove me into more of a frenzy of straining against the cuffs, screaming, pulling in every direction, but all this did was leave me panting. "No hope. You have nothing, demon's witch. And that is how it will stay either until you agree to work for me—"

"Never!"

"—or I kill you. After I've killed or driven mad the remainder of your friends, of course. Perhaps a little more blood on your conscience will change your mind. You are *so* easily motivated by guilt."

I glowered at him. "If you think I'll ever agree to make more hosts for you, you may as well kill me right now."

"We both know your morality is a little more flexible than that." Saranthiel reached around my waist, though I tried to twist away, and pulled my phone out from my back pocket. He dropped it on the floor and crushed it beneath his heel. "This has been fun, but I have guests to welcome and a blushing bride to attend to. I'll leave you some company, though."

He gave me a patronizing smile and went to the door to the wine fridge, holding it open as a hellhound prowled in. "Keep watch. Kill anyone who tries to come in." The beast growled in reply, and Bastien's hand chucked under its chin like it was a beloved pet. "No, but all your friends will be here soon enough." The hellhound whuffed and walked to the far side of the tasting table, out of sight of the door. Saranthiel addressed me again. "Consider the offer, McKenna. If you do, whoever remains of your loved ones may be spared." My eyes went wide in horror. Saranthiel smiled. It was Bastien's smile, but with nothing of him in it. "Once the screaming starts, I can't make any promises about the outcomes."

"No! No, stop, we—we can make a different deal, I—"

"I told you what I want and you turned me down, demon's witch," Saranthiel said, cutting me off. "Now you will learn the price of that refusal. We'll talk later."

I screamed in rage, pulling and twisting at the cuffs, and kept it up well after the cellar door closed behind him. I tried everything: pulling at the wine rack, squeezing my hand through the cuff, pulling at the links, working every potential weak point. Nothing. The hellhound stared at me with rotted, unblinking eyes, its breath rattling in its half-formed throat, unimpressed and stinking up the room with both its breath and its presence.

"Stop looking at me!" I snapped.

It did not.

Increasingly desperate, I cast my eyes around the room, looking for something, anything, to help, but anything that might've been useful was well out of reach. I could stretch my fingers enough to reach a few bottles of wine, but couldn't think of anything to use them for. My feet could barely reach the edge of the tasting table, but there was nothing useful there, either.

"A little magic would be really fucking helpful right about now." Staring at my wrists, I tried to force my magic out, throwing every ounce of my will behind it, calling out the words to unlock the wards along with a few others. Though I felt my power within me, as always, it couldn't get past the chains I'd placed on it. "Not using my magic really *is* gonna kill me."

Or was it? Maybe I could scrape my wrist deep enough, disrupt the line of the tattoo, break the wards through sheer brute physical force. It was worth a shot.

I wrenched my left wrist against the metal as hard as I could to cut into the skin, gritting my teeth in effort. A horrible, hot, biting pain erupted and blood spilled over my fingers, staining the sleeve of my shirt, but the ward held strong. I stopped with a cry, slumping back against the wine racks, my wrist on fire from the one attempt. Maybe if I had more time… but I didn't. I looked at the hellhound, wondering if

I could trick it into biting my wrist somehow. I didn't relish the idea of losing a hand, but I'd take it over everyone I loved being dead or driven mad.

Stupid useless tears spilled down my face. I was stuck here, I couldn't get out on my own, and no one was going to find me in time to make any difference. Years of running, a week of realization, days of careful planning, and all I had to show for it was a bloody wrist and a stockpile of magic I couldn't use.

*It can't end like this.* I couldn't even sit with my hands pinioned as they were, so I had to settle for slumping uncomfortably against the wine rack. *Not after everything. My mom, Cameron, Jackie. Even Brooke! And Bastien, seven hells.*

How had I not seen it? Saranthiel had hidden better than I'd realized. But with Brooke saying "her," I'd assumed. And Bastien had been so very Bastien-like. Kind, compassionate, practical. I'd even seen him use portal magic; I had no idea how Saranthiel had pulled that off. I wouldn't have expected her to have access even to Jackie's magic, much less cast outside the girl's specialty so easily.

Unless...

*Unless she's not Bastien!*

I struggled anew against the cuffs. But there was still nothing I could do to even loosen them. "Dammit! Okay, fine. Hey, hellhound, come on, you must be hungry right? Wanna snack on this?" I asked, flipping the beast off with my left hand. It growled at me, lumbering to its feet. Wait, was this actually going to work?

But it wasn't looking at me; it was looking at the door. I heard the door above open. Footsteps on the stairs.

"HELP!" I screamed, rattling the handcuffs against the metal. "HELP ME!"

The hellhound growled, taking a few steps forward, ready to go for the kill. The footsteps hastened and Laurent Lemaire appeared in the wine cellar, squinting over toward the refrigerated section and doing a double take when he saw me. Not quite the savior I was hoping for, but better than nothing. The hellhound growled and started to move.

"Laurent! There's a hellhound!" I warned him. As he reached the glass door, the hellhound sprang forward, the thick glass shattering around it. But Laurent Lemaire was no slouch; he sidestepped and easily opened a portal in its path, snipping it closed just as quickly after the beast's leap carried it through into whatever dark place sat on the other side. Laurent looked at the mess with a displeased look, stepping over the glass and brushing some from his suit.

"McKenna Ellerbeck?" Laurent said, his voice as gravelly and unhurried as I remembered. "What the hell is this?"

"Get me out of here. Bastien is about to marry an Archdemon and hand her the keys to Arcadia," I said, "and I'm the only one who can stop her."

# Chapter 21
# Between a Demon and a Dark Place

Laurent was utterly unimpressed by my warning as he approached. Where he'd once had a ring of white hair around his head, he was now completely bald, and his well-trimmed beard and mustache were fully white, all hints of the family blond gone. His gravelly voice was the same as ever, hard and unyielding as stone. "You go missing for ten years and then turn up in my hotel, handcuffed to the wall with a hellhound standing by, crying demon like the rest of your family? You're not going anywhere until you explain yourself."

"You think I did this myself? We don't have time for the long story. Your entire family's lives are in danger right this second. If I'm right, and I am, the entire town is in danger, and that's just in the immediate future."

He crossed his arms and waited.

"Salt and chalk, seriously? Fine, tell me what you wanna

hear so we can get out of here already!"

"You could start with why and how my grandson would be marrying an Archdemon," the old man said, "when I'm fairly certain he's marrying Mariposa Perez, a girl he's known his entire life."

"I don't know exactly what happened to Mari, but my guess is she's been dead since that cliff diving accident. That thing upstairs wearing her face is a demon in a human host body."

"That's not possible."

"I wish it weren't, but it's the truth."

"It isn't possible!" Laurent loomed up at me, angrier than I'd ever seen him. Even more than when a certain stubborn, self-righteous, know-it-all teenage girl had refused to bend the knee, so to speak. He raked his fingers over his short beard, and I was close enough to notice that the gesture was intended to mask their shaking. He wasn't just angry—he was *afraid*. "Unless, Miss Ellerbeck, you've got something else to tell me."

The idea that he knew sent a chill through me for a split second. But I'd refused to be cowed by him when I was sixteen and I wasn't about to start now. "I don't know, you wanna tell me how you know more about my magic than anyone in my family, Laurent?"

"Ladies first."

We glared at each other until I relented first, rolling my eyes. "We don't have time for this. Fine, yes, I unwillingly and unknowingly created a demon host ten years ago, and you're going to have to accept that I had no idea until a few days ago. You want the whole sordid tale, I'll step into your ring of truth and tell it if we live through this, but right now you need to *let me go*." I jangled the cuffs, sending bolts of pain through me. "Unless you'd rather wait until after the demon army marches through your hotel."

Laurent turned his eyes to the cuffs and then touched one with his finger. "*Dégage*." One cuff fell open, the other a moment later as he repeated the spell. I brought up my hands, flexing my fingers and gingerly rolling my wrists. I crossed them to align the runes, wincing.

"*Resera*," I said. The release of magic flowed freely through my body, and I cast a quick healing spell. "*Sana*." Healing wasn't my forte, but even the minor relief that the spell brought was welcome.

"You plan on telling me who we're up against?" Laurent asked.

"Are they married yet? Did they sign the grimoires?"

Laurent gave a curt nod. "They finished the ceremony just before I came down here."

"Shit." I stepped over the glass and power-walked to the stairs. "That means she has his magic already. It's Saranthiel, the Archdemon of—"

"Of Madness."

I shot him a look over my shoulder as we went up the stairs. "I'm not the only one who's going to have questions to answer after this." He grunted noncommittally. "She used my mom and brother to weaken the barrier over the last ten years, but the real plan was signing that grimoire and getting portal magic. And she mentioned some last-minute guests. Seems a pretty safe assumption she's about to rip open a portal to the Pit and walk her army of minions right into Arcadia Commons."

Laurent cursed under his breath. "In the flesh and ready to slaughter the most powerful witch families in the States." He ran a hand over his beard again. "You've really done it this time, girl."

I stopped short of the door to the kitchen and whirled on him so fast he backed down a step. "*Me?* If you assholes had listened to my mom or Cameron about the barrier, you might've caught on to this years ago!"

"This town didn't have a demon problem in over two centuries until—"

"Until *nothing*," I cut in. "Do you seriously think all this is on a choice a teenage girl made twelve years ago? That it has nothing to do with how you and yours shut out my family and told us nothing about our magic and how it was fueling the barrier? How you've looked down on hedgewitches for generations now? I made some bad choices, but don't think for a second you can blame me when you had all the power and choose to hoard it. But like I said, we don't have time for this, so either help me or stay out of my way."

His mouth was a line, his eyes hardening with hate. "Younger witches. Not a single one of you is worth the trouble you cause. At least your father had the sense to stay gone when he left." *What the hell does he know about my dad?* "But we don't have the time," Laurent replied, throwing my words back at me before I could ask.

He walked through the kitchen to the door that led to the ballroom. Everyone was seated for dinner, the sound of pleasant chatter and laughter mingling with dinnertime music over the speakers. "Since our interests are aligned, and I need your particular talents to get out of this, you can earn your keep and clean up the mess you made."

I had to clench my hands tightly to contain my fury. This asshole hadn't listened to a thing I'd said, didn't care for a second to consider that any of this might fall back on him. That's when I finally realized that he didn't have any answers for me and never would. He only had answers for himself. If there was any hidden truth to why my father left, to what my magic was really about, it was on me to find it for myself.

Didn't change the fact that, for now, I had no choice but to trust him.

"Not exactly death and destruction out there," Laurent said.

"Of course not. Killing you along with everyone else at the same time is part of her plan."

"Then there's not much reason for me to stick out my neck and get us all killed."

"Every hook needs bait." I scanned the room, searching the faces for my friends. I'd just gotten them back. I couldn't lose them again so soon. I stared at Mari, so convincingly human and beaming next to her new husband, and Bastien, smiling even though he knew someone here was a demon, because he had no idea it was his wife.

I shook off the distracting thoughts and found the face I was looking for: Tom Harwell. "Here's the plan."

Sure enough, when Laurent Lemaire walked back in and took his seat—after pausing briefly to say something to Tom—it was only moments later that the happy couple waved down the microphone from the DJ. I watched from behind the kitchen, waiting for the moment. Saranthiel and Bastien stood together, his arm around her waist as he held the mic in the other hand.

"Thank you everyone! Mari and I are so thrilled to have all our closest friends and family here," Bastien said, smiling at the room.

"We'll get to our first dance very soon," Saranthiel said in Mari's sweet voice. Now that I knew she was a demon, I finally had a legitimate reason for hating the sound of it. "But before we do, I have to beg your indulgence for a little demonstration."

*Already?* I straightened, glancing over at Laurent. Sure enough, he rose to his feet.

"No need to rush, we haven't even toasted the happy couple yet," he said, lifting his glass.

"We'll toast after, Laurent. We'll have even more reason to!" Saranthiel said, smoothly dismissing the protest.

"But—"

"Grandfather, please. This is important to Mari and me," Bastien said, motioning for him to take his seat. Mari led the way for the two of them to the dance floor.

My eyes went to Tom, his brows scrunched in concentration.

*Tom? Didn't you warn Bastien!* I thought, knowing he was listening.

*I'm trying, I can't get through! Something's blocking me, it's like I'm yelling into a pile of blankets, the sound's getting swallowed up,* Tom replied.

Looking back at Bastien, I took a breath and summoned a

touch of power, hoping Saranthiel was too distracted to notice it. It was barely even a spell, just enough to boost my vision and let me see the powers at play in his aura...

"As you all know, Mari had a terrible accident some years ago..." Bastien was saying.

Sure enough, there it was. Along with the blue pulse of his magic, brightest around his hands, a cloud of shadow circled Bastien's head. Saranthiel's power.

It wasn't infecting him, as it had Cameron and the werewolves, but it *was* interfering.

*It's her power. We can't get to him, and she might use it to mess with his head*, I told Tom.

*Can you get rid of it like you—ah!* What I could only describe as the equivalent of a spike in the telepathic feedback. Out in the ballroom, Tom cried out aloud, grabbing his head. His mother and father were rubbing at their temples as well.

*Tom! Are you okay?* Even as I asked, I felt the slithering along my skin, along my nerves, creeping into my blood as stars erupted in my vision.

---•---

The next thing I knew, I was on the ground, my vision fuzzy and my head pounding. I started to sit up and felt everything tilt around me, pain throbbing along the side of my head. I gripped the floor, panting for breath, trying to steady myself. Somewhere people were yelling. I gingerly touched my head and winced at the sticky feel of blood matting my hair, the tenderness of a bruise-to-be.

I remembered falling—I must have hit my head on the floor and knocked myself out. That explained a few things, and remembering why explained the rest. I gasped, jerking upward, and immediately regretted it as I fought a wave of nausea. Of course, given my hammering heart, short breaths, and the urge to run for my life because the thing of my nightmares was on the other side of the door, I had to conclude that my nausea was at least partly panic-induced.

*I have to move, have to go, have to run—no. Help. I have to help. But how the hell am I going to help now?* The last thing I'd seen, the thing that had sent my senses reeling and me crashing to the floor, was the true form of Saranthiel as she ripped open a hole in the fabric of the world to the Pit itself. I could still feel the corruption pouring off it and her, the glimpse of other demons, too many demons, her army ready to run us down—no, there was no hope for Plan B or C or whatever. *It's over, it's hopeless, the best any of us can do is run like hell. Why did I think I could help? I can't beat her!*

I struggled to my feet, hauling myself up along one of the kitchen counters. There, across the room, was a door with a lit EXIT sign above it. Saranthiel thought I was still chained up. I could get out of here, find a way to disappear again before she realized. Just had to lock my wards... I leaned against the counter and brought up my wrists, wavering as I tried to cross them. One word and I would disappear, I would be safe. Needed to concentrate. If those people would just stop yelling...

Not yelling. Screaming.

*"Once the screaming starts, I can't make any promises about the outcomes."*

I stared at the door to the ballroom. Then back at the EXIT sign.

I'd been the person who runs. If I left I'd live, sure. For a while at least. But this? This would never stop. Saranthiel would never stop looking for me, and in the meantime, she would kill everyone I loved. Or worse. And I knew now, deep down, that this was not the person I wanted to be anymore. I wanted to be the person who had a home, family, friends. I wanted my life back. To stop running and finally save myself and everyone else. To be my own black knight.

"*Sana.*" My head wound healed enough for me to reclaim my senses, as much as I could in the circumstances. Time for Plan...whatever letter we were on, call it Omega. Because this was absolutely our last chance. I kicked open the door to the ballroom and walked into hell.

---

The ballroom was chaos and noise. It all centered on the enormous portal, with ragged edges that oozed shadows into the air while hellhounds and other demons poured out into the room. Only the presence of so many powerful witches kept them from having overwhelmed the place entirely, but the witches were fighting at half strength. Some of them threw spells while others were unconscious, injured, or in the throes of madness. Lucca and Chris were in their wolf forms, throwing themselves against the demons, but their efforts were hampered by needing to avoid their claws and teeth or risk going mad themselves. I was more than a little shocked to see

Remi fighting alongside them, cutting down demons with her manifested shadowblade. I couldn't see Leo, Brooke, or a lot of the others, and I hoped that meant they were part of the group hiding behind the bar and overturned tables. From the look of things, I'd been knocked out for a minute or two at most.

In the center of the floor, the Archdemon of Madness stood triumphant, its form somewhere between its true self and Mari Perez, hands extended and surrounded by red-tinged shadows, a match to the edges of the portal she was holding open. Beside her stood Bastien, throwing spells of his own—it took me a second to realize that he was closing portals his family was trying to open, presumably to escape. Saranthiel had him under her control, making him see what she wanted him to see. The same thing she'd done to me when she tricked me into killing Jackie.

I was *not* about to let her do that to him.

With barely a thought, my power snapped to life within me, quick to answer the call, eager, a dog pulling at a chain it had been on too long. It, and I, had forgotten the taste of freedom, had believed the small space we had been occupying was all there was. Now it was time to let go and bring down the bitch who had shackled me. This time when I reached for my magic, I summoned it up in huge handfuls, more than I'd ever used at one go before. Wordless, I thrust my hands open, shooting golden threads of magic out into the room. The thin filaments latched onto the darkness, the infectious bits of demonic power on the humans in the room, and I felt it every shred of it through those lines. More than I'd felt in the woods, less than I'd felt from the barrier, but like both of those times, the power felt familiar, as if it had always been mine and could be again if I claimed it. Then, as I had in the forest, I *pulled*.

The maddening darkness shot out of the infected humans instantly. The darkness swirled around my hands, a mass of shadows interwoven with the golden threads of my magic, waiting to be claimed. The now freed humans and witches collapsed at the release.

All but one. At Saranthiel's side, Bastien cried out, doubling over and grabbing at his head. The darkness that infected him clung stubbornly; considering it came directly from the Archdemon herself, I wasn't surprised. I dismissed the shadows I'd already pulled out and sent the threads of my magic to weave and wrap around the strand connecting to him, reinforcing it. I grasped it with both hands and pulled again, physically and mystically.

"Mari!" he cried out as he staggered a few steps in my direction. "Help!"

Saranthiel whipped around. Her eyes, now full black, were surprised and then irritated. "Demon's witch! I didn't think you'd escape so soon. You may be cleverer than I gave you credit for." She let out a whistle, jerked her head at me, and three hellhounds coming out of the portal barreled at me full-tilt.

I had no choice but to release my hold on Bastien to defend myself, throwing out a hand at them. "*Repello!*" The blast of force sent one sprawling into a table. The other two kept coming. "*Prote—*"

But before the spell was done, the first of them slammed into me. I crashed into the wood parquet floor, sharp pain erupting along my rib cage and leaving me gasping. This hellhound was much more solid than the ragged, rotting ones I'd faced before, and those had been no slouches in a fight. Its frothing mouth lunged at me; I twisted, or tried to, but its teeth sank into my shoulder and I screamed. These dogs weren't messing around trying to infect me with madness this time. Then a second explosion of pain shot up my leg as the other one latched its teeth onto my ankle, trying to shred my boot and get to my flesh. My world was an inferno of pain, every breath, every scream and twitch; I couldn't stop it, I couldn't control it, and I realized I couldn't breathe for the weight of the demon on my chest. Stars shot through my vision, with darkness creeping in behind as I gasped.

"Bad dog!"

A spray of blood, a howl of pain, and the death grip on my shoulder suddenly let up. A dark line flashed through the air and the hellhound was bodily kicked off me. Air rushed into my lungs. Still horribly painful, but at least I could breathe. Lifting my head through a wave of vertigo, I saw Leo kicking the decapitated head of the hound that had been biting my leg away. She was holding a blood-covered carving knife in one hand, and her red dress was stained. She grabbed one of my arms while someone grabbed another; I dizzily looked to see Remi. Past her, I saw Lucca, in wolf form, rip the throat out of the hound that had been on my chest.

"You okay, Mickey?" Leo asked.

"Better now," I rasped as loud as I dared.

"I'll heal you," Remi quickly offered but I shook my head, wincing at the pain that set off in my shoulder.

"No. I need blood for this." That had been my mistake earlier, backward as it sounded. I'd been focused on being rid of the pain and confusion so I could join the fight, but too rushed to remember I needed blood for this to work.

Saranthiel and Bastien had turned their attention back to the rest of the room. She was yelling orders to her army, and he was back to canceling portals opened by others. A few of the minions were turning our way, however.

Lucca barked as he joined us, looking me over. "Thanks, Lucca. Can you keep them off me?" He barked again and lunged at the next hellhound headed our way.

"I'll back up the furball. You got this?" Remi checked. I nodded and with a last look, she spun her shadowblade in her hand and dove after him.

"What can I do?" Leo asked.

"Make sure I don't fall over," I said. "I've got an idea but I kind of can't stand on my own right now."

Leo secured an arm around my waist; I leaned against her, one arm around her in turn, taking the weight off my injured leg. I gathered my magic, reaching once again into that store within me. It was less than it had been, I could tell, but it was still considerable. Enough for this, I hoped.

With my good arm, I shot tendrils of light at Bastien once again. With my blood freshly spilled, the power was even more intense than before, even using only one hand. "Saranthiel!" I yelled, coughing. "I'm not done fighting over a boy with you yet!"

Snarling, Saranthiel spun on her heel, though her hands were still occupied with holding open the portal. I'd seen plenty of portal spells before; they're one and done, a spell to open and a spell to close. But she had to focus to keep this one going. There could be a dozen different reasons, from inexperience to opposition to impossibility, but what mattered was that she had to work at it.

"You are damn annoying, demon's witch." With one hand, she directed some of her power against me, renewing our war over the darkness infecting Bastien.

"Everyone needs a hobby," I grunted.

"I recommend you take up running and hiding again. You were good at that."

"Yeah, I guess I—needed a new challenge—" I gritted my teeth, fighting her as hard as I could with my focus split. Leo tightened her hold as the Archdemon's mystical force became physical, forcing us forward a step.

"You are outmatched, demon's witch," Saranthiel hissed.

"You know, on second thought, who am I to get in the way of true love?" Pulling my arm from behind Leo, I threw the magic I'd been concentrating in my other hand at her, releasing the threads on Bastien at the same time. "*Lux in tenebris!*"

The lack of resistance threw her off, followed by the light spell colliding with them both at once. The portal flickered, and the darkness around Bastien's head broke apart, the solid mass becoming cloudlike wisps. He blinked in confusion. "What...?"

I threw out the threads one last time and pulled them in. The shadows rushed to my hands, shot through with gold once again, and I didn't hesitate to dismiss them. "Bastien, the portal! Close it!"

The groom staggered to his feet, quickly taking in the situation and turning to the dark portal to the Pit. *"Ferme la porte!"* The blue light of his magic crackled along the edge of the portal, weaving unevenly along the ragged edges, and it began to shrink and close, but Saranthiel roared and threw her own magic back into it. Red and black and blue, witch and demon fought for control, neither gaining nor losing, until the demon lost her patience.

"Enough of this!" She backhanded Bastien, a blow hard enough to send him sprawling backward across the floor, landing a few feet from Leo and me. "You might've been useful to keep around, mortal, but I have what I need." She let the portal close behind her as she stalked forward, her skin growing mottled and her fingers extending into the too-long claws of her true form, darkness gathering and crackling along their edges as she drew her arm back to strike. Exactly what they'd looked like before she'd plunged them into Cameron's skull and driven him truly, irrevocably, mad.

"NO!" It wasn't even a choice. I threw myself forward, injuries be damned, landing on top of Bastien, placing myself firmly between him and Saranthiel, waiting for the spear of her claws into my head, my back, waiting for the madness to claim me.

It never came.

I opened my eyes, found myself staring into Bastien's blue-gray ones, wide as I'd ever seen them. "McKenna...?" His gaze flicked from my face to something behind me.

I slowly turned to look behind me. Saranthiel's claws had stopped inches from me, so close I could feel the sickening wrongness of them dripping onto my face, seeping into my eyes, threatening to blur my vision. But I fought it off, somehow. I looked up at the Archdemon of Madness, but this time, I didn't go mad.

It was then I finally realized why Saranthiel had never killed me, never driven me mad, not ten years ago and not now. She had harassed me, manipulated me, hurt and terrorized me, but despite knowing exactly where I was since the night I got back to this town, she had never truly threatened *me*. She couldn't. Because I was the *only* one who could make her host bodies, and she knew it.

For the first time, I looked at her and I wasn't afraid. She needed me and now *I* knew it. And that was something I could work with.

"Saranthiel. Let's make a deal."

# Chapter 22
# The Demon's Witch

Saranthiel's pitch-black eyes gleamed at my words, at the nervous tremor I put into them. She smiled like the cat who caught the canary, pulling back and lowering her claws. "You're finally learning. Good. Give me your loyalty as my sworn thrall and I will allow your friends and family to live."

I scoffed and tried to stand but ended up falling off Bastien and onto my ass. "Pass. Not my first rodeo, Your Madness. I'm not selling my soul without some fine print."

"McKenna, what are you doing?" Bastien said, helping me to my feet. "You can't do this!"

I had to sell this. "I have to, Bastien. We can't win, not now. I'm sorry I didn't get here in time."

He looked past me at her, his eyes bright with anger. "You have nothing to be sorry for. I'm the one who didn't see that I was marrying a demon. If anyone should be making a deal for the rest of us, it's me."

"No!" I turned, pressing my hands against his chest. His

whole body was tense, his glare unmoving, everything in him flipped to its darkest side. "This is on *me*. The only reason she ever got close to you was because I screwed up. I've been where you are right now, Bast. You saw what I did, you felt what I felt." Finally, finally, his eyes met mine, and it was like looking in a mirror straight into my past. "Listen to me. Pretty soon this is all just going to be before and after. But right now, you're in between, and that's exactly when the worst ideas seem like the only ones. Don't fall for it, don't screw up your life like I did. Don't make a choice you will never get to take back."

"And what about you? Taking it all on yourself alone is the mistake you made last time."

"I promise I'm not." I prayed he'd understand. "I have you. I have all of you. I know that now; I should've always known that. But this move has to be mine. Please."

Despite the yelling, fighting, and chaos around us, for a moment it seemed the room held its breath until his shoulders dropped and I knew he was relenting. Then he gave me a swift, unexpected hug. "Don't disappear again." Even at a whisper, his voice cracked.

"I won't."

He released me and I turned to face the Archdemon, carefully letting go of Bastien and standing under my own power. I hoped I didn't have to make any more sudden moves, or I'd be eating the parquet again. For that matter, I was also fairly tapped out magically. Most of my ten-year reserve had been used up in taming the shadows and freeing Bastien. "Let's talk terms."

"Very well." Saranthiel's eyes glinted, still full black though the rest of her had shifted back to looking like Mari. Something about the battle, or maybe the proximity of the Pit, had made her lose her hold on her human visage, host body or no. With the portal closed, the effect was gone, and so was her army. The wolves, witches, and Remi had finished off the last of the ones in the ballroom. Now the guests waited uneasily, witnesses for a second time today to a very different and unholy union. Saranthiel craned her neck to take them all in, unbothered by the numbers seemingly stacked against her. "Looks like we are not yet done with the 'I dos.' The fine print, then, is this: You will make more hosts for me, without question and without objection. After all"—she gestured to Mari's body—"your work is flawless."

The admission caused a ripple of surprise among the witches. More than a few of them were putting two and two together—including Mariposa's mother, Sofia Perez.

"You did this to her? You killed my baby and turned her into this abomination?" Sofia demanded, her face tearstained and furious.

I flinched, but shook my head. "No. I had nothing to do with what happened to Mari."

"But you secured this body for me all the same. Shall I tell them how, or would you like the honors?"

There was no getting out of this now, and if I let her do it, it would be the worst possible version of things. I glanced at the Harwells, at Tom, his father Doug and his mother Helen, then away just as quickly. "I'll do it."

Saranthiel made a sweeping gesture. "The floor is yours."

Scanning the faces of the gathered witches, I was suddenly a teenager on trial all over again. But this time instead of the local Council members, I stood before the judgment of every major witch family in this half of the States. I clenched my hands to keep them from shaking, and couldn't look anyone in the eye.

"I—I killed Jackie Harwell." I forced the words out. "I made her into a demon host."

"No!" Helen Harwell sobbed, the sound of it a stab in the gut. I risked a glimpse and saw her collapse against her husband; Doug caught her but stared at me in wordless horror.

"I'm sorry, I'm so sorry. Saranthiel—"

"That will do. On to our business," Saranthiel interrupted.

"No! No, that's not the whole story!" I objected.

"My patience is long but not limitless," she snapped. "And your friends are not invulnerable pending the execution of our agreement."

"Okay! Okay, I get it. Fine. I want your guarantee that none of them will be hurt. My friends, my family, anyone in this room is off limits."

Saranthiel eyed them like she was looking for a horse to buy. "A regrettable loss of talent, but very well. Those in this room and your existing friends and family shall not be harmed by me."

"Nor by your orders or by anyone who answers to you."

She rolled her eyes. "Very well. Agreed. They shall agree in turn to do the same for me—no harm shall be done to me and mine by those for whom you claim protection."

I shook my head. "No way. This is my deal, and none of them answer to me."

"Then they had best remember that if my safety is compromised, their own is no longer guaranteed." Her black gaze slid across the room, connecting with each person present and still breathing.

I swallowed. "... Fine. I also want my mom and my brother restored to full health."

Those black orbs connected to mine, and she gave me a sickening grin. "A life for a life, demon's witch. I can restore one of them, but you will have to choose."

"No. Both of them or no deal."

Saranthiel merely shrugged. "There are laws even I cannot break."

I ran a hand through my hair, taking heavy breaths. Casting about, I found Remi, who sadly nodded. Saranthiel wasn't lying. Dammit.

I closed my eyes, taking a moment before deciding. "Cameron. And you'll do it immediately, not ten or twenty years from now."

"Very well. Unless..."

I raised my eyebrow, wary. "Unless what?"

"It occurs to me that here you are, bargaining away your soul, for the protection of your peers. But they aren't really your peers, are they? They never were."

"What are you saying?"

"I'm saying that if not for them and how they treated you, you would never have been driven to seek out Forneus," she replied. The way she echoed what Bastien had said to me back at the Whale's Jaw was eerie. She turned to gesture at them. "Always setting you apart, letting your family live with the shame of lacking true magical power. Do you think none of them knew what your family sacrificed to protect this town? Of course they did. And they took it as a given that you were happy to continue bearing that burden. They didn't even have the courtesy to inform you, much less offer you a choice."

I looked at them. At Laurent, who had implied as much earlier in the night. He looked hardened as ever, but others among them were more easily shaken, looking away or at one another.

"Tell me, what have they done, any of them, to earn yet more sacrifice from you? In fact"—she turned back to me—"I'll make you a special offer. Choose one of them, any one of them, to be bound to me as well, and your mother will be healed. Seeing as how every resident of this town owes you and yours for keeping them safe, let's let them balance the scales. Laurent's a tempting one, isn't he?" My eyes darted to the old man. "He's the one who took your mother's magic. Wouldn't it be fitting for him to give her back her mind?"

"You—you can't do that. A bargain has to be made willingly."

"You think I can't make them willing?" she purred. "I can do many things, demon's witch. I can answer all the questions you have about your family. From dear old Thomasin Younger to your own mysteriously absent father. I can tell you more about your magic than any of them could dream of knowing. I can give you your mother and your brother back, and keep all of your loved ones safe forever. Give me a name, swear you'll make all the hosts I require, and it will be done."

I was tempted. I'd love to pretend I didn't scan those

gathered before me and think of all the things they'd done—or, more accurately, all the things they *hadn't* done. The loneliness and desperation I'd felt as a teenager; the tormenting endured by my brother and myself; the anger for the ten years I'd lost; the guilt for everything I'd been forced to do along the way, all in the name of keeping safe the town that had never welcomed me, and the people who had taken away my family's choice. The darkest parts of my heart whispered to me that they deserved it, that it was right, that they *owed* me.

But then my eyes fell on two people: Brooke and Remi.

Brooke had come to stand by her husband, looking as tremulous as she must have all those years ago in her family's flooded house, alone and about to die, with this same voice whispering promises of salvation in her ear, only to learn that all her choices had been taken from her. Brooke, who, despite finding love, a new family, new friends, was and always would be trapped.

And Remi, shadowblade still in hand as she stood near them, who despite her many faults and failings had protected the people she once would've preyed upon. Remi, who had fought to understand what it meant to be human, because of me, even though it was against her nature and every instinct; who had refused to take any thralls even though it left her vulnerable. Remi saw my gaze and lifted a fist to her heart, to that black knight tattoo.

We'd all been cast out, made to think we were alone, and we'd believed it. We'd let it run and ruin our lives, and not just ours, for that matter. It had to stop. We had to stop letting them—the Council, Saranthiel, anyone—dictate to us that we were in this alone, or that we deserved to be, just because they said so.

I faced the demon. "The only name you're getting from me is McKenna Ellerbeck. The only soul I have to sell is mine. Sorry not sorry you're getting sloppy demon seconds on it."

Saranthiel shrugged, unbothered. "Have your noble sacrifice, then. In that case, I believe we are settled: protection both ways for the aforementioned parties, your brother's health to be restored in full, and in exchange you will make as many demon hosts as I require, you will give me your full loyalty for the rest of your natural life, and your soul is mine to claim upon your passing. Are we agreed?"

"And you will never possess my body."

"Why would I when I have a perfectly good one of my own?"

A hundred other stipulations jumped to mind, but I knew I would either be shot down, be made to give up more, or finally try her patience too much and get us all killed. So I nodded. "Agreed."

"So mote it be." Saranthiel held out her hand.

"Oh, no," I said, shaking my head. "One more point of order. You will not physically touch me or anyone in my family ever again. I know what happens to people who touch you."

Her gaze narrowed. "The deal must be sealed, demon's witch."

"Then we sign it on paper like normal humans," I suggested.

"I grow impatient," Saranthiel said, her hand rippling as her long, shadowed claws emerged.

"Okay, okay! Paper copies take a while, I get it," I replied. I scanned the room, my eyes landing on the bar in the back. "How about we drink on it?"

After a pause, she nodded. "That will suffice. Brooke! Bring us two glasses of champagne."

Brooke started at suddenly being included in this. Exchanging an uncertain glance with Lucca, she let go of his hand and walked the path that cleared for her back to the bar. A series of champagne glasses had been set out, though many of them were now shattered, and none of those remaining were full. Brooke managed to find two unbroken ones, then popped open a magnum to pour as everyone watched her. I caught Laurent's eye briefly, then turned back to Saranthiel while we waited.

"So this was your real plan all along, even back then, wasn't it? Getting me to be your thrall?" I said, drawing her attention back to me.

She smiled Mari's smug smile. "Always. I knew where your real talents lay."

"Forneus must've known. Why didn't he ever make me create hosts?"

"It's a delicate thing, making a host. You were too new to take on that kind of spell from the start. He didn't want just any witch, he wanted a *good* witch. Well—a talented one." Her smile twisted into a smirk at the backhanded compliment.

"And why did *you* bother being a good witch? Why bother with any of this charade? You could've forced the grimoire ritual at any time," I asked.

"Are you always going to ask this many questions?"

I smiled stubbornly. She rolled her eyes. "Because it had to be real. Your human magic is influenced by your emotions, your thoughts. I wasn't going to take any chances, so I made sure it was genuine in every sense. The plan had been to get him to fall for his lifelong best friend, but you and Remiel ruined that avenue." Bastien glared at her, his hands twitching in anger at her speaking as though he weren't there at all. I credited his strong control for not blasting her with a spell on the spot. "But a new opportunity presented itself with the redemption of poor Mariposa Perez, sapped of her magic and turning over a new leaf," she cooed in a saccharine voice.

"So you did kill her? Or was her death just an accident?"

Her black eyes glittered. "Some secrets must be kept. But I should thank you—without you, this little love match never would've been possible."

My brow arched again. "What are you talking about?"

"She based Mari's change of heart on you." We both turned as Brooke answered the question. Two champagne flutes trembled in her hands as she held them out, her eyes downcast. "She, she asked me how to make Bastien fall in love with her and...and the only things I knew for sure were things about you. I told her everything I knew about you and your relationship with him. That was her model for pretending to be Mari." Brooke looked up, not at us but behind us at Bastien. "I'm sorry, Bastien, I'm so sor—"

"*Don't* speak to me." His voice was as cold as ice, as rigid as the rest of him.

Brooke looked away from him, tears slipping down her

cheeks. Saranthiel plucked one of the glasses from her, and I went to take the other.

"Don't do this!" Brooke blurted out as I reached for it. "You got free once, McKenna, don't do this again!"

Saranthiel hissed at her. "Traitor!" Brooke cowered; the Archdemon took the glass and shoved it into my hand. Some of the bubbles slopped over the edge and over my hand, but I made no move to stop them. "I've been too easy on your transgressions of late. We will discuss this later."

I touched Brooke's arm gently. "It's okay, Brooke. At least I know what I'm getting into this time. This is the only way."

Brooke blinked back tears but nodded and stepped back. Saranthiel and I faced each other, glasses in hand.

"We have a Bargain, demon's witch."

"We have a Bargain."

Our glasses clinked and we drank. I gulped down the entire glass and watched her do the same. I felt the heavy weight of my deal with the Archdemon settle upon me, and I prayed to whatever forces of good there may be that this was going to work. She threw the glass to the floor when finished. I did, too, because why the hell not? I was freshly damned.

"Is my brother healed, or do we need to go to him for that?"

"We'll need to go there, and as I did say immediately..." She gestured with her hands to open a portal, the same motions Bastien and his family used. A small tear appeared, red and black, blood and darkness ripping at the fabric of the world like an uneven wound. The washed-out lighting of a hospital room peeked out from behind it—but then the portal closed itself, winking out of existence before it could complete. "What is—" But her question was cut off by a fit of ragged coughing and she grabbed at her throat.

Brooke gasped. "What's happening to her? What did you do?"

"Dosed her with anti-magic elixir." I smiled darkly. "Which is canceling out the magic that keeps her body alive."

Saranthiel collapsed to her knees, one hand outstretched to me while the other still clutched her throat. "H-ho—"

"How? What do you think I was doing in that wine cellar? This was the plan all along, but instead of having to split the dose among everyone here, thanks to Laurent, we could split it all into two glasses. Probably why it's working so fast."

"But the bottle wasn't even open!" Brooke looked back at the bar.

"Didn't need to be. Ms. Ellerbeck gave me the elixir earlier. I only had to open a small portal in the neck of the bottle as you poured," Laurent said.

Saranthiel fell back onto the floor, losing her hold on the form of Mari. Her face became that of Jackie Harwell, and it felt like someone stepping on my own grave to see her again, the death mask that had haunted me for a decade, the nasty gash across her neck that I had put there. Wails echoed in my ears from around me, but I couldn't tear my eyes away from what I'd done.

*I'm so sorry, Jackie. And Mari. I hope you can both rest now. I hope we all can.*

The moment passed. Before our eyes, the body rapidly desiccated like some sort of instant mummification, until it was nothing but black, tight leathery skin stretched over bones, with an incongruous coif of copper red hair. Sobs and silence took over the room.

"Is it over? Is she gone?" Lucca asked as he hurried to Brooke's side, taking her in his arms.

"She's not dead, but she can't come back to Arcadia unless she's summoned," I said, and fixed an eye on Brooke. "Do us a favor, *don't* summon her."

"I don't know that I'll have a choice. And neither will you," Brooke said, her eyes still fixed on the corpse. "You both drank, McKenna."

"Yeah, but I've been taking that stuff for ten years. That dose was practically nothing to me."

"I mean you still made a deal with her," Brooke said. "Don't you feel it?"

The weight of that began to sink in, the truth of the matter. I may have killed her host body, but I hadn't killed Saranthiel herself. I could feel the tether that bound me to the Archdemon... a tether that still ended at Jackie's body...

Because I hadn't yet banished her.

"Get back!" I screamed.

The words barely left my lips when a mass of darkness burst from the body, coalescing into the true demonic form of Saranthiel. *"Next time you strike at me, demon's witch, make sure it is a killing blow!"* The roar of its voice, in both my ears and my mind, sent me spinning, vertigo hitting me like a brick wall. Or, more likely, hitting me like the floor I smacked into when I lost my balance. My ears rang, my eyes stung, the smell of sulfur filled my nostrils. I squeezed my eyes shut, panic roiling within me, once again certain the blow that was coming would end me at last.

Instead, I heard the shattering of glass as the enormous window looking out on the bay was smashed apart by the Archdemon's rage, the thundering crack of wood and plaster as she took out her rage on the room around us. "*Let it be on your head when they are crushed and buried alive!*"

"McKenna!" Someone grabbed me and hauled me several feet away as a chunk of ceiling crashed down where I had been. "She's bringing the whole place down!" Bastien yelled as he tried to pull me to my feet.

I looked up, warily, and saw that the Archdemon was indeed wreaking havoc all around us. But not touching a single person directly, even as they all screamed and ran to escape the room. "Sh-she can't hurt us! Her pact with me will be broken if she does!"

"That doesn't help the rest of the people in this building!"

He was right. And for all I knew, the ones in this room could easily end up excusable collateral damage somehow. "I have to banish her! I have to stop her!"

"Even you can't banish an Archdemon with no circle, especially after the spells you've been throwing around," Bastien pointed out. "We have to go, now!"

Saranthiel roared and we had to stop, the sound rendering us senseless, followed by a splintered piece of a wall being thrown down in our path.

Remi appeared next to us in a swirl of shadows. "Come on!" She grabbed our hands.

"*The littlest Archdemon! I've waited long enough to take you out. And I am truly done with you, Lemaire.*" Saranthiel's claws grew as she reached toward them.

"We had a deal!" I yelled, scrambling in front of Remi and Bastien. "You can't hurt them!"

"*We'll renegotiate.*" With a wave of her hand, she sent me sprawling. A spear of darkness shot out at the two of them.

I screamed, grabbing even though I was too far to reach it or them—and the shadow stopped in midair. I didn't pause to think, just twisted and threw, sending it back where it came from, stabbing through Saranthiel's body.

Saranthiel, however, showed no damage from the attack at all. "*You think you can harm me with my own power? You should be smarter than that, demon's witch!*"

She was right. I might be able to control the demonic power for some weird, unknown reason, but it would never be useful against her. My magic could be, but Bastien was right, too: I was too tapped out to banish her, even without a dose of anti-magic in my system. With no magic swords and no binding magic, the best I could do was play defense while we got out of here—

Except... I *did* have more magic. I had the magic of generations of witches, gathered for over two hundred years, sitting right outside that shattered window. A flicker of my will and I could see it, the great golden barrier of Arcadia Commons, glowing like a sun out over the bay, a glow mirrored in my eyes as I fixed them on my enemy.

"Get him out of here, Remi."

"Not without you!"

"Let me save myself!"

It must've been using her own words that did it, because Remi grabbed Bastien's arm. As he moved to protest, the two of them blinked away. Leaving me alone with Saranthiel.

Or, more accurately, leaving her alone with me.

"*Per magiam maiorum meorum,*" I chanted, rising to my feet, hands outstretched with open palms, summoning the magic of my ancestors. "*Per sanguinem magiam tuam ego evoco.*"

Like lightning, the magic of the barrier struck my hands and I *burned*. My body was on fire with it, every cell, every nerve alive with pure power. My heart hammered so hard, I could swear it was going to burst out my chest, but it didn't matter.

I was a *goddess*.

My blood sang as it coursed through me, made more of power than plasma, and I knew my eyes were lit and glowing again. Hell, my entire body glowed like a second sun. And I wasn't alone. Through the magic my ancestors had poured into the barrier, I felt each and every one of them, standing with me, beside me, within me. Their victories and defeats, loves and hates and sacrifices. The living tapestry of the Younger witches, the missing pieces that each of them had given up, including my mother, my brother, and myself, fell into place in me and I *knew*. I knew this was our purpose, this moment, this task. The barrier had been meant not as a shield but as a battery. Waiting for this day, this moment.

Waiting for me.

The blast of magic had thrown Saranthiel to the ground. The Archdemon righted herself, and I felt more than saw the panic in her featureless face. She struck out at me with her shadowed claws, a blow that should've ripped me apart. My magic went to work closing up the wounds without a word, with barely even a thought from me.

I twined my fingers together as threads of my power appeared between them. With every pass and weave between my hands, the threads grew longer, stronger. "Next time you strike at me, Saranthiel"—I grasped the strands, pulling them taut—"make sure it's a killing blow."

With a snap of my wrist, my magic lashed out like a whip and latched onto her, the threads of power burrowing in. She hissed and twisted, trying to pull them, to escape. Every attempt only tangled her further in the web of my magic, my power, and my will made manifest.

"Except there won't be a next time."

I *pulled*.

From every direction, my magic sliced into her, ripping out pieces of her power, tearing her apart. A death of a thousand cuts, puffs of shadows escaped her, swirling into the air like blood in water, piece by piece until she began to crack down the middle, a jagged line of darkness that filled with golden light. She screamed, howling, shrieking, an inhuman sound that thundered against my eardrums, shattered glass, and made the very walls of the world shudder until a final explosion rocked the room, plunging it into darkness.

Saranthiel was dead.

# Chapter 23
# Balance

Light crept back into the room. The threads of my magic, the ones that had ripped Saranthiel apart, were now wrapped around the mass of darkness that remained.

The unclaimed power of an Archdemon.

Inside its cage, the power writhed, restless, seeking a being to embody, an heir to belong to, but my power prevented it from escaping.

"What am I going to do with you..." I walked around the mass, fully healed and no longer limping. Most of the barrier's power was holding it in place, but that wouldn't last forever. I lifted a hand, touching the cage, and both sets of power responded: My magic glowed warmly, and the darkness jerked to the spot, pressing up against the boundary like an eager puppy looking to be adopted. Or a wild animal looking to make the kill, one of the two. If I wanted to, I could claim it. Claim it and use it to send a message to every demon out there that I was no longer their witch, but their worst nightmare.

All it would take was a thought, a small effort of my will. It would be that easy to surrender my humanity entirely. To become an Archdemon.

I yanked my hand away. Both sets of power calmed. However much of me was human—not a question I'd ever thought needed asking until now—I was not looking to give it up.

But then what? I scratched at my arm as I paced, feeling restless. The barrier? I could use Saranthiel's power to rebuild it, use what was left of my magic to lock it in place. But what would it mean to wrap Arcadia Commons in a cocoon of demonic power? Possibly the worst idea I'd had all day, and that was saying something.

I wiped my brow. I had to decide soon. I didn't dare risk freeing the power to go find its own home in one of Saranthiel's minions. The shadows in the globe began to follow me as I paced. They whispered to me, through the unnerving connection I had to it, throwing visions of my own greatness into my head. I could heal my mother and brother both. Wouldn't that alone be worth it? I was strong-willed; surely the temptation to use it for my own gain, or against my enemies, was something I could resist. Right? I could test it out, unlock the binding just a little, take out just a small piece of the power and see how it felt. Yes. A test, that would prove one way or the other...

"Stop it!" I jerked my hand from the sphere of magic, where it had gone once more almost of its own accord. Even from within, this power was tempting, too tempting. It was teasing me, just out of reach, the promise of a lover you know will betray you in the morning. But whose beckoning call you cannot resist all the same... maybe it wouldn't be so bad, maybe I could control it, like Remi had...

Exactly then, Remi appeared in the room beside me, blinking in surprise. "McKenna?" Had I summoned her? "You killed her—holy shit—" She looked at me then and whatever it was she saw, it shook her. She ran to me, grabbing my arms. "McKenna! What happened to you?"

"I used—the barrier to kill her—" I could only whisper, but my voice felt so loud and the rest of me suddenly so weak. I went to scratch my arm and was greeted with a stinging pain. I'd already scratched at it hard enough to draw blood. Blood that burned, in every vein, with every beat of my now racing heart. "...Remi?" I swayed and collapsed into her arms.

"McKenna, the magic is killing you!" she exclaimed. "You have to let it go!"

*That's* why this felt so familiar. Too much magic, poisoning my blood. The magic of the barrier that I had claimed, that I was still holding on to in order to keep Saranthiel's power bound. After all this, *using* my magic was going to kill me after all. Go figure.

"Can't. Her power, it, it'll escape—"

"It'll escape if you die, too!"

"Good point." The room was swimming, spinning, and I was burning up.

"McKenna, let it go. We'll deal with whatever comes next. All of us, together. But this isn't the way. I can't do this without you; none of us can." My head lolled against her arm. I felt so heavy, so weighed down. She grabbed my face, forcing me to meet her eyes.

"Pools of shadow and promise..." I murmured.

"Not the time for poetry, darling. Come on! This isn't how the McKenna Ellerbeck story ends. This isn't how *our* story ends," Remi begged.

My fingers lifted, touching her face. Her skin, always so warm, was so wonderfully cool right now. Of course. The answer was right in front of me. "...Fact."

"So glad you agree, now, *let it go!*"

"Don't hate me, Remi. *Recludo.*" The magic of the cage fell, and then, before the dark power could escape, I pressed my palm against her chest. "*I crown thee.*" Her eyes went wide.

Herded by my magic, the mass of darkness slammed into Remi, surrounding her, sinking into her body. She cried out, her form twisting, and she dropped me on the floor. In gaps between shadows, I glimpsed hints of her true form—horns, blood-red skin, ragged skeletal wings that could not fly—but never enough to truly see her. I was pretty sure I didn't want to. With one last yell and a puff of sulfur, Remi disappeared entirely, teleporting away to who knew where.

I rolled onto my back and lifted my hands to the sky. "*Vade in domum tuam*"—go home—I bid the last of the magic that was not mine. Find my family, reform the barrier, dissipate into the ether—whatever it called home, I sent it there.

And then, finally, I passed out.

———•———

When I woke up, I found I was being stared at by a very curious little boy with dark curly hair and a transforming robot in his hands.

"You must be Griffin," I said.

"MOMMY! She's awake!" he hollered, loud enough to make me cringe. I sat up from a couch I'd slept on countless times in my youth, a comfy old plaid number belonging to the Luppino household and still making its home in their basement TV room, it seemed.

Leo trotted down the stairs with a plate in hand. "Griff, not so loud! Sheesh, kid. Go on up, Nana's got cookies."

"Okay!" And with that, off he went.

"How're you feeling?" Leo asked, sitting down next to me. I gulped water from a glass that had been left on the coffee table and took account of myself.

"Shockingly all right," I reported. "Considering what happened last—night? How long was I out?"

"It's about five o'clock Sunday. You've been asleep for almost a day."

"Damn. Okay, maybe that makes it less surprising." There were some cookies on the plate she had set down, and I eagerly dove in, as ravenous as someone who hadn't eaten in over a day. "Salt and chalk. Your mom's anginettes are even better than I remember," I mumbled through a mouthful. "How's everyone else?"

"It varies pretty widely. Injuries of varying degrees of seriousness, plenty of trauma, and, well, two people died," she told me. "One of the older Lemaires—Bastien's great-aunt, I think?—had a heart attack, and Tobias Phillips. One of the demons got him."

"Mr. Phillips? But he had luck magic."

Leo shrugged. "I guess he was too busy focusing it on

everyone else. Hell, I'm pretty sure he's why I didn't get gutted at one point. He saved a lot of lives at the cost of his own. And of course, there's Mari and Jackie, in a way."

I ran a hand through my hair, but it caught on several knots and snags. "I should've figured it out sooner. They'd still be alive."

Leo lightly whacked me in the head with a couch pillow. "Would you stop that already? We were *all* fooled," she reminded me. "If the people here couldn't figure it out for five years, you can't expect to do it in less than a week."

"Doesn't make me feel any better."

"Then this probably won't, either: Laurent Lemaire called. He wants to see you as soon as you're up and about."

I made a face. "Ugh. You're right, it doesn't."

"On the other hand, this might: My mom's making lasagna for dinner, and she insists that you 'put some meat on your bones, all that European living has wasted her away'!" Leo smirked as she nailed an impersonation of her mother. "Don't worry, I told her you don't eat actual meat."

"And what'd she say to that?"

"Muttered some Italian prayer and said she'd double the ricotta." We both grinned. "Oh, and the couch is yours as long as you want, too."

"Thanks. Laurent can sit and spin till tomorrow." I emptied the water glass. "What about Lucca? And Brooke?"

"Well..." Leo started to reply, but a creak on the top stair brought both our eyes to see the couple descending the stairs. Lucca, Leo, Brooke, and me hanging out in the basement: If it weren't for the heavy dose of awkward and the recent deep betrayals hanging among us, it would've been like high school all over again. Then again, what high school experience didn't have its share of those, too?

"Hi, McKenna," Brooke said timidly.

"You feeling okay, Mickey?" Lucca asked.

"Surprisingly yes for someone who sold her soul, faced down an Archdemon, and tore down most of a magical barrier all in one night," I said with frivolity so forced even I winced. "I mean, yeah, I'm okay. You guys?"

Lucca nodded, and Brooke said, "We're okay. All three of us," as she rubbed her stomach. "And... and I owe you a huge apology and a debt I can never repay."

"Let's all do ourselves a favor and try to remove the word *debt* and all its synonyms from our vocabulary, okay?" I said. "I'll take the apology, but I didn't do that so you could try to pay me back. I did it because you deserved to be free— we both did—and that bitch deserved to die, and I realized I could make it happen. I'm glad you're free, I'm glad you're okay, and I'm glad the baby is, too."

"Does that mean you're staying for dinner?" Lucca asked.

"I don't think your mom would let me leave without at least three helpings," I said.

"Great. It'll be like old times," Brooke said, starting to smile.

I stood up from the couch. "...No, it won't. Apology accepted, but it's gonna take a lot more than that for us to be okay, Brooke. You don't owe me, but that doesn't mean you don't have things to make up for. I can't go back to being friends like all of that never happened."

Lucca bristled. "She had no choice, McKenna, you know that!"

Brooke put a hand on his arm; he backed down, though he still looked pissed. "I know. I'm going to do whatever I can to make up for everything. To you and to everyone else," she said.

"Good," Leo said. "For now, tell Mom you're taking your lasagna to go. 'Cause everything Mickey said goes for me, too."

"You can't kick us out, this is our home, too," Lucca growled at his sister. Brooke once again settled him with a light touch, however.

"We're not being kicked out, Lucca. They need space, and we're going to give it to them. That's fair," Brooke said. "My stomach's still a little off anyway, and I'd feel strange sitting through one of your mom's meals without eating."

We all knew that was a lie, but none of us called her on it. She was right about what Leo and I needed. I hoped one day things really would be better among the four of us, but I knew they would never be like old times again.

———•———

After a meal that anyone who wasn't in the Luppino family would call huge, I slept another night on the couch, and in the morning, freshly showered and dressed, I went to see Laurent Lemaire. He had me come to the Lemaire home, a large, stately Colonial manor on the bay, old enough to be an official historical home of Arcadia Commons. It had been in the

# THE TWICE-SOLD SOUL

Lemaire family since they had moved here and helped form the town, and was thus a popular stop for tourists and tours. Privacy was maintained via a wrought-iron fence surrounding the yard, complete with a callbox at the gate.

Their butler—which, yes, they had—took me to the living room, where Laurent was waiting for me. Despite the fact that it was before noon and a Monday, he was wearing a dark suit, though he didn't have a tie on yet, and held a delicate-looking china cup of tea. The butler poured one for me as well.

"Hello, Ms. Ellerbeck," he greeted. "You'll have to excuse my formal dress, but I've a funeral to attend later."

"Right, I heard about Bastien's aunt. I'm very sorry for your loss," I said contritely.

"Much appreciated. Though my aunt Dorothy—" *His* aunt? Wow. "—will be missed, she had quite a long and full life. There are arguably more tragic losses that will be marked in the coming week."

"I'm very sorry for those, too."

"You ought to be." My eyes flashed to him. "Don't look at me like that. You know exactly how much of this falls at your feet."

"I do." I lifted my chin. "I know how much of it doesn't, too."

He grunted. "Good. You'll need a balanced sense of blame."

I arched a brow. "I will?"

"If you're going to serve on the Witches Council, that is." He looked at me plainly, watching my reaction to this news.

"I—wait, what?" I sputtered. "You want *me* on the Council? No offense, but are you out of your mind?"

"I daresay with the Archdemon of Madness dead and no longer married to my grandson, I'm perhaps more sane than ever." He set down his cup. "Tobias Phillips's passing leaves us with an open seat. You've dealt more with demons than any of us, Ms. Ellerbeck. I don't like that about you, but it's experience we'll be needing. With the barrier practically gone, we're more vulnerable than ever, and two Archdemons have shown direct interest in this town and what it protects in the last twelve years. Speaking of, don't suppose you've got any insight to offer on what happened to the barrier, hm?"

"I do, but it's complicated," I said.

"Hm. You can fill us all in later." He picked up a tie from the back of a chair, turned to a mirror, and began tying it. "I suppose I can't say it wasn't within your rights to take it down. The magic did belong to your family, after all."

"That reminds me—you've still got some details to fill me in on, too," I said. "Is that going to happen anytime soon?"

"If you're accepting the position and returning to Arcadia, then yes, I can see fit to share some of what I know."

"Only some?"

"Some secrets are for the grave alone, Ms. Ellerbeck."

The Council. This wasn't something I'd ever thought would happen. Given my family and personal history with them, my instinct was to say no, but... there was a lot to be gained by saying yes, and information was only part of it. Still, one thing nagged at me about the offer.

"What about Bastien?" I asked. "It's an open secret you've been grooming him to sit on the Council for his entire life."

"Close. I've been grooming him to lead it," he corrected.

"And someday he will. Now isn't the time, however. Bastien's been dealt a great personal blow, and while the task would help distract him from his grief, he's not in the right mindset for it." He finished the tie and stroked his beard. I met his eyes in the mirror.

"That's not the reason. Not all of it," I said.

"No? Please, enlighten me," he challenged.

"You don't trust his judgment," I guessed.

Laurent gave me a hard look through the mirror. "The boy fell in love with a demon."

"So did I."

"True." He turned to face me. "But you did so knowingly, and while I'd never be so naive as to trust a demon, it cannot be denied that you did effect some degree of... *change* in Remiel. You then proceeded to kill Forneus while still a teenager and, two days ago, identified and helped kill Saranthiel. Whereas Bastien had no idea whom he was marrying."

*Helped* kill?

*That's right—no one was there when I killed Saranthiel. Laurent and everyone else must think Remi's the one who did it.* I decided not to correct him. What he was saying about Bastien, on the other hand... "That's not exactly fair—"

"Fair or not, it is the truth. He'll heal, he'll learn, and he'll do better. But this position is being offered to you." He buttoned his jacket, and I could hear the butler answering the door out in the hall. A moment later, none other than Bastien himself walked in.

He was wearing a black suit, pressed and crisp and perfect to the last detail. His hair was perfectly combed and his jaw freshly shaven, every inch the picture of somber respect. He wore his glasses, perhaps to try to hide the hollow, tired, and deep-set sadness in his eyes, but he blinked in surprise when he saw me.

"McKenna?"

"Bastien, I... I'm so sorry," I said, defaulting to what one says in those sorts of situations.

"Thank you. Aunt Dotty will be sorely missed," he replied mechanically.

"I'm sure, but, I meant..." What else could I say, after what had happened? *"I'm sorry* doesn't quite seem to cover it."

He nodded understandingly. "I know what you mean." He looked at Laurent. "Everyone's waiting for us in the car, Grandfather."

"Let's not keep them. Ms. Ellerbeck, if you'll excuse us."

"Of course. I'll let you know. Soon."

Laurent nodded at me once; Bastien looked puzzled but didn't ask, and they both left to pay their respects to the dead.

———————•———————

I meandered through town for a bit, driving the car that had been mine and was now technically Cameron's, until I came at last to a condo complex on the water, on the opposite end of the bay from the historical homes, where the newer construction in town was condensed. I knocked on the door of number 6 and waited to see if anyone was home.

With a burst of warmth and a wave of sulfur behind her, Remiel Blake answered the door.

To say she was disheveled was an understatement. Her hair was a mess, and half of it looked burned. One eye was pitch black, and one kept changing color. She was wearing an oversize men's button-down shirt over a pair of crooked panties and a bra with one strap slipping down her shoulder, and when the smell of sulfur passed, the smell of booze replaced it.

"Should I come back later?"

"Oh, no, you, *you*, are not going anywhere!" She snapped her fingers and her entire appearance changed, the messy twenty-something replaced with the sexy business-casual demoness. "What the hell did you do to me?"

"I thought that part was kind of obvious."

"Two Archdemons in one convenient package! Do you have idea how fucked up the last—how long has it been?"

"About a day and a half—"

"—how fucked up the last day and a half have been for me?" She pulled me inside. If her appearance had been messy, the inside of her condo was a downright disaster area.

"Really? 'Cause it mostly looks like you threw a rave in here," I said, surveying the place.

"Ha, right, if you can call dozens of minions coming by to pledge their loyalty a rave!" Remi snapped. She started making gestures, and the place began reordering and cleaning itself.

"Coming by? In person?" The reality of what I'd done started hitting me.

"In person, because yep, they can do that now. Well, some of them. The lower-level types. The bigger ones still can't get past what's left of the barrier, but believe me, it's only a matter of time." A snap of her fingers and a cocktail glass appeared in her hand, full of dark liquor. "Want one?"

"It's before noon."

"Like I care. Don't start panicking, most of the mess was me being pissed and trying to get drunk, if I'm honest," Remi said. "And every demon who's pledged itself to me has been sworn to keep the state of affairs vis-à-vis the barrier to themselves. Word among demonkind will let them all think it's still up, for a little while at least."

"Wow. Thanks, I...so..." I turned back to her. "...minions, huh?"

Remi chuckled, her ire breaking. "Yeah. Minions. I've got minions now. Everyone in the Pit's going all 'double Archdemon, what does it mean?' and it seems the safe bet is that I must be super powerful to have killed two Archdemons and stolen their power, so they ought to get on the winning team while they can." She looked at me, eyes glinting. "Of course, little do they know who the real power behind the throne is. The demon's wi—"

I cut her off. "Don't call me that. I am so incredibly over being called that."

Remi sighed. "I can't call you that, I can't call you darling, whatever shall I call you, then?"

I spread my hands. "McKenna works."

She smiled crookedly at me. "McKenna. Now, that sounds like someone worth keeping an eye on."

I smiled back. "I *am* sorry about not really giving you much of a choice, though. I was sort of out of options."

She waved her hand. "It's okay. I'd rather me be stuck with

this than you be dead. Although..." She looked at me from under her lashes.

"Although...?"

"I hope you aren't going to hold it against me this time."

I shook my head. "I won't. It would be pretty shitty of me, wouldn't it?"

"It was pretty shitty of you last time, too." Remi winced at her own words. "Sorry. I don't... well, no, I do mean it. But I also get it. Still, I sincerely hope that things will be different on the second go-round of you giving me Archdemon powers."

I looked at her and found myself grasping her free hand, squeezing her fingers. "So do I." Her surprise turned to warmth as she smiled and squeezed back, starting to move her hand to take a firmer hold of mine before I gently extricated it. "Especially since I've come here to ask a favor," I said before she could protest.

"Oh? Got your debt clear and you're already looking to re-up?" Remi said brightly.

"Not exactly. I'm here to ask you to repay the favors you owe me."

She blinked. "... Come again?"

"Don't look so surprised, Remi. You owe me. You were just talking about how you owe me for giving you the power of two Archdemons."

"Well... yes, but, we never made a deal about that..."

"But we didn't have to. You can grant deals retroactively," I reminded her.

She opened her mouth, then shut it again with a click of

teeth. "Me and my bloody big mouth." She downed the rest of the cocktail and put her drink down. "Right then. Very well. What'll it be?"

"My mom and my brother. Heal them, back to full health. You and Saranthiel both said it had to be a life for a life, and now I know it doesn't have to be my life. I've already given you two, and I want two in return."

Remi eyed me. "I don't know if I should be irritated that you're forcing my hand in a *very* big way or proud of you for figuring out how to do it in the first place."

I shrugged. "Why not both?"

"Very well. But after this, McKenna, we owe each other nothing," she said, stepping inside my personal bubble. "The slate is clear and the scales are balanced between us. Do you understand?"

"I understand. Should I also be worried?"

"I've got a whole set of problems thanks to your power move. So don't think I won't remember that when those problems come a-knocking. That said, you know where my loyalties are, my black knight, but you also know where my morality lies."

"In a gray and a shadowy corner."

"In pools of shadows and promise." She quoted my delirious words back to me, her painted lips forming around them and then lingering, parted and inches from my own.

I swallowed and rocked back on my heels, overdoing it and stumbling before I regained my own balance. "I know. I won't forget."

"Good." She stepped back, too, more smoothly than I, and

I wondered just how much I should worry about what I'd done to her. Too late to take it back now. "Before I do, one more question: Where do you intend to live? If we're going to miraculously heal your mother and get her out of the Harwell Institute, she's going to need a place to go, as will you, and Cameron's apartment won't hold you all."

I frowned. "I admit I hadn't thought about that."

"Might I recommend 134 Fox Hill Road?"

My eyebrow raised. "Our old house? Cameron sold it to pay for my mom's treatment."

"That he did, and he got quite a good deal for it. Despite it not being a seller's market, I might add," Remi said.

"Are you telling me *you* bought our house?" She nodded. "How? There's no way my brother would've sold it to you."

"He doesn't know that he did. I worked through some intermediaries, and it was being rented by a couple who kept it up quite nicely. They've since bought their own place, and it currently stands vacant."

"How convenient. But I don't have the money to buy it back."

"Ah, but with our slates freshly cleared, we could surely come to an arrangement," she invited.

I gave her a sardonic clap. "Wow. It took you under five minutes to cook up a brand-new way to get me in debt. Seriously, Remi? Thanks for the second reminder about your morality."

She scowled. "I'm trying to give you your home back the only way I know how."

"The only way, really?" I gave her a look. "Counteroffer:

We do this the human way. You get a lawyer to draw a fair rental agreement, with the additional caveat that, when the worth of the house has been reached in payments, ownership will transfer to the tenant—that is to say, Wendy Younger Ellerbeck."

Remi rolled her eyes. "That completely lacks finesse and flair."

"But?"

"But it'll do, yes," she sighed. "Very well. We'll do it the human way. You're lucky I like you."

I could think of at least a dozen replies to that, every one of them likely to get me in a different kind of trouble. I waited while she sent off a text. "There. There'll be a contract ready by this afternoon." She slipped it back into her pocket and looked up at me. "Ready?"

Ready to greet my mom with my own face? To tell my brother the fight was finally over? To catch up with the friends I never thought I'd see again?

To finally have my life back and truly go home, this time for good?

I smiled.

"Yeah. I'm ready."

The story continues in...

**THE TWICE-WANTED WITCH**

Book TWO of the McKenna Ellerbeck Series

# ACKNOWLEDGMENTS

While this book only got its start about a decade ago, my active imagination and I have been dreaming of this day since I was eight years old. To all my friends and family, thank you for helping to get me here at long last, whether through encouraging, indulging, or actively helping to shape the person and writer I am today. There are some in particular, of course, who are owed an extra-special shout-out.

My parents, Brian and Mary, for pretty much everything! For only ever loving, encouraging, and supporting me in all my impractical dreams, but also raising me to be able to follow them practically; for teaching me I could do anything if I worked at it; and for helping me do that work. I love you both, and I can never fully express the gratitude I feel for being so lucky as to have the both of you as my parents.

Brandon, for being my loving and ridiculous husband and partner in life, love, and family! For supporting the kid, nerd, gamer, and writer in me, being a fantastic father to our son, and making sure I could dedicate time to making this book happen. Thank you for being the corner piece to my puzzle. Witness me!

Rowan, my little guy! You amaze me every day, and I love

# Acknowledgments

seeing your kind, funny, creative spirit growing all the time. It thrills me how much you love creating, and I can't wait to see what you'll do next.

Mel, my real-life Leo, how lucky that we were neighbors freshman year! Thank you for all our adventures, stories, gaming, improv, and other creative pursuits together, and being my person over these many years. We may have started on the bump on the ass of BC, but we've risen pretty damn far ever since. Oh oh oh!

Cass, to whom this book is dedicated. I miss you every day. Thank you for so many things. As a person, as a friend, as a writer, your handprint is on my heart. Thank you for running that Monsterhearts game that inspired this story, because truly McKenna would not exist without you. I'd give anything for you to still be here, and I'm forever grateful you were in my life.

Joy, for your enthusiastic support and loving my book even though you're not a fantasy person, long talks on Cape nights, the ducks, and the snowflakes.

All the members of the Writers Cabal over the years: Eve, Greg, Cindy, Allyson, Mel, Henry, Cass, Miranda, Andrea, Julia, and John. Your feedback on this and other stories has been everything and made me a better writer, hands down. Thank you for that and for all the conjecture on "stories you're not writing."

The Loons! Thank you for guidance, support, spitballing, time slutting, and custom emojis. This thing would most likely have died on a terrible query letter and me flailing about with what to do next without you. I'll still flail about, but I'm grateful to have such a great group with which to do so.

## Acknowledgments

The Monsters: Cass, Mel, Scott, John, and David. That game was a roller coaster, but it was a great time and I wouldn't change a thing... okay, maybe one or two things. I mean, have you met us? We're kind of idiots.

Aaron, thank you for the memories, the laughs and even the heartbreak, your generosity, and the Black Knight custom cocktail recipe. You were gone too soon, but you are missed and remembered with a smile. I wish you'd been with us all longer.

My beta readers: Brandon, MT, Christine, Joy, Josh, TJ, Mel, Auston, Sandy, Michelle, and Serpico. My Futurescapes mentors and cohort: Lucienne Diver, Shiv Ramdas, Sarah Guan, Sean, Ash, Heather, Jayme, El, and Janet.

Thank you to Alessandra Bertolli and Amy Cortright for checking my Latin and French, Sarah Clark for the sensitivity read, and Dave Green for the headshots.

My editor Stephanie Lippitt Clark, thank you for picking this book! For loving it and McKenna, and getting both of us ready and out there in the world.

My agent, Brenna English-Loeb, for likewise picking me and McKenna, and believing I've got what it takes. It means so much to have a partner in making this happen!

Everyone who worked on this book from Orbit: Alexia E. Pereira, Lauren Panepinto, Bryn A. McDonald, Maggie Curley, and everyone else who helped to make this book a reality. Special thanks to Miranda Meeks for the cover art!

And you! The person holding this book right now! Thank you so much for coming with me and McKenna on this journey. I hope you enjoyed it as much as I did, and that we see

## Acknowledgments

you again for the next book. For reading this far, you've won a cocktail recipe!

## Black Knight

*created by Aaron Butler*

2 ounces dark rum
½ ounce Averna amaro
½ ounce Benedictine
Dash of orange bitters (angostura preferred)

Combine with ice and shake vigorously. Strain into a glass, smirk at the object of your affection and/or attraction, and enjoy!

# MEET THE AUTHOR

*Katie Hallahan*

KATIE HALLAHAN is a fantasy author who loves tabletop RPGs, vampire TV shows, corgis, dabbling in nail art, and pumpkin spice everything. She has designed award-winning narrative adventure games at Phoenix Online Studios, an indie game studio she co-founded. She lives with her husband and son in Boston, Massachusetts, where, shockingly, she actually uses her blinker when making turns. Katie is on Instagram, Bluesky, Threads, and X at @katiehal16; her website is katiehal.com.

Find out more about Katie and other Orbit authors by registering for the free monthly newsletter at orbitbooks.net.